Dictates of the Servators: Book 3

LEAVENING

Kallen Samuels

ISBN: 978-1-7779901-2-1
Imprint: Innov@t Publishing - https://www.innovat.org

DEDICATION

Thank you to my family and friends
for their feedback and support.

CONTENTS

ACKNOWLEDGMENTS

Cover design: Kallen Samuels
Editor: Theresa Rempel

Other books by Kallen Samuels

Leviticus – Dictates of the Servators: Book 1
Levigator – Dictates of the Servators: Book 2

Chapter 1

The discordant harmony of particles set Leviticus Radix's nerves on edge, even as it called to him. It was a sound that wasn't a *sound*, but the pull was real. It beckoned him like a promise — *a promise of discovery or regret?* He wondered.

The last few years had been a whirlwind of revelation. He was no longer an aspiring computational engineer, recently graduated from the Court of Learning in his home town of Denmount. Any thought of a career or a future along those lines had been irrevocably crushed. Instead, he was drafted into an ancient secret organization in a race against time to prevent the end of the world. More than that, he wasn't merely a Servator contributing to the cause. Somehow, he had become the Levigator. The last person who held that role died over seventeen hundred years ago. All eyes turned to the Levigator as the one who would save them. It seemed ludicrous. He felt a maniacal laugh threatening to break loose at the very idea. *Hold yourself together, Lev. Nothing shatters confidence so much as a Levigator cackling like a madman.* The Maker knew they needed hope and he would play along. It might be all he had to offer.

Levigator. Title aside, the word itself meant *one who eases a burden.* There was no denying the Servators had a heavy burden at the moment, but he had no idea what he was supposed to do about it. For now, he was following the path of his predecessors in the hope that an answer would present itself. He was looking for thin spaces where a rift might be formed.

Lev took a few tentative steps, first in one direction then another. The pull would be stronger in one direction, inexorably leading him to the source.

He had stopped denying that he was the Levigator. No one else possessed these impossible to believe abilities. He could sense the patterns of particles that permeated the world around him. He continually memorized those changing patterns and his place within them. He could call on those memories to form templates and materialize objects at will.

To the average person it might seem like magic, but Servators had been doing something similar with their quantum technology for years. Remotely materializing tokens using the Quantum Positioning Network, or QPN was something they took for granted. What made Lev special was that he didn't need the vast computational power of the QPN network. He didn't need the library of entangled templates stored in the memory stash. He was his own QPN and archive. It wasn't possible to hold that much information in a human brain, and yet he wielded that ability as easily as he wiggled his fingers. It was empowering and humbling at the same time.

Tark and Yori had taken up defensive positions and were scanning the horizon with their scopes, looking for some imagined adversary to test their skills. They went where he went. Not that he needed bodyguards, but they were also his friends. *They protect me from myself — they keep me sane.* Nico was among them, a lifelong friend from his childhood. By some strange turn of events, or perhaps by the Maker's will, his best friend had also been dragged into this world-spanning drama underpinning their reality. Like his own, Nico's choices had been ripped away. He was denied access to his family's business, framed for a murder, and on the run until he could prove his innocence. *None of that matters if I fail and the world comes to an end.* Lev shook the dark thoughts from his mind and looked at his friend standing a few cubits away. He was grateful Nico had agreed to accompany him. It didn't hurt that he was now a fully trained Servator. Even Tark and Yori acknowledged Nico's new skills. He'd thought they would object when he named Nico as his assistant, but they assured him they had tested Nico themselves. Lev smiled, imagining what that testing involved. No doubt Nico managed to land a few blows to win their respect.

"The percentage of discordant particles is increasing." Lev noted.

Nico called up the map that Analyst Hemish had given them and stared at the coordinates on his wrist Q-view. "According to Hemish's calculations, the thin space should be within a league's radius of this position. Do you have any idea what it looks like, Lev?"

Lev had studied several of the original rifts formed by his predecessors, but this was his first attempt to find a thin space to create a new rift. They hoped to discover a more advanced kin world and gain a new technological advantage against the Breacher threat. "A thin space? No. The journals of Rushoen Nu Lon didn't describe thin spaces, only the rifts that were formed from them. Hemish thinks I may be the first who can sense a thin space in a way that is more than a vague feeling of discomfort."

Nico grinned. "From the expression on your face, it looks like you may be feeling some discomfort yourself. Unless that's from the porridge Tark served this morning." Nico made a pained expression of his own.

"I heard that!" Tark yelled from a distance. "Oats with mead is a beloved family recipe. It's wasted on your spoiled palate, Callan!"

Nico turned to Lev with a bewildered look and whispered, "How could he have heard that?"

"I hear everything!"

Lev shook his head and shrugged, chuckling at Nico's incredulous countenance. Tark liked to tease and was very good at guessing how people might react to his comments. It was unlikely Tark had actually heard the whisper, but tormenting Nico was one of Tark's favourite pastimes.

"The particles seem to be coming from that direction." Lev pointed vaguely to the east and began walking.

After twenty minutes of walking, Lev was certain they were on the right track. The air held a constant flow of the twinned particles that formed when a kin world was bleeding into their own. From his experiments with the known rifts, he had learned that this concentration only occurred within one hundred cubits of a rift. The thin space had to be very close.

"It's here. Yori, can you head back and bring the ground transport?"

"On it."

Lev continued walking. The sound grew in intensity until he thought he'd go deaf from the roar. Nico and Tark seemed oblivious as they trudged a step behind him. "Can't you hear that?" Lev wondered aloud.

"Hear what? Why are you yelling?"

Right. Lev reminded himself it wasn't actually a sound. It was the closest thing his brain could offer to interpret what he was sensing. He decided to immerse himself fully into pattern sight. Perhaps it would diminish the auditory illusion.

The world snapped into sharp focus and the sound disappeared, replaced by a visual representation of a breeze as particles flowed from a specific point. He could see it off in the distance and started to jog toward it. Within three strides, he found himself moving in the same direction as the flow of particles, *away* from the point of origin. He had passed it. Lev stumbled as he jerked to a halt. He spun around and found the thin space once more. Carefully backtracking, he stopped at the point where particles seemed to be streaming away from him in every direction. He took one large step backward and then traversed a slow circle around the spot where he had been standing. His eyes grew wide in realization. He hadn't been sure what to expect, but it wasn't this. The rifts on Servator bases were large enough for a man to walk through, if such a thing were possible. What he was looking at now appeared no larger than his fingertip. No wonder thin spaces were so difficult to find. "This is it."

Nico walked to where Lev was standing, hoping to see for himself. "You're looking at it now? I don't see anything."

"you're standing in the middle of it. I can see particles flowing from the top of your head."

Nico yelped as he jumped to the side, furiously brushing off his arms and legs as if he were covered in ants. "Why didn't you warn me?"

"I think there's more on your back." Tark offered helpfully.

"Get it off!"

Tark grinned as he vigorously thumped every spot on Nico's back.

Lev rolled his eyes. "There's nothing on you, Nico. The particles are out of sync with our world, flowing through you as if you weren't even there. They can't do you any harm."

Nico glared at Tark who was laughing hysterically. "I wish you could have seen the expression on your face."

Yori arrived with the ground transport and hopped out. "What's going on? What did I miss?"

"Nico... was attacked... by ghost ants." Tark managed between guffaws.

Lev sighed. "I bet this is why Rushoen Nu Lon travelled alone. This is supposed to be an historic moment."

Yori nodded at Tark who quickly sobered. "What's next?"

"Now I form an arch and hope someone or something on the other side is watching."

The way Lev understood the science, a rift would only form if both sides of a thin space were observed at the same time. Creating an arch would provide a mechanical means to continuously observe the thin space on their side. It increased the odds that a rift would form from a random observation on the kin world side.

Lev noted the position of the fingertip sized hole between worlds. He had memorized the pattern for creating an arch and set it to materialize with those coordinates at the centre. The arch quickly formed, marking the thin space location for his travelling companions. They all stared at the spot, willing something to happen, but the arch remained inert. After half an hour, Yori broke the silence. "Well that was anticlimactic. I guess we set up the marker beacon for the analysts back home and move on?"

"Hang on a moment." Lev was staring intently at the spot that made up the thin space in the centre of the arch. He could see the particles flowing from the gap clearly. According to Hemish, no one had been able to do that before. He knew the exact dimensions of that tiny gap between worlds. His mind had already mapped the coordinates. Once a rift was formed, analysts routinely materialized tokens through the rift to transfer information. He was the first to witness a thin space as a hole. *Does that mean I could pass a token through that gap?*

"Nico, can you find a pattern for a micro sight token that would fit through a hole the diameter of a crossbow shaft?"

"Let me check." Nico's fingers danced over the screen on his wrist Q-view. "I think I found something. Yes, this seems to meet the requirements." Nico initiated the template with coordinates to materialize on the ground before them. A tiny viewcorder appeared.

"That should work. Disassemble and re-materialize it a few more times so I can memorize the pattern."

Nico did as he was asked.

"Okay, I have it. Yori, do we have any stiff, thin wire in the transport?"

"Yes, we always carry a roll of wire in the toolbox. I'll get it."

"Thank you."

There was one other thing he had accomplished which had never been done before. He had passed his arm through a rift and retrieved a token that had been placed on the other side. That was theoretically impossible. Tokens could be formed on the other side of a rift because they materialized using particles from that side. Direct passage of an object or transmission from one side to the other was a different matter altogether. The particle frequencies didn't match and the two were repelled. It was the reason why sharing data between worlds was so painstakingly slow. A form of written material needed to be transferred as a token, whether parchment or writ weave in nature.

Yet he had done it. Lev's mentor, Akhen, had surmised that he was so familiar with the way his body moved through the pattern that he had somehow been able to match the frequency of the particles that made up his flesh with those of the other world. If he could do that for the view token — if he could enable it to exist on the other side of the thin space for just a moment, maybe they could be the observers for both sides and trigger a rift formation. He had memorized every particle of the sight token's template. He'd need that knowledge to shift the frequency of each particle as it passed the threshold between worlds.

Yori returned with the wire and some cutters. Lev wrapped the wire around the sight token to secure it. He played out a foot of wire to use as a grip and cut the wire. After a minute of bending and shaping, he had a suitable handle.

"Nico, can you establish a connection with the viewcorder?"

"Got it. Point it at me, will you, Lev? Yes, I can see myself. it seems to be working properly."

"Okay, I'm going to try to pass it through this hole in thin space."

"There's already a hole? I thought rifts couldn't form on their own."

"They can't. I'll explain later. Right now, just keep your eyes on the screen."

Lev knelt before the arch and began feeding the micro sight token through the spot that only he could see. He immediately met resistance. *What exactly did I do that first time when I passed my arm through the rift?* He couldn't recall since he hadn't been paying attention. Lev set the viewcorder aside and pressed the tip of his pinky finger through the gap. There was a moment of resistance and then his finger slipped through. He pulled it out and repeated the experience using pattern sight to bring the finer details into focus. *There!* He could see the particles shifting frequency to adapt to their new surroundings. Lev grabbed the viewcorder and placed the handle end of the wire against his finger to pass it through at the same time. His finger passed through, but the wire stayed behind. He tried to imagine the wire as part of his body, or rather, he imagined his finger was thicker than it was. This time the wire passed through as well. *Yes!* He needed to visualize the coordinates of the wire in relation to his body.

Lev turned the wire around and tried feeding the camera end through. The lens was facing him to match the perspective of someone viewing the thin space from the other side. It was working. The sight token was completely on the other side. "Nico, what do you see?"

"Nothing. I could see you for a moment and then I lost the signal."

"Of course, the signal."

"Uh, yeah, that's what I said."

"Never mind, keep watching. Let me know when you have a signal and when you don't." Lev pulled the token back.

"I have a signal" Nico reported.

Lev pulled deeper into pattern sight until he could see an oscillation representing the viewcorder signal moving through the pattern. He memorized the wave form and then pushed the sight token back through.

"Lost signal." Nico responded.

Now Lev could see the signal pattern from the other side. It had shifted and was being repelled. He concentrated on the plane of transition. He needed to switch the wave pattern frequency at the moment of translation. He only needed to maintain it long enough for Nico's wrist Q-view to pick it up.

"Signal is back."

In the time it took for Nico to report, the arch began to shimmer as the thin space enlarged. "It worked! We have a rift." Lev's excitement evaporated as the implications of what they were seeing dawned on him. The other side of the rift was a wall of water. It was a flood world.

The four of them stared in silence. They all knew the prophecy. This was what they were trying to prevent on their own world.

Yori spoke first. "I'll grab the transmitter to mark the rift."

"Don't bother." Lev disassembled the arch. We can't afford the resources to monitor a dead end. Mark the coordinates and record the location as a flood world." Lev did his best to mask his disappointment. At least they knew that Hemish's map held promise, and now he understood how to speed up the process of forming a rift. He had to believe that sooner or later they'd find what they were looking for.

"Nico, plot our next destination. We have a lot of ground to cover."

Chapter 2

"That should be it." Kade began his descent of the ladder, looking past the rungs at Selica below him.

"You remembered to set the transmission frequency this time?"

Kade rolled his eyes. "Yes, I remembered. Run a signal check and you'll see for yourself." Kade smiled as his wife picked up the diagnostic panel and did just that."

His wife — Kade still couldn't believe that Selica had agreed to marry him. He felt like he had nothing to offer her, but she accepted anyway. Their life on Chellea had been idyllic. It was beautiful, but there was a reason it was considered a rehabilitation island. He was a felon by Servator standards and a prisoner here for another year before he'd be given the option to leave. For her part, Selica had lived a life in slavery and deserved her freedom, not more confinement. He'd made bad choices and deserved the consequences, but she'd been forced to obey the Breachers. That made her a victim, not a felon.

Selica told him repeatedly that she was content to spend the rest of her days on the island. She felt more freedom in the safety it provided than she would looking over her shoulder on the mainland. The wounds from a lifetime of Breacher oppression ran deep. Kade still felt guilty. It troubled him that he couldn't offer her more than an open-air prison. A cage was still a cage, no matter how exotic.

He had to admit that he also enjoyed the security offered by the island. All the more now that he was about to become a father. He smiled fondly at his wife. She was just starting to show. After all they'd been through, they were finally building a hopeful future, if a limited one.

Kade knew Selica would never have considered a child if they were still among the Breachers. Children born of Breacher slaves were considered property. She had lived that life and would sooner die than put a child of her own through those same horrors. He understood such conviction. His childhood was nowhere near as bad, but his father had been verbally abusive and controlling. He vowed that he would be different. His children would receive the love, support and protection they deserved. It was the one thing he could offer Selica.

In the meantime, he would prove himself useful to the Servators and show them he was repentant for his mistakes. He held no love for the Breachers and wanted them stopped. The thought of them using the algorithm to kill more people nauseated him. He could never atone for the lives that were lost, but he could help to ensure it never happened again.

Leviticus Radix had asked him to replicate the Breacher network here on the island. A working copy would give them the means to explore ways to impair the system. Kade wasn't confident that the network security could be breached, but Radix had proposed a novel strategy to prevent the network from identifying any more Servator agents. They wouldn't need more than limited access to the network for the plan to work.

Previously, he and Radix had covertly communicated by injecting ambiguous characters directly into the viewcorder feeds. It was possible because the facial recognition algorithm expected viewcorders to return results. Radix had exploited that expectation to respond to Kade's call for help. Since then, Kade had been able to provide the Servators with appropriate keywords they could append to bits of expected information. The algorithm would recognize the injected content as legitimate, and dutifully format it into appropriate records. Servator analysts had been accessing Breacher viewcorders in remote locations to slowly insert profiles of non-existent people into the Breacher network. All they needed now were manufactured faces to assign to the profiles. That's where their current efforts were focused.

"That was the last one. We have viewcorders set up on all of the main paths."

"Do you think the residents will be upset?"

Kade sighed. "They'd be furious if they knew, but we've gone out of our way to make sure these look nothing like viewcorders. The islanders are under the impression that these are improvements to the local tote-comm network."

"I don't like lying to them."

"Neither do I, but we don't have a lot of options — it's a small community. Besides, the images will be altered, so no privacy will be lost. We're only doing what the Servators asked us to do and it's not like the original images can be taken off island, isolated as we are."

"I know, but these people are our neighbours. Many are becoming friends. I don't want to lose that."

"These aren't just viewcorders. I've included improved repeaters that really *will* increase the speed and range of the tote-comm network. That's going to make a lot of people happy. It's not all a lie."

Selica didn't look convinced. "So you keep telling me, but it doesn't change the way I feel."

Kade placed his hands on her shoulders. "You know I'm the only one who can provide the facial markers used by the algorithm for identifying citizens. It shouldn't take long to collect enough images to build the generic composite faces Radix asked for. Once that's done, you can help me disable the viewcorders, leaving only the tote-comm improvements."

"What about the images themselves?"

"Once we've created the composites, I'll let you personally delete the originals. Deal?

"Deal. That can't happen soon enough. I'm sorry for adding to your stress, Kade. I know you're only doing this to help stop the Breachers. I want that as much as you do. It's just that we're building something special here, a life with a community of caring people. I've never had that before and I don't want to put it at risk. It still feels fragile to me, like someone is going to take it away."

"Are you still having those nightmares?"

"Yes, it's always the same. Breachers come to the island and destroy everything we've built here."

"That's one of the reasons I'm working so hard to blind them. To protect our little family." Kade placed a hand on Selica's belly. She covered it with her own and held it there. "These islands have remained hidden for centuries. If we can give Radix the means to create masks, he can use them to hide the identities

11

of Servator agents. If the algorithm can't track them, it will be a lot harder for Breachers to find these islands."

Selica leaned into his embrace. "I hope so."

"I've seen Radix apply one of these masks. They're very convincing. I don't see any reason why it shouldn't work." Kade held her tight. He wished he could take away her nightmares. He wished he could promise her everything would be alright, but only time could do that. He lifted her chin and looked into her eyes, willing her to see assurance there. "We're as far away from the Breachers as we can get. This island will be the last place on their radar, even if they learn of its existence. We're safer than we ever imagined we would be. On top of that, we've been given an opportunity to fight back with no risk to ourselves or our child. We're doing good work here, Selica. Important work that can save lives. I've made a lot of mistakes in the past. This is my chance at atonement. I don't want our son or daughter to be ashamed of their father. I want them to know that we fought for good."

"You've already proven that, Kade. You work harder than anyone on the island and everyone here knows it. You've gained the respect of those who used to blame you. Our children will see that."

"Children? Plural? Shouldn't we see how we handle this one first?"

Selica laughed. "You know what I mean, but you're right, we need to do this."

It warmed Kade's heart to see the shift in her mood. He kissed her forehead and they walked hand-in-hand back to the lab for a romantic afternoon of testing viewcorder feeds.

Chapter 3

Tenika scowled. "I can't work like this, Isau. I need full access to the network."

"Second Anarch Jax."

"Excuse me?"

"You will refer to me with the proper title accorded my rank."

Tenika rolled her eyes. "Are you serious?"

The Second Anarch's desk sat on a raised dais elevating him, even when he was sitting in his chair, above those who entered his office. Tenika would've thought it an affectation of a weak leader, were it anyone else. He was leaning against the front of his desk, forcing her to crane her neck to see his face.

"Don't forget your place! You're mine to command and not the other way around." Isau Jax straightened to his full height and looked down at her. He was an imposing man with a comfortable command of his authority. She found that both infuriating and alluring at the same time.

"You've proven yourself valuable, and I've allowed you to rise in rank faster than anyone before you, but don't presume my favour will overlook impudence."

Tenika didn't understand her relationship with Isau. He could be aloof or intimate. The latter made no sense to her as he was her senior in rank and quite a few years her junior in age. The age difference didn't seem to bother him. She didn't believe he was particularly attracted to her, assuming instead that it was a form of control. Historically she would have laughed at such an attempt. It wasn't possible to manipulate someone like her. She didn't have feelings or emotional attachments like normal people. Yet somehow, things were different with this particular man. It was confusing. Her intent was to use and discard him as she was certain was his plan for her as well. It was to be expected in these types of alliances — a dance she knew well. Still, she found that she didn't want this association to end. It was ridiculous. He thought he owned her. That assumption filled her with indignant rage. She had proven herself to be more than his equal. She most certainly would surpass him.

"Yes, Anarch." The easy compliance angered her even more. How had he attained this influence over her? She would analyze her feelings later — again. Right now she needed something from Isau.

"The network."

"No one is hindering your access."

"No one is.... I have to make a trip to this facility and request a time slot for the simplest of queries! When I'm in the field, every minute is critical. By the time I've jumped through *your* hoops, my target is often lost."

Isau raised a cautionary eyebrow.

Tenika pressed her lips together and tilted her head forward in acknowledgement of her disrespect.

"You've placed me second to yourself in the chain of command, yet I have no more access than any other agent. How am I supposed to prepare a proper strategy without knowing all of the parameters? How can I effectively coordinate the people you've placed under my command?"

"You've shown yourself to be a formidable strategist despite those limitations. I've always provided the details necessary to succeed."

Tenika raised her voice despite his previous warnings. "You're limiting what I can do for you! I could accomplish so much more."

Isau gave her a wry smile. "Of that I have no doubt. What might you accomplish were I to give you the keys to the kingdom?"

"Is that what this is about? You don't trust me?"

"My dear Tenika, you are brilliant, bellicose, and ambitious. It would be an insult if I failed to respect your abilities. Only a fool would consider you anything less than a threat."

Is that why I'm drawn to him? Tenika wondered. *Is it because he doesn't underestimate me?*

"I've succeeded in everything you've asked. Surely I've proven myself trustworthy."

"You've proven yourself highly effective with what you're given. You have no need for more than I provide. Or am I to assume that you don't trust me to know how to run my own affairs?"

"Of course not, Anarch. I'm not questioning your leadership."

Isau barked a laugh. "Oh, I see. You don't question my ability to lead. You just think you would make better decisions?"

"Not better, just different."

Both of Isau's brows rose this time.

This wasn't going as she'd hoped, but she never really expected Isau to grant her more access. Even if he had, it still wouldn't have given her what she truly desired. She didn't want more access to the network in Caralithica alone. She wanted access to the shared intelligence from all of the international networks. Only the anarchs could access that information. She'd learned that the shared content was stored and regularly updated in a memory stash archive hidden at a secure location. If she could find the location of that archive, she could take the information for herself. That was the real reason for pestering the Anarch like a petulant child.

Tenika bowed submissively. "I defer to your wisdom, Anarch. Might I ask a small boon?"

Isau snorted derisively. "I say no to your first request and you immediately ask for something more? Your audacity is unparalleled. I don't believe there's such a thing as a *small boon* where you're concerned. Let's see if you can prove me wrong this time."

"You have a private terminal here in your office. If my access must be supervised, I'd prefer *your* supervision. The underlings who oversee the network don't have the authority to permit my request, or your wisdom to see its value."

Isau's eyes narrowed in suspicion at her sudden tractability. "The only access that can't be granted by the network chief has to do with international requests for information. That's strictly for my eyes only."

"I understand, Anarch. Indeed, this *is* an international request. You'd save me a great deal of time if we could handle this now — while I'm here."

"Always manipulating — what are you requesting?

"As you know, I've had some conflict in the past with the former head of

Callan International. He's vanished and I was going through our network archives trying to locate him. I've discovered a recent viewcording which appears to show him at a location near the border. I'm trying to ascertain if Nico left the country, but of course I can't track his movements beyond our own network."

"Why are you still searching for Nico Callan?"

"Apart from my own personal vendetta? With Nico missing, Qas Dugarish is not able to fulfill his assassination contract. That's a loose end we need to tie off in order to protect our assets among the magistrates and City sentries."

Isau nodded. "I appreciate your tenacity in continuing the pursuit, but I can't give you access to my terminal."

"I understand. I'm only asking you to check on my behalf."

"I don't have time to sift through archives."

"I can provide the location of the viewcorder immediately beyond our borders and the time stamp for the moment in question. All I need to know is whether Nico Callan is visible in the viewcordings from that location. It should only take you a moment."

Isau leaned back in his chair and folded his arms across his chest as he considered the request. "I'll do this if you let go of the campaign to increase your network access. I weary of it."

If you do this for me, I won't need to ask any longer. Tenika gave the impression she was considering. "Can I approach you for similar requests in the future where international information is concerned?"

Isau shook his head in disbelief and sighed. "If your requests are relevant, infrequent and not at an inconvenient time, then yes." Isau hastened to add, "I'll revoke that offer if you abuse the privilege."

"That will be satisfactory, Anarch."

Isau looked to his terminal and began entering his authorization.

Tenika reached into her pocket at the same time and pressed a button on her tote-comm. It was a signal to her personal team to begin tracking signals. They had spliced into the Caralithican network to monitor usage for the past several days. Enough of the signals had been catalogued to confidently identify local traffic. Now they were looking for something unique representing the Anarch's request to the shared international archive. If they were lucky, they could track that signal to its source.

Isau quickly found the viewcording for the date, time, and location identified by Tenika. He spun the screen around so she could see and beckoned with his fingers, indicating that she should join him on the dias. She took a seat at a chair in front of his desk and Isau replayed the viewcording.

"There's a lot happening quickly in that scene.... Could you play it again?" Tenika asked, stalling for time. Isau played it a second time at a slower speed. The tote-comm in Tenika's pocket remained silent. No response from her team. *Come on guys.*

Tenika pointed to one of the men on the screen. "That looks a bit like Nico, but it's hard to tell from this angle. Are there other cameras in the area?"

Isau shot her an impatient look, then pulled up a feed from across the plaza.

She stared silently at the screen, watching Isau's patience wear thin out of the corner of her eye. He was about to say something when her tote-comm chimed twice. That was the pre-arranged signal. They'd located the archive!

Tenika sighed both in relief and for the sake of her little drama with Isau. "This viewcorder has a much better angle. That's not Nico."

Isau glowered at her. "Shall we waste more of my time while you answer your tote-comm, or are we done?"

Tenika took a knee and put on an appropriately chastised expression. "No, Anarch. Sorry, Anarch. I appreciate you taking the time to do this for me."

Isau turned the screen back towards himself and disconnected. "Then you're dismissed — and Tenika — wear something nice tonight."

Right, they were having dinner together later. More conflicting messages. Tenika huffed silently. He'd be reminding her how generous he was, all evening. It was a small price to pay to pay for what she'd just gained.

"I'll wear the green dress that I know you appreciate. Oh, and I found a cask of that Kemetican wine you're fond of."

Isau's eyes brightened. "Something to look forward to. I'll have the kitchens prepare a suitable accompaniment." He waved her away, turning to the parchments scattered across his desk.

Tenika smiled as she left. She'd be on her best behaviour at dinner. After all, she had something to celebrate. She was about to get a place at the big table, even if none of the anarchs realized it.

Chapter 4

A week had passed since Kayla's inauguration as Chief Sentry of Caralithica. Every day had been filled with bureaucratic legalities and command structure training. She wouldn't have guessed there would be so much more to learn after a lifetime of shadowing Cello Vantos while being groomed for the role. Now she wondered how her mother had managed any of it. Thankfully her mother's former assistant was continuing in that role for Kayla's benefit. Kayla was happy with the decision. Joff Persif excelled in his role and she had always gotten along well with him. At least theirs was one relationship she didn't need to cultivate. She planned to heavily lean on him in the months to come.

This was the first break in her schedule and she'd invited Nico and her mother to her new living quarters. It was also her first time hosting guests. There wasn't much to do in preparation. The base kitchens were preparing a meal for them and since she had done nothing but drop into bed and pass out from exhaustion each day, the place looked as clean as the moment she first walked through the door.

When they arrived, Kayla offered wine to her two guests and retreated to pour some for herself. Nico and Cello chatted amicably about trivial matters. Cello congratulated him on being named as assistant to the Levigator and they talked a bit about what that would entail. Nico likewise congratulated Cello on her recent retirement.

Kayla was still reeling from the implications of her new standing among the

Servators. How could she be their leader? She was younger than the vast majority of the people on the base. Almost everyone had more experience than her. Hearing Nico congratulate her mother's release from those responsibilities brought it all storming to the surface against her will. Without thinking, she blurted out the first thing that came to mind. "How could you do this to me?"

Cello's shoulders slumped as though she'd anticipated this conversation and hoped it could be avoided. "I believe I did it to myself, not you."

Kayla gaped at her mother. "What's that supposed to mean?"

"It means *I* retired. That was *my* prerogative."

"But you didn't ask me!"

Cello snorted. "I was the Chief Sentry. I most certainly did *not* need your permission."

Kayla looked over at Nico with a *help me* expression on her face.

Nico glanced first at Kayla, then at Cello who raised an eyebrow which clearly meant *keep your opinions to yourself*. "Um, I think I'll go stand over there." Nico slowly backed away with one hand raised, the other clutching his wine mug protectively against his chest. Now there were two sets of raised eyebrows hastening his retreat.

"Stop deviating from the point, Mother. You know that's not what I meant. You named me as your replacement — without considering my wishes!"

"Kayla, I know you've been away from Servator influence for a while, but have you already forgotten your vow?"

"Of course not!"

"Repeat it to me."

"You're just trying to change the subject again!"

"Declare your vow!"

Kayla glowered at her mother's insistence. The conversation wouldn't continue until she complied. She ground her teeth and voiced the familiar words. "I give my life in service to the Maker's Way and promise to obey the dictates of the Servators even to death, placing the lives of others before my own."

Cello smiled, triumphant. "There you have it."

Kayla threw her arms out, shook her head and raised her shoulders in an *explain yourself* posture.

"You gave your life to service and obedience, placing the needs of others before your own."

19

"I promised to follow the Maker's Way, obey the commands of my superiors and save others even if the price was my life."

Cello nodded. "That's certainly part of it."

"Part of it? What other interpretation could there be?"

"Kayla! Don't act the simpleton. You grew up as the daughter of the Chief Sentry. You know full well the vow applies to far more than obedience and a willingness to die for the cause. If that were the limit of its meaning, the vow would only apply to those who face danger in battle. What do you suppose it means to an analyst or administrator? What does it mean to an archivist? What of the recruit who declares that vow before she even knows what role she will play? We put the needs of others before our own. We obey the dictates laid down in our laws — all of the dictates. We follow the commands of those who uphold them — all of the commands, not just those associated with battle."

Kayla held her tongue, duly chastised.

"I didn't make this decision alone. It was made by all of the Chief Sentries together. It was made after consulting with your past instructors and those who know your character well. It was made in consideration of what you've already accomplished and what we believe you will yet do. It was a unanimous decision. That is something which rarely happens and you should be humbled by their opinion of you. The process follows ancient dictates and the conclusion is law. No one *chooses* to become a Chief Sentry. They're always appointed. Did you believe I had a choice in my own naming? I was filled with grief after the death of your father. The last thing I wanted to do was pick up that mantle, but I accepted because of my oath. I promised to obey and serve. Others see in us things that we don't see within ourselves. Sometimes we must accept their joint wisdom, even if it makes us uncomfortable"

Kayla couldn't remember the last time her mother had spoken at such length. Never had she heard her mother speak about her own choosing. She didn't know how to respond.

Cello softened her voice. "Kayla, you must have known that you were being groomed as one of several potential candidates for leadership."

Kayla looked at her feet. "Yes, I knew," she whispered.

"Then why are you responding with surprise and outrage?"

"I didn't expect it to come so soon! I thought it would happen in some distant future after you'd passed on having lived a long and happy life. I'm not ready and you're still needed. I can't do what you do."

"You underestimate yourself. Establishing Port Callan and Port Vantos was a massive undertaking. I've never taken on a project of that magnitude. I'm not certain I could do what *you did*."

"Of course you could, Mother…"

Cello held up a hand to forestall Kayla's protest. "Perhaps when I was younger, but not now. You saw a need where I was content to maintain the status quo. You and Nico brought forward innovative solutions beyond anything I would imagine on my own. Your actions were swift and decisive, adapting as necessary to changing conditions. You made sound decisions with limited access to mentors for feedback. These are qualities of a leader. Qualities that have been slipping away from me of late. I feel blessed that a clear replacement became apparent well before a transition became an absolute necessity."

Nico found his voice and joined the conversation. "She's right, Kayla. Don't forget that you did all of that while also running a multinational company. I never doubted your ability to oversee Callan International. And you managed it under an alias, no less."

Kayla gasped. "Nico, your company! I can't stay on as head of Callan International if I'm the Chief Sentry. I'll have to resign. What will you do?"

"It's taken care of. On the day you were named, I spoke with our Servator lawvocate. A working command structure has been in place for a week. Enis has set things up so he can act on my behalf. He's happy to continue in that role. He told me that things have been uneventful since Tenika was removed from the equation and he's been enjoying the challenge."

"You're certain?"

"Absolutely. I never expected you to continue in that role indefinitely. Enis has been looking for a long-term solution since I went into hiding. This just means he's had to move the timeline up a bit, but that's not a problem. He already has a few good candidates in mind. The company is in good hands. You need to focus on your new responsibilities."

"Well, then — I guess I'm doing this."

Kayla's resigned expression bought a sympathetic smile from her mother. "I know all of this feels overwhelming at the moment. I remember how it was for me, but it becomes routine before you know it. Wasn't that the case at Callan International?"

Yes, that was true. Kayla nodded as she recalled those first few months. It did become second nature, sooner than she would've thought.

Cello continued, "... and you were never groomed for that position like you were for this one. These are your people. You know what the expectations are. In many ways, this should prove an easier role to step into, even if the stakes are higher."

"This time you won't be working in secret." Nico added.

"That's right," Cello agreed. "Joff knows my job better than I did. He won't let you fail. The man is a stickler for detail. Nothing slips through the cracks on his watch. Besides, I'm not going anywhere. If you ever want advice, I'm here. You won't be doing this alone."

"Thank you both. That does help a bit. I haven't had a moment alone with my thoughts this past week. Everything has been happening at breakneck speed. Logically, I know that this pace won't last forever, but right now it feels that way."

"Do you want me to talk to Joff and see if he can slow things down a bit?"

"No, that's okay Mother. I'd rather get this initial rush over with. I just needed a reminder that things will settle down. Thank you. I don't know why I didn't think to talk with you sooner."

"You didn't have time, dear."

Kayla laughed. "Right!"

A knock sounded at the door and Nico moved to answer it. "Food's here."

Kayla's stomach growled in anticipation. She hadn't found time between meetings to eat a mid-day meal. Anxiety had kept her hunger pangs at bay, but now they were making themselves known. "Thank the Maker. I'm starving!"

The remainder of the evening passed in the blissful comfort of a familiar routine. It was just what she needed before taking on the world.

Chapter 5

Kenric abruptly disconnected from his conversation with the Second Anarch of Arapanus. Arguing with Samitar Patix was a pointless exercise. Logic was lost on the man when his temper flared. It prevented him from seeing clearly.

Since the gathering of the anarchs, Kenric had increased the surveillance of his peers. He had long ago infiltrated their inner circles. It was one of the benefits of patience and long-term planning. With the exception of Isau Jax, all of the others were careless and shortsighted. It was possible that Isau was aware of Kenric's agents, keeping an eye on them and feeding false information. Kenric did something similar with the clumsy efforts other anarchs made to infiltrate his own organization. It didn't trouble him overly much in Isau's case as he was generally an ally. The others, however, were irritants, and right now he was thoroughly irritated.

Kenric's Sicari had been sending him reports of Servators dying at the hands of his fellow anarchs. He'd expected a few such occurrences and planned for it in advance, but there had been an escalation in recent weeks.

It was infuriating. The entire plan relied on the Servators remaining complacent. Too many deaths would put the Servators on alert and send them into hiding. They needed to catalogue as many Servators as possible before moving against them in a single coordinated effort.

The networks were all up and running. The technology was working flawlessly, they'd already located more Servators in a few months than all past efforts combined. Everyone was pleased with the results. Kenric had invested heavily in the effort, selling the technology at cost and providing expertise. He'd even given away the facial recognition algorithm for free. All he asked for in exchange was a little patience. Now it appeared that they considered the price too high. The ingrates!

They had all agreed at the gathering that no one would move against the Servators prematurely. Kenric understood that a Breacher's word couldn't be trusted, but they all stood to benefit from this plan. The Servators had been a thorn in their collective sides for far too long. They hindered Breacher efforts and diminished opportunities for illicit income. He'd thought the anarchs' greed and personal ambition would be enough incentive to work together on this one course of action. It was a once-in-a-lifetime chance to end the Servator interference permanently.

Why couldn't they wait? They had an estimated two thirds of the Servators located already. What harm would it do to wait a few more months until the algorithm was no longer providing new leads? What benefit could be gained by diminishing their advantage? It wasn't as though the Servators were meddling more than usual. The Breachers weren't gaining any new income streams, but they weren't losing any either. Everyone had been satisfied with the status quo before he had offered this technology. Now the other anarchs were acting like children without enough self-control to delay gratification. He'd counted on their greed to stay the course, but instead it had fostered recklessness.

As far as he could tell, Isau Jax remained committed to the plan, but the rest had followed Kivar Bantoo's example. The man had always been impulsive — led by his appetites. It wasn't a surprise that he'd been the first to give into temptation, they all knew him to be a fool. Why look to his folly for direction?

It was a rhetorical question. Kenric could piece it together well enough from the details he had gleaned from Kivar's recent tote-comm conversations.

Kivar, The Second Anarch of Kemetica, had a well-known hatred for a particular Servator who had bested him on many occasions. It was Kivar's own fault, fool that he was. Kivar had been very vocal in his threat to end that Servator's life the first chance he got. That opportunity presented itself when the algorithm located Kivar's nemesis. The Second Anarch of Kemetica had reacted in his predictably impulsive way and slaughtered the ranger, along with his entire family.

Kenric expected this type of conduct from Kivar. Neither did it come as a surprise to the Servators. Other than the horror of the attack itself, it didn't raise any red flags regarding a change in Breacher behaviour. Kivar had publicly repeated his death threats on several occasions and finally followed through — end of story. There were no serious consequences to the greater plan as far as Kivar was concerned.

The lack of repercussions wasn't lost on Samitar Patix. The Second Anarch of Arapanus, a vengeful and ill-tempered man, already had a long list of enemies. Kenric could picture him stewing in his blood lust, as one after another of his enemies became viable targets. The temptation was too great and the precedent had been set. If no one complained when Kivar did it.... Of course, the second error was nothing like the first. Samitar wasn't impulsive like Kivar. He was deliberate in his planning, making his actions all the more alarming. Worse, he didn't just hit one enemy, he hit several of them over the course of a weekend. It looked exactly like what it was — a well-planned large-scale attack against the Servators. It was the very thing they needed to avoid, and Samitar had been completely unrepentant when Kenric called him to account.

Then there was Loo Vishar, Second Anarch of Jaihuwan. Always deferring to the majority. The fellow would never intentionally put himself in harm's way. He liked Kenric's plan. It meant that he could get rid of his enemies all at once with very little risk to his life or livelihood. When he learned about the actions of Kivar and Samitar, he feared he would lose the low-risk outcome that he coveted for himself. In his cowardice, he chose to attack his own targets before he lost the advantage of surprise and anonymity. His list of enemies wasn't as long as Samitar's, but it was every bit as calculated — an obvious attack against the Servators.

They could at least have tried to obfuscate by being less specific in their targets. How hard could it have been for them to stage a street gang battle with excessive collateral damage? Any number of fictions might have worked to avoid illuminating their plot. His peers had no imagination. It galled him to even admit they were peers, so low was his opinion of them.

It was at times like this that Kenric wished for the oversight of a First Anarch. Unfortunately, as best anyone could tell, there was no such person or position. At least, Kenric had never heard of anyone being contacted by a First Anarch, not in recorded history. The working theory was that fear of a greater authority would keep the Second Anarchs from attempting to claim each other's territory. Infighting was bad for the greater cause, after all.

No one knew if the threat of First Anarch discipline was real, but all Second Anarchs feared what that might look like. The First Anarch was believed to be a vessel for the wastrels, those non-corporeal beings called overlords by the Breachers. Kenric quailed thinking of the madness he heard whenever he came near the doors to overlord realms. The thought of one of those terrifying beings taking a human host and walking among them was enough to prevent a Second Anarch from pushing their luck.

No, Kenric would never wish to meet a First Anarch, but such an authority would likely prevent the very lack of cohesion he now had to deal with. His operation was falling to pieces before his eyes. The damage was done and now he had to find a way to salvage his plans as best he could.

His informants, along with viewcordings from the Breacher network, painted a picture of frantic movements among the known Servators. They were on high alert and would be going into hiding very soon.

The algorithm would track them to some of those hiding places where they'd likely gather in large numbers. That might make it easier for kill squads if it came to that. Unfortunately, it would also make it harder to expose them to the short-lived virus he had prepared. He needed to move soon while he could infect the greatest number of people.

Kenric did some quick calculations. Having targeted almost two thirds of the identified Servators was a good start. That was how many had ingested the toxin being distributed covertly by the Sicari. Once he released the highly contagious but otherwise harmless virus, it would trigger the toxin, killing only those who had been targeted. Servator numbers would be reduced to such a degree that they would find it difficult to mount a defence when the remainder were hunted down.

The network would continue to track their movements. Sooner or later he would find the rest of them. It would take much longer, but he could still have the victory he coveted. He could still be immortalized in the Breacher histories.

He considered the ramifications of an early release of his virus. He had already arranged the means by which he would demand command authority to coordinate a mass attack. The other anarchs would have no choice but to agree when they learned that they had ingested the toxin and that he held the antidote.

Once Breachers from around the globe were organized and ready with their pre-planned targets, he'd no longer need the other anarchs to move ahead with his plans. They would discover soon enough that there wasn't really an antidote, but it would be too late.

If he released the virus now, they'd die before he was granted command over the allied hordes. He had enough spies in place that he might still gain control, but it wasn't a guarantee. Kemetica and Jaihuwan would quickly fall into line. Their leaders were too weak to garner any real loyalty. Arapanus would prove more difficult, but that was where he had the most embedded resources. Samitar had always been the biggest threat.

Caralithica was the only unknown. Most of Isau's senior staff was aware of the alliance between Kenric and their master. He hoped that would work in his favour, but Isau was also the hardest to read. He'd have to worry about that later.

Actually, there was a second unknown. The threat of a possible First Anarch. If Kenric took global command of the horde, it would certainly be cause for such a person to make an appearance. In his original plan, Kenric had hoped to corrupt the Third Anarchs of each nation and prepare them to replace the Second Anarchs, following their deaths. It would allow him to rule from the shadows without technically breaking the Breacher hierarchy. His global command was supposed to appear to be a temporary posting. If he set the virus free ahead of schedule, he wouldn't have time to make those arrangements.

There was no obvious solution. His peers had ruined everything. It would've been better if he'd never included them in the first place. That realization crystallized his resolve. It would *still* be easier without them. He gave further thought to the possibility of gaining authority without the other anarchs around to get in the way. Considering his inability to control them, it was more appealing to take them out of play sooner than later. Perhaps it was hubris, but he became convinced he could manipulate the hordes if their masters were not around to countermand him. It was a gamble, but no worse than the one he had begun with. Kenric picked up his tote-comm and made a call.

"Accelerate your efforts to administer the toxin to all known targets. I'm advancing the deadline."

If there was a First Anarch, Kenric might soon die for his overreach. *Better than living with failure* he decided. If the First Anarch was a myth, then Kenric would have the resources to accomplish all of his goals and so much more. Either way, he'd learn the truth.

Chapter 6

"First the death of a ranger and his family in Kemetica, then the slaughter of my people in Arapanus and the targeted attacks in Jaihuwan. The Breachers are clearly targeting Servators." Jokan Pizzar stood over the conference table, balanced on his fingertips as if leaning forward would add weight to his words, "I thought we were monitoring their network viewcorders and staying clear? How are they finding our people?"

"The viewcorders we've been avoiding are not the issue, it's those hidden micro-corders. They're nearly impossible to spot. Finding them all is hopeless," the Chief Sentry of Jaihuwan responded.

"Micro-corders? I've heard nothing of this. Why weren't we informed?" Jokan demanded.

"It was in the weekly briefing notes, Jokan. You have to read them if you wish to remain informed." Chief Sentry Suul remarked.

"Well, pardon me for being a little preoccupied with funeral plans, Talia!"

"Forgive me, Jokan. I meant no disrespect. I too lost friends this past week."

Kayla took that moment to interject. As the host of this meeting of the Chief Sentries, it fell to her to moderate. They had chosen Caralithica as the safest place to meet due to her recent security innovations at the Denmount base. "Everyone, please be patient with each other. This has been a very trying time. It's been many years since we've faced such aggression from the Breachers. Every lost life is a blow to us all. Jokan, Talia, Beniti, I'm sure everyone here wishes to convey their condolences for your losses. We're here to help as best we can."

Heads nodded in agreement around the table.

"I'm sorry, Talia — everyone." Jokan lowered his head. "My emotions are getting the better of me. I feel like I've let my people down — like I should have done more."

Desi Yorubi, Chief Sentry of Sumakad spoke into the silence that followed. "There was nothing you could have done, Jokan. The attacks came without warning. You've no need to apologize. Each of us at this table holds the same fear for those under our command. We want to protect them, and when we're unable, we feel the weight of that responsibly. Everyone here can attest to similar feelings of helplessness. One death is already too much. No one wishes to suffer additional loss." Desi looked around the table at those gathered. "Yet we know that it is inevitable. We will lose good people. The best we can hope to do is minimize risk and that's why we have gathered here today, is it not?"

"That's correct, Chief Yorubi. The purpose of this emergency meeting is to identify risks and implement solutions. You all know that we've incorporated some cutting-edge security initiatives here at the Denmount base. I've put together a task force to stress test and expand on those systems. Those efforts, and some novel ideas from the Levigator, have led our analysts to some fascinating new uses of QPN technology. I'll be distributing our findings later on in the day, but to begin, I'd like to discuss the possibility of pooling our resources to implement these new security measures at all of our bases as soon as possible. It will require sending teams of your own people to study under our analysts. Together they will work on the security details of each base, critiquing and refining as necessary."

Kayla held up a hand to forestall the inevitable objections. "Now before you say anything, I am aware that no one is keen to expose their security measures. However, I think we can all agree that current measures are long overdue for an update. In order to uncover any existing weakness, we need fresh perspectives. That means exposing yourself for a short time, but only to your fellow Servators. In the end, you'll all have a more robust response to our common enemy. Once your people understand the possibilities, I have no doubt they will be able to expand on them in creative ways to make your security measures your own once more."

Silence ensued and Kayla second-guessed her decision to place this particular topic as the first item on the agenda. "I, uh, expected a little more discussion. I didn't mean to minimize the effectiveness of your existing protocols."

Beniti shook his head and chuckled. "You misunderstand, Kayla. I think we're all just a little surprised that you felt it necessary to get a consensus on this. Everyone here has had an opportunity to see the changes you've implemented and are suitably impressed. I, for one, have been waiting anxiously for you to offer to share your findings so that I can upgrade our own facility. There is no question that our existing defences are sorely lacking compared to your own. Considering the new threats we face, we need every advantage we can get. If you need to see a consensus..." Beniti raised his hand and others immediately shot into the air. "You have our unanimous agreement, Chief Sentry Vantos."

Kayla's cheeks coloured. She was decades younger than her peers at this gathering and a little intimidated by their wealth of combined experience. "Thank you. Well then, in light of recent events, I'd like to begin as soon as possible. I've scheduled a start date for next week. The sessions will be held at Port Callan. When you have a moment during the day, please provide a list of ten names to my assistant Joff, who will prepare for the arrival of your staff. We'd like you to send a mix of analysts and security experts familiar with any facilities you feel would benefit from an assessment."

A few hands began scribbling names on parchment as Kayla continued. "With that out of the way, I yield the floor to Chief Sentry Abrax for an update on the micro-corders."

"Thank you, Kayla. We've been able to find a few of these devices." Beniti held up a tiny transparent device. "As you can see, they're easy to miss. Their transparency allows them to blend into the background. The ones we've found have been located on patterned or busy surfaces where they're all but impossible to spot unless you're specifically looking for them. This one was inside the office of a chief magistrate. We have been focussing our search on locations with a high chance of revealing sensitive information as the most likely targets. That said we've also found them outside in public locations and oftentimes in areas near existing Breacher viewcorders. That is disturbing because it suggests that they're using the existing viewcorders as decoys to lull us into a false sense of security while these secondary devices continue to track our movements."

Jokan interrupted, "That's why my people were found despite our precautions."

"That's what we suspect, yes."

"The micro-corders are not directly connected to the Breacher viewcorder network. Instead, they use the public tote-comm network to transmit to an unknown location. We assume they connect to the Breacher network from a transfer hub."

"Can we interfere with the signals?"

"Not without disrupting tote-comm service to the public as well. We're working on a way to create a temporary disruption for emergencies, but it's not a sustainable long-term solution."

"Then what are we to do?" Talia asked. "It seems pointless to consider disabling individual micro-corders knowing it's unlikely we'd find them all. Worse, they've been active for months without our knowledge. We have no idea how much intelligence they've already accumulated. What if these recent attacks are just trial runs for something bigger? How many of us are already compromised?"

Beniti nodded. "Agreed. We have to make plans based on the assumption that many of our people are being targeted as we speak. That means everyone goes into hiding as soon as it's possible to do so safely. we'll have to be very careful in how we move people. We can't have everyone travelling at once to the same locations. Each of us will need to do an inventory of recent paths taken to bases and safe houses. We have to find out which are the most used points of ingress and assume that one or all of those points of entry have been compromised or are being carefully watched."

Faces sobered at that revelation.

Chief Sentry Yorubi voiced the thought on everyone's mind. "We need to plan for evacuation in the event a base is compromised."

"I've been discussing that possibility with Chief Sentry Vantos. Currently, Port Vantos and Port Callan are the only Servator facilities with covert means of ingress far from viewcorders." Beniti turned to Kayla and nodded.

"We've already begun tunnelling for emergency housing in the caves riddling the cliffs around Port Callan. The undersea entrance grants us a great deal of security for moving a large number of people. Nico Callan has reserved sea transports dedicated to carrying Servator passengers and transporting emergency supplies. We recommend you make plans to evacuate your people to the nearest international seaport. Look for Callan International vessels with a yellow stripe on the bow. You'll know you've arrived at the right place if you see a small Servator symbol to the right of the boarding ramp."

"The vessels are already docked at the ports closest to your main bases." Beniti added. "If you feel it's safer to travel to a different port, let me know. I also recommend you send someone to coordinate with the captain of the vessel in your port. You'll need to find a way to load passengers without raising suspicion. I'll leave those details to you."

Kayla thanked Beniti as he sat down.

Chief Sentry Pizzar brought up the next item on the agenda without Kayla having to present it. "We need to find out what the Breachers know. We're just reacting right now. We need proper intelligence to plan effectively."

Several heads around the table were nodding in agreement.

Beniti rose again. "We only know for certain the location of the memory stash archived in Sumakad. That information was given to us by Kade Brixton when we saved him from the Breacher base where he was being held. Kade has intimate knowledge of the network as its architect."

"How do we know we can trust him?"

"The Breachers forced Kade to build the network. We all know how they operate. He wants to see the network brought down as much as any of us and has been working tirelessly to help make that happen. The problem is the network can only be accessed from within a very secure base."

"If we try forcing our way into a Breacher stronghold, we could lose as many people as if we did nothing." Talia noted.

"The Levigator has a plan." Beniti grunted. From the look on his face, it was a plan he didn't agree with.

Kayla spoke into her Q-view and the door to the conference room opened a moment later.

Shouts of alarm and outrage filled the air as Second Anarch, Kenric Trantor, sauntered into the room.

Chapter 7

Hands flew to Q-views and defensive weapons materialized. A few who leapt from their chairs thought to initiate the newer emergency shields developed by Lev and a team of analysts. Lev was glad to see his idea put to practical use, even as he raised his hands to assure everyone they were unnecessary.

Lev held up his hands in a submissive gesture. "Everyone, please — you're not in danger."

"Who let *him* in here?" Jokan Pizzar demanded. As the Chief Sentry of Arapanus, he was all too familiar with the face of Kenric Trantor who operated in his city. "What's the meaning of this? That man is a murderer! Where are the rangers? Why is he not confined to a cell?"

"It's okay, Jokan." Beniti assured him.

"No! it most certainly is *not* okay." Jokan was on his feet, with a stun baton pointed at the interloper. He was jabbing his finger at his Q-view attempting to summon security. "Why is no one responding?"

"Beniti cocked his head to the side as he looked at their visitor and shrugged. "I told you this was a bad idea, Levigator. I think you'd better end your demonstration."

Leviticus disassembled the token that was masking his face.

Jokan stopped in his tracks, confusion on his face. "Levigator? How did you... What... I think I'd like an explanation."

"I'm sorry for the theatrics. When I first proposed my idea, it met with a great deal of skepticism." Lev glanced at Beniti who shook his head, making clear his opinion. "I needed to make sure you saw the potential before sharing my plan."

"This is unnerving." The Chief Sentry of Jaihuwan lowered her shield, but kept her eyes riveted on the Levigator. "If such technology exists, how do we know you're the Levigator impersonating Kenric Trantor and not the other way around?"

That idea hadn't occurred to the others who shared uneasy glances.

"Talia, would you ring my Q-view please?"

Talia complied and everyone heard the chime on Lev's wrist.

"It's not possible for anyone but the owner of a Q-view to enable it. You've just heard confirmation that Talia contacted my personal Q-view. If that's not enough proof...." Lev materialized a portable mask generator on the table in front of each Chief Sentry.

Talia smiled and bowed her head in acknowledgement. "I concede that you are indeed the Levigator. Now, what are these devices?"

"You're all aware that I've been spending time on the rehabilitation island of Chellea to consult with Kade Brixton. We've been exploring ways to counter the Breacher network. These masks are one of the interim solutions. Kade has created generic facial composites that line up with key facial mapping points of the Breacher algorithm. These are coordinated with QPN intersections that I've identified for each composite image. Without going into detail, it reduces the computing power required to generate a token. This in turn allows us to eliminate a need for the Quantum Positioning Network. The headbands you see in front of you are designed to scan the contours of your face and map local coordinates to create a token mask using one of a hundred generic faces we've compiled. Those faces and associated fictional details have been painstakingly uploaded into the Breacher network through an exploit of the Breacher viewcorder reporting system. Unfortunately, we're limited by the kind of data the network can accept, so we can't use it as a backdoor for writ contagions or other methods of invading the network."

"So this is a way for us to impersonate others as you've just demonstrated?" Desi asked.

"Not exactly. What I've shown you isn't possible with these devices. Since I don't rely on the QPN, I can reconfigure tokens quickly enough to animate the features for myself. Unfortunately, the QPN doesn't have enough capacity to provide a similar function for the many people who may be using these masks at any given time. These devices will only be capable of a static image."

"So — it won't fool a person on the street?"

"Anyone using one of these devices will be able to mask their identity from the Breacher viewcorders. They'll appear to the algorithm as one of the fictional characters we've created, but you're correct. If a person is looking right at you, it will be obvious something is strange about your appearance. I would recommend using the masks only when travelling quickly from one location to another. In areas where you'll be engaging with others, it should be avoided."

"That will severely restrict its use." Jokan noted.

"True, but it's the best we have to offer at the moment. Besides, our primary goal at this point is to limit the ability of the Breachers to track us. The masks will be useful when travelling to Servator bases or meeting with fellow operatives. In those instances, we would be trying to avoid the public regardless, so this provides some added insurance."

Desi turned the thin band over in her hand, marvelling at its smooth lines and light weight. It was similar in appearance to a recent fashion trend and wouldn't look out of place in the street. "Yes, this will be helpful. It will offer some comfort to know we can escape watchful eyes when necessary. What about friends and families of Servator agents who don't have access to Q-views?"

"That's part of the reason for taking this route. There's a small button on the side to turn it off and on. It's completely self-contained with no access to the Servator network. They can be distributed to those we trust as needed. We've been telling people the headband is an image projector. There is no need to mention anything about Servator token technology. The mask cycles on and off so quickly that it never becomes a true solid — users can still touch their own faces while it's active. So far, people seem satisfied with the projector explanation."

"How soon can we have access to these devices?" Talia asked.

"I'm sending you the token templates now." Lev tapped his Q-view and the Chief Sentries glanced at their wrists as chimes filled the room. "You can begin producing your own immediately."

"Thank you for these, Levigator." Kayla added. "These will be useful in any evacuation efforts. I'm sure the revised security protocols our working group comes up with will benefit as well."

"I think we can agree these masks will be useful," Beniti affirmed. "However, we still don't know the extent of our current exposure. I believe we were discussing the difficulty in gaining access to that information when you made your dramatic appearance earlier. Perhaps you'd like to share your plan with the rest of the group?"

Lev hesitated, somewhat abashed.

"Appearing as a notorious Breacher does seem a poor choice considering recent tensions." Jokan agreed. "Why not lead with the portable masks?"

"I apologize for startling you. As I mentioned earlier, I needed you to see how realistic the effect could be before sharing my plan. As for choice — it took quite a bit of time and effort for the analysts to gather the necessary images to create a realistic template with an acceptable range of expressions. It took an equal amount of work on my part to become familiar enough with the template to effectively animate it. I didn't have time to prepare an alternative before this meeting."

"What possible reason could you have to choose that particular face?" Jokan wondered.

"I thought that was obvious. I intend to impersonate Second Anarch Trantor in order to gain access to the information we seek."

If an anarch walking into the middle of a meeting of the Chief Sentries created an uproar, it was nothing compared to the consternation that followed Lev's announcement.

"Unacceptable! The Levigator cannot put himself in such a dangerous position." Desi insisted. "There has to be..."

Jokan didn't let her finish before voicing his own dismay. "There must have been others you could have chosen to impersonate — someone with a high enough security level to access the network. Pretending to be the Second Anarch in his own backyard? It's madness!"

Beniti stared at Lev with a smug *I told you so* expression on his face. Lev ignored him, waiting patiently as objections circled the table. Eventually someone noticed his silence. One by one the voices fell away.

"Kade already warned us of Kenric's plan. He wants to track down all Servators and destroy them in one coordinated effort. We all agree that we can't continue operating in the dark. We need to know how far his plan has progressed.

We can't afford to wait or we risk losing everyone and everything. The Sumakad location is the only one we have intelligence on. I've given this a lot of thought. We can only attempt this once and the only person with unfettered access is Kenric himself. His people fear him and are not likely to question my actions in his stead. This *will* work as long as we can identify a time when Kenric will be away from the base."

"Going in there alone would be suicide." Kayla shook her head. "It's far too dangerous. It's not worth it."

"Isn't it?" Lev locked eyes first with Kayla and then with every other person in the room. "Isn't it the Levigator's job to ease the burden of oppression? Is there anyone else who could hope to pull this off? Are there others better able to protect themselves? You know I'm the only person capable of this and you know it needs to be done. From my perspective, if I can save one life it will be worth it. We all know that we have far more to lose."

No one had a response.

"I'm grateful for your concern, but for all you know, this is what the Levigator was meant to accomplish. The Breachers won't expect such a bold move. You were fooled by the disguise. They will be too, and if things go sideways — they won't expect the other things I can do either.

"I didn't come here to ask your permission. I'm doing this with or without your blessing, but I do hope you'll help. Kade has provided a writ contagion that may shut down the network permanently. I'll attempt to deploy it from within after I've accessed their memory stash for the information we seek, but first I need to get through the front gate. That's going to require some intelligence about Kenric's whereabouts and possibly a distraction. Can I count on you to help me work out the details?"

"If you've already decided, then you know we won't refuse you. What do you need, Levigator?"

Lev shared the basics of his plan and they spent the better part of four hours considering scenarios and refining details. When no more could be done from the conference room, people began to leave. Beniti remained behind as Lev stared at the mess of parchments and kofa mugs strewn about the table.

"I still think it's a bad idea."

Lev smiled at the expected reminder. "I know, and to be honest, it confuses me."

"How so?"

"From the moment you discovered I was the Levigator, you refused to offer advice when I asked for it. You kept saying it wasn't your place to

influence the choices of a Levigator. That hasn't stopped you from repeatedly admonishing me whenever you felt I was putting myself at risk with my *Levigator choices*."

"I'm not trying to prevent you from trusting the Maker's lead. I'm offering you advice in the only way that's left to me."

"How do you figure?"

"A Chief Sentry has to learn to rely on more than himself to accomplish a goal. He has to trust his people to follow his commands and come up with solutions. Just because a course of action is the right one, doesn't mean its execution can't be improved upon. If I can reduce your risk by encouraging you to consider alternative plans of attack, I will continue to do so."

"Ah, so no influence at all then."

Beniti offered a self-deprecating shrug. "I hope you know by now that I'm your friend and I care about your well-being."

"I do, and I'm thankful for your friendship despite the confusing hypocrisy."

"You think I'm a hypocrite?"

Lev regretted his choice of words, realizing how harsh that sounded. "I'm a beneficiary of your good will, so it feels wrong somehow to use that word, but isn't that what it means to say one thing and do another?" Lev asked. "Of the people I've met who follow the Maker's Way, most have been pleasant and earnest. However, I've noticed a smaller subset of individuals who appear to have a different understanding of what it means to follow the Maker. They tend to be people I greatly respect and admire, like yourself. At times their views seem to be in conflict with Servator dictates."

Beniti nodded. "Is it hypocrisy or perspective?"

"I suppose my perspective could be skewed." Lev conceded.

"Actually, I was suggesting that the differences you've noticed may be a matter of Servator perspective. The Maker's Way is ultimately about our relationship with the Maker and each other. Those who try to live by the dictates alone will appear different than those who use them to seek deeper relationships."

Lev was taken aback by that admission. "I've noticed that some people strictly adhere to the dictates while others follow those that suit them. Some don't seem to follow them at all, and yet they still claim to be following the Maker's Way. That sounds like hypocrisy to me."

"Oh? Do the dictates seem oppressive or evil to you?"

Lev shook his head at the sudden change in direction. "I don't think anyone could deny that the world would be a better place if everyone followed the dictates, but some would argue that there are circumstances and times when they can't be followed."

"Do you agree with that assessment?"

Lev shrugged, noncommittally.

"Assuming that was true," Beniti continued. "It would still be better to at least try to follow the dictates and fail, wouldn't you agree?"

"I suppose."

"So, who is the hypocrite? The person who recognizes the value of the Maker's Way, and fails to uphold it, but keeps trying and maturing? Or is it the person who says 'I'm already good and I don't need to change, so none of the dictates apply to me?'

"There's a saying in the ancient texts. 'When I was a child, I reasoned like a child — when I became an adult, I did away with childish things.'

"Children don't like being restricted by rules. They say to themselves, 'I won't treat my own children this way when I grow up,' but they end up imposing the same rules. They know better, having gained an adult perspective. Likewise, we don't understand the Maker's rules unless we mature to a point where we become like the Maker in our desires. When we have a heart like the Maker, we want what's best for everyone. We begin to think of others more than ourselves.

"When following the Maker's rules willingly, the dictates become unnecessary. That's because we make better decisions and end up doing what the Maker would have wanted in the first place. True freedom comes not in following the dictates or avoiding them. It comes with a change of heart that leaves us wanting the same things as the Maker. The dictates provide guidance while we're learning. When we finally understand their wisdom and benefit from their employment, they are no longer necessary. From that point on, they become a truth of our reality that we respect in the same way we respect the force of gravity while standing at the edge of a cliff."

Lev considered Beniti's words. "So you're saying I'm noticing a difference in the level of spiritual maturity?"

"Partially, perhaps. More importantly, I'm telling you that understanding the character of the Maker provides context and greater insight. The dictates of the Servators can be summarized by saying that we should care for each other. It goes without saying that the Maker cares for us or there wouldn't be Levigators.

"As for your confusion about my actions — I can recognize your authority and have confidence in your ability as Levigator while still worrying about you. There is no contradiction because caring about others is at the core of the dictates."

Lev finished the thought, "...and at the same time, you're not perfect, but you're trying."

Beniti smiled. "Precisely."

Chapter 8

The pounding of the surf was muted by the stone work above her head. Tenika sat alone with her thoughts, staring at the blank viewscreen in front of her. It had been some time since she'd visited this particular property, but soon it would be a regular destination. It was the perfect location for covert access to the Breacher network. The ruins of an ancient lighthouse sat perched on the edge of a rocky promontory a few leagues north of Denmount. It was hidden from the highway due to its lower elevation on the sea cliff wall. The lighthouse was accessible only by a narrow rut-filled path that could barely be called a road.

She'd noticed the ruins during a meeting with Bode Garushe on his sea transport. He had sailed them to a location just offshore, but far from prying eyes and alert ears, or so he thought. The lighthouse ruins had been barely visible in the dark, but moonlight reflected off some broken glass among the rocks. It caught her eye as they floated past. Something about the structure struck a chord. Solitary, abandoned, but still standing in defiance of whatever the world threw at it. It had taken her some time, but eventually she found and purchased the land where it sat, forgotten.

It was ironic. That meeting on Bode's sea transport resulted in her temporary capture by Servators. It also allowed her to find this place which she now hoped would lead to the Servator's undoing.

The entire seaward face of the lighthouse had sheared away. The cliff it sat on had collapsed in some long-ago landslide. The remaining structure contained an air shaft that ran the full height of the tower. The shaft provided a perfect place to conceal an antenna. A below-grade room remained intact and was now filled with high tech equipment and other creature comforts. Tenika told no one about the place. It was for her alone, a place to escape and think.

She thought back to a recent report from her informants within Callan International. Seri Quin had resigned from her position as temporary head of the company. That bit of news didn't trouble her so much as the fact that Seri had also effectively disappeared. Tenika still had a score to settle with that woman and not knowing where or when she might be able to extract her vengeance was galling. She had imagined a number of pleasing scenarios where she destroyed Seri's credibility, thus ruining her career. Now that Seri was no longer working for Callan International, those options were off the table. It was like the woman knew when to dodge and weave before a blow was even directed her way.

Tenika had ordered her people to find out where Seri had gone, but they kept hitting dead ends. It was like she never existed. That only proved what she'd thought all along. Seri was hiding something and Tenika was determined to find out what it was. When she learned the truth, she'd discover a new avenue for vengeance.

Nagging doubts popped into her mind as she recalled the arrogant confidence Seri had displayed at one of their last meetings. *What if I never hear of her again? Is it possible that I've met my equal?* No, that couldn't be right. Seri didn't have a calculating presence. *Unless she's a far better actor than I imagined.* Tenika had lost so much over the past year. This drive to hurt Seri was petty and served no real purpose, but she couldn't bear the thought of losing a single thing more. She deserved some good news for a change.

Tenika forced her attention back to the reason She was here. If everything had worked as planned, she'd have full access to the international Breacher Network. She would then have the inside information she needed to plan properly. It was the edge she'd been trying to gain since she first accepted Isau's invitation to join the Breachers. Isau.... She was still confused by her feelings about the man, but it didn't matter. She refused to remain under anyone's control. That meant gaining leverage and she couldn't do that while she was being kept in the dark.

To make herself invaluable, she needed advantages that others didn't have. She'd already used some of them to gain her current standing. None of her fellow

Breachers knew about the technology she had stolen from Callan Biologics. She reserved its use for her non-Breacher crew, preferring to keep those two worlds separated. That arrangement had worked well for her so far. The contacts from her past had no idea who the Breachers were and they didn't know the true purpose of the viewcorder network. It was enough for them to know that gaining access to it meant more intelligence for their own endeavours.

As she had hoped, when Isau logged into the network with his higher security privileges and made an international query, Tenika's team had been able to follow those unique signals. It wasn't precise, but it gave them a general area to begin their search. It didn't take long to locate an isolated facility with transmission towers and a suspicious amount of security.

Tully had provided still-view images of the men guarding the facility and Tenika immediately recognized several of them as Breachers. She didn't know for sure that this was their target, but it was a reasonable assumption and at some point they needed to find out what was inside.

She'd given Tully the go ahead to infiltrate. After a few more days spent observing the comings and goings of facility staff, they were able to determine the optimum time to make their attempt. They decided on a pre-dawn shift with only two guards and one network operator.

The Energy scythes Tully's team had developed from stolen Callan Biologics technology were used for the first time in a live operation. The EMP pulses had a thirty-cubit range. With her men evenly spaced, they quickly created what looked like a general power outage rather than a targeted attack. The long-distance application worked flawlessly. Apart from their long-range abilities, the scythes could cut through flesh at close range, hence the name. Combat use wasn't practical for this exercise. They couldn't leave behind any evidence of their infiltration. Tenika had been concerned about how they would accomplish the required stealth. She had been doubly pleased when Tully told her they had identified a pulse pattern for the scythes that could temporarily scramble human synapses from a distance. That frequency was used to knock out the guards and staff. After that, the downed men were quickly administered a sedative that would keep them asleep for several hours. The Breacher security detail never knew what hit them. Tenika knew the type. When they awoke, they wouldn't admit that they'd fallen asleep on duty. Since the temporary network failure looked like a localized power issue, the staff would report nothing amiss and avoid the ire of their superiors. The viewcorders were down after all, there would be no record to suggest anything suspicious.

It was a small matter to lift keys from the sleeping men and enter the building. The network technician had a terminal open when he passed out, so Tully didn't even need to break into the system. He had full access and was able to install intercept weaves and hidden transmitters well before their mission deadline. The entire operation was executed swiftly and successfully.

Tenika was proud of her team. They were highly skilled professionals who put their Breacher counterparts to shame. It was an organization-wide shortcoming she'd need to address as she rose in the Breacher hierarchy, but right now it worked to her advantage.

Her fingers hovered over the command pad. This was the moment of truth. She was the only one with access to the transmitters, so the connection hadn't been tested yet. This had been her first opportunity to escape from her Breacher duties. She entered her password and stared at the viewscreen in anticipation. Text scrolled past her eyes and paused at a blinking message — *Establishing connection... Signal lock...* The screen went black and Tenika was about to scream in frustration, but then the familiar Network interface appeared.

"It worked!" Tenika jumped to her feet and threw both fists into the air. She quickly sat back down realizing her celebration might be premature. She had general access, yes, but did she have full access to the international archive? She quickly typed in a few queries for access to viewcorders in Jaihuwan. *Let's see what Laki Shung is up to.* There he was. Someone had placed a micro-corder in his office. *My old boss is slipping, or maybe he was never as clever as I thought he was.* It made her feel good to know that she could monitor the man who had once monitored her. She definitely had access to the international viewcorders, but what about the collected information? A few more queries gave her the answer. Still-views of faces and personal details filled the screen.

"I'm in!" Tenika completed her victory dance. She took advantage of her solitude to let out a rarely displayed lack of constraint. Catching her breath, she returned to her seat in front of the viewscreen.

She was uncertain where to begin. The possibilities were truly global in scope. Then suddenly, she knew exactly where to start.

Tenika switched the interface to search mode and entered a query -S-E-R-I-Q-U-I-N-.SEARCHING... NO RESULTS.

That didn't make sense. The network was up long before Seri left. She had to have been captured on a viewcorder somewhere. Unless she was somehow able to make that information disappear as effectively as *she* had. No, that would be impossible unless she happened to be a highly placed Breacher. That seemed very unlikely. Tenika snapped her fingers as she remembered that a face could be in the system without an associated name. She split her screen and called up her personal files. She had a copy of Seri's personnel file from Callan International. It contained a fairly recent still-view which she copied and entered into a query using the facial recognition algorithm. SEARCHING... MATCH FOUND.

Tenika studied the image on her screen. The face that stared back at her had long dark hair, and at first she thought the algorithm had found an imperfect match. Even so, there was something familiar. She tried to imagine the face with lighter hair and a shorter cut. Then she saw it. That arrogant confidence that so infuriated her. It was Seri alright, but the results said she was Kayla Vantos. *Why is that name so familiar?* She read more. -KAYLA VANTOS - HIGH PRIORITY TARGET - DAUGHTER OF CELLO VANTOS, CHIEF SENTRY OF THE CARALITHICAN HOST-.

Cello Vantos? That was the name of the Servator woman who interrogated her! The same woman who sentenced her to life imprisonment without a trial. Seri Quin was her daughter? No wonder Seri had looked so smug. Tenika had been right when she sensed that Seri was more dangerous than she appeared. She was a Servator agent! *How long were they watching me?* Tenika wondered. She screamed with fury at the thought of being played a fool by Seri. No, Kayla, she reminded herself. She had to imprint the correct name in her mind.

Kayla had been an irritant who got in the way of her plans, but Cello had imprisoned her. Both needed to pay. Her need for vengeance fused into a single name — Vantos. The Servators had stolen everything from her and that effort had been led by the Vantos family. The flames of her hatred for the Servators was fuelled by the revelation.

"You can't hide from me, Kayla Vantos. I have your face, I have your name, and I have the means to find you anywhere in the world. Sooner or later you'll have to surface and I'll be waiting."

Chapter 9

Everything was in place. Lev waited patiently in the black ground transport, watching the citizens of Sumakad go about their daily business. The Chief Sentry of Sumakad had provided a duplicate version of the model used by Kenric Trantor as his personal conveyance. Rangers had been monitoring Trantor's movements and determined that he chose this particular day each week to tour a number of restaurants and unassuming businesses. Judging by the types of people Trantor met, it was likely he was gathering reports from his agents and informants. Regardless, it typically kept him away from the compound for most of the day. It would give them plenty of time to complete their objective.

Once Kenric left the compound, they'd wait fifteen minutes and then pull up to the gates, giving the impression that Kenric had forgotten something. Lev would pose as Kenric from that point on.

Tark was driving. He wore a masking headband that mimicked the face of Trantor's regular driver. It wouldn't fool anyone up close, but as long as no one tried to speak with Tark directly, he'd be okay. After Lev exited, Tark would park the ground transport a few buildings away and take up position in front of the compound to watch for Kenric's return or any other unexpected surprises.

To avoid detailed explanations about why Kenric appeared to be returning prematurely, Yori would provide a distraction, giving Lev an excuse to send the Breacher guards off to investigate. The guards would report Kenric's return without having time to obtain an explanation. It would alert the staff of his presence without Lev surprising anyone or needing to explain himself to every person he met. That was the hope anyway. If Lev ran into complications, he intended to play the role of a frustrated leader ready to snap at his minions. A bad temper would go a long way in keeping people away from someone as infamous as Trantor.

The Breacher base operated under the guise of a diplomatic embassy. It allowed them to maintain secrecy behind the compound's walls. However, as Kade had informed them, a marketplace opened up within the compound walls during daylight hours. Citizens could ply their trades under the watchful eye of Breacher security. The bazaar was their choice of location for a distraction. Yori had purchased a stall at the edge of the bazaar that looked like it was about to collapse. At the proper moment, he'd set it aflame and run through the bazaar shouting in alarm. He'd left several buckets of water at the site so others could douse the flames. They only needed a few minutes of excitement, not a catastrophe.

Lev sat up in his seat as Yori reported in. "Trantor is on the move. His ground transport is pulling away from the compound. Wait for confirmation of his arrival at his first destination."

Rangers had been placed at a few locations where they expected Trantor to visit. They didn't know for certain where he might go. His routine hadn't been consistent. They hoped to have at least a few correct guesses to provide advance warning of any changes in his itinerary.

"Understood," Lev replied. The minutes passed quickly and confirmation was received. Tark pulled the vehicle up to the front gates. Lev glanced at his reflection in the transport window. Kenric's face looked back at him. He quickly exited the ground transport and waved Tark away. By now Yori would've initiated his distraction.

The guards looked at each other as Lev approached.

"Second Anarch!" One of them stiffened. "Is there a problem —" At that moment shouts could be heard from the bazaar. The volume increased as the crowd took up the alarm. The guards alternated their attention between Lev and the commotion, not sure what was expected of them.

"Well, don't just stand there!" Lev barked. "Find out what's going on." The startled guards turned as one in the direction of the noise. "Not both of you!" Lev rolled his eyes." He pointed at one of the guards. "You! Go and check it out!"

To the second he said, "You stay here to guard the entrance. What were you thinking? Call for backup and let the staff know I don't want to be disturbed. I've seen enough incompetence for one day. Can you handle that?"

"Yes, Anarch!"

As Lev walked through the gates, he saw the man talking into his tote-comm with a worried expression on his face. *Good*. Lev waited until he was alone in a hallway before giving his status. "I'm in." He was on his own now. In the event that things went really wrong, Yori had arranged for another distraction. It involved putting a hole in one of the compound walls with some explosives. Hopefully it wouldn't come to that or lives could be lost. The thought of it made him squirm. The whole purpose of doing this himself was so no one else would be put in harm's way. He didn't think his soul could handle any more loss of life. He'd argued against outside assistance, but of course no one was going to be talked out of coming to their Levigator's aid. He knew they would try even if he told them not to. *I just have to make sure it doesn't come to that.*

Kade had provided him with a layout of the compound. Lev had two objectives. The first was Trantor's private quarters. Staff wouldn't find anything suspicious about that. Kade said that Trantor had a private terminal. It was expected to be secured, but that didn't matter. Kade built the system and he had a master access code. It was his first objective because it would give him time alone to search the archives and determine how badly the Servators were compromised. If all went as planned, he'd make a copy of the archives and move on to his secondary objective. That would be trickier.

The second part of their plan was to infect the network with a writ contagion. He'd need access to a maintenance terminal within the network operations room. Kade had warned him that the operations room was always manned. If Lev was found out, he'd have to run. It would be too late to search the archives by that point, so the network attack had to be the last thing he attempted. Kade assured him someone would notice quickly if a contagion was deployed — counter-measures would raise an alarm.

Lev walked with brisk purpose as he made his way toward Trantor's quarters. He was prepared to scowl at the people who crossed his path, but everyone averted their eyes at his approach and hugged the walls to stay out of his way. *I guess guard number two got the message out.* It was what he needed, but a part of him was horrified at their fear of him. *The man must be a monster.* That thought spurred him on. He had to stop the Breacher threat. He was the Levigator.

Lev was taken aback by the opulence of the room as he entered Trantor's chambers. It was a monument to decadence and abuse. He wasn't sure what he had expected, but it affronted his senses anyway. *Focus Lev.* A quick scan of the place led him to a desk with a view screen off to one side. He hurried to the terminal and entered Kade's access code.

It didn't take long to find what he was looking for. He was already familiar with the system. Kade's designs were based on his own after all, and he'd spent time on the version that Kade had reconstructed at Chellea Island. Lev connected his wrist Q-view and initiated a copy as he scrolled through the entries. It was far worse than he imagined. Using *Servator* as a query, he was presented with a list of thousands of photos alongside names and locations around the globe. He recognized several of those locations as secret Servator facilities. The blood drained from his face as he considered the implications. They needed to respond immediately. "Tark, I need you to contact Chief Sentry Abrax and have his analysts turn their attention to the contents I'm uploading. It's worse than we thought. Immediate evacuations are in order."

"Understood."

Lev was startled by a loud bang. It echoed through the room. He stood, prepared to defend himself, but was hampered by the cable connecting his Q-view to the terminal. He was still alone. *Bang.* Lev's eyes darted about the room trying to find the source of the noise. *Bang. Bang.* It seemed to be emanating from behind a large, heavy and very ancient looking door.

The Q-view chimed indicating that the copy was complete. Lev disconnected the cable and moved toward the door to investigate. A wailing began to accompany the pounding. It was definitely coming from beyond the door. Did Trantor have some poor tormented soul locked away? He looked around for a key, but found nothing. Maybe there was another way to get it open. He looked around the edges and at the hinges for some weakness. Then he realized he hadn't tried the handle to see if the door was actually locked.

His fingers brushed the handle and the door began to shudder under repeated blows. An otherworldly howl grew in volume until he had to cover his ears. Lev's skin crawled and he took three quick steps backward. *That wasn't human.* All of his senses screamed for him to run. He dropped into pattern sight and tried to see beyond the door. What he saw, or rather what he didn't see, startled him more than the sound.

The entire world was filled with patterns, but here there were none. It was a dark void that looked like a wound. He perceived it as pain and recoiled. His attempt to look beyond the door with pattern sight elicited a roar of anguish and rage, followed by a more aggressive attack on the door. The wood splintered under one of the blows. Lev wasn't about to release whatever lay beyond. He had enough trouble to deal with for the time being. Hemish might have some answers, but those would have to wait. Lev ran from the room, eager to get away. Once in the hall, he took a few moments to settle his nerves and then headed for the network operations centre.

Kade hadn't exaggerated. The operations centre had no less than fifteen workers busy at various tasks. All eyes turned his way when he entered the space. He couldn't afford to hesitate and made a beeline for someone sitting at a terminal. He wasn't sure how he would release the writ contagion with so many witnesses, but first he had to find out if it would even work. Kade had escaped before the technology was released to other anarchs. No one knew how those additional networks had been deployed. Were they all tied together or did they run independent of each other?

"How may I help you, Anarch?"

Lev said the first thing that came to mind. "Recent intelligence warns of a potential breach of one of our international networks."

The technician looked confused. "I just checked the status of all international networks a few minutes ago and they were all functioning normally."

Lev searched frantically for a reply. "I said *potential* for a breach. I didn't say it had happened yet," he snapped. "If one of the international networks went down, how much information would we lose?"

The technician looked at him strangely. "As per your orders, we have nightly backups of the archives from all international networks."

Lev waved that away as if he had momentarily forgotten. "Right, of course, but how long would an individual network be down if it was attacked?"

"Assuming the damage was physical, the backup equipment would need to be installed. That might take a few days. If it was an attack on the writ weaves, then it would only be down for a matter of hours. All networks hold copies of the entire archive and any one copy can be used to restore others. Barring a coordinated attack that simultaneously takes out all networks around the globe, we're very secure, Anarch."

"Excellent." Lev nodded as he looked over the man's shoulder.

That was disappointing. Kade's writ contagion wouldn't do the damage they had hoped. The best they could hope for would be a delay in the use of this particular network. Lev's Q-view vibrated with two pulses indicating a warning. He was out of time.

Lev raised his voice. "Everyone leave the room immediately."

Technicians looked uncertainly at each other. One brave individual voiced the unspoken concern, "Anarch, you warned us to never leave the network unattended."

"Did I say I was leaving with you?"

"No Anarch, but — are you okay? your voice sounds strange."

Lev was surprised it had taken this long for someone to question that particular irregularity. He hadn't intended to speak at all, but that wasn't an option anymore. "My voice is hoarse from yelling at incompetent fools all day long! Leave! Now, or your families will receive an unwelcome visitor." Lev hated the sound of the threat as it left his lips, but it had the desired effect. Technicians raced for the exit, fighting each other to get through the narrow doorway.

"Status." Lev spoke into his Q-view.

"Trantor has returned. Repeat — Trantor has returned!"

"What? Why didn't we receive an advance warning?"

"Uncertain," Tark said, "however, Trantor and the guards at the front gate are having a lively discussion. Now Trantor is yelling into his tote-comm. You need to get out of there, Levigator, we've been made."

Yori cut into the conversation. "Guards are swarming from the compound into the front entrance. Get out of there, Lev, now! Head towards the south wall. I'll use our backup diversion to give you an alternate escape route."

"I need a minute."

"You don't have a minute!"

Lev plugged his Q-view into one of the terminals and initiated the writ contagion. While he waited, he disassembled his Trantor mask. They'd be looking for an impersonator now so there was no point in maintaining the disguise. It would do more harm than good at this point.

His Q-view chimed, acknowledging completion of the contagion download. Lev unplugged and ran.

He'd seen his own face while searching the archive. They knew who he was and had labelled him as:

-LEVIGATOR-HIGH-VALUE-TARGET-

The chance that they wouldn't recognize him was slim, but if security were focused on a Trantor look-a-like, perhaps he might slip away.

"It's the Levigator!" Someone yelled while pointing in his direction.

So much for slim chances. "Directions!" Lev demanded. Yori was tracking the location of his Q-view through the QPN.

"Take your next right, two lefts, and then exit the building."

Lev looked over his shoulder. Several guards were on his tail. He materialized a stone wall across the corridor in his wake. Yelps of surprise were followed by growls of frustration as he left them behind. "I'm outside. Where to next?"

"Turn right and head between the two buildings. It opens to a plaza. Continue between the buildings on the other side and you'll enter a clearing that leads to the south wall of the compound. I'll let you know when it's about to blow."

"Understood." Lev raced between the first two buildings and almost tripped in his haste to come to a stop as he entered the plaza. Security was pouring in from two sides. A glance backward showed more approaching from the rear. They were blocking his way. He was surrounded.

"Stand down!" one of the guards warned. "If he moves, shoot him." Multiple weapons were raised and trained on him. The one in charge took a moment to answer his tote-comm. Everyone stood in tension, waiting. After a few minutes the crowd parted and Kenric Trantor himself sauntered into the clearing.

"Look what we have here. The *so-called* Levigator of the Servators has come to pay me a visit." Trantor sneered. He turned to his men. I know you've been hearing rumours. Some say the Levigator has super strength or mysterious powers. See for yourself. He stands at the mercy of your weapons like any other. He's only one man. What do you have to fear? Set your weapons aside. He's not going anywhere and I plan to show him my *hospitality*. That would be difficult if he were full of holes. I have questions, Mr. Radix, and you will answer them."

Kenric turned to the guards and waved toward Lev as though he were unworthy of further consideration. "Take him."

The guards surged and Lev ran toward the exit they were blocking. He formed a wedge of shielding and threw them to the sides as he cleared a path between the buildings. Running all out, he yelled into his Q-view. "Yori! Blow the wall!"

"You're too close! you'll get caught in the blast radius. You need to take cover."

Some of the Breachers had regained their feet and were chasing him between the buildings, unaware of the threat.

"There's no time. I won't get another chance. I can protect myself. Blow it!"

Lev had just finished his sentence when chaos erupted. He'd barely had time to materialize a five-cubit thick wedge of granite close to the wall he was approaching.

He entered pattern-sight and the whole world felt like it was slowing down. Lev saw the front of the pressure wave as it was forming. The granite wedge parted the wave, allowing him to maintain his forward momentum, but it wasn't enough to protect him from the hailstorm of stones that fell from the sky as gravity reasserted its influence.

With an adrenaline rush of impossible speed, his mind calculated the velocity and trajectory of each fragment as it hurled towards him. Some he side-stepped, others he obliterated with steel spheres flung at their targets with matching velocity. Smaller fragments bounced off the body armour he formed as he ran. His mind captured every movement of the intricate dance. It felt like an eternity, though it happened in a fraction of a second. By some miracle, he suffered only minor scratches — nothing that would slow him down as he ran toward the hole in the wall of the compound.

His pursuers weren't so fortunate. They were about halfway through the passage when the blast sent them hurtling back.

Lev glanced over his shoulder, amazed that he could have traversed such destruction virtually unharmed. He would try to unpack what had happened later. For now, he could only shake his head in wonder as he passed through the wall and into the waiting ground transport.

Tark veered their transport away from the compound at high speed while Yari looked at Lev with concern. His mouth moved in agitation. Lev gestured to his ears, unable to make out the words. He assured Yori that he was okay, despite the ringing in his ears. At least he thought he spoke — he couldn't hear the words coming out of his mouth. Yori seemed satisfied and turned his attention back to the road in front of them. Lev slumped to his side in the back seat and stared out the window at the sky as the tops of buildings and trees flew by. They had the information they needed, but the writ contagion would only gain them a few hours. Now that Trantor knew the Levigator was on to him, would he accelerate his plans? Lev prayed it wasn't too late.

Chapter 10

Kenric glared at the group gathered in his chambers. "What do you mean he escaped?" Kenric demanded. "I was there. The Levigator was weaponless and hopelessly outnumbered. When I left you to your duties, he was at your mercy and you let him go?"

"We didn't let him go, Anarch, he escaped."

"Explain to me how a man surrounded by guards and contained within the walls of this compound was able to leave without opposition."

"Apologies, Anarch. There were some... inexplicable occurrences and then the explosion —."

"Oh yes! Let's not forget the gaping hole in our primary defence. I'd like an explanation for that as well. We were attacked by an external force of unknown size that was able to breach the compound wall unimpeded. This kind of infiltration is an undertaking that requires prior surveillance and a great deal of planning. Yet no one noticed anything unusual in the days prior to the attack? No one was around to see charges being placed on the walls or to question suspicious characters lingering in the vicinity? How is that possible?"

The head of security wisely held his tongue.

"So we don't know how many people were involved besides the Levigator and one of them could still be among us disguised as me. I understand that this imposter was allowed to just walk through the front gates and no one thought to ask why I had returned so soon?"

"My men are not accustomed to questioning their Anarch."

"I understand that things were different under Villecrest's leadership, but I realize now he wasn't fully to blame. Your incompetence defies imagination. I should have replaced you all the moment I took over." Kenric looked at the head of security with disdain. His mouth puckered into a frown as he clenched his jaw.

"Make sure your men are aware of a potential imposter in our midst. If anyone is approached by someone who looks like me and is given an order, they are to confirm that order by calling my tote-comm. If I answer, but the person they face does not have a tote-comm against their ear, that individual is an imposter and should be taken into custody immediately.

"You will also question all staff to determine if there are traitors in our midst. See to it that the compound wall is sealed by end of day. Now get out of my sight!" He spat. "I'll deal with you later."

To his credit, the fellow was out of sight in less than twenty seconds. Kenric made a mental note to replace the head of security with one of his own men. Ural, he decided. Ural would whip them into shape.

He turned his attention to the network technicians who were looking suitably cowed. "What have you found?"

A thin looking engineer with a ring of gray hair made a nervous squawk as his coworkers pushed him forward.

Kenric sighed. "At ease. I don't hold you responsible for base security. I'm hoping you can provide some insight. Do you have information beyond what has already been discussed?"

The engineer nodded his head. "Yes, Anarch. We've looked through viewcordings from the past two weeks. The algorithm has identified several known Servator rangers in the vicinity on numerous occasions."

"What about Leviticus Radix, the Levigator?"

"We have no viewcordings showing the arrival of the Levigator. It's unclear how he appeared within the compound." The engineer's expression held a look of awe or perhaps fear.

Kenric rolled his eyes. "He didn't magically materialize out of thin air. What about the imposter?"

The engineer nodded his head vigorously, happy to share something more concrete. "The imposter arrived in a black ground transport matching your own.

It was parked a few buildings away from the compound just prior to your morning departure. We were able to follow it to a location a few leagues away where we saw Levitius Radix and two rangers climb into the transport. We were unable to find any other recordings to show where that transport came from."

Kenric rubbed his chin in thought. "So Radix was in the ground transport when it arrived at the compound?"

"Yes, Anarch. The only place it stopped was at the location where it parked immediately beforehand. One of the rangers left the vehicle at that point. Leviticus Radix remained inside along with the second ranger."

"What about the imposter?"

"The first sighting we have of the imposter is when he leaves the transport to enter the compound. We suspect the Levigator and two rangers joined him in the transport. Perhaps the imposter was the person who delivered the vehicle."

"Then how did the Levigator get into the compound?"

"Unknown, sir."

"So there were at least four people involved, possibly more. I want you to go through those same viewcordings and look for other suspicious activity in the neighbourhood."

"Yes, Anarch!"

"Oh, and arrange for the placement of micro-corders throughout the base. That was an oversight that needs to be corrected immediately. We wouldn't be floundering for information now if we had viewcordings from within the compound."

"I'll see to it."

"Good. All of you can return to your terminals. Report anything else you find, directly to me."

Relief was palpable from the network crew as they left to return to their work.

Kenric considered options as his Sicari contact stood silently nearby. The room was otherwise empty and Kenric was grateful for the silent reprieve.

Radix had been in Kenric's private chambers. He had no doubt. His terminal was open to the international networks. No one on the base had access to that information apart from himself. Only someone with Radix's considerable writ weaving skills could have circumvented his security.

It was unlikely the Levigator could have made it to his chambers unchallenged. Unless he really could appear out of thin air. No, the obvious answer was that Leviticus Radix was the impersonator. Kenric wasn't about to share that possibility with his superstitious underlings.

Additional evidence of Radix's presence was the agitation of the overlords who were still howling. The door to their domain had splintered under their protests. He had never heard them so enraged. It could only be from the proximity of a Levigator. There would be no sleeping in his chambers tonight. A hot rage flushed through his body at the thought of his personal space being violated. He hated how impotent it made him feel.

Kenric turned to the Sicari at his side. "Contact your brothers who are supporting Decar. Tell them that they're no longer required to bring the Levigator to me. If they find him, they are to kill him. He's become a direct threat to our plans."

The Breacher turned to leave.

"Oh, and I'd consider it a personal favour if you *dismissed* the head of security for me."

The man nodded once and left.

Kenric sighed deeply. "Why can't I find anyone reliable to handle things in my absence?"

It was bad enough that his fellow anarchs couldn't see the big picture, but now his own house was in disarray. It was an embarrassment. Now the Servators would be on high alert. Kenric pulled out his tote-comm. He couldn't wait any longer.

The voice on the other end of the connection was terse. "Yes?"

"Release the virus."

Chapter 11

Hemish disappeared into his thoughts and Lev waited patiently for his answer. The archivist tended to forget the world around him when he was chewing on a problem.

Lev picked up one of several journals open on the table and continued to read. It was written by a Levigator named Yuul Neem. Yuul lived hundreds of years before the more famous, Rushoen Nu Lon. He read the passage for the third time, finding it no less puzzling.

Our contact with this kin world has shed little light despite the new technology we've gained.

He set the journal aside and picked up another penned by an even older Levigator named Bon Weiloos. He read it aloud in a soft voice. "This rift was our window to the prophecy. We witnessed the destruction of a world and now we wait for the answer to present itself." *What answer was he waiting for?* Lev wondered. *It was a dead world.*

Many of the journals written by previous Levigators contained similarly cryptic passages. Lev looked up with a question on his lips, but Hemish was no longer in his chair. Apparently Lev was picking up some Hemish-like habits. He didn't notice the man get up to leave even though Hemish didn't move without a great many grunts and the subsequent popping of joints.

Looking around, Lev spotted him beside some shelves near the windows. He was perched precariously on a stool, stretching to reach a scroll from the upper shelf. "Ah, there you are."

Lev rose to assist, worried Hemish might fall. He returned to his seat just as quickly, not wishing to embarrass the older man. Hemish had found his way safely back to earth and was waving his find like a victory flag. He wore a toothy grin on his face. "I haven't thought about this scroll in years. I think we may find some answers here."

Hemish unfurled the scroll and laid it out on the table, his fingers running down the columns with both familiarity and reverence. "Here it is. This is one of the few references we have on the subject. It's the only thing I can think of that might explain what you've described."

Lev twisted his head trying to read the upside-down text from across the table, until he realized it was in a language he didn't recognize.

"What does it say?"

"It describes a wraith-like entity called a wastrel. Nasty creatures from the sound of it. Apparently they can possess a body and use it for unspeakable things."

Lev held his tongue, waiting for more.

"You mentioned that the noises you heard came from behind a massive door in the Second Anarch's chambers?"

"Yes, and when I touched the door, whatever was on the other side became outraged and desperate to break through. It reacted as though it wished to destroy me. I felt a wave of pure evil. I don't know how else to describe it."

Hemish considered the description. "Evil *is* the word used to describe a wastrel, but I'd always thought them to be fictional characters — stories to scare errant children. There have been rumours in the past suggesting that wastrels and Breachers are allies of a sort. If such creatures actually exist, and there is one in the Anarch's chambers, that would be very distressing news."

Hemish shook his head. "It doesn't make sense that a wastrel could be held in a locked room within the Anarch's quarters. You can't contain a wraith in such a manner. According to the texts, they're not corporeal in nature. Look here." Hemish pointed. "Because of their great evil, they were confined in the empty void. That doesn't sound like someone's bedchamber."

"Are you translating that correctly?" Lev asked. "The empty void part, I mean?"

Hemish looked at the words again. "Yes, that is the closest approximation I can make in our language. Why?"

"Because when I tried to see past the door using pattern sight, there was nothing there."

"That follows. A wastrel has no corporeal body, as I've said."

"No, I mean there was a void beyond that door. There was nothingness. No pattern, no particles, just... emptiness. The space was entirely lifeless — like a hole in the universe."

Hemish paled. "Are you certain?"

"I know what I saw, or rather what I didn't see. In all that I have perceived of the world to this point, I have never seen a blank space in the pattern."

Hemish shuddered. "The ancient texts speak of a great evil shadowing the hearts of humanity just before the end comes. If the Breachers are in league with wastrels... If they have control of a rift leading to the void...."

"We may be jumping at shadows." Lev offered.

"Yes, perhaps we should move on to matters within our control. You had some questions about previous Levigators?"

Lev rolled up the scroll. The action served to remove an uncomfortable subject as much as to uncover the journals below. "I've been reading the notes of past Levigators, as you know. Something strikes me as odd."

"What might that be?"

"Before I answer, perhaps you could give me your perspective on the reason we search for thin spaces."

Hemish straightened as one preparing to deliver a memorized lecture. "The rifts provide us histories to compare with our own so we can better determine how to prevent the prophesied flood. On occasion, the Maker uses it to give us new technology which helps in the fight against the Breachers. Turning a Breacher tide forestalls the coming flood."

"So, from a Servator perspective, would you say that the rifts serve as a means to prevention?"

"Yes, that's a fair assessment."

"Have we benefited more from the histories, or more from technology?"

Hemish scratched his temple. "Well now, that is an interesting question. Servators have vowed to uphold the Maker's Way. We recognize that the dictates guide us and preserve order. Without the dictates, we tend towards chaos and yet we know that the dictates in and of themselves do not create order. There must be a desire to obey — a longing to change."

"Chief Sentry Abrax said something similar. He told me there are those who follow the dictates and those who follow the Way."

"Yes," Hemish nodded, "Precisely. We search the histories of kin worlds to see how we might avoid mistakes and become better people. It's not enough to follow dictates if we don't understand the reasons for their existence."

"So the histories obtained through a rift are more important than the technology?"

Hemish frowned, "I wouldn't say that. The histories provide a measure to validate the need for the dictates. Without the dictates, we hasten our demise. However, the speed of our demise is compounded by the efforts of the Breachers to eliminate the Maker's Way. Do you see?"

"You're saying we wouldn't recognize the Breacher threat without the dictates or the histories and we need a way to combat that threat."

"Correct." Hemish smiled. "The histories and technology are two sides of a coin. One gives us the reason and the other the means. Does that answer your question?"

"Not at all," Lev sighed. He picked up one of the journals. "When I began looking for thin places at the coordinates you provided, I was under the assumption that I was ultimately looking for technology. You're well aware that we've met with nothing but disappointment in that regard. Every world I've located has been in a state of flood — or post-flood and devoid of life."

"Don't give up yet, Levigator. There are still many coordinates left to explore. Rushoen Nu Lon himself found only a handful of useful rifts among all he discovered. A single advanced kin world could make the difference."

Lev brushed that concern aside with a wave of his hand. "I'm not giving up, but I've been studying these journals to see if I might find a way to refine my search. What I'm reading doesn't add up."

"I think you need to provide a little context."

"In most of these journals, the Levigators seem disappointed when technology is found, but expectant when a dead world is discovered. They don't appear to be interested in the technology *or* the histories."

"Can you show me?"

Lev pointed out passages in several journals.

Hemish leaned back in his chair. "A new mystery to solve. Still, we can't ignore that many of the past Levigators eased our burdens with previously unknown technology. Those advances helped us keep the Breachers in check for thousands of years. That seems to weigh heavily in its favour, don't you think?" Hemish placed a hand on his back and exhaled slowly. "I'd love to continue our discussion, but you'll have to excuse me." He rose in what sounded like a painful snapping of twigs. "For now, these old bones need a rest. We can talk more in the morning. Stay as long as you wish. Please lock up when you leave."

Lev watched as Hemish slowly shuffled to his sleeping quarters. He hoped to be as sharp of mind in his own declining years. *If I live that long.*

He shuffled through the pile of parchment until he found volume four of Rushoen Nu Lon's journals. He wasn't sure why he felt drawn to this particular volume, but he leafed his way to a passage he'd underlined. Hemish would be mortified at the vandalism. Lev smiled, picturing Hemish's reaction to his sacrilege.

Returning his attention to the passage, he read it again.

Another rift, another failure. The analysts are overjoyed with their new-found distraction. Their preoccupation lacks in sight.

Lev stumbled over the last words. He imagined the author had meant to write 'insight' not 'in' and 'sight'. It reminded him of something else Beniti had said.

'Understanding the character of the Maker provides context and greater insight.'

The words tumbled around in his head, refusing to leave. Context — insight — context — insight — context... in... sight. A shock coursed through his limbs. "No," he whispered. "It couldn't be."

With shaking hands he held the journal in front of his eyes and entered pattern sight. There, embedded within, was a string of letters formed from particles that made up the parchment. A message visible only to another Levigator.

Chapter 12

Nico fingered the scar on his temple where the knife grazed him. Several weeks had passed since his encounter with the Breacher assassin. He'd held his own for a few minutes, but the Sicari was clearly the superior combatant. If Tark and Yori had arrived a minute later, he'd be dead. It took all three of them to fight him off. Nico hadn't told Kayla. He didn't want her to worry. Truth was he didn't want her to know he needed to be saved either. His warkata skills were improving daily, but he still had a lot to learn.

Seeing your life flash before your eyes changed a man. All Nico could think about was Kayla and the things he still wanted to say to her. The life he hoped to share with her. *She's the Chief Sentry now — she doesn't need you getting underfoot.* Nico knew she didn't have time for a relationship at the moment, not with the growing Breacher threat. For that matter, he had his own responsibilities as the Levigator's assistant. Still, he missed her. Their separation ached like an open wound.

With the international contract on the Levigator's life, they were constantly in a state of high alert. It was wearing on them all. Somehow, the Breachers kept finding them. It was inevitable, he supposed. Who knew how many micro-corders the Breacher network employed by now? Nico, Yori, and Tark used the new face cloaking masks as often as they could, but sometimes it just wasn't possible. In a large crowd, the masks drew unwanted attention. The rigid features were just too unnatural. For his part, Lev had learned to animate one of the composite faces provided by Kade Brixton. However, that didn't help the rest of them and they couldn't afford to be separated. Nico's brush with death was proof of that.

Nico had developed some strategies that seemed to be helping elude their pursuers of late. It involved a lot of backtracking and changes of transportation, but that was easy for him to accommodate as the owner of an international mega-company. He had resources almost everywhere and enlisted Brokar Luge to provide full-time coordination of their transportation needs. As his Servator contact within Callan International, Brokar could commandeer any type of transport at a moment's notice. More than once, they had escaped capture by taking flight with a roto-wing conveniently located on top of one of his company's buildings.

He was grateful for the respite of this recent trip. The thin space coordinates were located on a remote island, accessible only by sea transport. It had been a restful trip. They couldn't hurry if they wanted to. Nico opted for a sailing rig. His travelling companions were pleasantly surprised when they boarded a leisure craft. He'd thought they could use a little comfort along with the sense of security that came with being miles from anywhere or anyone. Nico closed his eyes as he leaned against the railing and inhaled the salt air. Sailing was in his family's blood. *I needed this too*, he realized.

"Nico!" Tark yelled from a deck chair where he was lounging. "I need another one of these fruity drinks. Where's the serving boy? What kind of an operation are you running here anyway? The service is sorely lacking."

"I believe Yori brought you that one. If you'd like to complain to the server, I can go get him. I imagine his response will be very entertaining. He hasn't done any sparring yet today."

At least someone is enjoying himself, Nico thought.

"Ha! Yori's punches feel like a massage. I might allow it, after he brings me a fresh drink."

Nico looked up to see Lev approaching from behind Tark's chair.

Tark noticed the direction of Nico's gaze. "Um... is Yori behind me? He's behind me, isn't he?"

Lev barked out a laugh that made Tark jump, then handed him another mug of fruit juice.

"Yori's on the radio for some reason. You're safe for now," Lev assured him.

It was good to see Lev smile. Nico was supposed to be keeping Lev grounded, but that was getting harder by the day. He could feel Lev's growing frustration. They'd located over half of the thin spaces on Hemish's list and the one on the island they'd just left had proven to be another disappointment. The rift led to a dead world like all of the previous ones. Lev was growing despondent from their lack of success. Something else was bothering him as well, but he refused to talk about it.

Lev pulled up a chair of his own and sat with a heavy sigh. He put his hands behind his head and turned his face to the sky, watching a seagull fly in lazy circles. The three of them allowed the moment to stretch. The only sounds were the lapping of water against their transport and Tark's noisy slurping as he enjoyed his drink.

For a precious few moments none of them had a care in the world — until Nico saw Yori standing in the doorway leading to the communications room. His face was ashen.

"What's wrong?" Nico asked, pushing away from the railing. All of his nerves were jangling. They hadn't seen another sea transport in days. It couldn't be an attack.

"It's the mainland," Yori choked.

Both Tark and Lev were on their feet in an instant.

"What about the mainland?"

"It's... There's a..."

"Come on man. Spit it out, you're making us nervous."

Yori shook his head in disbelief. "There's a plague. Thousands have died. It happened so quickly. The healers have never seen anything like it. One minute people were fine and within two hours they were dead. No one realized what was happening until it was too late. There was nothing anyone could do."

"What are you talking about? People don't die that quickly from a plague!" Lev insisted.

Nico didn't know if that was true, but he wanted to believe it.

"You must have heard wrong." Tark suggested. He lifted his Q-view to try for himself.

Yori shook his head. "Why do you think I was on the radio? No one's responding on the QPN network. I was finally able to contact a radio enthusiast at Kemetica base for confirmation. The plague affected people all over the world.

Some seem to have nothing more than a slight cough and the sniffles while others... It makes no sense. How could it affect people so differently?" Yori slumped to the ground.

"The bases are below ground. Were Servators spared at those locations?"

Yori grabbed fistfuls of his hair. "The Servator host is devastated. We've lost over half our global compliment, at last count. The numbers are still coming in."

A tear streamed down Yori's face. "My sister and her kids are gone."

"My parents?" Tark whispered. Yori shook his head. Tark moved towards the bow and turned his face out to sea.

Nico was rooted to his place with shock. "Are you kidding me? Now we have to deal with a plague on top of everything else?" he shouted. Nico knew it was the wrong thing to say, as soon as he said it. Lev's shoulders slumped under the weight of an additional burden. "Don't do that to yourself, Lev. This isn't your fault."

"Maybe not my fault, but my responsibility. I'm supposed to ease burdens, but so far all I've done is watch while things go from bad to worse." Nico's heart ached for his friend. He'd lost so much — given so much of himself. it was too much of a burden for one man to carry.

"What should we do?"

"We stay on course and head for home as quickly as we can."

"Is that wise? You might get infected. We can't afford to lose you, Lev."

Lev spun, anger and frustration competing for dominance in his eyes. "I'm *not* floating around on a pleasure craft while thousands of people die! I'm the Levigator, I have to be able to do something."

"What, Lev? What will you do?"

"I don't know! Okay? Something. Anything. I'll figure it out when we get there."

"That's not a plan."

Lev stared at Nico with his mouth hanging open. After a minute he snapped it shut, breathing heavily.

"Look," Nico said. "We're not that far from Chellea island. We can get there within the hour. They're isolated and probably fine, but if they're in trouble, they may not see another sea transport for a very long time. We need to at least check. Maybe by the time we get there things will have settled enough that we can get a response on the QPN network. At the very least, they must know more than we do by now. We can decide where to go from there."

"Fine. Set course for Chellea."

Chapter 13

The walls were covered with charts. Lines connected dots. Circles inscribed everything within a one league radius of hot-spots in various locations. Tenika paced the small room, eyes never leaving the map that had most recently caught her interest.

She noted the time on the wall chrono. There was still an hour before her appointment with Qas. She'd arranged to meet him at a food stall in a local market not far from the lighthouse.

She'd been spending as much time as she could in her secret research station. The international archive of the Breacher network was a treasure trove of information if you knew what to look for. Her peers didn't have an eye for detail. They spent their time focusing on the obvious. In Tenika's experience, it was far more lucrative to look at inconsistencies and anomalies. Like the ones she had been chewing on for the past several weeks.

It seemed pointless to wade through the catalogue of suspected Servators. There were already Breacher agents tailing those individuals. Tenika was more interested in the ones who had not yet been found — specifically, Kayla Vantos. As the daughter of a Chief Sentry, she wouldn't be easy to track down. Finding Kayla would require unorthodox methods.

Tenika decided to focus her search on those in the archive who had been identified as -LOW-PRIORITY-. Her instincts paid off. A handful of individuals appeared in the logs far more often than the average citizen. That could have been explained away as a delivery person, or perhaps someone who lived on the street. She might have left it at that except for a curious anomaly. One of those individuals appeared in two different places at the same time, leagues apart. On closer inspection, she found other instances of the same phenomenon. It wasn't an error. When she checked the viewcorder footage, the same individuals could indeed be seen at several locations with the same timestamp. She remembered thinking *surely, there aren't that many identical twins in Denmount? Perhaps someone was intentionally using look-a-likes to confuse the algorithm*. Tenika knew at that point she was on the right track. The only people who knew about the algorithm were Breachers and Servators.

She used the viewcordings to track individuals to specific buildings, but with each investigation, her target failed to emerge again. Others would leave the building, but not the person she was tracking. It was possible the viewcorders had been confused by a hat or a shadow and simply failed to identify the target leaving, but she thought not. There was something else going on. She could feel it.

One day she got incredibly lucky and spotted one of the now familiar faces on the street leaving the market. She followed him. Just before he turned onto a different street, he stopped and tapped the side of his head. It struck her as odd and she noted the time on her wrist chrono as well as the street. When she rounded the corner he was gone.

Later that afternoon she called up the viewcordings for that intersection and was shocked by what she witnessed. She had a good view of the man's face. It was the same person she had been following... until it wasn't. She reviewed the viewcording multiple times and there was no mistaking what she saw. The man tapped the side of his head and then he was gone, replaced by another low priority individual. They were using masks!

It didn't take much time after that to identify over thirty similar anomalies. She created a list of suspected masks and had them monitored by the algorithm. That was when she discovered a serendipitous quirk of the system. The algorithm was designed to flag any individual who came in contact with a priority suspect. Whenever a mask was removed, the system identified the remaining face as a contact of a priority suspect. Flagged individuals were automatically captured as a still-view image. Looking back through the logs, she discovered that those images had later been identified as known Servators. It was the lead she needed, but she wasn't ready to share it with the Breachers. Leverage was something to be hoarded.

Tenika immediately began the task of locating potential Servator strongholds. Every time a mask disappeared, she recorded the termination point. Cumulative termination points narrowed the radius of possible destinations. So far, Tully and the boys hadn't been able to pinpoint a Servator facility, but it was only a matter of time. Then she'd start making the Servators pay. For now, she had one lead that might pay off sooner. A common termination point for masked Servators was located at a specific berth at the Denmount sea port. During her surveillance, she had seen a man escorted there under guard. A review of viewcorder footage showed the prisoner to be a Breacher operative who had gone missing a few weeks ago — presumed to be in Servator custody.

She had a pretty good idea where he was being taken. That Vantos woman had sentenced her to life imprisonment at a rehabilitation facility on an island. She'd said that Tenika would be taken there by sea transport. If transports to the island left from the Denmount port, there was a good chance the Breacher prisoner was headed to such a facility.

Oh, what delicious irony if she could destroy a facility like the one where they had hoped to imprison her. That thought had led to a plan and that plan involved Qas Drugaresh. Speaking of which, she needed to leave if she wanted to make her scheduled appointment with him.

The drive was a short one and she used the time to go over the arguments she hoped would convince him. There were two reasons she had chosen Qas, the first being that the Vantos family was specifically looking for him and the second, that she'd learned Qas's brother had been captured by the Servators and was likely serving time on a rehabilitation island.

When she arrived at the food stall, Qas was already waiting. He handed her a spear of meat and deftly steered her away with his hand on the small of her back as if they were a couple out for a stroll. She knew he'd have scouted out a private place to talk, and he didn't disappoint her. They stopped at a bench far from the crowd near a babbling creek and a flock of noisy ducks. He pulled out a bag of breadcrumbs and began tossing them about to make sure the noisy fowl would stick around. She wasn't sure if noisy ducks were the best way to go unnoticed, but her conversation with him certainly wouldn't be heard. As it turned out, the aggressive birds also chased away anyone who came too close to their free meal.

"Why have you contacted me? I have nothing new to report. Nico Callan still — eludes me." That had been difficult for Qas to admit. Tenika was aware that completing a contract was a matter of pride for him. It was a humiliating mark on his otherwise unblemished record.

"That's not why I called you here. Well, partially perhaps, but not in the way you might imagine. I have a proposition for you."

"I haven't completed the first task."

"What if you didn't have to?" Tenika flinched at the scowl he gave her.

"Do you think I can't fulfill my task?" The question sounded more like a threat.

"I am confident that you can do whatever you set your mind to do. I meant no disrespect, however Nico Callan is no longer a concern. I wish to cancel the contract on his life."

Qas stiffened. "You dishonour me!"

"Are you trying to tell me that no one has ever cancelled a contract?"

"It's a shameful thing for a Sicari to fail. Even if you wish it, I will not stop until Nico Callan is dead."

"You didn't answer my question."

Qas gave her another scowl before answering. "Sometimes a contract is dissolved if a higher priority target is determined. There is no shame if the original task is replaced by a greater challenge at greater risk."

Tenika quirked an eyebrow.

"You have such a task in mind?" Qas looked at her suspiciously. Or was that hopefully?

"As I was saying, Nico is no longer an issue, but there is a greater threat that you are uniquely suited to address. If you accept this new task, I will consider your contract complete. I warn you, it will be risky."

"Explain."

Tenika pulled a small electronic transmitter from her pocket. "This is a new type of tracking device. It can send a signal from anywhere in the world. I would like to embed it under your skin so you can be tracked. Then I'd like you to allow yourself to be captured by the Servators."

Qas was on his feet in a flash, searching his surroundings for threats. "What have you done?"

"This isn't an ambush..."

73

"Wait." Qas held up a hand as he spoke quietly into his tote-comm. She should have known he'd have other eyes watching this meeting, as well as an exit strategy. Qas didn't make it this far by being careless. Part of her was irritated that he had so little regard for her own sense of honour.

"As I was saying... this isn't an ambush, Qas, but it might be a chance to save your brother."

That got his attention. "I'm listening."

"You recall that I was in Servator custody."

Qas nodded.

"I was on my way to a rehabilitation facility when I escaped. During my interrogation, the Chief Sentry of Caralithica was very determined to learn your whereabouts. Of course, I had nothing to tell her. She seemed to be personally invested in your capture."

Qas nodded impatiently as though none of this was news to him.

"Yes - well, I have reason to believe that those who are convicted by Cello Vantos are directed to a rehabilitation facility by sea from the port in Denmount. The Chief Sentry let that information slip while she was sentencing me. I was headed for that transport when I escaped and I have seen other Breacher prisoners led there as well. If your brother was convicted by Cello Vantos, then it is likely he was sent to the same facility."

Qas completed the thought. "...And if I were convicted by Cello Vantos, I might be sent to be with my brother."

Tenika smiled, "You see why I'm coming to you with this. It's a certainty that you'll stand before Cello Vantos if you're captured."

"I've been searching for my brother for over ten years. No one has ever discovered the location of a Servator rehabilitation facility."

Tenika held up the tracking device. "We can change that, but there's only one way to find it — in chains and under guard."

"How do I know my brother is even still alive? What's to prevent the Chief Sentry from demanding my immediate execution?"

Tenika shook her head. "When I accused Cello Vantos of seeking my death, she told me that the Servators didn't have a death penalty. It goes against their dictates. The maximum sentence is life imprisonment. If your brother has died, it won't have been at the hands of the Servators.

"Once you've arrived, we'll finally have a location. I'll send a strike team to retrieve you and release any captive Breachers."

Qas tilted his head and looked directly into Tenika's eyes. "If I'm any judge of character, you care little for my brother or your fellow Breachers. What do you hope to get out of this?"

Tenika's expression turned cold. "I want to make them pay. I want to see every Servator suffer for what they did to me. I want to end their existence and I want to start at the heart of their *so-called* justice system."

Her eyes never wavered and Tenika thought she saw a kindred spark of anticipation in Qas's expression. "I can't guarantee you'll find your brother, but you can be the hero who struck at the heart of the Servators. Once the prisoners are released, you'll lead the charge to purge that place of our enemies in whatever way best honours your code. Together we can utterly destroy them. It will be glorious."

Qas drew his knife and cut into the flesh of his forearm. While Tenika was gaping in surprise, he snatched the tracker from her hand and embedded it into the fresh wound. A wicked grin spread across his scarred face. "This is a worthy task. I accept."

Chapter 14

This was the first time Kade had been allowed into the Servator communications room. Leviticus Radix and Nico Callan were already there, along with two dangerous looking men whom he remembered meeting on the sub during his escape from the Breachers. What were their names again? Oh right, Tark Laywood and Yori — something. Administrator Lasa Na Tuni was pouring himself a mug of kofa from an urn near the door.

Kade still couldn't believe how much Radix had changed. People deferred to him for reasons Kade couldn't understand. Physically he had become far more imposing than Kade remembered, but the biggest change was in his demeanour. The man was clearly a leader. *Then again*, Kade thought, *I've changed as well. People on the island trust my leadership, to a lesser extent. Circumstances forge people*, he thought. *They force you to look at who you are and what you're becoming. To seek redemption for past mistakes.*

Kade surveyed the room. He'd never seen equipment like this before. It seemed far too advanced for this isolated place. *More things I don't understand.*

Lev was speaking with Pasch, one of the Servators who worked with the island's communications equipment. "Ask them to provide a breakdown of the deaths by geographic location."

Lev glanced at Kade, noticing him for the first time, and returned to his conversation.

"They say they don't have all of the numbers yet," Pasch answered.

"Ask for estimates. We don't need exact figures, we just need a sense of what's happening so we can plan a response. No, wait, they're obviously overwhelmed at the moment. We're in a better position to do that kind of digging. Tell them to send everything they have."

Details scrolled across the viewscreen. This was no simple communications array, Kade realized. It shouldn't have been possible to return that amount of data so quickly after it was requested. Not over so great a distance.

"Can you put it up on the large viewscreen, Pasch?"

Everyone turned to stare at the numbers flowing across the enlarged display.

"According to this," Nico read, "the plague appears to be largely benign in the general population. People report headaches and sniffles. So why are others dying in a matter of hours after exposure?"

Yori was first to notice a trend. "Look. The largest number of deaths are among Servators."

"At least fifteen percent of the deaths are regular citizens," Nico added. "Pasch, can you display the names of those who died that are not Servators?"

On a hunch, Tark made a suggestion. "Just display casualties from Ebot and Denmount. It might help to see if we recognize names from our home towns."

Pasch updated the results.

"There!" Tark exclaimed, "and there!"

"I recognize several names as well." Yori confirmed. Faces fell as each of them identified friends and acquaintances. The full weight of the disaster dawned on them in turn.

"I'm not the only one who sees the connection — right?" Yori asked.

Nico held a hand over his mouth in horror as he mumbled a response. "All of the names I recognize belong to people who are Servator supporters."

There were silent nods around the room.

Administrator Na Tuni voiced what they were all thinking. "This was a targeted attack. It explains why no one on Chellea has died. As far as we know, the Breachers are unaware of these islands."

"Kenric's plan was for a single coordinated attack," Kade whispered.

Lev locked eyes with Kade. "Did Trantor ever say anything about a virus?"

"No, but he seemed adamant that the other anarchs not use the algorithm to plan independent attacks. He insisted that this needed to be a single coordinated operation. That would be difficult to accomplish among the

Breachers. They don't trust each other — who would lead? A plague would avoid the need to rely on Breacher cooperation."

"Pasch, have there been any postmortem examinations?"

Lev's eyes skipped over the new information as Pasch updated the viewscreen. "The analysts identified a known airborne pathogen. It had some unique markers, but nothing potentially dangerous."

"What's that?" Tark asked.

Lev shrugged in confusion waiting for Tark to elaborate.

"One of those files is flagged for further investigation. It doesn't look like it's been reviewed yet."

Pasch selected the indicated file and they all absorbed the contents.

"Postmortem examinations discovered a toxin in Servator victims. That same toxin wasn't present in survivors. It's too small of a sample group to form a definitive conclusion, but very suspicious."

"Pasch, send this report back with instructions to confirm the presence of this toxin in as many of the fallen as they can manage," Lev ordered.

"That would be very effective as an attack vector," Kade offered, "a toxin triggered by later release of a virus."

"It still doesn't make sense," Nico mused. How would Trantor target only Servators and their allies with a toxin?"

"Taint the water supply?" Tark offered.

"That would infect everyone."

"Not if an antidote had been administered beforehand."

"The problem remains the same. How would you distribute an antidote to part of the population without raising suspicion?"

Tark shrugged in defeat. "Through the water supply?"

A nervous laugh escaped Nico's lips. It was a welcome reprieve from the tension building in the room.

"Kenric would never have let the other anarchs in on such a plan," Kade insisted. "If the Breachers were offered an antidote, they would immediately suspect a poison. It's a common way to eliminate Breacher competition."

"The alternative is to administer the toxin to each target individually," Nico shrugged. "Trantor couldn't coordinate such an effort quickly and quietly."

Kade pursed his lips and slowly shook his head. "Kenric Trantor isn't like other anarchs. He's skilled in subterfuge and feared for the breadth of his intelligence network. He's known for playing the long game."

"When I infiltrated the Breacher network in Sumakad, I downloaded their archives," Lev interrupted. "They already had a massive list of identified Servators from all over the world. We don't know how long they possessed that information, but I suspect long enough to administer the toxin to individual targets. It would explain why Trantor wanted the other anarchs to wait."

Kade gaped at Lev in shock. "You managed to break into the Breacher base in Ankhora? Did you use the writ contagion I gave you? Did it work? What happened?"

Lev held his hand up and Kade fell silent, surprised by his obedience. *Since when do I defer to Radix? We've both really changed.* Kade realized that he no longer felt animosity towards Leviticus. In fact, he trusted the man.

"I did use the writ contagion, Kade, and it worked. Unfortunately, it only offered a temporary reprieve. If any single country network goes down, it can be rebuilt from other Breacher network backups. We'd have to infect all of them at once for a permanent solution — assuming we knew where all of the memory stash archives were located. That will be impossible now that they've been alerted."

Kade's shoulders slumped in disappointment. Lev's expression softened. "It's okay, Kade. We struck a blow and obtained the information we needed. Learning how much we were compromised accelerated our security efforts. The masks we developed using the composite faces you've compiled have been instrumental in slowing Kenric's identification efforts. This plague could have been so much worse. You've kept your word and worked continuously to oppose the Breacher threat. We're eternally grateful for your help." Lev reached out to clasp Kade's hand in a firm grip. "You've earned our gratitude and, speaking for myself, I forgive you for past transgressions."

Kade felt a tear forming. For so long he'd sought forgiveness, but he hadn't anticipated how strongly it would affect him. He wanted to hide himself away and weep like an infant. He looked at Leviticus's face for sincerity and was rewarded with a soft smile, warm eyes and a subtle nod. Kade struggled to speak past the lump in his throat. "I don't deserve..."

Lev squeezed his shoulder.

"Thank you," Kade whispered.

One by one, each of them offered a hand of fellowship.

"You've done well here, Kade," Administer Na Tuni assured him. "I've been keeping the Levigator apprised of your progress. The reports have all been favourable. I'm proud of you." Pasch was the last to approach. He wasn't privy to what was going on, but wasn't about to refuse a handshake to someone the Levigator was commending.

The poignant moment was broken with a gasp from Yori and everyone immediately turned back to the viewscreen.

"What is it?" Tark asked.

"Look, there are anarchs reported among the dead!"

"But no Breachers," Administer Na Tuni amended, "and one anarch is notably missing from this list of the deceased."

"Trantor," Kade guessed.

Administer Na Tuni nodded in affirmation. "As you said, poison is a preferred Breacher method for ridding oneself of competition."

Kade groaned. "This is bad. Trantor wants to destroy all Servators. If he consolidates power, all Breachers world-wide will have the same agenda. The viral attack may have been stunted, but this is only the beginning."

"We have to assume that's true and plan accordingly," Lev agreed. "Pasch, I need you to transmit some instructions to all Q-views by order of the Levigator. All surviving Servators are to remain in lockdown until the virus has run its course. We don't know who might have been exposed to the toxin. Coordinate the movement of Servator allies to safe houses.

"Send an additional message to the highest ranked Servators among the survivors. If it turns out that the toxin is present in all of the dead, then we have our answer. I'll want all remaining individuals tested for presence of the toxin in their systems. Those who carry the toxin will need to be quarantined for their own protection. Start with our allies. Those who are cleared can go back to their homes if they choose, but they'll need to be warned about the Breacher threat. Have the analysts develop toxin test kits and face mask tokens that can be quickly materialized as needed. Better yet, see if they can develop an anti-toxin and an injector token. We'll also need some way to test food and water for contaminants to protect against future ingestion of the toxin.

"Have those in charge contact me directly with recommendations over the next few days."

"Composing the message now, Levigator."

"What about us?" Yori Asked. "What are *we* going to do?"

"We're leaving for the mainland as soon as possible."

"We don't know if you've ingested the toxin, Lev. You could catch the virus. We can't afford to lose you."

Lev sighed in frustration. "Can you afford to have the Levigator sitting on an island while everything falls apart?"

Yori scowled at the thought.

"It will take us more than a week to travel back to the mainland," Lev reminded him, "by that time, the virus may have run its course. Regardless, I'm anticipating that the analysts will have a solution by then. We can be tested before we set foot on shore. If not, at least we'll be nearby when a solution is available. I know you, Yori, you don't want to be stuck here while there's a fight brewing any more than I do."

Yori inclined his head in acceptance. "That will be acceptable."

Administrator Na Tuni cleared his throat. "What about those of us on the island?"

"I don't imagine there will be a supply transport available for some time. How self-sufficient is your island, Administrator?"

Lasa straightened and pulled back his shoulders. "We will miss some of our indulgences, but we can survive just fine on our own for however long we must."

"I'll try to send a smaller transport with medical supplies and spare parts for critical equipment. I'm not sure if I can do more than that before assessing the damage on the mainland."

"We'll be fine, Levigator."

"I'm sure you will, for the most part, but you won't have access to engineers or technicians for a while."

Lasa frowned. He hadn't considered the need for equipment repair.

"There is one other thing I could do to help in that regard," Lev continued. "Kade! Could you come over here for a moment?"

Lasa seemed confused as Kade made his way across the room.

"Kade is an inventive and accomplished engineer as you well know."

Lasa broke out in a grin as he realized where the conversation was headed.

"Kade, this is highly irregular, but I'm prepared to offer you a field commission." Lev looked over at Lasa. "That is, if the Administrator approves?"

Lasa nodded enthusiastically.

"A field promotion?" Kade wondered aloud.

"If you accept, your sentence would be rescinded, but I'd have to ask you to remain on the island."

"Selica and I have already decided, we will remain here when our sentences are complete. This has become our home."

"This island will need someone who can keep Servator equipment functional. You'd have access to technology you've only dreamed of."

Kade's eyes wandered over the mysterious communications equipment. "Yes! I mean, of course. I'll do whatever I can to help."

Lev smiled, remembering his own inner child when he first set eyes on Servator technology.

"Joining the Servators isn't a trivial matter. If you accept, you're tied to the cause for life," Lev warned.

"I'm already tied to the Servators. I have no life away from this island. I'd continue helping the cause regardless of my status."

"Are you willing to take an oath?"

"I'm willing."

"Very well," Lev cleared his throat and began the traditional rite. "Kade Brixton, is it your wish to join yourself to the Servator cause, giving your life in service to the Maker's Way?"

Kade looked to Administrator Na Tuni, not sure of the proper response. "Um, yes?"

"Will you obey the dictates of the Servators even to death, placing the lives of others before your own?"

"Yes."

"Then by my authority you are joined to the Servators." Lev placed his hands on Kade's shoulders. "Welcome to the cause."

"That's it?"

"Were you sincere?"

"Of course!"

"Then that's it," Lev grinned. "you're going to love your new toys."

Lev turned to Administrator Na Tuni. "I'll leave his Servator education in your hands. I doubt he'll need any help with the technology side of things, but make sure he receives a crash course on the QPN and token templates. I want him up to speed quickly so he can help with the defence of this island, if it should become necessary. I'm also curious what innovations he may come up with to help on the mainland."

"I'll see to it, Levigator."

"Kade — your perspective is about to change. I'm sure you've had many questions about things you've seen and heard. You'll get your answers. You're going to be tempted to experiment with what you learn. I need you to promise that you'll focus on practical solutions. I need you to use the technology for defence and you may not have a lot of time to prepare."

"You have my word."

Lev smiled. "There was a time when that would've meant very little to me. I know better now."

"Nico! Where are Tark and Yori? We need to get going."

Nico laughed. "Don't you think we know you by now? They left fifteen minutes ago to provision our transport. They'll probably be done by the time we get to the docks."

"Then let's go." Lev shook hands with Administrator Na Tuni. "Lasa — thank you for your hospitality. I'll do my best to keep you updated."

"It was my honour. Don't worry about us, Levigator. You need to concentrate on fulfilling your role in the Maker's plans."

Lev inclined his head and then turned toward the docks, wishing he knew what those plans were.

Chapter 15

The viewscreen glowed in the dim morning light. Tenika rubbed the sleep out of her eyes. She'd made the drive to the lighthouse ruins during the predawn darkness, wanting to make sure she arrived before the world awoke. It would be another long day of monitoring — the third in a row. Qas had been in the custody of the Servators for five days. They had agreed that Qas would do his best to delay the interrogation for three days. Beyond that, Tenika had no idea how long he'd be held before sentencing.

Based on her investigation of past viewcordings, Breachers who went missing were typically dispatched within a week or two of capture. So here she sat — day six into her lonely vigil. She needed to witness Qas boarding the sea vessel she hoped would take him to a rehabilitation island. They needed the island's location before they could make a move. The tracker embedded in Qas's arm had already proven its value by revealing the location of his interrogation. From a Servator perspective, it was conveniently located in one of the dockside warehouses, a mere stone's throw from the vessel that transported prisoners to the rehabilitation island. From Tenika's perspective, it was an unwelcome inconvenience. It meant there would be a very short period of time to witness the transfer of Qas.

She could just go through the recordings at a later date, but that would still take time and she wanted to be able to act immediately on a second objective. Qas would give a signal once he was in the open, on his way to the ship. The signal would let her know if he had been interrogated by Cello Vantos. If he gave that signal, she planned to move on the warehouse as soon as Qas was aboard the sea transport. There was a small chance that they could capture the Chief Sentry before she left. It would give her leverage over Seri... no, it's Kayla Vantos she reminded herself. Once she lured Kayla into her trap, she'd have her vengeance against them both. "That's *if* I can catch Cello." Tenika sighed. She knew it was a long-shot. The Chief Sentry had no reason to loiter in a dirty warehouse after sentencing Qas, assuming she'd even be there.

"Cello would want to look into his eyes." She assured herself. "She'll be there."

Tully had offered to have his men monitor the warehouse and alert her of Qas's appearance, but she couldn't afford to have him distracted from his other task of preparing a kill squad. This first operation against the Servators needed to be done without Breacher involvement. Someone else would try to take credit otherwise. It left very few resources at her disposal.

Thanks to Tully's efforts, they had accumulated enough of the new energy scythes to supply a small army, but they didn't have a sufficient number of men to wield them. Tully was in the process of recruiting mercenaries — men driven by greed who wouldn't ask questions. They were being offered very generous compensation — wealth they couldn't collect without returning the scythes she was lending them. At the same time, the scythes provided a guarantee of payment for the mercenaries. It was the only way she could think of to retain some level of control over the technology for the time being. She needed to gain more authority before revealing such weapons to the Breachers. If Isau learned of the scythes, he would force her to hand over the technology immediately and she'd lose valuable leverage. Tenika snorted, "That's not going to happen."

Finding mercenaries was proving to be a slow process. Tully was forced to look far abroad to avoid drawing Breacher attention to her activities. The travel, vetting, and scythe demonstrations took time. *Too much*, Tenika thought, but they didn't have other options. Tully's time and that of his men was too valuable to waste on a warehouse stakeout. Besides, it took her mind off of the frustration of waiting and gave her something to do.

Tenika's tote-comm chimed. She smiled as she recognized Tully's identity code. It was like the man knew when she was thinking of him. "Tully, what have you got to report?"

"It's potentially good news. I've managed to contact Zahn Quor, the largest mercenary group in Arapanus. They're available for hire and can provide enough men to fill our ranks, but...."

"They want more money?"

"No, actually they're more interested in the scythes than the money."

Tenika sighed. They were running out of time and they needed the manpower, but much hinged on keeping the new weapons under wraps until the right moment. "How circumspect is this organization?"

"They were very difficult to track down. Most information about them is just rumour. I didn't find them so much as they found me. It seems I did a little too much digging."

"Are you okay?"

"Things were a little tense at first, but one of their men recognized your name from a past operation in Jaihuwan. Apparently, the two of you went head-to-head and he was very impressed. To hear him tell the tale, he tried to recruit you. Anyway, their suspicions diminished after that, but it was the scythes that convinced them to consider your offer."

Tenika quickly assessed the risk. "Ask them if they're willing to commit exclusively to my service for a period of ten months. That means no other operations without my approval. I will compensate for their time at twice the standard rate of pay, not the higher amount you initially offered. If that's acceptable, then pending the success of this initial operation, I'll allow them to keep the scythes. At the end of the contracted ten-month period, I'll offer to equip the rest of their organization with scythes for a reasonable price."

"One moment."

Tenika continued staring at her viewscreen while Tully presented her offer.

"Tenika?"

"Go ahead."

"They've already arranged a contract with a different party seven months from now. They're willing to accept your terms of exclusivity for a period of six months provided we can produce additional scythes within two weeks of completing the contract."

Tenika shook her head. "They're eager to get their hands on scythes for this upcoming contract."

"That's my read on the situation as well."

"How's manufacturing? Could we fulfill the obligation?"

"It depends on the distance."

Distance. Others were listening to the conversation and Tully obviously didn't want them to understand, but what did he mean by distance?

"Tully — are you saying you haven't shown them the long-range capabilities?"

"I like to save that for the hard sell."

"Tully, I could kiss you!"

"Thanks boss, but you're not my type."

Why do people keep saying that?

"Anyway," Tully continued, "I'll have to ask for specific numbers, but I believe we can handle the request for this type of *limited* production run."

Tenika smiled. By equipping Zahn Quor with less capable scythes, she would still retain an advantage. "Tell them that if they're only willing to commit to a six-month term I will only compensate at the standard rate of pay."

"They agree to those terms."

"Excellent, I'll leave it to you to arrange for their arrival and supply of the inferior scythes."

Tenika disconnected her tote-comm and leaned back in her chair. Six months wasn't a lot of time to accomplish her goals. Still, she'd been fighting impossible odds her entire life. She'd make it work somehow.

Now that she had her temporary army, she just needed Qas to complete his part. They'd carefully orchestrated his capture. An infamous assassin who had eluded authorities for decades didn't suddenly get caught. He'd insisted on a course of action that would allow him to retain his peculiar sense of honour. It began with a brazen attack on the Chief of the Watch in the City Sentinel barracks. An eight-hour standoff followed. Qas performed a mysterious disappearing act from the barracks and then popped up at various public locations throughout the city — shuttled here and there by Tully and his men. The City Sentinels were led on an elaborate goose chase ending with Qas finding himself surrounded at the base of the statue of one of the City's founders. There he'd hidden a stash of weapons and incriminating documents that would be the downfall of several corrupt officials. The ultimate confrontation had been a bloody one. All but two Sentinels fell before Qas finally submitted.

Tenika rolled her eyes recalling the unnecessary drama, but that had been

Qas's price. "If this plan of yours doesn't work out and I find myself imprisoned for the rest of my life," he said, "then I want my final act to be glorious and legendary."

"It was certainly memorable," Tenika mused, "but we have very different definitions of glorious." Still, he'd come through. Shortly after his capture, he disappeared from Sentinel custody, adding to his mystique and assuring Tenika that he was now in Servator hands.

She'd been gazing dumbly at the viewscreen for so long, she was startled by the sudden activity at the warehouse. A side entrance opened and a man, bound in shackles, was roughly pushed ahead of two guards. It was Qas. She'd recognize his frame anywhere. If there was any doubt, it vanished when he somehow managed to bloody the nose of one of his minders despite his chains.

Tenika quickly found a viewcorder angle that allowed her to zoom in on Qas. He found the same viewcorder and stared straight at it with a wink and a defiant smile. Tenika laughed despite the tension.

"Come on Qas, was Vantos there or not?"

Qas raised his shackled hands to his chest, gave her two thumbs up and continued to harass his captors.

"Tenika muttered to herself in frustration. "We don't have time for this Qas. Be a good little prisoner and get on the sea transport. You can have your fun later."

With Tully tied up in other affairs, Tenika had to recruit six low level Breachers to storm the warehouse. They were waiting for her command. She pulled out her tote-comm and made contact. "Prepare to engage. You're not to harm any females you encounter. I leave the rest to your discretion, but I would prefer prisoners to corpses. Wait..."

Qas was now moving with quick compliance. They led him to the same ship she'd seen other prisoners board. She waited until he crossed the gangplank and yelled into her tote-comm. "Engage now!" She switched her view back to the warehouse. Qas was forgotten. He was on his own now. Tense minutes passed as she waited for a report. Her tote-comm chimed.

"Report!"

"The building is secure. No women on the premises."

Tenika sighed. She always knew it was a long-shot. "How many prisoners have you captured?"

"There were two men on security detail who put up resistance."

"Are you telling me that six of you couldn't take two of them alive?"

"They had some strange type of weapon...."

"Never mind, leave the building and bring me the weapons, then head back to base."

"What about the bodies?"

"Leave them."

Fools, Tenika thought. *When I'm in charge, there will definitely be training.*

It was disappointing to have Cello Vantos slip from her grasp, but it wasn't a total loss. There were two less Servators in the world. Cello would learn that the warehouse was compromised, depriving her of an asset. Best of all, Qas was on his way. She'd soon have the location of the Servator rehabilitation island and she now had the manpower to attack it. Today's victory was small, but a bigger victory was coming.

Chapter 16

When Tenika returned to the Breacher base, she was greeted by chaos. Fights were breaking out all over the compound. The door to the kitchens stood open, barely hanging from its hinges. When she entered to investigate, she could see that the pantry was almost empty. Someone had been looting the food stores, or rather, someone was emptying the shelves at that very moment.

"What do you think you're doing?" Tenika demanded. The fellow answered her with a shove. Her temper flared as she bounced off the wall. A quick strike to the throat and a second to his solar plexus had the brute doubled over and gasping for air. "I asked you a question." She waited as he tried to suck in enough air to answer.

"What's it to you?" *Gasp*, "mind your own business."

"The Anarch's business happens to be my business. If I'm not mistaken you answer to him. Yet here you are stealing from the hand that feeds you. The Anarch doesn't deal kindly with those who cross him."

The thief began to laugh. "I recognize you now. You're that woman who has the Anarch's favour. Or, you were. You could do better. In fact, I could use an assistant...." He made a clumsy lunge and his nose connected with her fist.

"You broke my nose!"

In one smooth motion, Tenika had him in a head lock with a knife to his throat. "You'll lose a lot more than that trickle of blood from your nose if you don't answer my questions."

"Okay, Okay!"

"What's going on around here? What did you mean when you suggested that I no longer have the Anarch's favour?"

"He's dead!"

"Who's dead?" She pressed the edge of the knife firmly against his throat.

"Second Anarch Jax! The servants found him dead on the floor in his chambers."

Tenika slackened her choke hold in shock and her captive began twisting in her grip. A sharp rap at his temple with the pommel of her blade sent him sliding soundlessly to the floor. *Isau's dead?* That couldn't be right. She needed to find Nash. If anyone knew what was happening, it would be Isau's assistant.

Tenika made her way as quickly as she could to the offices of the Second Anarch. She recognized the two Sicari guarding the door. Qas had recruited them as part of her covert task force for the operation to free him from the Servator rehabilitation island. They nodded and opened the door for her to pass.

Nash was pacing the floor. His hair was a mess and he looked like he hadn't slept in a week, but she'd only been gone a few days.

"Nash."

His eyes darted in her direction and took on a hopeful expression like a dog who'd just lost his master.

"Tenika, you're back! You have to help me. I don't know what to do!"

"Calm down, Nash, tell me what's going on. Someone said Isau is dead. That can't be true, I just saw hi..."

"...It's true," Nash interrupted, "and he's not the only one. All of the Second Anarchs are dead except for Kenric Trantor."

Tenika couldn't believe it. Nor could she deal with the feelings that were bubbling to the surface. She wiped a hand across her cheek, confused by the moisture she found there. *What's wrong with me? I've watched people die for my entire life. This shouldn't matter to me. He was only an obstacle in my path.* Her voice shook as she asked, "Who did this?"

Nash looked confused. "Tenika... there's a plague. Thousands of people died. Where have you been?"

"Thousands of..." Tenika's voice tapered off in disbelief.

Nash snapped his fingers to get her attention. "Never mind, we can talk about that later. Right now we need to get things under control. No one will listen to me!"

"Where is the Third Anarch?"

"He's trying to consolidate power, but no one is listening to him either. He's a..." Nash bit his tongue before he could complete the sentence.

"He's a fool," Tenika offered. "Don't worry, Nash, I completely agree. Where is Third Anarch Fin, now?"

"He's holed up in the armoury with a few men."

Tenika looked to the Breachers in the doorway and raised an eyebrow in question. Both answered with a sharp nod. The Sicari answered to no one. They had no pre-existing agreements with the Third Anarch, nor were they likely to. Adar Fin didn't inspire fear or confidence and the Sicari held nothing but contempt for weak men.

"Come with me," Tenika ordered. She was surprised by Nash's quick obedience. He had been her handler, yet now he seemed happy to follow her lead. It appeared that his confidence came, not from his own initiative, but from the Second Anarch's backing. Without Isau's authority propping him up, the man seemed unfit to lead. She strode out of the offices and headed to the armoury with Nash in tow. The two Breachers followed in their wake.

Shouts echoed from the walls as they neared the armoury. A group of men demanding weapons were being held at bay by Adar's motley crew. As Tenika entered the atrium, she took in the bloody scene. Several men had been cut down trying to gain access. She stepped over one of the bodies and began to shove her way past those still standing.

"Hey! Who do you think you are?" One of them made to grab her and instantly regretted his decision as a Sicari twisted his arm with a sickening snap. The second Sicari drew his sword and held it at arms-length, slowly turning in a circle as he pointed it at everyone within range. The challenge in his eye had the desired effect and the room quickly cleared. Tenika continued to the entrance of the armoury only to be challenged a second time.

"Stop where you are. Entrance is by invitation of Anarch Fin only."

"Is that so?" Tenika bared her teeth. "Do you think you can stop me?"

The guards were overconfident in their position. Judging by their stance and the casual way they held their weapons, they were obviously untrained. They were little more than undisciplined bullies. Tenika disarmed her challenger before he could register what was happening. After a moment of shock, the second guard thought to raise his own weapon in time for a Sicari to step in front of it. "You would be wise to hand that weapon over to me and leave. If you're foolish enough to pull the trigger, I guarantee that my partner will be on you before I hit the ground. If you face one Sicari, you face us all."

The fellow blanched. Everyone knew that killing a Sicari meant death to the one responsible as well as everyone they cared about. Sicari were relentless in their pursuit of vengeance for a fallen comrade.

"That goes for all of you except the Third Anarch himself. We have business to discuss."

"Come on people!" Tenika interjected. "You heard the man. Surely none of you are so dimwitted that you would defy the Second Anarch's Sicari."

One of the Sicari raised an eyebrow. Tenika shrugged. She had overstated things. The Sicari belonged to no one, but these usurpers didn't know that and it had the desired effect. Soon both the armoury and the atrium were silent and empty of bodies except the slain that littered the floor.

Adar Fin was apoplectic. "How dare you!"

"It was easy," Tenika smiled. "I just walked up and took charge of the situation. Someone had to. You seemed to have found yourself in a bit of a siege situation. Sooner or later you would have been overwhelmed. I think a little gratitude is in order."

"Gratitude!" Adar sputtered, "You — I had everything under control." Adar clenched a fist and took a step toward Tenika. He had second thoughts at the sound of a low growl from the Sicari behind her. He looked from Tenika to the Sicari and back again.

"You have no authority here. I am the Anarch and you will follow my command." He looked at the Sicari as he said it. The fool didn't even realize how little authority he had.

"Third Anarch, as I recall. You have no say over the Second Anarch's holdings."

Adar glared at Tenika. "I'm next in the chain of command, that makes me Second Anarch."

Tenika turned to Nash. "Is that true?"

"It's true that he would be in the running," Nash replied, "however, the choosing of a Second Anarch is decided by his peers. They may select anyone whom they deem to be a suitable leader. It's not a given that a Third Anarch will be chosen. There must be a gathering of the Second Anarchs to make that decision and no single anarch can make that decision alone."

"There, you see? You have to be a leader, and in order to be a leader, you need followers," Tenika looked around the room and shrugged. "I don't see any followers, do you?"

"This is outrageous!" Adar shouted.

Tenika placed a finger on his lips to silence the man. He almost exploded in impotent rage as his eyes darted to the threatening Sicari at her side. "Tut, tut. I wasn't finished. Nash, isn't it true that Third Anarchs are usually chosen because of their incompetence? If I'm not mistaken, a Second Anarch will generally choose someone they see as no threat to their authority. Do I have that about right?"

Nash had difficulty suppressing a grin. "That does tend to be the case."

Did Adar Fin have authority over you as the Second Anarch's assistant?"

"Certainly not."

"Huh. So, no followers or authority. Things aren't looking very promising for your candidacy, Adar."

"I suppose you think yourself a better choice?" Adar sneered. "Is that what this is about? Isau's little pet project thinks she can fill her master's shoes?"

Adar's sneer fell as his jaw dropped in shock. His eyes wandered to the knife in his stomach. Tenika grabbed the back of his neck and placed her forehead against his. "As you can see, Adar, I already have one follower and two very powerful allies. By the end of the day, I will have many more. You've just learned too late that you don't have what it takes. Don't worry, I'm more than capable of filling the shoes of Isau Jax."

Adar slumped to the floor as Tenika released him.

"How do we go about declaring my ascendancy, Nash?"

Nash struggled to find words at the sudden turn of events. "The other anarchs…"

"Yes, yes, I know that part, but as you said earlier, all of the other anarchs are dead except for Kenric Trantor. You also said that no single anarch can make that decision alone. I don't believe for a minute that the transition to power is as civilized as you make it sound."

Nash swallowed hard. "There are two ways to become Second Anarch. One is through a series of back room deals and the other is through bloodshed."

Tenika grunted. "I thought as much. Option one is not open to us and I've already chosen option two. So, how do I complete the transition?"

"I can call an assembly, but you'll need to provide a show of power."

Tenika faced the Sicari. She already had an inkling on how to entice their secret order. "Consult with your brothers. I have a proposition for them. If they accept, I'll make it worth their while in plunder and bloodshed."

The Sicari bowed and quickly departed.

"Nash, gather anyone you trust and meet me in the Second Anarch's chambers. We have a lot of planning to do.

Chapter 17

Kenric wasn't accustomed to waiting, but these were delicate times. With the sudden death of his Second Anarch peers, an inevitable power vacuum threatened the stability of the Breacher hordes. The petty warlord mentality so prevalent in criminal organizations always reared its ugly head whenever opportunity arose. The largest, and often least intelligent, were always the first to try and take power by brute force. It seldom lasted for long, but resulted in an unfortunate loss of manpower. Sooner or later, those with more cunning would put down the rabid dogs among them and claim a position of authority. It was why he had waited a week before arriving in Kemetica. It was also why he was waiting now for an audience with the Third Anarch who had claimed the leadership role as Kenric knew he would.

Most Second Anarchs chose men of little threat to serve as Third Anarch. It was hard enough to hold on to power — giving an intelligent and ambitious underling too much authority was suicide. That presupposed a man of wisdom at the top. No one would choose that label for Kivar Bantoo. The recently deceased Second Anarch of Kemetica was dull-minded and rash. Anyone could have told him that his choice of Lobar Chad for Third Anarch was a mistake, but he wouldn't have listened anyway.

Kenric had placed informants within Kemetica base decades ago. It turned out that keeping an eye on Kivar was unnecessary. The man was his own worst enemy. Lobar was another matter. It was, in fact, Lobar who Kenric dealt with while setting up the viewcorder network in Kemetica. Kivar allowed Lobar far too much control over his holdings. Not that it mattered, Kivar would never learn the error of his ways now.

Kenric hadn't even bothered to approach Kivar to discuss battle strategy for their global offensive against the Servators. He went directly to Lobar and convinced him to take on an extra contingent of Sicari to facilitate the final destruction of the Servators. He knew a man of Lobar's ambitions would find the offer of a Sicari contingent far too tempting to decline. Kivar had a few Sicari working with him, but these new warriors would be answering to Lobar. The eagerness in Lobar's eyes blinded him to the source of those warriors.

As it turned out, those Sicari enabled Lobar to gain control of the Kemetica horde far more quickly than he might have otherwise. *He's probably riding quite a high at the moment.* Kenric decided to let the man have his moment in the sun and tamped down his growing impatience.

After another hour of waiting in the antechamber outside the Anarch's office, a small man scurried into the room. Kenric recognized him as the former Second Anarch's assistant.

"You there!"

The man startled, not expecting to be addressed.

"What is your name?"

"My name is Omir, Anarch."

"If I'm not mistaken, Omir, you were Kivar's administrative assistant."

"Yes, Anarch, that is correct."

Kenric began raising his volume and intensity in the practiced manner he used to intimidate. "Then I assume you're aware that it's not wise to keep an Anarch waiting!"

Omir dropped to his knees, shaking.

"Apologies, Anarch Trantor. I was told to wait..." Omir swallowed, stuck between a rock and a hard place as he looked over his shoulder at the open door to the office where the Third Anarch waited. "...I mean, Anarch Chad will see you now."

Kenric snorted. "A privilege to be invited into his presence, I'm sure. I expect you to remain here in the antechamber until my business is concluded. Do you understand?"

"But, sir, Anarch Chad told me to..."

"I'm going to stop you right there, Omir, because I think the excitement of recent events has addled your memory. Do you know who I am?"

"Yes sir. You're Second Anarch Trantor."

"Has there ever been a time in your life when you placed the orders of a Third Anarch above those of a Second?" Kenric held up a hand to forestall Omir's response. "That was rhetorical. We both know you wouldn't be here to answer that question if you had. So let me be clear. You *will* remain here until I release you."

"Yes, Anarch!"

Lobar, having heard the entire exchange through the open door, would be fuming at what he surely considered an abrogation of his authority. Kenric had just dismissed Lobar's display of power as irrelevant and reminded everyone within earshot that a true Second Anarch was in the building. Kenric waited several minutes before entering to face the scowling Third Anarch.

The office of the Second Anarch was a bit of a misnomer. It was, in fact, a series of rooms surrounding a large circular common area approximately thirty cubits in diameter. Lobar was orbiting a gilded statue of Kivar Bantoo in the centre of the room, the head of which was lying shattered at the base. Sicari lined the perimeter of the common area. At a quick count, there looked to be at least thirty of them. The space was quite large, but even so, it felt crowded with so many assassins in one place.

"What are you doing here, Trantor?"

"That's Second Anarch to you, Lobar. Have you so quickly forgotten your place?"

Lobar sneered, but held his tongue.

"I should think it obvious why I am here. I've come to check on your progress. Are you prepared for our attack of the Servator bases?"

The Servators had been cautious, but they were unable to keep the base locations a secret. The facial recognition algorithm was tireless in its pursuit. Known Servators would eventually meet other Servators, each one being tracked until several common locations were isolated. The Servators would always disappear in certain zones. Those areas were then blanketed in micro-corders until there was no place left unobserved. Eventually, it was discovered that the Servators were using masks of some kind to try and hide their identities. It became relatively simple to track them after that. The Servator bases were being uncovered one by one. So far, he knew the location of the Servator Base back in Sumakad and the one here in Kemetica.

With the other Second Anarchs dead and their organizations in chaos, it was no longer possible to attack all of the Servators in one coordinated operation. Instead, Kenric would have to settle for a few bases at a time. Everything was in readiness back in Sumakad. His horde waited for word that the attack in Kemetica had begun. In preparation for this two-pronged attack, he had been sending Lobar instructions, but Kenric wasn't willing to trust that the man had followed his direction. Now that it was time to strike, he couldn't afford mistakes. The plan required precision.

War was an effective way to claim loyalty and he felt certain that Lobar understood this as well. The attendance of Sicari at this meeting suggested Lobar had plans that weren't in alignment with his own. By now these warriors should have been stationed at the Servator base, waiting for Lobar's order to proceed.

"Why would you travel all this way? I have everything under control."

Kenric pointedly gazed around the room. "If that's true, then why are your most critical operatives here in this room instead of preparing for battle?"

Several of the Sicari turned their heads in Lobar's direction, apparently equally interested in his answer.

Lobar lifted his chin in a childish expression of defiance. "Your strategy was problematic. I've made some revisions."

"It's not your place to question the orders of your superiors."

Lobar stepped on the crushed head of Kivar's statue and ground it under his foot. "I no longer answer to Kivar Bantoo."

Kenric was growing impatient. "That may be, but you *will* answer to me as the last remaining Second Anarch!"

"You have no authority here. Return to your own country, old man."

"The chain of command is not bound by borders," Kenric retorted, "there's a dearth of oversight in Kivar's absence."

Lobar spread his arms. "Here I stand, to fill the void."

"You cannot claim that station for yourself! It requires the unanimous approval of the Second Anarchs."

Lobar offered a smug grin and a meaningful sidelong glance at the circle of assassins. "Indeed, and I've gathered witnesses to observe your unanimous approval of my elevation."

Kenric scoffed. "I'll do no such thing."

"If you don't, I'll order these men to remove you from my presence — in pieces."

Kenric noted the confusion on the faces of the Sicari. He'd made agreements with them and they expected those arrangements to be honoured. "Plans are in place, Lobar. Agreements have been made. The operation must continue or there will be consequences."

Lobar laughed. "I don't think you're in any position to make demands."

Kenric slowly shook his head. *Does this fool really believe he controls the Sicari?* "Lobar — I'm going to ask you a question and I'd like you to think very carefully about how you answer. Do you intend to uphold our agreement to attack the Servator base?"

"Since you've asked so politely, the answer is no. I have no intention of wasting my men or my resources on your pointless vendetta. In fact, I've decided I don't need your endorsement or the status quo. I think it's time for something new, but don't worry, Trantor, I'll take good care of Sumakad. Once I've..."

Lobar slapped at his neck in irritation looking around the room for the offending insect. A look of bewilderment crossed his face as he pulled his hand away and regarded the tiny dart in his fingers.

The Sicari began filing away until only one remained.

"Are the plans still in place?" Kenric asked him.

The assassin looked at his wrist chrono. "We can be in position within the hour. If you can gather the horde to give them orders within that time, we can still do this before nightfall." He handed a tote-comm to Kenric. "I'll call you when the horde is in place and we're ready to execute."

Kenric nodded and the assassin strode quickly from the room.

Kenric sighed as he looked down at the lifeless form of Lobar. "Don't worry, Lobar, I'll take good care of Kemetica."

Kenric knelt to pluck the dart from Lobar's fingers.

"Omir! come quickly. The Third Anarch has collapsed."

"What happened?" Omir asked in alarm.

Kenric pocketed the dart and pointed to the ugly welt on Lobar's neck. "A hornet bit him and he's had a very bad reaction. Quickly, call for a healer."

Omir narrowed his eyes as he considered the scene — then wisely took up the narrative as he felt for a pulse. "It's too late, Anarch. These kinds of reactions are swift. He's already dead. "

"That's unfortunate. We're in the middle of an important operation. I'll need to take command. Omir, can you explain the circumstances to the Commander of the Horde and send him to meet me here immediately? Tell the rest of the horde that I'll make an emergency announcement in the main hall in thirty minutes."

"Of course, Anarch. I'll attend to it at once."

The Commander of the Horde arrived within five minutes, impressing Kenric with his punctuality.

"You requested my presence, Anarch?"

"Yes — Omir explained the situation?"

"He did, Anarch. The timing is bad as we were completing preparations for the operation."

"That's actually why I called you here. I'd like a report on our progress. What do the final plans entail?"

"As per the intelligence you provided, we knew to look for an underground bunker. Using points of ingress located with the viewcorder network, we were able to estimate the rough area of the compound. We drilled several test holes spaced fifty cubits apart near the centre of the region. We chose locations where we could excavate discretely. Three of the test holes came into contact with a roof structure. The holes have been widened at those locations and explosive charges placed.

"Our instructions are to follow the orders of the Sicari. When the charges are blown, units of the Sicari will drop through each of the three holes allowing them to enter the base far from any defensive measures that may exist at the entrances.

"Once they've cleared the initial drop zone, half of the horde will join them. From there, we'll divide the horde and systematically move outward in all directions. Any Servators who try to flee the base will encounter the remainder of the horde who are waiting at all known points of egress. Of course, there is a chance that we have not discovered all of the exits, but we hope to move swiftly enough that the majority of the Servators are dead long before they know what hit them."

Kenric exhaled slowly, letting out some of the tension that had been building. It appeared the plans remained unchanged and that the important preparations had been made. Lobar's attempt to intimidate him must have been a last-minute plan instigated by Kenric's sudden appearance.

"Excellent, Commander. We will proceed as planned. The Sicari are heading to the Servator base as we speak. I'm hoping the horde can join them within the next forty-five minutes. Assuming they've already gathered, do you think that's possible?"

"It can be done, Anarch. We've been training for this and can leave at a moment's notice."

"I realize that this is a sudden change in command structure, Commander. Will we have any trouble with the horde following orders?"

"If you're asking whether my men have any loyalty to Lobar Chad, the answer is no." The commander grimaced. "No one in the command structure holds any love for the man and all are aware that this is a joint operation based on your planning. Your reputation precedes you, Anarch. No one will question your authority."

"Then if you don't mind showing me the way, I've asked Omir to gather your men in the main hall where I'll address the horde."

The hall wasn't far from the Anarch's offices. Kenric smiled. Some things remained the same wherever you went, like the conveniences afforded to those with privilege.

The auditorium was packed with men, and more flowed out beyond the entrances. He was pleased to see that the Commander hadn't been exaggerating their state of readiness. The warriors had arrived, armed and ready. Kenric supposed that might have something to do with the current political uncertainty, but whatever the reason, he was glad to see it.

Kenric lifted his voice so it could be heard to the far corners. "Breachers of Kemetica, you are a sight to behold. When your commander spoke with pride about his mighty horde, he was not exaggerating. Here you stand, a mighty army ready to crush your adversaries."

The crowd roared in approval.

"For those of you who have not yet heard, the Third Anarch has perished." Kenric paused for a moment to gauge the crowd. These were hard men and none of them seemed bothered by the revelation. He decided to take a chance. "It seems the man had a weak constitution. He was undone, not by a piercing sword, but by a reaction to the tiny sting of a hornet."

Laughter filled the auditorium as men jostled their comrades at the joke.

"Perhaps Lobar failed to recognize your hard work or give you the praise you deserve."

The comment started heads nodding in the crowd.

"I want you to know how proud I am of what you've accomplished in so short a time. Here you stand, ready for battle. You know our enemy. How many of you have lost a comrade to the so-called justice of the Servators? How long must they continue to be a thorn in our sides, interfering with our livelihoods? Your preparations were not in vain. No longer will you wait, for the moment has come. We'll march against our enemy and purge them from Kemetica. Today is a day of revenge and plunder. Are you ready?"

The auditorium shook with the stamping of feet and the approving roar of the bloodthirsty audience.

"You know the plan, you've trained for this moment, and now I give the order. Go and conquer!"

The resounding shouts were deafening and the volume hardly seemed to decrease as the warriors filed out of the hall. Kenric hoped they had sense enough to keep quiet when they approached their objective. The commander seemed to sense what he was thinking.

"Never fear, Anarch, they know silence is required for this operation. This was only a temporary emotional outburst. I don't believe the former Second Anarch has ever spoken to them in anything other than a dismissive and derogatory manner. They've been treated as dogs for so long, your speech was bound to have an effect. That was well done."

"Thank you, Commander." Kenric glanced at his wrist chrono. "The Sicari will be in place by now. I'll leave you to join the battle."

The commander's cape flared as he turned to leave.

"Oh, and Commander?"

"Yes, Anarch?"

"Once your men have had their fill of sport and plunder, I want that base incinerated. Leave nothing for the Servators to return to. I want anyone who might escape to remain exposed."

The Commander nodded once and departed.

Kenric pulled out his tote-comm and called the Commander of his own horde in Sumakad. Similar preparations had been made there. This day, two

Servator bases would cease to exist.

The conversation was brief. "You're cleared to engage."

"Acknowledged, Anarch."

Kenric smiled. He could still make this work. By tomorrow, the world would be a very different place.

Chapter 18

The sea transport listed slightly as it crested another wave. The vessel had been hastily loaded and the weight was poorly distributed. The ship's provisions and crates of armaments were ported by the warriors who wandered above and below decks. Tenika couldn't fault them for their lack of knowledge in lading protocols. She'd seconded several of the fighters to begin redistributing the load and the listing became less of an issue with each passing hour.

Tenika nodded to a pair of Breachers engaged in a game of dice near the prow. She liked to come here to escape the noisy sparring sessions that seemed to sprout at regular intervals in the broader spaces amidship. It had become a routine to scan the horizon searching for their target. Qas's tracker had remained stationary for several weeks. Either he was dead at the bottom of the ocean, or he had arrived at his destination. Tenika wouldn't have been surprised if Qas's strange sense of honour had driven him to take on an entire crew of his captors, only to die at their hands in what he would undoubtedly consider a glorious final chapter to his life. She liked to believe that his desire to free his brother would override that temptation.

The first few days of their journey had been filled with anxiety at the possibility that Qas might be dead. She needed this victory to seal her position as Second Anarch. Those concerns were put to rest now as she gazed at the dark spot in the distance. The tracking signal pointed directly to the island in their path. Dead or alive, Qas has successfully completed his objective. They had the coordinates for one of the Servator rehabilitation islands.

Tenika felt a little thrill. Not that long ago she was sentenced to a lifetime of imprisonment on just such an island. Soon she'd have revenge on the Servators for their arrogance in assuming they had the right to judge her based on some moral imperative outside of regular legal channels. She was far from innocent, of course, and regular legal channels would have seen her executed rather than imprisoned, but that was besides the point. What galled her was that she was expected to abide by a set of Servator rules she never knew — rules she never agreed to submit to. She hadn't even heard of Servators or Breachers before her sentencing — not that she'd have chosen a different path had she known.

The island was lost from sight for a moment as the transport slid into a wave trough. A curse erupted from one of the Breachers behind her following a throw of the die. The vessel's sudden descent sent one of the dice tumbling across the deck. It came to rest against her boot. Neither of the players seemed to notice as they argued about whether or not the roll should be counted. She placed her foot atop it before it passed through the railing and disappeared into the sea. Tenika snorted. It was a perfect metaphor for her current circumstances. She was throwing dice in an unpredictable game with uncertain outcomes and at risk of being crushed under the boot of an overpowering force. The stakes were higher than anything she had chanced before. Much of it was out of her control, something that didn't sit well with someone who preferred meticulous attention to detail.

Her mind drifted to Isau Jax. The unwelcome feelings he brought to the surface was another thing out of her control. Was he the reason she was being so uncharacteristically reckless? Now that he was gone, did some suicidal impulse drive her? *No, it's revenge, pure and simple.* She couldn't afford to believe otherwise for the moment.

Following her murder of Adar Fin, she had announced her claim to the position of Second Anarch before the full assembly of the horde at Caralithica base. The outrage at her declaration was more because of personal ambitions than anyone mourning the death of Adar. By that time, several factions had already formed. Each group imagined themselves the obvious successor. Their surprise at learning several other groups disagreed with those assumptions was amusing to Tenika, and proof that they were unfit to lead. None of them had properly gauged the political landscape, too caught up in their own self-importance.

She, on the other hand, had done her due diligence. Those loyal to Isau Jax were guaranteed leadership positions in the new power structure. Others were bribed or blackmailed using the bounty of Isau's war chest or the wealth of incriminating evidence Nash was able to provide. That left the inevitable bloody conflict among those who remained. That was where her Sicari connections came into play. They had agreed to her terms and made a show of force in support of her claim. Hundreds of them had mixed in among those assembled and when the challenges came, they were quickly and brutally quelled. The formal ceremony of fealty was a foregone conclusion long before Tenika claimed the throne. Any who had eyes to see could have foretold the outcome. The wilful blindness of her opponents made the task that much easier.

Now that her authority was firmly established, she would need to fulfill the pledges she'd made. The most important of those was her deal with the Sicari. She had promised a series of ongoing campaigns of bloodshed against the Servators, their common foe. They were also promised all of the associated plunder.

Tenika held no illusions. These warriors were not following her, they were watching her. It was a test to see if she could hold up her end of the bargain. Not a few of them were here on the possibility they might free some former comrades from a rehabilitation island, Qas foremost on that list. Even so, she sensed that most of them had their doubts about her insistence that she had the location of such an island. Failing a rescue, they hoped for battle at the very least. If Tenika failed to deliver one or the other, she was certain they would end her life. She felt surprisingly calm about the threat to her existence. She was more worried about the future if she survived. Tenika needed allies who wouldn't question her at every turn. To obtain that kind of trust, she had to pass this test.

It was easy enough to locate Servators with data gathered by the Breacher network. Anyone with access could isolate that kind of target to attack. If that were her only play, she would be replaced sooner or later. She needed to accomplish something far more audacious — something never done before. Striking at the hidden heart of the Servator justice system would more than prove her worth. Beyond that, it would feed rumours that would grow into legends, the type of mystique that surrounded great leaders.

Tenika needed this to work. She glared at the island willing it to cooperate, then sighed at her childish attempt to control the future.

One of the Breachers was searching for the missing die. Apparently, they had agreed to accept the number that was showing when it was found. She lifted her foot, picked up the die and handed it to him. "It was a three." She gave him a half-hearted smile and headed back to her cabin.

***

Tenika woke with a start as a crab crawled over her hand. She shook it off in disgust and sat up, shaking sand out of her hair. Others were already busy pulling boats into the taller grass at the edge of the beach and brushing away their tracks with branches. She hurried to find a branch of her own. This was it. Today she would either prove her worth or die for her failure.

The ship was anchored far enough from the island that it wasn't visible to the naked eye. They'd made the long final leg of their journey by small craft under cover of night. They had chosen to land on a beach located a few miles from the lights of the main village. By the time they arrived, there were only a few hours remaining before dawn. Everyone did their best to get what sleep they could.

The previous day, Tenika had stood on deck before the gathered warriors to share details of the operation. To her right were the mercenaries that Tully and the boys had hired. Among them were a number of hand-picked men, previously loyal to Isau Jax, who now made up her personal guard. Those men would follow her lead. To the left were a surprising number of Sicari who comprised an army far beyond what she imagined for this operation. She could not command them and acknowledged the same when she made her case. She and her men would follow their own objectives. The first was to find and free Qas. She explained how he had put his life in danger so that she could bring them all to the island for this moment. She had promised Qas that he could lead the assault as his reward, but she didn't know if the other Sicari would agree. Her worries proved unnecessary. It appealed to their code. Those who put themselves at greatest risk deserved more honour, and no honour was greater than leading in battle. It didn't hurt that most of them knew Qas personally or by reputation. There were no objections to having Qas lead. That settled, Tenika had held up her arm to expose the Breacher symbol branded there. She looked first to the Breachers. "No harm is to come to any who bear the mark of the Breachers," then she turned to her mercenaries, "or those who wear a red arm band. All others are fair game."

A roar of approval had come from the Sicari. The mercenaries were more sedate, merely smiling as they imagined the plunder to be had. The plans hadn't progressed much beyond that. A few scouts would be sent out at first light and once Qas was located, they would free him. After that, it was Qas's show.

Tenika had given the scouts her tracker when she first woke and they had returned surprisingly quickly with Qas in tow. He had been out for a morning walk. Evidently, the prisoners were not kept in cells.

Qas stopped in front of her. "You made it."

Tenika smiled. "You doubted me? From the look of things, this has been more of a vacation than a hardship. Maybe I should have just left well enough alone?"

Qas grimaced. "My brother was here, but I was informed he died under the gentle ministrations of these Servators. They denied him a glorious death in battle, and they will pay for it with their own blood."

"I assume that means you have a plan of attack?"

Qas nodded. "I've had plenty of time to consider their defences and weaknesses. Shall I fill you in?"

"That won't be necessary. I've brought some men to help me obtain maps, memory stash archives and any other intelligence of value. As for conquering this island and extracting your revenge... I leave that in your capable hands, as promised."

Qas frowned. "I don't suppose you've reserved a few men and some weapons to help me in my endeavour?"

"I can't really spare any of my own men, but I did find a few others who agreed to help you."

Qas looked around. "I don't see anyone."

Tenika looked over her shoulder. "Oh, they're just on the other side of that dune over there. See for yourself."

Qas gave her a stern look. He didn't like playing games, but she couldn't help herself. She would have loved to see the expression on his face when he saw the hundred fully armed Sicari and mercenaries on the other side, but she contented herself to wait. She didn't have to wait long. Tenika had seldom seen Qas smile, but when he turned, he was grinning from ear to ear. His smile faded as he grew serious. Bowing deeply, he nodded to her and without another word headed down the dune to make battle plans.

Tenika crested the dune and waved to Tully who gathered the mercenaries to meet her for some planning of their own. She almost felt sorry for the island's inhabitants. Those thoughts were quickly suppressed as she revelled in her success. She'd passed the test and won the respect of the Sicari. Nothing could stop her now.

Chapter 19

"That was a cheap shot, Yori!"

Blood was streaming from a gash on Tark's scalp.

"There are no rules during a life and death battle. You need to be prepared for anything. I've lost enough friends — I'll not lose another due to sloppiness. Defend yourself or suffer the consequences." Yori came at Tark again with uncharacteristic aggressiveness. Their sparring sessions had become more violent of late. Tempers were high and fear drove them to push themselves — fear and guilt.

All of them were still reeling with news of the fall of the Servator bases in Kemetica and Sumakad. They still hadn't recovered from the loss of Espor Island. So many good people — gone. Yori's entire family was lost in the defence of Kemetica Base. When he wasn't venting his frustration in a sparring match, he was silent and brooding. It was discouraging to watch such a dramatic change in someone as rock steady as Yori.

Tark was further along in his grief, having lost his only remaining family in the plague, but fear and survivor guilt were beating him down. He second-guessed himself at every turn. More than once, Nico had caught him making a tactical mistake that could have cost them their lives.

The Breachers had made it clear that they could attack both their most secure and their best hidden locations. There were no guarantees of safe harbour any longer. Speculation about whether the Breachers were engaged in a coordinated attempt to exterminate the Servators was now an undeniable fact.

On the heels of tragedy, Lev accelerated their schedule. They were pushing through a gruelling weeks-long marathon to open the remaining thin spaces. It was a desperate wish that some technological advantage from an unknown kin world would reveal itself. Hope was renewed as they arrived at each location on Hemish's map, only to be dashed at the discovery of one dead world after another.

Thankfully, there were no Breachers harassing them at this location. It was a small comfort knowing that it meant they were likely busy elsewhere threatening Servator friends and family. This was their final destination. Hemish had acknowledged that there could be other thin spaces, but this was the last on the list that Hemish had provided. They didn't have time to wander about, blindly seeking. If they didn't find anything here, they wouldn't find anything at all.

The possibility of failure was too uncomfortable to contemplate, but they all knew the odds were against them. While Yori and Tark vented their frustrations by sparring, Lev sat on the ground facing a thin space only he could see. He hadn't moved all morning. Nico didn't know if he was praying or paralyzed with fear.

Nico wasn't handling things any better. With Servator bases being attacked, his fear for Kayla was constantly at the front of his mind. He felt terrible worrying about Caralithica base more than the others, but he couldn't help himself. His heart and mind were there at the best of times, so they were there even more so now. These new threats drove him to distraction. He knew Kayla was more than capable of handling herself, but the thought of her dying while he was so far away was maddening. If there was even the slightest chance that his presence at her side could make the difference between her life and death, he wanted to be there. If she died in his absence it would haunt him for the remainder of his days. Every moment they were gone increased his anxiety.

He knew it was illogical. Just before they'd left, he'd helped install additional security measures. Besides, Caralithica base was already the strongest of the Servator holdings. Port Vantos was hidden in the mountains far from civilization and Port Callan was accessed by sub-aqua transport. It was safe to say that the Breachers had no viewcorders in either of those locations. Even so, Nico knew that Kayla was working hard to take in Servator refugees. The viewcorder network could still track people to the docks. From there the Breachers could follow one of the sea transports. It was true they could only follow to the sub-aqua transfer station, but if someone managed to stow aboard and learned of the underwater manoeuvres, they would lose the biggest advantage they currently had. It kept Nico awake at night. They had been overly confident in the inaccessible nature of the undersea caves. Who would think to look for a hidden base below the dangerous waters crashing against the cliffs? Unfortunately, with the increased traffic of Servators, there would be a great deal more scrutiny. Sooner or later someone would put two and two together. *Stop it, this isn't helping.*

Nico looked over at Tark and Yori who were now yelling at each other, then to Lev who continued staring off into space. What they all needed was to get back to base. The sooner Lev opened this last rift, the sooner they could head for home. They might not return with a solution, but at least they could contribute to the fight in a tangible way. Nico walked over to Lev and sat beside him.

"Is this some new technique for opening rifts?"

"Ha, ha, you're hilarious."

"You know you're going to have to open it sooner or later."

Lev gave Nico a *how stupid do you think I am?* look and returned to staring at nothing.

They sat in silence for a few moments before Lev spoke. "What if the rift leads to another dead world?"

Nico played along. "So what if it does?"

"Nico, I could've made a real difference in the defence of Servator bases over the past few weeks. If there's nothing on the other side of this last rift, that means I've wasted weeks chasing a fool's dream instead of saving lives. I'm the Levigator, saving lives is what I'm supposed to do."

"Actually, I think you're just supposed to ease the burden. You can't be everywhere at once. Besides, if we hadn't checked out the remaining thin spaces, you'd be beating yourself up over every future loss of life, worrying that one of these rifts could have had the answer. It's a no-win scenario, Lev. No more bases have fallen in our absence. We still have time to get back and make a difference. Every minute you sit here doing nothing increases the likelihood that will change."

Lev shook his head. "I don't understand. Akhen was certain that I would find something. Hemish was convinced as well. If I'm not supposed to discover a technological advantage, then what's my purpose as Levigator?"

"They did express concerns early on about influencing your choices."

Lev cast a dark look at Nico. "Is that your idea of a pep talk?"

"I'm just saying what you've been told from the beginning — only the Levigator will know the correct path. No one has questioned any of your actions. Everyone knows that the path of the Levigator is seldom what people expect. If you don't find anything here, then everyone will know that this wasn't what the Maker intended when he chose you."

"How can you be so sure?"

"Leviticus Radix, I've known you for most of my life. You've always been exceptional, but you currently surpass anyone alive. You're probably more powerful than all previous Levigators combined. Why would the Maker increase your potential if it was only to repeat what has gone before?"

"I helped bring this about by contributing to the facial recognition algorithm! What kind of Levigator puts people at risk like that?"

"You had no way of knowing, and look what you've done since then. You created the masking technology which hampered the effectiveness of the Breacher viewcorder network. You saved Kade, robbing the Breachers of their most important computational engineer. At risk to your own life, you entered a Breacher compound to obtain a copy of their memory stash so we'd know how exposed the Servators are. While you were there, you temporarily corrupted one of those databases, granting the Servators an important reprieve. Because of your help, the Servator base in Caralithica is more secure than it has ever been and we now have a safe place that Servators can flee to. If that were not enough, you are giving people hope in a hopeless situation. Leviticus — you've eased so many burdens already — when will you understand that you've already accomplished enough? If it weren't for you, the Servators would never have learned about the facial recognition software. We could have been completely wiped out before we even realized there was a danger. We've been beaten down, but now we have a chance to rebuild."

Lev grunted. "Your second pep talk was much better than your first."

"Nothing's over until it's over."

"I'm not sure about everything you've said, but you're right about one thing. We need to get back and I'm only delaying the inevitable." Lev hooked his thumb in the direction of Tark and Yori. "I'd better get on with this or those two will kill each other before a Breacher has the chance."

Lev pulled his tools from his tunic and began the process that would allow him to simultaneously observe both sides of the thin space, forcing a rift to open. He'd become quite adept at the process over the last few weeks — it wouldn't take long. They had their answer a few minutes later.

Tark and Yori noticed the disturbance and joined them. All they saw was water. Yori, always the pragmatic one, spoke first. "That's it then. We still have light. I'll go break camp."

No one seemed disappointed and moods shifted dramatically. Tark and Yori worked side by side, joking with each other as if they'd never had a disagreement. Nico noticed he had a bounce in his step as he packed his own gear. If they hurried, they could be home by nightfall. The thought of being there for Kayla lifted a weight off his shoulders. He was already considering ways to improve security at the remaining bases. Only Lev remained somber. He didn't look defeated exactly, it was more that he seemed — lost. Nico prayed Lev would discover his purpose soon, or he feared his friend would never find his way back.

Chapter 20

Selica set her lantern down and consulted her rudimentary map. She carved a mark in the stone wall where the tunnel diverged.

"How many connecting tunnels are there?" she sighed.

Chellea island was formed by a long dormant volcano. The village was built on the interior of the caldera, but on the sea facing side there were a few vents that she had noticed while helping on the fishing boats. She'd made a mental note of the approximate location for one of the vents, hoping to explore it at a later date. As it turned out, there was no way to access the entrance without rock climbing gear and little chance of her scaling a cliff in her current condition. She chuckled to herself imagining her pregnant belly pressed against a rock face while she tried to reach a handhold.

That initial failure to find a point of ingress spurred her curiosity and eventually she found a vent that she could reach. It was well hidden from view, and a little precarious to access, but the discovery had been exhilarating. Since then, Selica had spent a little time each day mapping the lava tubes.

Several of the tunnels seemed to be connected, but so far none of the tunnels she explored had brought her to the first vent she'd spotted from the sea. That was good. If they weren't all connected, it would make things more difficult for searchers if someone came looking for her.

Selica was determined to create a proper map. She'd already had a fright when she tried to pass through a narrow gap and nearly fell down a vertical shaft.

Her current girth had impeded her passage and prevented a sudden plunge into darkness. She was doing this for the baby, but the child had inadvertently saved her instead.

No one knew about her exploration. If she became lost or trapped, she might never be found. Selica wasn't sure why she never told anyone about her discovery. At first, it was just nice to spend time alone with her unborn child. She felt less self-conscious singing and talking to her child knowing no one could hear her — or maybe it had something to do with the fact that she'd been a slave most of her life and she liked having a secret place to escape to. Over the past year she'd grown comfortable with the idea that no one knew about these islands. She embraced the thought that she'd never need to fear the Breachers again. Even though she was island bound, she felt freer here than anywhere else on the planet — safe in obscurity.

A few days ago, however, that sense of security was abruptly ripped from her like the dressing from a wound that wouldn't heal. All of the painful memories came flooding back. If she couldn't feel safe here, then where? And it wasn't safe, not anymore. Kade's confession ended any hope of that. She understood why he'd kept it from her. She could still see the anguish in his face when he told her the truth. He wanted to protect her and he felt that he'd failed. It wasn't his fault, but he couldn't help his feelings or reactions any more than she could. They were both damaged souls.

He had told her he was going for a walk that morning and when late afternoon arrived, she'd begun to worry. After hours of searching his usual haunts, she eventually found him at one of the spots they shared as a couple. It was a special place for the two of them and neither were inclined to spend time there alone. That he was there suggested he was thinking about both of them. He'd been distant the last several days, but she thought he was just immersed in one of his current projects. He looked upset. A knot formed in her stomach.

A pile of half-finished carvings lay at his feet. Selica was instantly on alert. Kade whittled to calm his nerves, but there was nothing relaxed about his furious motions or the misshapen scraps of wood strewn about. Some had clearly been thrown down in frustration or anger. She tentatively walked up behind him and placed a hand on his shoulder. He stiffened and stilled his hands.

"You found me."

"Kade? What's going on?"

Her question seemed to undo whatever tentative control he had and his shoulders slumped — then they began to rise and fall as he shook with heaving sobs.

"I'm so sorry, Selica."

"Why? What's happened? Kade? You're frightening me!"

"A few days ago we received some terrible news from a sea transport making a delivery to Espor Island."

Espor was home to another Servator rehabilitation facility. The islands had close ties as they were all within days of each other. They'd become interdependent, each island producing different necessities so they wouldn't be too reliant on the mainland. If a disaster struck one of the islands, it wouldn't cripple the others, but the effects would be felt. Selica jumped to the obvious conclusion. "Did they get hit by the plague?"

Kade shook his head and looked at her with defeat in his eyes. "They were slaughtered. Their crops were burned, the animals killed. No one survived."

Selica clamped a hand over her mouth and shook her head in denial. She sat beside Kade, wrapped her arms around him, and joined his weeping.

When their tears were spent, she asked for details. "How could such a thing have happened?"

Kade held her gaze with a ferocity that unnerved her.

"The crew of the sea transport found a symbol carved into the door of the administration building, it..." His voice failed as he searched her face — for what she couldn't imagine.

"Enough, Kade! just tell me already. What did they see?"

He spoke so quietly she couldn't make out his words.

"Kade!"

"It was the mark of the Breachers!" He shouted in anguish.

Selica was filled with horror. She wrapped trembling arms around her unborn child. "How did they find it?" She whispered.

"I don't know, but, Selica, they cleared out the communications room and the administration offices. They have shipping records, travel times, and written communications."

Selica paled as the implications settled in. "Then they can find us, too." She began to shake uncontrollably. Her heart was pounding in her chest and she couldn't seem to get any air. How could this be happening? She couldn't go back to the Breachers, it would destroy her. "No," she whispered." "Please, no. No, no, no, no, no."

Kade's face was a mask of misery. "It's only a matter of time. Selica, I'm so sorry, I thought we were finally safe."

She didn't hear the rest of what he'd said. It wasn't fair to Kade, but her flight response kicked in and she ran. She ran with no idea where she was going until her lungs were burning. The baby sensed her distress and was moving in agitation. A few sharp kicks caught her attention, and she worried she might harm the baby if she didn't calm down. She took deep calming breaths and slowed her pace.

Eventually she found her way to the only place she truly felt safe on the island. The lava tubes. She'd spent the night there, needing time to process the threat.

Kade was worried sick. When she finally returned home the following morning, he held her tight. She had to forcibly push out of his embrace to look into his face. She assured him she was okay, but didn't tell him where she had been.

That was over a week ago. Something had changed in her that night. She didn't fear for herself anymore. She remembered the sacrifices her own mother had made to spare her life as a child. It brought a deeper appreciation for what her mother must have been going through. She would protect her child from those monsters at any cost.

The baby was due sometime in the next few weeks. She prayed that the Breachers wouldn't arrive before then. The last thing she wanted was to give birth in a dark tunnel without the presence of a midwife in case there were complications. Once the baby was born and she had a little time to heal, she'd be better able to defend that precious little life. She would shield their child with her own body if it came to that. In the meantime, she was determined to build a fortress. Mapping these tunnels was part of that plan. She needed to know every danger and every possible escape route in case the Breachers discovered the lava tubes.

Several of the tunnels had depressions that captured run off when it rained, so drinking water shouldn't be a problem. Food was another matter. It might not be possible to leave their hiding place to forage. Stockpiling food was top priority. Thankfully, she'd been preserving excess produce from her garden and drying fish for months. The villagers thought her odd. The island was tropical and had crops year-round. Whatever wasn't eaten went to the other islands or was thrown away when it spoiled. Perhaps it was the uncertainty of her childhood, but she just couldn't bring herself to throw away food. That instinct was serving her well now.

No one noticed or cared that her personal larder was slowly emptying. She'd managed to move two weeks worth of supplies into the tunnels. By the time her larder was empty, there would be food for several months. She just needed time.

Arriving at another fork in the tunnels, she was pleasantly surprised to find a pre-existing mark carved into the wall. She'd been there before. Consulting her map confirmed that she was close to *home* as she'd begun to call it.

As part of her explorations, she'd found a side tunnel that formed a cavity without an exit. This became her primary base of operations and she'd outfitted it with the basic comforts — a straw mattress, bedding, lamps, some cooking utensils and a portable stove.

Now back at her starting point, Selica stretched and placed her hands on her sore back as she looked over her handiwork. There was only so much she could do alone. Sooner or later she'd need Kade's help to develop some kind of fortifications in case it became necessary to defend themselves. Leviticus had granted Kade access to Servator technology, and what Kade had shared with her sounded like magic. He'd been hard at work finding new ways to use that technology in the Servator's fight against the Breachers. She was confident he could find a way to use it to defend their little family as well.

I'll tell him tomorrow, she promised their child. Honestly, she wasn't sure why she had waited so long. Part of it was that she didn't want him to think she was being driven by irrational fear. At the same time, she wasn't sure how to explain the protective instincts she was fostering. *It doesn't matter*, she decided. *If he won't help — If he won't promise to keep this a secret — I'll do it myself.*

She shook her head. Of course Kade would help. He'd give his life to protect her. It wasn't in him to abandon her in her time of need. He felt just as protective of their child. She just hoped that when the time came, he'd put his responsibility for his family over his duty to the Servators.

Chapter 21

The entire surface of the table was covered in parchment — a tablecloth of words. He moved scrolls from one side of the table to the other trying to find a particular text. Hemish had warned him that messy research could be more frustrating than fruitful. As he groped, his hands bumped into a hard object demanding his attention. It was a plate loaded with cheese and bread rolls. A mug and flagon of water sat next to it. Lev smiled as his stomach reacted to the sight with a growl. When had he eaten last? Hemish had stopped asking what he was looking for several days ago after Lev snapped at him in frustration. Hemish hadn't interrupted him since. Despite Lev's rebuke, the elderly archivist continued to bring meals throughout the day. He always left them just within reach, so Lev would notice them sooner or later. Hemish had also set up a cot between two rows of shelves where Lev dragged himself when he could no longer keep his eyes open. He reminded himself again that he needed to apologize to Hemish and thank him for his ministrations.

Three days had passed since he first entered the library, invading Hemish's sanctum with single-minded determination. He intended to read through every journal written by previous Levigators. He'd discovered a subtext embedded within the journals that was only visible to someone with pattern sight. With that revelation, a hunger to devour every word consumed him. He'd been feeling adrift, not knowing his purpose, and hoped the answers were somewhere within the words of his predecessors. *If I don't find answers soon...* Lev didn't want to finish that thought. Too many people were counting on him. Too many people had already lost their lives because he didn't know what he was doing.

Lev tore open a bread roll and stuffed it with cheese before taking a bite. He chewed thoughtfully as he leaned back and let his gaze drift over the mess of parchments and scrolls. *There!* He reached across the table for the document that had eluded him. It was the journal of a Levigator named Yuul Neem. Lev had combed through a particular passage in that journal at least a dozen times, hoping for new inspiration with each reading.

"The true danger lay not in the Breachers, but the wastrels. They must remain contained. If even one escapes, that one will release others, then all is lost."

That critical piece of information had been passed through a rift just before the fall of a certain kin world. Yuul Neem had learned that the escape of a wastrel was the point of no return — the event that precipitated a world destroying flood. It comforted Lev somewhat to know that while his algorithm was a sign of the cataclysmic event drawing near, it wasn't the actual cause. He wasn't the destroyer of worlds, the wastrels were.

Lev read the remainder of the passage from Yuul Neem's journal. "So much has been lost over time, but I now know the truth, having discovered it in the writings of Bon Weiloos."

Lev looked at the stack of scrolls to his right. Hemish had managed to collect quite a collection of Bon Weiloos's writings over the years. It was a daunting pile and Lev had been hunting through them off and on for the past two days.

The obvious question that sprang to mind was how wastrels are contained. From what he'd learned about wastrels, Lev was convinced he'd encountered one such prison in Kenric Trantor's chambers. Goosebumps formed on his flesh as he recalled the mad whispering of the wastrels when he placed an ear against that ancient door. It couldn't be so simple as a regular prison cell, could it? The question had puzzled him for most of the previous afternoon, but he'd had better luck today.

Bon Weiloos wrote that the wastrels were contained in an abyss. It was formed by opening a rift to nowhere. Early Levigators created many of these void rifts until all of the wastrels were contained, preventing destruction of the world.

Lev nodded as he considered the implications. The Levigators who formed those first void rifts would likely have created them wherever they encountered swarms of wastrels. That there were several voids created suggested that Breacher bases could harbour other doors, just as there were rifts to kin worlds on many Servator bases.

Yuul mentioned that if one wastrel escaped, it would release others. The thought of those doors under Breacher control at bases all over the world sent shivers up and down his spine.

He read the next words of Bon Weiloos aloud. "It's impossible for a wastrel to resist the initial pull of a freshly opened rift. They're drawn inexorably into the void. It's far easier for a wastrel to enter the abyss than to leave it, but the flow from a rift tends to slow after an initial breach. Given enough time, the wastrels could eventually escape. For this reason, entrances to the abyss were sealed with heavy doors formed with a particle frequency capable of diminishing flow." It explained a great deal and helped Lev to better understand the level of threat.

Perhaps more disturbing was what had come to pass after those prisons were created. Further reading explained how the original anarchs were once Servators who were placed as doorkeepers for the abyss. They were slowly driven mad by the whispering of the wastrels through the rifts they guarded. Lev could commiserate. The little he'd heard still haunted him at night. The corrupted Servators began to serve the wastrels and eventually formed the organization known as the Breachers. It was surprising that the wastrels had not escaped in all of this time under Breacher control, but thankfully enough fear and superstition had grown through the centuries that the anarchs never opened a door longer than necessary — Perhaps for a moment to offer a sacrifice or dispose of an enemy, but no more.

That the wastrels were currently all imprisoned was the one thing Servators unknowingly had in their favour since the ability to create a new void rift was lost to history. Akhen expressed his belief that Lev was possibly the most powerful Levigator ever, but considering what previous Levigators had accomplished, Lev had his doubts. He wasn't sure what he would do if the wastrels escaped. He did know that he wouldn't feel comfortable until he learned how to create a void rift. Unfortunately, over time, the Servators began to focus on technology as a way to control the Breachers instead of worrying about the real enemy — wastrels. Now that knowledge was gone and he had no one to teach him.

Lev slowly ran his hand over his head. He had sensed that he was missing something and now he knew just how skewed things had become. The assumptions held by many Servators about a Levigator's role were completely wrong. He now understood that the focus was always meant to be on containing the madness spread by the wastrels, not Breacher activities alone. The whispered influence of a wastrel in proximity to an anarch was far more dangerous.

On some level, Servators knew that Breachers weren't the primary threat. The Maker's Way suggested as much. In fact, the whole premise of a rehabilitation island was that Breachers could change if they were removed from negative influences and shown a better path. One of his best friends was proof. Yet, as often was the case, people became complacent.

Lev yawned. The shadows in the library suggested it was late afternoon. He'd made his way through all of Bon Weiloos's scrolls except the one he was currently holding. He rubbed his eyes and read the final entry.

"Wastrels are drawn to those with power — heads of state, military or religious leaders, financiers — it doesn't matter what form of power, so long as it provides influence. They twist minds and darken souls, driving out self-control. They cleave the waters of reason, leaving madness in its wake. The power of a Levigator is like a beacon to the wastrels. We must not give in to fear as we draw them to the void."

Lev tossed the scroll in frustration. "How am I supposed to do that if the knowledge for creating a void is lost?" He decided to change tack and move on to something different. His current train of thought was frustrating him.

Before he had headed off on a tangent with the Weiloos journals, he'd been trying to understand why all of the past Levigators were more interested in post-flood worlds than pre-flood ones.

Lev had learned to look for trigger phrases in the writings of the Levigators, signalling the start of pattern sight text. He was looking at one now in a later journal written by Rushoen Nu Lon. The trigger phrases often hinted at a fascination with post-flood worlds. A common sentence was, "It is not the end, but a new beginning". Another example was from the Yuul Neem journals, "This rift was our window to the prophecy. We witnessed the destruction of a world and now we wait for the answer to present itself." It was these cryptic statements that had puzzled Hemish over the years. Lev would need to share his pattern sight discovery with Hemish at some point.

"What were you looking for?" Lev whispered into the fading light. He decided to read for one more hour and then call it a night. Twenty minutes later, he had his answer. Rushoen Nu Lon theorized that a rift could be closed. If it were possible to close an existing rift, a new rift could be opened to a different location on that same world. If they could accomplish this on an empty world, Rushoen felt sure they'd discover what they all suspected — that human life existed post-flood. Unfortunately, no one had discovered how to close a rift. Neither did they know if a new thin space would present itself, allowing a rift to that world to be formed once again.

Conviction filled Lev in a wave of heat. "That's my purpose — to clear a path to the truth. I need to learn how to close and reopen a rift on a dead world." It was never about finding new kin worlds or technology. If he could find survivors on a dead world, he'd be able to learn the truth about how they survived. They could prevent what had always seemed inevitable.

Lev wasn't sure where to begin. He'd consult with Hemish and Akhen in the morning, but right now he needed rest. He stumbled to the cot and felt a glimmer of hope as he quickly fell into the most restful sleep he'd had in months.

Chapter 22

Everyone was on edge knowing it was only a matter of time before the Breachers located Chellea Island. With two Servator bases destroyed on the mainland, help from that quarter would be slow in coming - if at all. Kade had attended a recent council meeting where he insisted that they needed to prepare based on the assumption that they were alone and that any help would come too late to make a difference. The silence following that proclamation showed just how heavily the loss of their sister island weighed on each of them. That same fate awaited them all if they sat on their hands and did nothing.

As the only engineer on the island, it fell to him to devise what defences he could. Not long ago, Lev had given him full access to Servator technology. It was an unprecedented act to grant such a thing to someone who wasn't officially a Servator, but their present circumstances called for extraordinary measures.

He'd been like a child exploring toy stalls at the bazaar. It was like being asked to imagine something, only to see it magically form before your very eyes. The possibilities were mind-boggling, yet somehow the Servators didn't seem to fully grasp the creative potential. They'd used the technology for so many years that people seemed to assume it had already reached the pinnacle of innovation. Kade supposed they were so mired in tradition that it blinded them to the building blocks that made it so exciting. Proof of that conjecture was evident when Radix showed him how he'd used the technology to create masks that hid people's identities. It was such an obvious application for intelligence gathering that Kade couldn't understand how no one had thought of it before. Then there was Lev's novel uses of Q-tech to help Kade and Selica escape from the Breachers. It showed just how much could be accomplished with a new perspective.

Like Leviticus, Kade had no preconceived notions to hold him back. The technology was brand new to him and he wasn't just a technician modifying existing templates. He'd examined the foundations of the technology until he understood its limitations. He could see how templates were developed in ways that were not so different to writ weaving. It became quickly apparent that Servator analysts had never gained enough understanding to do much more than modify existing templates. When he asked questions in an attempt to fill in some gaps, it was acknowledged that the technology had been given to them — they had not developed it themselves. That raised many more questions, but it also explained the lack of progress.

As a computational engineer, Kade was able to write his own templates after a substantial amount of trial and error. He thought he had enough of a grasp on it to improve on the existing templates. It would have to do for now, he didn't have the time to become proficient. Lev had encouraged him to use the Servator technology to find creative solutions to the Breacher threat. Given a year, he felt he could come up with the applications that would once again give Servators a technological advantage over the Breachers. As it was, they were barely keeping ahead of the threat with not a moment to spare for experimentation. Right now, he had to focus all of his energy on using the Servator technology as best he could to save this island.

The first limitation he encountered was a time lag between requesting a template and seeing it materialize at a selected location. The Servator Quantum Positioning Network ran on a massive memory stash housed in a few locations on the mainland. The island was too far away from the memory stash. The result was a large transmission delay between the repeater towers. It would affect the response time of any defensive measures he incorporated. Thankfully he'd upgraded the island's local network when Leviticus had asked him to work on a special project. The objective had been to capture facial data for Lev's masking application, but Kade had improved the communications network at the same time.

Lev had provided him with shipments of equipment to address almost any need. Kade used some of that equipment to implement his own memory stash on the island. Its storage capacity was too small to serve effectively as a QPN, but it was large enough to hold a few templates and several specific island coordinates. That upgrade would provide a fast response time for a limited number of objectives. It wasn't much, but used judiciously, it could be a game changer.

They'd need to run cable across the island and hard-wire viewcorders at strategic spots to monitor incoming vessels and troop movements. They couldn't rely on spy tokens because of the same time-lag issues. A large portion of their defences would need to be materialized in advance at predetermined locations. Those would need to be physically triggered like a traditional animal snare. That limitation meant a large part of their efforts would be finding ways to funnel the Breachers along the most defensible routes.

Having only two beaches and sheer cliffs around most of the island, Chellea was in a better position, defensively speaking, than some of their sister islands. Knowing the Breachers, Kade didn't think that would be enough to discourage a determined force, but he did think them lazy enough to try the beaches first.

The main beach route offered a few places to set up an ambush that could decimate the Breacher ranks and give the islanders a fighting chance. The problem was that the residents were averse to the idea of that kind of violence. They knew that they would have to fight for their lives at some point, but they'd insisted that lethal methods should be a last resort. He understood the sentiment, but knew the Breachers would offer no such mercy. It put Kade in a difficult position. He was being asked to make their first line of defence a deterrent, when in fact those were the places they needed to be decisive. If the Breachers made it past the initial defences, it would become next to impossible to control what followed.

Kade hated how quickly he was reverting to the fatalistic attitudes of his time as a Breacher captive, but it served to remind him of their ruthlessness. He knew at some point he might have to take matters into his own hands if he hoped to protect his family and the people of Chellea. No one else needed to know if he decided to take lethal action, the guilt would be his burden alone.

Kade's job during a Breacher incursion would be to remotely monitor their movements and trigger defences as necessary. The council insisted that someone needed to be kept out of the fray to view the engagement objectively. The defences Kade was developing required coordination and timing. It couldn't be left in the hands of someone who might make a panicked decision on the battlefield. Kade had initially refused, but he realized he was the only logical choice. No one else could modify templates on the fly should a plan require a sudden revision, or inspiration struck. It was for that very reason he was reserving template space on the local archive — for quick response options. What those options might be, he hadn't decided yet.

Against his better judgment, Kade conceded to the counsel's wishes for non-lethal deterrence. The first line of defence was based on an early discovery Kade had made. Despite what it might look like, Q-tech templates didn't materialize matter from nothing, rather it brought particles together from the surrounding environment in a localized radius. The QPN used those constituent elements to assemble matter according to the template specifications. The radius from which elements were drawn was determined by the amount of mass required for the template. The technology was designed to draw only from inanimate objects and in such a way as to prevent the compromise of existing structures — that was to say, not too much material from any one spot. Typically, this would be in the form of surfaces that would naturally erode from the elements.

The process worked well for common objects — not so well for exotic materials. In certain locations, where required elements were in short supply, the technology was smart enough to make substitutions. It was an incredibly advanced, elegant solution and Kade was very curious about the people who developed it.

The safety protocols were robust, but Kade had discovered it was possible to force a reduction in the draw radius. By collecting from a tight radius near a forming mass, he could essentially displace material from one place to another, as long as the elements being collected were the same as those being used. In this case, he formed earthen reefs in the water beyond the beach to prevent large sea transports from getting too close to shore while drawing earth from below the beach surface. It was a slow and tedious process. The excavation ended just short of the waterline where he materialized a gate that would allow water to flood beneath the beach, creating a mass of quicksand. If Kade couldn't stop the Breachers from coming, at least he could slow them down by preventing a gathering of troops on the shore. He repeated those entrenchments at the second beach.

For their second line of defence, Kade climbed to the top of the cliffs on either side of the path that led down to the main beach and took coordinates along the cliff edge. He called up a template he'd designed the previous day and materialized a massive cradle filled with rocks — one at each end of the path. If they timed it right, they could trap the Breachers between the rock falls, forming a natural prison. For now, it was set to drop the load from a remote command on the wrist Q-view he'd been given. If they had time, he planned to run more cable to viewcorders located at both ends of the path and set up proximity triggers.

As for weapons, they had the existing templates for Servator short range stun batons, flash charges, and sonic cannons. They were the weapons of a police force meant to subdue individuals and disperse crowds. It was hardly a suitable response to the ballistic weapons that the Breachers would carry, but it was better than nothing. If flash charges were used judiciously, it might allow the villagers to get closer to the Breachers to use their stun batons more effectively. Those who weren't busy erecting a large fenced structure to contain stunned Breachers, were preparing prisoner restraints.

The production of weapons was proceeding nicely. Kade had discovered that if he provided a good source of raw material close to the production room, the templates were able to materialize items at a faster pace. He had the village children collect silica and mineral rich stones that he taught them to recognize.

Weapons would be available to everyone, but they were limited in their use by the need to be recharged at intervals. Each baton was good for about five shots. They were never designed for a prolonged battle. The island had several Exotic Particle Reactors, but the weapons needed time to charge. He'd looked through the template library to see if it was possible to materialize portable EPRs. Unfortunately, their construction required too many exotic materials that weren't readily available in most environments. As an alternative, he modified the handheld weapon templates to accept a low-tech portable battery that could be swapped out. That modification created its own challenges because the battery packs were heavy and each person could only carry a limited number. Still, it increased their capacity from five shots, to thirty.

The sonic cannons were a different matter. They required a dedicated power source and the island only had two portable EPRs. Kade decided to place one at the second beach. Access to the smaller beach was by way of a series of narrow switchbacks and steps carved into the cliff face. A sonic cannon manned in shifts could keep the enemy at bay indefinitely.

The other cannon would be placed in a tower overlooking a hastily built wall surrounding the village. It wouldn't prevent a concerted rush, but it might give the villagers time to escape to their defence of last resort.

If all else failed, they would flee to the edge of the lake at the bottom of the Caldera. There, they had constructed a large motorized raft with a wall of sandbags for protection against projectiles. The raft would move as necessary to stay out of reach for as long as possible. At that point, Kade would relocate to a predetermined high point on the island where he would man a radio and continue to call for help, or in the worst-case scenario, warn others away. It all felt like too weak of a response, but it was the best they could do with what they had.

After completing all these hastily prepared defences, they would hold onto the hope that none of this had been necessary and the Breachers wouldn't find them after all.

Chapter 23

They met in the offices that formerly belonged to Isau Jax. Tenika had taken possession and made the space her own, but a bit of Isau remained — a painting here, a sculpture there. She couldn't bring herself to erase him completely. Lately, she found herself filled with anger at his death. His demise robbed her of the opportunity to — *to what?* At first, she wanted to wipe the smug grin off his face and prove that she was better than him. Later, she grew to respect him and her ambitions changed into a desire to be his equal and... *and what, Tenika? Rule at his side? Really?* She shook her head. She'd always been a lone wolf and the position she now found herself in was exactly what she wanted. For some reason, her rise to power felt hollow without Isau around to witness it. Whether that was because she wanted to gloat or for some other consideration, she wasn't sure. Regardless of the reason, she couldn't get the man out of her head.

Tenika became aware of Tully's eyes on her and shook herself out of her reverie. "Were you able to reverse engineer any of the weapons we collected from the island?"

Tully compressed his lips. He didn't like admitting to failure. "No. The technology possesses some kind of self-destruct feature. Any attempt to tamper with one of the devices causes it to disintegrate. It's a most peculiar thing to witness."

Tenika shivered. *Servator sorcery.* It reminded her of her interrogation under the penetrating eyes of that terrifying Servator, Akhen Hor. He made

132

things appear and disappear in a similar manner. It was... unsettling.

Tenika was equally disappointed that they couldn't access the Servator memory stash archive they'd retrieved. The archive had been the first to disintegrate. At least they had the parchments. The maps were a bit of a puzzle without a proper frame of reference, but Tenika felt certain they would become meaningful in time.

The shipping manifests, on the other hand, provided a wealth of inferable data. They included lists of cargo, along with times and dates.

"How successful were you at the docks?"

Tully brightened. "The dockmaster was very accommodating, thanks to your generous donation. He was more than happy to lend us the shipping manifests for several hours. You were right in your assumptions."

Tenika leaned forward. "You found some matches?"

"Yes, several sea transports have delivered cargo over the years that are similar to those we saw on manifests taken from the rehabilitation island."

Tenika grinned. The parchments from the administration office on the island recorded dates of departure and arrival of sea transports. That would help estimate the time required for a return trip. Tenika could compare those estimates with what they already knew about the length of their own journey to the island.

The island manifests also suggested some kind of inter-island trade. Considering the necessity for secrecy, it was probable that such trade would only occur between Servator interests. Based on the short duration of those trips, the islands had to be relatively close to one another. If those assumptions proved true, they should be able to use the travel times to estimate distances from Caralithica and between islands. That still left a very large area to search, but Tenika hoped to narrow the possibilities even more.

"You mentioned several sea transports."

"Four transports are recorded as leaving port with almost exactly the same cargo over the past two years."

"And you have the names of those transports?"

Tully matched her grin. "I do. Two of them are at the docks this very moment, and one of them is taking on a similar load."

"This is very good news, Tully! I want you to place trackers on the hulls of both of those ships before they leave, and keep an eye out for the arrival of the remaining two."

"I've already made arrangements for trackers to be placed tonight."

"I might have guessed. There's a reason I keep you around after all."

"Probably because of my impressive physique." Tully flexed the twig-like arms of his thin frame.

Tenika handed him a platter with cheese and meat left over from her mid-day meal. "How many times do I need to tell you to eat?"

Tully accepted the offering, rolled a slice of cheese and popped it in his mouth.

"On to other business. How fares your investigation into the only surviving Second Anarch?"

It took Tully a few moments to finish chewing and swallowing before he could answer. "That has been an eye-opening inquiry. This Kenric Trantor is greatly feared among the Breachers, informants, and street urchins alike. He has a formidable intelligence gathering network that has gained an almost mythical status. If one were to believe the rumours, the man sees everything."

Tenika dismissed that notion with a wave of her hand. "No one in the criminal world has that much control. Loose tongues, greed and sheer stupidity provides a constant stream of information for those clever enough to filter fact from fiction. Trantor's information is no less subject to that kind of discernment. Nor is he personally immune to the escape of his own secrets."

"True enough, though he plays the game very well. The fear he sows is backed up by Sicari alliances and, while no one can prove it, all who cross him end up dead sooner or later."

"So, he's a strategist who likes to keep people guessing. That makes him a formidable opponent. However, I know Isau had a loose alliance with the man and didn't display any of the fear that you've uncovered. It tells me that Isau was immune to Trantor's machinations, which means he's less of a threat to someone equally skilled in intrigue."

Tully nodded. "I've come to a similar conclusion. You're more than his match, but we'll need to be cautious when dealing with the man."

"Agreed. Other than gossip, did you learn anything more about his mysterious survival from the plague that killed his peers, or about his plans?"

Tully crossed his arms and began pacing as he expressed what they both were thinking. "It's highly suspicious that he's the only surviving Second Anarch. It is rumoured that he was away on business at the time - a convenient alibi, but not difficult to fabricate."

Tenika redirected his thoughts. "I agree, but if he's guilty of murdering his peers, he must have had a reason. Even if he's innocent, a strategist would certainly begin to make plans now. Someone needs to take control of the Breacher factions. Trantor will believe himself the only logical choice. I disagree. It will come down to Trantor or myself, he just doesn't know it yet. I need to understand how he thinks, how he operates, what plans he's set in motion. I need to know who will side with him and who can be swayed."

Tully grimaced. "His Sicari alliances put him in a strong position."

"But not a stable one." Tenika interrupted. "If I've learned anything from our interactions, it's that the Sicari don't maintain any particular loyalties. They'll change alliances if it better suits their purpose. I need to offer something more enticing than what Trantor brings to the table. To do that, I need to know what agreements he has in place. This is like a complex game of Jumkano. We need to stay three moves ahead. If we can sway the Sicari, Trantor will lose his most prominent game piece."

Tully's nostrils flared in that way he had when he was trying to reserve a promising piece of news for the right moment.

"I know that look, Tully, what are you holding back? Spit it out."

"You do have a negotiating tool not available to Trantor."

Tenika sighed when Tully paused for dramatic effect. "Tully...."

"I'm referring to the energy scythes. Since our victory on the rehabilitation island, word has spread among the Sicari about the formidable weapon. They place a high value on traditional methods of assassination. Bladed weapons demand close proximity which necessitates a high degree of skill. It's a mark of distinction for a Sicari to ensure his assassinations are up close and personal. If there's no personal risk, there's no honour. The Sicari are not averse to using technology, but the idea of an energy-based weapon that functions like a blade appeals to them on a fundamental level. The next time you're among Sicari, watch their eyes when the energy scythes come up in conversation. The avarice is impossible to miss once you've seen it."

"I've noted their interest. Qas is constantly pestering me about obtaining more. You know better than anyone that I've been dangling that carrot for a while now."

"Yes, I've recently used that particular carrot myself."

135

Tenika furrowed her brow, not liking where this was headed. "Tully...." She warned.

He suddenly seemed to realize how it sounded. "Oh! Tenika, no, I would never compromise your position by making a side deal. Let me better explain myself."

Tenika nodded for him to proceed.

"This relates directly to our intelligence gathering efforts. We'd been following an individual who we knew worked for Trantor. We didn't know in what capacity, but he often had Sicari in tow. On one occasion, we found him alone in a local market. We approached him much as we'd done with others, playing the part of some street thugs looking to join the Breachers. We told him we'd seen him leaving the Breacher compound and asked questions about what it was like to work for the famous Kenric Trantor. The hatred in his face at the mention of the name led us to believe we were on to something. He told us if we cared for our friends and families, we'd stay far away from Kenric Trantor.

"I asked him if his family was in danger and he immediately grew suspicious. He demanded to know who we were and craned his neck to search in all directions. His face was awash in panic. I assured him we didn't work for Trantor. He didn't believe me until I mentioned that we had travelled from Caralithica. He latched onto that new piece of information and asked what we knew about the rehabilitation islands. I suppose the shock on our faces must have given us away, because his demeanour changed completely. He seemed to know who you were and begged us to save his family. It was then that we learned his name, Decar Tosh, and that he's an assistant to Kenric Trantor. It seems he lost Trantor's favour and was given an impossible task to complete in order to redeem himself. Decar has resigned himself to his fate and is desperate to save his wife and daughters."

"That's all very interesting, and of course I'd like to pick this man's brain, but you still haven't explained what this has to do with the energy scythes."

"I told Decar we would help him if he'd come with us. He refused. Decar explained that his Sicari companions were tasked with making sure he completed his mission. He said it would be impossible for him to escape and that he wouldn't put his family at risk by trying. I asked him if he'd reconsider if we could leave with both him and his family. He didn't think that was possible, but agreed that he'd be willing to try if we could make that happen."

"Tully — the energy scythes?"

"Right. We decided to approach the two Sicari who were serving as Decar's keepers at a time when Decar wasn't with them. The opportunity arrived three days later. They ignored us until I asked if they knew a man named Qas Drugarish."

"That was a very foolish thing to do, Tully."

"It was a calculated risk. When they asked how we knew that name, I told them that we had access to some of the energy scythes used in a recent operation. When I explained that we were looking for a buyer, they were positively drooling at the prospect. I agreed to meet with them again in two weeks time with proof of our claims."

"And now you'd like my permission to carry out a plan you've yet to share with me."

"You know me well, Tenika. I'd like to offer them two energy scythes in exchange for their help in delivering Decar's family to us and turning a blind eye to their escape."

Tenika was skeptical. "Do you really think they'd agree to such a thing?"

"They were very eager, but I was wondering if you might be able to convince Qas to join us when we meet, in exchange for a few more of those energy scythes he's been pestering you about. I'm certain his presence would seal the deal."

Tenika snorted. "If you think I can convince Qas to do anything, then you haven't been paying attention. Still, I do want Qas to accept that those scythes come at a price, and if he agrees, it would get him off my back for a while. I'll ask, but if he says no, I need you to come up with another plan to rescue Decar and his family. He could be exactly who we're looking for and if he feels indebted to us, so much the better."

"We can still offer the scythes without Qas's presence."

"No, It's too risky. If they decide to deliver you to Trantor, he'll connect the dots and come after me before I'm ready. If Qas is present, they'll be honour bound to hold their end of any agreements, or keep silent if they refuse."

"As you wish."

"I do, and Tully, about those energy scythes — I've been meaning to ask you to look into a modification. I've had you disable the long-range capacity of the scythes we provide the Sicari. I'd like the option to remotely enable the long-range abilities of future models. I'll need a way to send a signal via tote-comm that will enable the feature for ten uses. I intend to be the only one with the pass code."

Tully nodded in understanding. "You wish to increase the value of your currency with the Sicari, while at the same time ensuring your safety."

Tenika rose and patted him on the shoulder, signalling the end of their meeting. "You know me well, Tully."

Chapter 24

Kade stumbled along looking up occasionally to make sure he was still following Selica. She'd already chastised him several times for ignoring her commentary as they walked. He didn't really have time to go for a walk with everything that was on his plate. Administrator Na Tuni had asked for an update on their defensive preparations this morning and Kade promised he'd have a report ready by late afternoon. He still had to come up with some creative distractions for emergency use should their other deterrents fail.

Selica had been standing patiently beside his workbench for a full ten minutes before she gave up waiting for him to notice and tapped him on the shoulder. She was carrying a full pack on her back. When he asked about it, she said it was food and insisted he take a break and join her for a walk.

Kade had been about to decline, but the look on her face suggested that refusal was an unacceptable response. He sighed at the distraction, imagining she had a picnic in mind. It seemed a frivolous waste of time given the threat hanging over their heads.

In the end, he realized that he'd been ignoring his hunger pangs and that he hadn't really accomplished much anyway. It was probably a good idea to take a break and clear his mind. He might have a fresh perspective after stretching his legs. So he reluctantly rose to join her and found himself trailing after his wife. He should have been spending some quality time with the one person who meant most to him in this world, but his mind kept chewing on problems.

"Kade!"

"Huh?"

"Are you even paying attention to where you're walking? I'm surprised you haven't tumbled off a cliff."

Kade took a surprised look at his surroundings, only now realizing they stood on the high caldera path. *How long had they been walking?*

Selica huffed at the look on his face. "You haven't heard a word I've said, have you?"

"I, uh...."

"Never mind, we're here."

Kade's confusion grew. They were nowhere in particular. This part of the trail wasn't wide enough to step off the path, let alone spread out a blanket for a picnic lunch. He turned back to Selica with a question on his lips just in time to see her head drop below the edge of the path on the sea cliff side.

"Selica!" Kade rushed to the spot in a panic and peered over the edge. Selica was shuffling along a narrow ledge towards a hole in the cliff face. She stopped to look up at him. "Don't just squat there gawking. I know you don't have all day. Come on, this is the place I was telling you about."

Kade wracked his brains trying to remember snippets of conversation he'd only given a tenth of his attention to. Selica disappeared into the opening and Kade followed.

When they had both moved several cubits into the tunnel entrance, Selica held her arms out and took a slow turn. "What do you think?"

Kade's face turned crimson realizing he'd have to admit he hadn't heard a word she said during the entire walk. *What kind of a lousy husband am I?* "It's ... a very nice lava tube?"

Selica said nothing, hands on her hips, head cocked to one side like a bird contemplating a worm.

When she finally spoke, it followed a resigned sigh. "I know you've been under a lot of pressure Kade, but this is important. I need you to think about our family." Selica's hands moved protectively to their unborn child.

"Why do you think I've been working so hard?" Kade asked in exasperation. "Everything I'm doing is for our family!"

"That's not what I meant. If you'd been listening on the way up here, you'd know that."

Kade hung his head at the admonishment. "You're right." He settled to the floor of the tunnel. "Tell me what's going on."

"If the Breachers come...."

Kade covered her hands with his own, tugging her to a seated position facing him, "We'll be ready for them. I won't let them hurt you."

"Don't make promises you're not sure you can keep, Kade. We both know what the Breachers are capable of. They've already razed one island and now they know how little resistance they can expect. We don't have the resources to stop a determined assault."

"We're far better prepared than Espor Island was."

"Even so...."

Kade turned to look out the tunnel opening. "What do you want me to say? That we should give up? I can't do that, Selica. I'll fight for our family until my last breath."

"I know you won't give up. I'm not asking you to, but I can't return to the Breachers, Kade. I won't let our child suffer the kind of childhood I endured. If our baby is a boy, I can't live with the thought of Breachers raising him — turning him into a monster. If it's a girl — you know what that means as well as I do. No child should have to live a life filled with that kind of despair."

Kade was uncomfortable with the direction of the conversation. "What are you saying?"

"I'm saying that I'm not content to sit idly by while you try to defend our family alone. This is my fight, too. You'll be expected to oversee the island's defences when the time comes. If something were to happen to you, I need to be able to protect our child. Where will the baby and I be while you're busy trying to save Chellea?"

"I — I'm still working on that. I hoped we could find someplace safe for you to hide."

"That's what I've been trying to tell you. You don't have to."

"I don't understand."

Selica stood, reached for his hand and pulled him upright. "Come with me."

She picked up a lantern that was sitting on the tunnel floor and turned it on before walking confidently into the darkness. Kade lost all sense of direction as they wound their way through the inky blackness surrounded by a little bubble of illumination. He ran into her when she suddenly stopped. Kade muttered an apology for the collision as she stepped through a seam that opened into a cluster of small cave-like spaces.

Selica walked around the cave and turned on several more lanterns until the space was filled with a soft glow.

Kade let out a soft whistle as he surveyed the cozy surroundings. The floor was covered in reed mats. A woven mattress sat along one wall, neatly folded blankets resting on top. Colourful tapestries decorated the walls to deaden echoes and add some warmth. In an adjoining cave, the walls were lined with bamboo shelves holding woven baskets filled with dried fruits, fish and other preserves. Selica set her backpack on the floor in front of the shelves and began placing the contents on the shelves.

Kade let out a chuckle. "So the food wasn't for a picnic?"

Selica gave him a wry smile and tossed him an apple.

He took a bite and talked around a mouthful. "How did you manage this? I know I was preoccupied, but these are a lot of items to carry. Did you have help?"

"No!" Selica responded a little too fervently. "No one knows about this place and you can't tell anyone!"

"Whoa! Maybe you should fill me in a little more. I promise you have my undivided attention."

Selica pulled out her crude map and showed him her extensive exploration. She explained how the lava tubes were isolated from others she'd seen while fishing off the island coast. The tunnel entrance they used was the only point of ingress. She gave him a quick tour of important features like the rainwater depressions, and a few interesting vents that were too small for a person to climb through, but provided fresh air and a window out to the sea.

When the tour was over and they were back in the living area, Selica sat down on the mattress to rest. "What do you think?

Kade stared at his wife with pride. She was always surprising him with her resourcefulness. "This is amazing! I can't believe all you've accomplished in such a short amount of time."

"It's been over a month, Kade."

"Has it been that long? Still, when did you find the time?"

"I brought a little with me on each of my daily walks. No one noticed anything strange about my comings and goings. I've always gone for walks in the morning and early evening. It adds up."

"I can't believe you were doing this for a whole month and I never noticed. You must have a very low opinion of me right now."

"No, you were very busy, and I wasn't ready to tell anyone about this place until now. When you first told me about the attack at Espor, I was in shock. It triggered something in me, and I needed to run and hide."

Kade nodded his head. That wasn't a figure of speech. She literally had run away. When she didn't return by nightfall, he'd spent that night wide-awake, worrying.

Selica guessed what he was thinking. "This is where I spent the night when I ran. After I found this place, it became my sanctuary. I felt safe here. It gave me the security I needed to think things through. I learned that the desire to protect our child was stronger than my fear of the Breachers. That's when I decided to make this place into a stronghold. I've done all I can do to stockpile the necessities for a prolonged stay, but I need your assistance to fortify it. Will you help?"

"What kind of question is that? Of course, I'll help. I can't tell you what a weight off my mind this is. I've been having trouble focusing on the island defences because I keep worrying about you and the baby. This is a perfect solution. It's well hidden, and with the Servator technology, I can make this place invisible and impenetrable. In fact, this will solve a major problem I've been struggling with."

Selica looked uncomfortable. "What problem is that?"

"If everything falls apart, I'm expected to relocate to a high point on the island and transmit distress calls. We know the Servators won't be able to help anytime soon, but we might be able to find a passing ship that could offer assistance. Quantum transmissions won't be heard by non-Servator sea transports, so I need to set up a more limited traditional transmitter. It needs to be high enough to clear the caldera lip while still remaining hidden. That cave you showed me with the vent to the sea would be perfect. It's hidden, protected from the elements, and I can push an antenna through the hole to transmit. Most importantly, I won't need to worry about finding you because you'll already be here. In fact..."

Selica interrupted him. "Kade! You can't tell anyone about this place! I know it's selfish, but I did this for us. I can't protect our child if I have to worry about other people too. This island has taken my husband from me these past weeks. I'll not let them put our child at risk while they use you up to prepare their defences. You spend every waking hour working to save our friends, while they go home and make preparations for their own families. What about us?"

"I'm so sorry, Selica. I didn't realize you were feeling this way. What do you want me to do? I can't just turn my back on the people who gave us shelter."

"I'm not asking you to. These people are my friends as well. If you did any less to help them, you wouldn't be the man I fell in love with. All I'm asking is that you allow us to have our own preparations, just like everyone else. I want you to keep doing what you're doing. I just hoped you could help a little with the finishing touches."

Kade scratched his head as he thought about it. "You're right. If my defences fail, the villagers will still need to resort to the raft on the lake as a final refuge. There isn't enough room in these tunnels for everyone to fit. We've always known anything we do by that point is just a delaying tactic while we pray for help to come. Even so, that doesn't mean this can't still be the place I set up transmitting equipment."

"What are you thinking?"

"The council agrees that no one can know where I set up. They don't want to risk someone divulging that information while under duress. If we're to have any hope of rescue, the transmission location needs to remain a secret. I can prepare a motorized cart to help me move the equipment here on my own. Come to think of it, this also solves another potential problem. I was uncomfortable with the local QPN sitting exposed in the administration building. If we lose that to the Breachers, we lose any chance of a last-minute solution when an opportunity presents itself. If I move that here as well, I can solve two problems at once."

"As long as you can do that without revealing the location, I'm okay with the idea. To be honest, I'll feel better with you here if things get bad."

Kade rubbed his chin as he switched into problem solving mode. "Okay then, here are my initial thoughts. First, I'll widen the path to the entrance. Then I'll form a wall around the tunnel opening to match the cliff face so it's not visible from the sea. The Servators have this system of creating false walls that can materialize as needed - a high tech door, so to speak. I'll create one of those to block the way to the entrance so it's not possible to see the path, or enter the tunnel without a pass code once it's been erected.

"Next, I'd like to form a cistern where the water collects so we can store a larger reserve. We'll also need a latrine of some sort. Oh — and I could bore more vents to allow some natural light to penetrate and brighten this place up a bit. If we have enough time, I'd also like to try excavating an internal staircase down to sea level and create a little undersea tunnel. It might be possible to coax some fish into a little fishing hole. It could also provide us with an emergency exit that's not visible from the exterior of the island."

Selica laughed. "Those are just your *initial* thoughts?"

"You kind of put me on the spot."

"I love it. Thank you."

"I'll tell Administrator Na Tuni that I've found a location for the transmitter and explain my plan to move the QPN there as well. I'll let him know that I need a week to complete the installation. He'll post guards on the main path to make sure no one follows. I'm sure we can start in the next day or so."

Selica's face blanched. "Oh, no."

"What's wrong, I thought you liked the idea — Selica?"

He turned to see Selica, hunched over with a hand on her pregnant belly.

"We might have to wait a few days. My water just broke. I need to get to the midwife."

Selica waved her hands in front of Kade's shocked face and snapped her fingers several times. "Honestly, Kade. You can defy a murderous Breacher and overcome your fear of heights during a life-threatening escape. You can throw yourself into preparations to save an entire village of people from a Breacher horde with the odds stacked against you, but you freeze up at the thought of a tiny little baby entering the world?

"Never mind. I'm headed back to the village. Follow when you're ready." Selica patted him on the cheek and smiled. "Maybe you need a little time in this sanctuary to contemplate why your fear of childbirth is greater than your fear of the Breachers."

It took Kade a moment to realize he was alone. "Selica? Selica, wait!" Kade shook off his stupor and rushed to catch up. It wasn't lost on him that once again he was following her lead. This time it didn't bother him at all.

Chapter 25

"Let me do the talking," Qas insisted. They were nearing the appointed meeting place. He'd already scouted ahead to ensure there would be no surprises. It seemed the two Sicari Tully had approached a few weeks ago were genuinely interested in the energy scythes he had offered.

Tully was confident they would agree to his terms once they laid eyes on the latest version of the weapon. The original was little more than a smooth baton for a handle with a narrower, cubit-long spar, extending the baton's length. Emitters dotted the spar to create a cutting edge when power was applied. During their incursion on the Servator rehabilitation island, Tully had noticed that a number of the Sicari had affixed sharpened points to the end of the spar so they could also use it without power. That, and the love the Sicari had for bladed weapons, inspired him to make additional changes beyond the modifications Tenika had asked him to incorporate.

The revised weapon was now truly a blade, about the length of a short sword. The circuitry was in the pommel, protected by a proper guard. He'd found a very talented bladesmith hoping to make a name for himself, who agreed to produce the blade and tang. The man was confused by Tully's request for a hollow channel in the back edge of the work. He'd also asked for regularly spaced holes originating from that channel and exiting on one side of the blade. When Tully refused to explain why, the bladesmith shrugged, deciding not to pursue the matter further, and threw himself to the task. The finished product was a work of art. The single edged blade had a subtle curve with a reinforced tip. The holes required for the emitters were accommodated by decorative scallops that managed to smooth the transition to the thickened back edge while giving the blade a threatening appearance. Tully had requested a finish that could withstand high temperatures. The final result was a blade with a gleaming black ceramic coating broken only by the thin silver line of the honed edge.

The bladesmith was pleased when Tully doubled the agreed upon payment, but was close to ecstatic when offered a contract for a hundred just like it. Tully promised the man that if he could ramp up production, there would be additional larger contracts on the horizon.

Back in Tully's production facilities, his team fine-tuned the fussy task of installing circuitry in the hilt and blade. Emitters were placed within the scallops on one side of the blade and tuned to extend just beyond the sharpened edge. They were able to match the curve of the blade and the arrangement resulted in a serendipitous energy shield covering the flat of the blade. Tully wasn't sure how that might be used, but he was confident the Sicari would think of something.

The sheath was made of a metal alloy and housed a battery to keep the weapon fully charged when not in use. Additional battery packs could be swapped out as needed.

Tully smiled as he recalled the meeting where Tenika asked Qas for his help with this operation. He had outright refused to get involved in anything that might jeopardize a contract held by his fellow Sicari, but Tenika's offer of a few energy scythes got the better of him. He'd agreed to meet, but made no promises.

After Tenika explained what they were planning, Qas seemed doubtful that the Sicari Tully had approached would be easily swayed once they heard the details. A lot depended on the specifics of their contract. He'd used his reticence to try to increase the number of scythes Tenika was offering for his help. When Tenika refused to offer more than four, he threatened to leave. It was at that point that Tully mentioned they had dramatically improved on the design and Qas would be getting the new improved version. Tenika had raised a brow at that, concerned that he might be about to divulge the hidden long-range capabilities. Tully hadn't told Tenika about his additional improvements and just winked at her while placing the sheathed weapon into Qas's hands.

Qas furrowed his brows at the unexpected package, then looked up at Tully who nodded for him to unsheathe the weapon. The expression on Qas's face as he did so was worth the effort Tully had put into its design. He'd known there would be value in making the weapon esthetically pleasing to Sicari sensibilities. However, he wasn't certain whether he'd been successful until he saw the naked lust in Qas's eyes. The involuntary hiss from Qas's lips harmonized with the sound of the blade sliding from its sheath. When Tully showed Qas how to power the weapon by striking the end of the pommel, his eyes grew wide. Stepping back to gain some space, Qas put the weapon through a series of forms, testing the weight and balance. He reluctantly switched off the power and placed the scythe back in its sheath and held it lovingly before his eyes.

Tenika snatched it from his hands and took full advantage of her newfound leverage. She reiterated her offer of four of the *original* scythes, or two of the updated version.

The dismay on Qas's face was comical, if not predictable. He suggested that it was unnecessary to involve the other two Sicari, suggesting he could do the job himself for four of the newer scythes.

Tenika reminded Qas that he was a known associate of hers and she couldn't risk his being identified in an operation against her biggest potential adversary. Qas reluctantly agreed and Tenika mollified him by returning the weapon to his eager hands with the promise of the second one — if he could successfully convince his peers to participate.

That was a week ago and now they were back in Sumakad waiting for their Sicari contacts to appear.

"What do you think our chances are?" Tully asked.

Qas grunted. "They'll go out of their way to make it work once they lay eyes on what you're offering, so keep it hidden until we first explain what we want in exchange. We need to gauge how difficult this may be and understand their existing contractual agreements before tempting them needlessly."

Tully looked at Qas strangely. "Surely they wouldn't be so easily swayed from their duty?"

"Not normally." Qas admitted.

"So how would this be any different?"

"I've been meaning to ask how you came up with the design for the updated energy scythes." Qas responded. "What made you decide to use that particular pattern of scallops on the blade?"

Tully frowned at the unexpected question. "There was no thought put into it at all. I gave the bladesmith the necessary specifications and left it to him to decide how to make it work. Not knowing what they were for, he was concerned about the holes required for the emitters and the hollow space in the back edge. His solution provided a way to strengthen the area while satisfying his sense of aesthetic. It was a simple mix of practicality and artistic expression. Why?"

Qas held Tully's gaze for a full minute, searching for the truth in his words. Qas sniffed. "If I didn't know better, I'd think you've been sneaking around the headquarters for the Order of the Sicari."

"What on earth are you going on about?"

"Your new energy scythe bears a striking resemblance to the sword of our revered founder."

"Huh."

"Yes — huh. Since no outsider has ever stepped foot in Sicari headquarters or knows where it is, I'll have to accept that you speak the truth. It's just a stroke of good luck that you possess technology for a weapon that suits Sicari tactics and happens to look like the most coveted blade in Sicari tradition. Every Sicari initiate has dreamt of wielding the founder's blade and here you are offering the closest alternative."

"I assure you it's a total coincidence."

"I don't like coincidences, but I'm content to leave it alone. The weapon has merit on its own, but if I ever find out you've been lying to me...."

Tully shivered at the implied threat. "I swear to you, I'm telling the truth. Do you think I'd lie to an assassin?"

"You'd be surprised by the falsehoods that come out of the mouths of someone pleading for their life. People turn on their loved ones in a heartbeat. It's despicable."

Tully thought it best not to point out the hypocrisy of a killer assuming moral superiority. Besides, it wasn't as though someone like himself who provided arms to assassins could judge.

The two Sicari arrived precisely on time. They'd agreed to meet in a squalid district where the homeless lived in makeshift tents or roughly assembled shacks constructed of whatever refuse was available. Qas and Tully were led to a tent on the periphery, far enough away from the others to offer some privacy. One of the Sicari handed two silvers to the occupant who smiled broadly and invited them graciously into his ramshackle kingdom before disappearing.

"Who do I have the honour of greeting?" Qas began.

"This is Xiten, and I am Kanoi. You honour us with your presence, Qas Drugarish. When we were approached by your companion, we didn't believe he really knew you. We were prepared to dispatch him today if we determined that he was disparaging your name for personal gain."

Tully turned pale at the admission.

"Thank you, my brothers."

The two Sicari nodded and spoke the ritual phrase, "For the preservation of the order."

Qas provided the expected response. "Integrity must be maintained."

"You vouch for this man, Qas?"

"I do"

"We've heard many rumours. Have you wielded one of these energy scythes? Can you verify its effectiveness?"

"I used one in the campaign against the Servator rehabilitation island. Our success speaks to its effectiveness, but I guarantee what you've heard doesn't do it justice."

Xiten and Kanoi both looked like they wished to discuss that campaign in detail, but it wasn't the time or place. "May we see the weapon?"

Qas held up a hand. "We'd like to discuss payment first."

The two Sicari frowned.

"Don't misunderstand me, brothers. The client isn't interested in financial currency so much as a favour. I warned my contact that you would not jeopardize any existing agreements in order to help, so I thought it best to explain the request before taking this any further."

"Prudent. Continue."

"I'm told that you have been known to tail a man named Decar Tosh."

"That is no secret," Xiten acknowledged.

"What of his family?"

"Decar Tosh has a wife and two daughters who work in the textile mill for Kenric Trantor," Kanoi answered. "He likes to keep a close eye on the families of his assistants as an incentive."

"Do you have contractual obligations to watch over Decar's family?"

"No, it's enough for Trantor to know where they are. The family's activities are not monitored and they carry on with their lives without interference."

"And what of Decar?" Qas pressed. "How do your agreements pertain to him?"

"We accompany Decar whenever Trantor has intelligence on the location of the Levigator. Decar's task is to eliminate that Servator threat, but we know he isn't up to the task. It will fall on us."

"You're to assassinate the Levigator?" Qas asked in surprise. He thumped his chest with his fist. "That is a worthy risk."

The two Sicari bowed their heads in acknowledgement of the honour Qas showed them.

"So you're bound to watch over and protect Decar Tosh?"

"You misunderstand, Qas. We have no long-term commitments to Kenric Trantor. When we agree to an assignment, the contract is implied for the duration of that mission and no longer. Trantor is away on business and there has been no new intelligence regarding the Levigator. Decar's task is on hold until those circumstances change. We keep an eye on Decar now, only so he's easy to find when the time comes for his task to resume. We have no current obligations to Trantor in regards to Decar."

"I see." Qas scratched his scalp.

"What is the favour you're asking?"

"The client would like to take possession of Decar and his family. You would be given two energy scythes in exchange for your willingness to turn a blind eye, or to refuse any other assistance you may be tempted to offer. Tully, show them a scythe."

Tully unwrapped one of the scythes and pulled it out of its sheath. The transformation on the faces of the two Sicari was instant. Tully slapped the bottom of the pommel to power up the scythe. Xiten's mouth gaped, and Kanoi's hand involuntarily reached for the weapon. Tully quickly turned it off, not wanting to accidentally sever any fingers.

Qas spoke again, reclaiming their attention. "I understand that this request is beneath hunters of the Levigator. If you would rather not be involved, I can handle this myself," Qas assured them. "In that case I ask for the professional courtesy that you not interfere."

Tully wanted to object. Qas was off script and Tenika had specifically warned him not to get involved. Qas cast a warning look at Tully, demanding his silence. Tully noticed the conflicting expressions on the men's faces and realized the clever thing Qas had done. He'd acknowledged their skill and that the request was beneath them. Then, the famous Qas suggested maybe he, himself, should be the one to do it. The implication was either that they were less capable or that they thought themselves greater than Qas. He gave them an out that wouldn't dishonour them while delivering a perfect mix of passive aggressive challenge.

Tully handed a scythe to each of the men to inspect. Each unsheathed a blade and tested the balance. *There's no chance they will hand those things back.*

"We see no conflict of interest," Xiten blurted at the same time that Kanoi exclaimed "We accept." The two of them looked abashed at the sudden lack of professionalism.

Qas smiled. "Feel no shame. I had a similar reaction the first time I held one."

"That's an understatement," Tully muttered. Qas shot him a look filled with promises of pain. Tully pursed his lips and found somewhere else to direct his attention.

Tully moved to reclaim the scythes, but Qas prevented him. "The payment is theirs. They won't dishonour the contract." Tully nodded and stepped back while two very pleased Sicari strapped their new toys to their belts.

"How and when should we go about this?" Tully asked.

Xiten shrugged. "Now would be good."

"Now?"

"Trantor is away, we are free of commitment and Decar's wife and daughters are just about to complete their shift at the textile mill. Kanoi can guide you to an appropriate spot where you can intercept them. I'll find Decar. Meet back here in an hour and you can be on your way."

"Can it really be that simple?" Tully wondered aloud.

"There will be no consequences for us." Xiten assured him. "It's Decar who takes all of the risk by fleeing. Kenric will ask us to hunt him, but we'll refuse, this time around. We like to keep Trantor guessing."

"Sometimes it's that simple." Qas smiled. "Let's get going. I have a scythe of my own to collect."

Chapter 26

Kade stepped back to critique his handiwork. He'd spent the morning in the lava tubes assembling a surprise for Selica. It was a crib. The corner posts and rails had whimsical carvings of fish and birds. Bamboo spindles surrounded the woven mat at the base.

He still couldn't believe he was the father to a beautiful baby girl. Kade yawned, rubbing his eyes. Neither he nor Selica had been getting much sleep. Little Kuisa clearly had the tenacity of her mother, crying nonstop for what felt like days.

Kade nodded in satisfaction at his craftsmanship. He couldn't wait for Selica to see it. Their little hide-away was coming along nicely. The task of widening and enclosing the entrance had been completed a few days ago. No one would find this place without explicit directions. Strategically cored ventilation holes now provided enough light that the main areas of the tunnels were illuminated during the daytime. He'd completed the cistern which was already half full of water and had even managed some rudimentary plumbing to carry water to the latrine. Forming a staircase down to the waterline was a much larger task that would need to wait.

The memory stash for the QPN templates and the transmitting equipment were already sitting in the small cave he'd chosen for that purpose. Kade tapped into the internal power source of the memory stash to power the transmitting equipment. The memory stash was connected to a Q-view workstation that was up and running, but he hadn't tested the transmitting equipment yet. *No time like the present.* Kade sat in front of the transmitter and dialed in the frequency to a second unit sitting at his workbench in the administration building. Hitting the power switch produced an audible hum. The smell of hot dust assailed his nostrils as the unit warmed up. This was an old transmitter that had been sitting unused in a corner for years. Kade put on the headset and nearly jumped out of his skin from someone yelling into his ear.

"Kade! Kade! Where are you?" It was the panicked voice of Administrator Na Tuni.

"Kade here. Is there a problem?"

"Kade! Thank the Maker! I've been trying to reach you for hours. Ships are approaching the island. We need you here. Now!"

"I'm on my way!" Kade ripped the headset off and ran for the exit. *This can't be happening. We're not ready.* His body threatened to overtake his feet as he ran recklessly downhill on the path to the village. He forced himself to slow down before he risked a twisted ankle. *This was a mistake, putting so many key responsibilities in the hands of a single person.* Even as he thought it, he realized they didn't have a choice. He was the only person on the island with the required expertise.

Relief washed over Kade as he met Selica coming up the path with Kuisa curled up in a sling. She was moving slowly, but steadily. "Kade! I was coming to get you. You heard?"

"Yes, Administrator Na Tuni contacted me on the radio."

"Oh, Kade, I'm so frightened. This is really happening."

Kade wrapped his arms protectively around his little family. "It'll be okay. Can you make it to the lava tubes on your own? Do you need help?"

"I'll be okay. It will be a few more hours before the ships arrive. I have time, but you need to go. Here, you forgot your tote-comm on your workbench. I have mine with me as well. Keep me updated."

Kade took a moment to study Selica's face and burned the image into his memory. He looked down at his newborn daughter and hardened his resolve. *The Breachers can't have them. If I have to die to keep them safe, I will.* He gave Selica a quick kiss and hurried to the village.

Kade burst into his workspace where he found Administrator Na Tuni staring at the viewscreens on his workbench.

"Three sea transports!" Kade exclaimed. "Why so many? Don't they know how few of us are on these islands from their attack on Espor?"

"What do we do?" Lasa whispered.

They weren't ready. They still needed to set up viewcorders on the path from the beach to monitor the Breacher's passage. They needed to time the rock falls if they hoped to trap the invaders.

"Who's our fastest runner?"

"That would be Ren."

"Good, send Ren to the top of the cliffs on one side of the path. Give him a tote-comm and instruct him to call me when he sees the majority of the Breacher force between the two rock falls. He'll need to stay there long enough to determine whether it succeeded and to run back to the village as fast as he can if it fails."

"I'll go get him now."

"Send Jon and Gren to man the acoustic cannon at the far beach, too."

Lasa nodded and hurried off at a jog.

They did have viewcorders set up at each of the beaches to watch for sea transports, since those were the obvious places to land a party. He'd be able to spring those first traps without assistance.

Kade pulled out his tote-comm and took a moment to contact Selica. "Where are you?"

"I just sealed the tunnel entrance. We're safe inside."

Kade breathed a sigh of relief. "I'll do my best to let you know what's happening. You may be able to see some of it from the viewscreens I set up in the transmitter room. Do you remember my instructions on how to operate the workstation?"

"Yes. Kade, please be careful. Your daughter is going to need her father and I don't think I can do this alone."

"Don't worry about me. Get some rest. That was a long hike so soon after childbirth." Kade felt a lump growing in his throat. "I love you, Selica."

"And I love you."

"They've dispatched landing craft. I have to go."

Kade turned his attention back to the viewscreen, just as a call came in from Jon and Gren. "If you're going to try something, Kade, now would be a good time."

"Yes, I can see them. They're amassing on the beach. I'm about to trigger the first deterrent. It will only slow them down. After that, I'll be too busy to contact you. Do what you can to keep them at bay with the cannon, but if it looks like you can't keep up, return to the village. Don't try to be heroes."

"Understood."

The main beach was filling fast. Kade triggered the gates at both beaches to let the sea water flow beneath the sand. At first it didn't look like anything was happening. Kade checked to make sure he had actually triggered the gates. By the time he returned his eyes to the viewscreen, the results were rapidly becoming apparent. Men began sinking to their waists in the sand — arms flailing. A few who had tripped were dragged under and quickly retrieved by their comrades. They began to slowly form two lines. *What are they doing?* Kade watched them struggle for a moment and then turned his attention to the second beach. The results there were much the same, but the distance from the water to the path was shorter and Breachers had already found their way to the cliff face. Kade saw several fall over as the sonic cannon was turned on them.

"Yes!" His enthusiasm was short-lived as he saw some Breachers setting up a projectile cannon on the prow of one of the landing craft. *How could I be so stupid? I should have guessed they'd bring large ordnance.* They were aiming for the sonic cannon. He grabbed his tote-comm to warn Jon and Gren. A puff of smoke belched from the Breacher cannon. Kade waited breathlessly for an answer to his call. When Breachers began ascending the path unimpeded, he had his answer. It was an hour-long hike from the second beach. They still had a chance. Kade yelled in frustration and turned his attention back to the first beach.

More landing craft were streaming from the anchored sea transports. His blood ran cold as he watched the Breachers unload planks. The first group who were still mired in the wet sand had managed to move themselves into parallel lines, facing off in pairs. They were passing planks to the front of the line, resting boards on the shoulders of each opposing pair to form a human bridge.

Kade rubbed his temples vigorously. His first deterrent had only gained them a few hours.

"Ren!" He yelled into his tote-comm. "They're coming, get ready. I'll stay on the comm. Let me know when they're two thirds of the way to the village."

Kade was sweating. What had he been thinking when he agreed to take on this role? He had no military training and it was showing. His strategy failed to account for long-range heavy weapons and the ingenuity of his enemy. They were moving through his deterrents as if they were just a minor inconvenience. Kade hadn't found time to think of any creative options for tokens on the local memory stash. *What am I going to do if the second deterrent fails?*

His tote-comm squawked. "Now, Kade! Now!"

Kade triggered both rock falls at the same time. The roar could be heard a half-league away and the ground trembled with the impact. Kade ran to the door of his lab and saw a giant plume of dust rising into the sky.

It took fifteen minutes before the dust settled enough that Kade thought Ren might be able to see what the results were. "Talk to me Ren, what's happening?"

"I —" cough... "It's hard to make out details, but the rocks must have rolled quite a distance." Ren paused for a coughing fit. "The pile isn't anywhere near as high as we'd hoped. I'm trying to get a little closer to see if — they're climbing! Kade, it didn't work! I think they see me."

"Run, Ren!" Kade heard a loud crack through the tote-comm. "Ren? Ren... Ren!"

The tremors started in his fingers and moved up his arms until his whole body was shaking. He couldn't get enough air. He didn't notice Administrator Na Tuni's hand on his shoulder at first. Words began to filter through his panic.

"Kade? Kade! We need a report. What's happening?"

"They're coming. The deterrents failed. Breachers are moving in our direction from both beaches. Get everyone behind the walls. I'll be out shortly."

Kade grabbed a pack and tossed in anything he thought might help. His notes on token templates, his wrist Q-view, and the toy he'd been carving for Kuisa. He was about to leave the lab when he remembered that there were still Servator weapons in the manufacturing area. Hastily gathering up as many as he could pile on a cart, he dragged them out the door. Kade tossed them here and there, throwing some in the surrounding bushes hoping the Breachers would be tempted to search for the easy plunder. The futuristic looking Servator weapons would disintegrate if someone tried to use them without the proper codes, but maybe curiosity would gain them a few more minutes as the Breachers investigated. That done, he ran to the gate in the wall they'd built around the village and ordered it shut.

The villagers had gathered and were waiting for him. He let his eyes drift over the nervous crowd.

"The Breachers are coming."

Chapter 27

Qas could be frustratingly vague when it came to the Sicari. Tenika decided to come at it from another angle. "How have you been enjoying your new energy scythes?"

Qas drew one from the pair of scabbards on his back, and looked at it fondly. "Tully really outdid himself. The scythes are functional works of art and the envy of Sicari everywhere."

"I could increase our production capacity. There's no need for Sicari to lack what they desire. I'll happily provide one to every Sicari warrior."

"For a price," Qas amended.

"For a price," Tenika agreed.

"That's where we begin to run into problems, Tenika."

"I don't see a reason for concern. It's a fair trade. If I understand correctly, the Sicari have no interest in Breacher politics or who's running the show. You can help me get what I want — something that is of no threat or value to the Sicari. I can give you what you want — something of value that serves to increase the effectiveness of the threat represented by the Sicari Order. We both win."

"It's not as simple as that."

"Then help me understand."

Tenika studied Qas's furrowed brow as he tried to think of a way to placate her without revealing too much about his secretive order.

"The Sicari are not governed by a ruling authority in the manner of the

Breachers. We answer to no one, not even to each other. We're bound by our craft, our oaths and our honour."

Tenika mentally rolled her eyes. *There is no honour among thieves ... or assassins.*

Qas continued, the questioning lift of her brow ignored.

"Even if I wanted to convince the Sicari to back your bid for power, there is no leader I could approach who can enter into a contract of agreement representing all Sicari. I would have to convince each Sicari to decide for themselves."

"Do that, then."

"Very funny."

"I'm serious, the rumour mill seems to be alive and well among your ranks. I noticed that word of the scythes travelled quickly, as did your exploits on the Servator rehabilitation island. Surely that gives your opinion some weight."

Qas shook his head. "Weapons and tales of glorious battle are standard fare at Sicari gatherings, but those reflect individual prowess that have nothing to do with politics. No Sicari will be swayed to join a cause. All that matters is the opportunity to prove oneself. To do that there needs to be...."

"...great risk. Yes, I know."

Qas nodded. "You begin to understand. The Sicari honour their contracts, but we don't enter into them lightly or long-term. Those who gain the most prestige in our order, do so by careful consideration of potential future contracts. One can gain skill and a level of prestige through continuous battle. Indeed, some spend all their time as mercenaries for hire to various armies. However, the level of skill required to compete in a military exercise, while providing risk, is relatively predictable. More prestige is gained for a solitary assassin using an arsenal of skills against a superior force. A well-protected target provides a high risk, high value contract. In that sense, we value politics merely for the intrigue it provides."

Tenika set down the mug of kofa she'd been nursing and leaned forward, placing an elbow on the table so she could prop up her head. She'd spent a long night going over the intelligence Tully had gathered on the movements of Kenric Trantor. The Second Anarch successfully destroyed two Servator bases and commandeered two Breacher hordes. She couldn't allow his expansion to continue if she hoped to succeed in her own ambitions.

"You're saying that Sicari are motivated to preserve or grow opportunities to test their skills?"

"That's putting it in very simplistic terms, but not entirely inaccurate."

"You're also suggesting that the lure of a shiny toy isn't enough to risk future opportunity."

Qas grinned. "Oh, don't get me wrong, we Sicari like our toys and you could convince many to join a single campaign in order to obtain a scythe. The recent detachment you sent to attack a second Servator island is proof of that. You had to turn some Sicari away, if I recall. However, that won't get you preferential consideration for future contracts. In order to do what you're contemplating, you need a consistent supply of ready soldiers. If you want some of those forces to be Sicari, they need to be confident in consistent returns. No Sicari is going to turn down a sure contract from a proven source on the uncertain promises of a newcomer."

Tenika scowled. "Surely those two campaigns account for something! Those islands have remained hidden for centuries until I uncovered them — something none of your previous benefactors have been able to accomplish."

Qas waved away her objection. "The scythes were a strong incentive, but you wouldn't have had so many volunteers if that had been the only value. As you've noted, there is some prestige in sharing the conquest of the mysterious Servator rehabilitation islands. As a result, your name is now known among the Sicari. That is no small feat, but we both know there is a limited supply of such islands, if there are even any more to be found. Many Sicari will now be wondering if you can repeat your success on the mainland where victory isn't so easily assured. More importantly, you're not the only player, there are others with a long history of providing significant contracts to the Sicari."

"You're referring to Kenric Trantor," Tenika's nostrils flared. Kenric's name was coming up in conversation more often than she'd like.

"The Sicari are not contracted solely by Breachers, but Kenric is a suitable example. He has provided many Sicari with contracts over the years, and now he has gained control of a second horde, promising more to come."

"I control one of the hordes."

"That's true, but the Breacher factions are in turmoil. You could lose control of the horde just as quickly as you've gained it. Trantor retains his traditional hold on one horde and will surely succeed in retaining control of the other. He *is* a Second Anarch of some renown, after all. Your record isn't yet established."

"So what do you propose I should do?"

Qas smiled. "You're already doing it. Continue to generate opportunities. Consistency is key. Your name will grow with the number and types of challenges you provide."

"Providing enough targets will do the trick?"

"No. That will keep you in the minds of Sicari, but if you want a reliable pool of recruits, there are only two sure ways to gain that foothold."

Tenika placed her face in her palms. Talking with Qas was exhausting. Why couldn't he just give her all of the details instead of waiting for her to ask specific questions? "May I ask what those two sure ways might be?"

"One way would be to gain and maintain control over more hordes than Kenric."

Tenika sighed. "And the other way?"

"If you undermine Kenric's authority in a way that makes him look less competent than you, it could shift Sicari preference in your favour."

Tenika rose to get another mug of kofa. She offered to get a mug for Qas, but he declined. "If you were to choose a target that would appeal to the Sicari, what would it be?"

Qas was ready with an answer. "Minimally, you should duplicate Kenric's success. You'll need to claim a second horde and destroy two mainland Servator bases. If you can do that, your success with the Servator islands will give you an advantage that Trantor can't duplicate. Even so, if you allow him to take one more horde, that may no longer matter."

Tenica was rubbing her temples now as she considered the speed at which she'd need to plan and the logistics involved. "Where is the nearest unclaimed Breacher horde located?"

Qas stood and walked to a map of the world on the meeting room wall. He drew a finger across the sea from Caralithica to Jaihuwan and tapped it twice with his index finger. "If you can claim the horde in Jaihuwan and reinforce it with the horde from Caralithica, then you'll be the same distance from Arapanus as Trantor. Arapanus will be the only game piece left on the Jumkano board."

"Do you have any Breacher contacts in Jaihuwan who would be willing to meet with me?"

"I might. Have Tully investigate the situation at the Breacher base there. I'll see if any of my Jaihuwan contacts are still in place. If they are, I'm sure I can arrange for a meeting if you have a few of those scythes to offer them. No promises beyond that, but they're always interested in intrigue if you can provide a suitable challenge."

"Can I ask you one more question, Qas?"

He nodded for her to continue.

"If the Sicari are as careful in their commitments as you say, why are you helping me at all?"

Qas thought about it for a moment. "While it's true that Trantor is the safer choice for most Sicari, I've seldom accepted a contract from the man. Too often I've seen him turn an operation into something slightly different than what was agreed upon. That may seem like semantics, considering what the Sicari do, but I'm not a fresh warrior who can afford to blindly rush into battle trusting on the strength and reflexes of youth. Fortunately, I've built my reputation elsewhere, so I don't need what he has to offer. I've also worked with you on several occasions — enough to understand your motivations. Let's just say, I would prefer to work with you over Trantor, and since I have nothing to lose either way, you offer a better potential future from my perspective."

"Well, aren't you the charmer."

"Make no mistake, Tenika. If you fail in your goals and no longer have anything to offer, I'll turn from you just like any other Sicari."

"I know that should sound ominous, but I appreciate your honesty far more than you know. Let the word out discreetly that I may be planning a raid on the Servator base in Jaihuwan with the help of the Breacher horde there."

"Isn't that a little premature?"

Tenika grinned. "Ah, but think of the intrigue."

Qas laughed as he glanced at his wrist chrono and shook his head in admiration of her scheming ruminations. "I have another appointment to get to." He said his goodbyes and left her alone with her thoughts.

Jaihuwan... my old stomping grounds. Perhaps it was time to return to the place where it all began and renew her contacts there. She had power now and understood the criminal landscape. Her debt to Laki had been paid by Isau, and she held the keys to Isau's kingdom. If her characterization of Laki was accurate, he'd be eager to gain a powerful ally. He might be able to give her the edge she needed for a creative takeover.

The more she thought about it, the more convinced she was that it could work. She needed sleep more than anything else now, but first thing in the morning she'd send Tully to Jaihuwan to start fleshing out this new plan.

LEAVENING

Chapter 28

Kade saw the fear in the villager's eyes and found he had no comfort to offer them. There was no easy way to share the bad news, so he gave it to them straight.

"The Breachers have made it past our defences and are coming from two directions. We're outnumbered at least ten to one. They have cannons capable of shredding the wall around the village. We can't stop them here. At minimum, they could surround our village within the half hour. We can't wait until that happens. We need to get to the raft before they arrive, which means we need to leave now."

Everyone stared at him in silent shock. Many started weeping. Children clung to their parents' legs, knowing something was wrong, but unable to understand.

Kade clapped his hands to get their attention. "Gather the children at the shoreline. I'll take them with me to safety when I leave for the transmitter."

Someone shouted from the crowd, "If there's a safe place for the children, why are you only telling us now? Why don't we all go there?"

"You all agreed that I should find a secure location for the transmitter and use it to keep calling for help. I found such a place, but there isn't enough room for everyone. There's enough space for the children, but no more. You also agreed that no one should know the location. That's even more important now if you want to keep your children safe. I'm sorry, that's the best I can offer. If you feel you can protect your children better with them at your side on the raft, I can

165

understand that decision. Either way, you need to make a choice quickly."

There were a lot of hugs and tear-filled eyes, but all of them chose to send their youngest children with Kade. A few of the older children refused to go, demanding the opportunity to fight alongside their family and friends.

That settled, Kade made one last request. "I need a few volunteers to remain in the village. The rest of you, head to the raft — now."

The crowd turned as one and began moving as quickly as they could toward the lake. Ten men stayed behind and waited for further instructions.

Kade nodded at them sombrely. "Everything we do from this point forward is a delaying tactic. If we have an opportunity to confiscate some of their long-range weapons, we might be able to win a war of attrition from the safety of the raft. Unless I can contact someone to bring help, that's really our only hope at this point.

"We still have a sonic cannon mounted on top of the wall. One of you will use it to knock out a swath of soldiers while the others slip through the gate to gather as many Breacher weapons as they can. That will only work briefly before they take it out with their own cannon. Once the sonic cannon has been disabled, start using the flash cards. The first time will be the most effective. Get everyone to arm a card and toss it over the fence at the same time. The Breachers won't be expecting it and you can temporarily blind many of them. Take advantage of the confusion to gather more of their weapons.

"One of you should load a cart and bring whatever you can gather to the raft. It won't take long for the Breachers to figure out how to counter the flash cards, but you might be able to surprise them a few times. Last of all, I need one of you to splash fuel on the walls. When the flash cards are no longer working, ignite the wall and head for the raft. Hopefully the fire will hold them off a little longer."

Kade saw the determination in their eyes. He knew he'd probably never see them again.

"Does everyone understand what they need to do?"

All of them nodded in affirmation.

Kade felt guilty leaving them, but there was nothing more he could do here. He might still come up with an idea for something he could do with the QPN.

"I need to get down to the lake. I have to lead the children to safety and I need to prepare one last surprise."

"Go. We've got this. We'll buy you as much time as we can."

Their bravery was inspiring, but Kade couldn't think of anything to say, so he turned and started running for the lake located at the centre of the island's caldera.

***

It took longer than he would've liked to lead the children up the long path to the lava tubes, their little legs could only carry them so fast. He could hear the sounds of battle long before they reached their destination, but they were able to arrive safely. Kade took a final look around as the last child entered and then he sealed the entrance behind them.

Selica greeted him with a firm embrace. "Kade, you're safe. I was so worried! What are the children doing here?"

"I'm sorry, Selica, I know you wanted me to keep this place secret, but I just couldn't leave them there."

Selica took in the frightened little faces. "Of course, you couldn't. None of these little ones should have to face the Breachers. They would've all become slaves. I wouldn't wish that life on any of them, you know that. You did the right thing."

"Can you get them settled? I need to start transmitting and see if there is anything else I can do to help."

Selica sat on the bed and was already surrounded by little bodies seeking comfort. "We'll be okay. Go — the others need you."

Kade was already halfway to his remote workspace before she finished her sentence.

It only took a minute to warm up the transmitter and start the pre-recorded loop requesting assistance from any sea transports that might be in the vicinity of the island. If anyone received his message, they would be surprised by the coordinates. These islands had remained a secret for centuries.

Kade turned on his screen and selected a viewcorder facing the interior lake. It was worse than he expected. The villagers were already out on the raft, floating near the far edge of the lake. Breachers had pulled down the walls surrounding the village and were lashing them together to form several rafts of their own. The Chelleans were doing some damage with the weapons they'd collected, but they couldn't keep up. There were too many Breachers.

167

How could I have failed to consider that possibility? Kade felt tears of frustration welling up. *I've doomed them all.*

He stood and began pacing. There had to be something he could do. "Think, Kade!" He still had blank templates held in reserve on the local memory stash. Once programmed, he could quickly form and reuse them, but how could he hope to make a dent in the Breacher ranks? If he could somehow frighten them away....

Kade pounded his fists against his thighs, praying the Maker would rain fire on the Breacher horde. He froze mid-step as a thought occurred to him. Kade couldn't cause fire to fall from the sky, but this island had obviously been an active volcano at one time. What if he could fool the Breachers into thinking it was about to erupt?

Kade ran some quick calculations. "Yes! This could work." The templates were simple and he had them entered in less than ten minutes. He chose random locations in areas where Breachers had gathered in the village. He selected more on the lakeshore and some in the shallows of the lake.

For his first wave, he began displacing coconut-sized cavities of earth just below the surface to a point in the air at shoulder height. The combination of a divot in the ground and soil in the air gave the impression of explosive eruptions.

For the second wave, he set pockets of iron particles to rapidly materialize a hair below the surface. He overrode the safety margins to allow more iron particles to materialize at the same coordinates, repeating the process in a continuous loop. The particles, unable to share the same space at the same time, were forced outward as friction raised the temperatures exponentially. He had just enough memory in the jury-rigged QPN to create fist sized lumps of exposed molten iron before the archive reached its limits and the process stopped.

For the third wave, he displaced water to the same coordinates as the molten iron, creating bursts of steam. He materialized more molten iron in the shallows of the lake, creating small pockets of boiling water.

The three-wave process was set to cycle at random locations for as long as the system could sustain it.

Kade's eyes were glued to the viewscreen, willing something to happen. He knew it would take some time before enough of the reactions occurred that everyone would start to notice. The viewcorder he was monitoring was too far away to see much detail, but eventually the horde became frantic. As more earth was displaced, the ground began to rumble.

Kade switched to a viewcorder closer to the action in the village. From that new perspective, he could see Breachers frantically fleeing jets of steam and falling earth as they did their best to avoid stepping on molten material they could only imagine was the lava of a volcano about to erupt. Kade was pleasantly surprised at how much chaos he'd managed to create. He was also humbled by the potential damage that the Servator technology could cause. He had a new respect for the safety protocols.

Within a half hour, the Breachers were all headed back to their ships. Kade worried that they might return when his tactics cycled down, but an hour later they picked up anchor and left.

"What do we do now?" Selica asked. She'd slipped into the room with Kuisa in her arms and three of the youngest villagers huddled around her legs.

Kade leaned back in his chair and sighed. "Now we wait for a few days and watch for signs of survivors, or any Breachers left behind. Now that our QPN resources are no longer dedicated to building defences, I can try to materialize sight tokens around the island to monitor for movement. It will be a random affair since we don't have coordinates mapped for the whole island. With enough time, we may get lucky and obtain some useful views."

"Do you think you were able to deter the Breachers in time?"

"I'm not sure. The raft is too far away from the one viewcorder we had pointed at the lake. I'll try placing a sight token on the raft if I can, but…"

Selica finished his thought, "…but the raft is a moving target, and you don't have coordinates. You might end up filling the lake with useless sight tokens."

"Right. Finding an empty raft may not mean much anyway. If the villagers were out of options, they would've tried swimming to shore. I want to believe that some of them escaped."

Selica nodded. "You'll be staying at the viewscreen to monitor, then?"

Kade gave her an apologetic look. "I know you could use some help with our wards, but I want to be ready to deal with any threat to the remaining villagers."

"It's okay, Kade. I'll manage. Those are our friends out there. If anyone can help them, you can."

Selica left Kade to his work. Her parting words were meant as encouragement, but they felt like condemnation. He'd already failed their friends. *What if they're all dead? How will I explain to these children that I'm responsible for the loss of their parents?*

Kade had struggled with guilt for months after learning the Breachers used his facial recognition algorithm to target people for assassination. Those deaths weighed heavily on his soul. Now he had more blood on his hands. Intellectually, he understood that it was the Breachers who had done the killing. Unfortunately, that mental exercise didn't prevent his emotions from pointing a self-recriminating finger. In both instances, his failure resulted in the death of innocent people and he couldn't find a way to escape that terrible fact. Kade prayed for survivors.

***

On the third day following the exodus of the Breachers, Kade had decided it was time to scout the island. In a state of utter grief, he discovered that everyone was dead. Kade insisted that Selica and the children remain in the lava tubes for another week. He spent that time in mourning as he marked the coordinates of the slain. Recovering the bloated remains of bodies afloat in the lake was the most grisly part of the task. Those were brought ashore and marked as well. He gave each victim his heartfelt apology, swearing to the parents that he would protect their children. When all the victims were accounted for, Kade set the QPN to excavate earth from beneath the bodies and replace the soil on top. Then he materialized memorial stones over each, recording the names of the fallen.

That was two weeks ago. Kade had surrounded the island with sight tokens pointing out to sea. If any sea transports appeared on the horizon, an alarm would warn them in time to return to the lava tubes. He didn't really expect anyone to return. The Breachers accomplished what they set out to do and the Servators on the mainland were likely facing similar attacks. No one would be visiting Chellea any time soon.

Kade stood with Selica and the children at the edge of the ruined village. It was time to begin the task of rebuilding. They couldn't live in the cramped confines of the lava tubes forever. The administration building was the largest, so they decided to start their repairs there. They needed something big enough to serve as a boarding house for their fifteen wards.

Selica leaned against Kade with a wry smile on her face. "When we decided to start a family, this wasn't quite what I had in mind. I guess I was destined to become a house mother after all."

"We'll make a life for them ... somehow," Kade promised.

Selica noted the pain in Kade's voice. "You were placed in an impossible situation. Against insurmountable odds, you saved these precious lives, Kade.

None of these children will suffer the horrors of slavery that I endured. The parents of these children would be grateful. Remember that."

Kade knew she was right, but it would take a lot of whittling to work through his pain. At least working with his hands would prove productive — carving toys for the children could be another opportunity for penance."

"We're all alone now," he whispered.

Selica gestured toward the children. "But there's hope for a future."

Chapter 29

Tenika wracked her brain trying to remember if she was missing any pertinent details. This had to go off without a hitch. Tully had arranged a meeting, and three weeks ago she'd returned to Jaihuwan for the first time in decades.

She'd had to flee the wrath of Laki Shung all those years ago. At the time, she'd been part of a street gang run by a low-life named Tibor who was continually making unwelcome advances. One day he took things too far and in the struggle that followed, he wound up dead at her feet. It was only later that she learned his full name — Tibor Shung. Things quickly went downhill when she discovered that his father was chief of the largest criminal organization in Jaihuwan.

Laki had many sons, born to many women. Tibor, in particular, was an embarrassment and his loss wasn't mourned, but Laki couldn't let the insult to his family name go unpunished. Laki, first and foremost a businessman, was aware of Tenika's talent for making a profit. So, he'd given her a choice — die, or leave Jaihuwan forever and pay him an exorbitant sum of money as reimbursement for the death of his son. If she was unable to pay by his deadline, she'd die. Tenika had spent decades working to purchase her life. In a strange twist, her debt was paid by Isau Jax when she joined the Breachers.

Considering her historical baggage, Tenika wasn't certain how her return to Jaihuwan would be received by the Shung family. They answered to the

Breachers, but they were also a very large and powerful organization in their own right. The Breachers of Jaihuwan were in disarray after the death of the Second Anarch, Loo Vishar. Tenika had no way of knowing if the Shung family would take advantage of the circumstances to make a break and strike out on their own.

As it turned out, the Shung family was undergoing its own transition of power — from father to son. Old age hadn't treated Laki well. At the start of their meeting, Laki had seemed somewhat confused. He pointed Tenika to his eldest son, muttered something about going to bed, and then shuffled off, showing little interest in current affairs. The conversation was enlightening.

"Forgive my father. He's become forgetful of late. My name is Quento Shung. I've been — transitioning into my father's role at his behest. How may I help you, Second Anarch Sheridan?"

That was interesting. She hadn't used a formal title when setting up the meeting. The only name she'd dropped was that of Isau Jax. This young man seemed very well informed.

"You know who I am?"

"Of course. You are the new Second Anarch of Caralithica. I presume your presence here has something to do with the power vacuum following the death of Jaihuwan's own Second Anarch."

"You presume correctly. What is your perspective on that vacancy, if I may ask?"

Quento smiled. "Let's not beat around the bush. I prefer direct discourse. I know that you're responsible for the death of Tibor. Let me put your mind at ease. I despised my brother. You did me a favour by killing him — one less competitor for the throne, not that Tibor was ever in the running. I've been handling affairs for my father for several years now and am well aware of who we answer to — if that's what you were wondering. As for your other unspoken question — I have no wish to venture into Breacher politics. I have enough on my plate trying to cement my position within our own organization. There are a few brothers who refuse to accept Father's wishes."

"I see. Yet you agreed to meet with me despite your disinterest in Breacher governance."

"There are currently four factions vying for control of the Breachers in Jaihuwan. The lack of resolution is spilling over into our own enterprises. As you can imagine, the confusion is encouraging brash decisions that threaten a long-standing agreement among the crime chiefs. It increases the challenges to my authority, and the timing couldn't be worse."

Tenika thought she understood where this was going. "You believe we may be able to help each other."

Quento bowed his head in acknowledgement. "That's assuming you're not here to name a new Second Anarch, but wish to assume that role for yourself."

It was Tenika's turn to bow her head. "You're an astute man, Quento Shung. Perhaps you could tell me what sort of assistance you feel I could offer."

Quento didn't hesitate. "A show of Breacher force in support of my leadership."

Tenika was impressed with Quento. He understood the shifting winds and his place in the hierarchy. He seemed to grasp the importance of the established structure, while recognizing the need to modernize it. More importantly, he wasn't greedy or overly ambitious. He struck her as intelligent and pragmatic, precisely the type of person she'd want working for her. "I suppose that depends on what you bring to the table."

Quento had clearly given it some thought beforehand. "Until you command the horde in Jaihuwan, you'll need enforcers to gain control. Can I assume that you have access to such a show of force?"

"I do. Although it may prove difficult to bring a few hundred Breachers and fifty Sicari into Jaihuwan without drawing attention." Tenika wasn't sure she could secure that many Sicari, but it was important to establish the narrative. Rumours would spread and that worked to her advantage.

Quento grabbed onto her words. "You're backed by the Sicari? With the force you've described, it shouldn't be difficult for you to take control, considering the current state of things. There will be a great deal of bloodshed, however. May I offer a solution?"

"Please."

"My informants have provided me with names of the four leaders fighting to claim the position of Second Anarch of Jaihuwan. Loyalty among the Breachers is low and I've been able to bribe several within the ranks of each faction. If you wish, I can have these leaders assassinated in their sleep."

"How do you know you can trust your insiders to do as you ask?"

"The men I approached are convinced that the Breacher organization is crumbling. They were already planning to abandon the Breachers altogether. I've encouraged them to stay a little longer by promising them positions in one of my ventures."

Tenika considered the proposition. Quento had saved her some work by identifying her targets, but she wasn't comfortable trusting the men he'd bribed. If even one of them backed out, the faction leaders would be on guard, complicating matters.

"Here is the price for my endorsement of your leadership. Provide me with the names and locations of the faction leaders. You will not give a kill order. Instead, I will have the Sicari deal with the matter. Apart from any intelligence you can provide on the current Breacher situation, you will provide me with an additional fighting force of fifty men. Can you manage this?"

Quento stroked his beard as he performed the mental calculations. "Yes, I can provide that many men who are loyal to me."

Tenika wasn't done. "I'll need you to quickly spread a rumour among the Breachers. This will be the task of the men you've bribed. They're to let every Breacher know that the horde is ordered to gather in the main hall at the base to receive instruction. Tell them that the insurgents will be punished by decree of the Second Anarch of Caralithica. We'll need to strike fear into the hearts of the Breachers of Jaihuwan. Tell them..." Tenika paused to consider something suitable.

Quento provided a suggestion. "Perhaps we could say, *the Butcher of Caralithica is coming*. It provides an appropriate amount of dread anticipation."

Tenika huffed. "Yes, I suppose it does. Very well."

"Perhaps I'm missing something obvious," Quento ventured, "but if you give advance warning for this gathering, won't the factions see it as an opportunity to assassinate you and claim leadership in a show of power?"

"I'm counting on it," Tenika replied. "There's one more thing, Quento."

"I'm listening."

"Once I've gained control, I will be naming you as the Third Anarch in charge of the Breacher horde in Jaihuwan."

Quento went very still. "I have no desire to take part in Breacher politics."

"Can you think of a better way to cement your leadership? All of the criminal organizations in Jaihuwan will have no choice but to recognize your authority or face the wrath of the Breacher horde. Your power will be established immediately."

Quento looked very uncomfortable. "I'm not a Breacher."

"I can easily remedy that. It will mean taking a vow and accepting the mark." Tenika displayed the brand on her arm."

Quento swallowed. "Won't the Breachers take issue with an outsider ruling over them?"

Tenika gave him a hard stare. "Those who might take offence will all be dead."

Quento didn't appear convinced, so Tenika explained.

"This is the only way. Once I'm done, the Breachers who remain will largely consist of soldiers who will fall in line with the new establishment. You have a large criminal organization in place, able to police any remaining resistance while you establish your authority as the Third Anarch. It will align our interests and provide me with someone I can trust to run things in my absence. Trust is perhaps too strong of a word — better to say I am more familiar with the Shung family than the Breachers in Jaihuwan. I know you won't cross me because the Sicari will be watching and reporting back to me."

Quento seemed taken aback by the threat. It served the purpose even though Tenika couldn't really command Sicari to maintain such a vigil.

"Don't look so distressed, Quento. This will give you what you want. I have no interest in spending more time in Jaihuwan than necessary — too many bad memories. You'll be able to build your family empire in ways you've never imagined, with very little interference from me. As long as you can maintain control and keep me informed, we'll get along fine. Agreed?"

After a moment of silence, Quento reluctantly nodded, "Agreed."

Tenika sent Tully to work out the details, having him remain in Jaihuwan to prepare for their second objective as well, an attack on the Servator base. Tenika spent a week searching the data collected by the facial recognition algorithm in Jaihuwan. By tracking Servator movements, she had determined that their base was located in the lower levels of an ancient temple, which was now a museum. It was clever of them to hide in plain sight. That revelation reminded her of a report about a possible Servator safe house beneath the Denmount Centre for Learning — another historic structure. The Caralithica Servator base continued to elude her, but now she wondered if that initial suspicion hid something much larger. She made a mental note to investigate further.

With the help of Quento's men, Tully discovered a forgotten underground aqueduct that had once been part of the temple. They'd found a spot where part of the tunnel gave way to a stone wall that appeared to have been constructed at a later date. Careful clearing of the mortar granted them a peephole that confirmed Servator movement on the other side. They had their point of ingress. The Servators would be taken by surprise.

Which brought them to today. The auditorium was packed. Quento had done his job well. She technically had no right to call a meeting of the horde in Jaihuwan, but she knew enough of the soldiers would comply out of habit. That would force others to attend, if only to observe.

A portion of the Caralithican horde had been relocated to Jaiwhan over the course of two weeks. They were waiting in the city for an order to attack the Servator base. The horde would follow Sicari through the aqueduct and Quento's men would make sure there were no people wandering around the museum within a radius of three city blocks. Once the attack began, Quento's men would capture anyone who appeared in the vicinity, assuming them to be Servators fleeing their base. Tenika would verify their identities later.

In a pleasant surprise, Qas's contact in Jaihuwan had found fifty local Sicari willing to contract with her for the Breacher takeover. She was beginning to believe that Qas had played down the appeal of her scythes.

Looking out over the auditorium, Tenika spotted the four men identified as faction leaders. Sicari were mingling with the crowd, disguised as Breachers. They had the targets, and their followers, surrounded.

It was time. Tenika squared her shoulders and strode onto the stage as if she owned it. Black clad Sicari flanked her in an impressively threatening display.

Tenika stopped in the centre of the stage and raised her voice. "How has it reached my ears that you've forgotten your place?" She demanded. "Not only have you failed to follow procedure in finding a replacement for your Second Anarch after his death, but you fight among yourselves, killing your fellow Breachers and weakening the horde. The rebels will be punished. Order will be restored."

"Who are you to claim any authority here?" A voice shouted from the crowd.

Tenika recognized him as one of the faction leaders. She gave him a wicked grin. "I am the Butcher of Caralithica." The Sicari flanking her pulled out their scythes and powered them up. The glowing blades produced a satisfying response among the crowd. Several of the faction members looked like they were having second thoughts.

The man who challenged her seemed to think he had the world on his side. "I see two Sicari with you. Did you really think you could come here with that pitiful show of force and intimidate us?" He swept an arm toward his men to emphasize the point.

Tenika lifted her arm and pointed at him. She knew his name, but wouldn't give him credibility by using it. "You! You will come to me and submit."

"Oh, don't you worry, I'll be right there." He drew his weapon and the auditorium erupted. The other factions also pulled weapons, fearing they'd lose an opportunity to gain the throne for themselves. In that same moment, fifty energy scythes came to life and every Breacher who drew a weapon was dead before anyone could make sense of what was happening.

The faction leaders were momentarily spared and roughly carried to the stage where they were forced to their knees before Tenika.

"I told you the rebels would be punished." She said nothing more. The finger she drew across her throat spoke clearly enough.

At that prearranged signal, four heads rolled off the stage into the audience. The fifty Sicari took up position around the perimeter of the auditorium, scythes glowing with menace.

"Are there any others who refuse to submit?"

The remaining Breachers took a knee and shouted in unison. "No, Second Anarch. Command us."

Tenika walked off the stage and began raising Breachers to their feet. "Stand and attend your Anarch. No more will you fight each other. Tomorrow we will fight the Servators and rid ourselves of their arrogant interference. Those who distinguish themselves will be rewarded."

Heading back to the stage, she signalled for Quento to join her. He'd already given his vow and received the Breacher mark as well as the surrounding scars that granted him authority. "Take a good look at this man. Memorize his face. This is Third Anarch Shung. He will be my eyes, ears and hands in my absence. You will obey him as if the orders came from my own lips."

"Yes, Second Anarch! Command us Third Anarch!"

"Go and prepare for the battle tomorrow. Follow the lead of these Sicari who will give you instructions. You are dismissed."

LEAVENING

It was done. The horde of Jaihuwan belonged to her. In the eyes of the Sicari, she now matched Trantor in numbers of Breachers. Soon she'd have the destruction of one Servator base and two Servator islands to her account. On top of that, she had the criminal families of Jaihuwan acting directly on her orders. The coveted energy scythes were just the filling in a pastry. If she wasn't seen as a threat before, she certainly was now. Trantor couldn't ignore her any longer. It was time to take things to the next level.

Chapter 30

The mood was sombre around the large meeting room table. A buffet along the back wall remained untouched. No one was in the mood to eat.

Beniti Abrax was inconsolable. The Chief Sentry had lost his entire Host. He refused to forgive himself for his absence during the attack of Kemetica base. He'd been discussing strategy with Akhen Hor and Leviticus Radix in Caralithica at the time. No one blamed him, but he steadfastly avoided the eyes of his peers.

As the Chief Sentry of Kemetica, Beniti was first to learn of the attack on his home base through an alarm triggered on his wrist Q-view. He left immediately on the fastest LTA available, but by the time he arrived home, there was nothing to save. The base lay in ruins.

Shortly before the attack, Beniti had ordered all of his people back to the base to make preparations for dealing with the growing Breacher threat. The intent was prudent, but too late. They hadn't expected it to come so soon or Beniti never would have left. The assault must have been brutal and swift — there was little evidence of resistance. If Kemetica base had begun fortifications even a week earlier, they might have had something in place to prevent the catastrophe, or at least given them an opportunity to escape. What should have been a time of reunion turned into a death sentence.

Beniti had put out repeated messages in the vain hope of finding someone still alive, but there was no one to respond. The slaughter was shockingly thorough. A contingent of rangers from Caralithica flew out to help in the aftermath. Beniti was too stunned to handle the situation on his own — the victims were all family and friends. Every silent body felt like an accusation. The Chief Sentry needed time to come to terms with the enormity of the tragedy. Recognizing that need, the visiting rangers took the burden from him. The dead were too numerous to deal with, so they sealed the breaches, capped the ventilation system and filled the base with a preservative gas. It was a temporary solution to prevent decay while providing a makeshift tomb. It would grant them some time to make appropriate arrangements.

Now they were gathered back in Caralithica, mourning the loss together. It was another in a series of blows. First the plague had reduced their numbers by over sixty percent, and now Sumakad, Kemetica and Jaihuwan bases were gone, further reducing the few thousand Servators that remained. The magnitude was difficult to grasp.

Jokan Pizzar, Chief Sentry of Arapanus placed a hand on Beniti's shoulder. There was nothing he could say. Knowing the terrible burden of losing even one soldier, he couldn't imagine what it would feel like to lose all of his people in one fell swoop. Arapanus hadn't been attacked yet and he prayed it never would.

Kayla looked around the table. With only three Chief Sentries left, she had requested the presence of former Chief Sentry Cello Vantos. She also invited a few senior staff who were currently at Caralithica base to attend this strategy session. Chief Analyst Akhen Hor and TokenLead Deak Bosto rounded out their number. Levigator Radix and Second Chief Strategist Nico Callan were on a mission, unable to attend.

Kayla didn't want to seem indifferent to the suffering, but they couldn't afford to delay this meeting any longer. She cleared her throat, immediately gaining everyone's attention in the otherwise quiet room.

"You know why we've gathered. The analysts have identified the toxin that decimated our ranks as well as how the plague was used as a trigger. The fact that so many Servators were exposed to the toxin in advance of the plague tells us that the Breacher's facial recognition algorithm is far more effective than we first thought. The discovery and destruction of three Servator bases makes two things abundantly clear. The Breachers have declared war, and we can no longer move freely in populated areas without exposing ourselves further. Worse, our reduced numbers and self-imposed seclusion means our intelligence gathering abilities have been hampered to the point that we're practically blind to Breacher activities. We don't know what they're planning or where they'll strike next."

Beniti lifted his head and spoke for the first time since entering the room. "We know exactly what they're planning — the annihilation of all Servators to bring about the destruction of the world. They may not realize the consequences of their actions, but the prophesy is clear."

"We don't know for certain that things have progressed to that point," Cello interjected.

Deak Bosto, the only one at the table who had no context for what seemed like a radical departure from the topic at hand, looked about in confusion. He peered questioningly at Cello in particular, who apparently had been keeping secrets from him. Kayla noted the familiarity in that silent back and forth. She approved of the flourishing relationship between the former Chief Sentry and the Lead TokenWard. Deak was a beloved family friend and her mother deserved some happiness now that she no longer held the responsibility of leading the Caralithican Host. Still, Kayla had no doubt there would be some interesting conversations in her mother's immediate future. A former Chief Sentry was just caught keeping secrets from the current Lead TokenWard who happened to be in charge of intelligence gathering.

Cello cast a warning glance at Beniti who merely rolled his eyes. "There's little point in keeping secrets any longer, Cello, the flood is coming and nothing can stop it. Ask Akhen if you don't believe me. Everyone at this table should know the stakes."

Deak looked to Akhen who nodded his head and filled him in. "Our information from the rift worlds is consistent with what Beniti suggests. There is a common denominator that precedes the flood."

"And that is?" Deak queried.

"Facial recognition technology leads to the destruction of the Servators."

Deak sat back in his chair with a shocked expression on his face. "As Lead TokenWard, I'm responsible for security and no one thought this was something I should know about?" His face began to flush with anger as he realized the former Chief Sentry — his current love interest — had withheld the information from him.

Cello had a contrite expression on her face as she tried to explain. "It wasn't my place to share those details. The chief sentries agreed as a whole that it would be detrimental to share that information before it was absolutely necessary. Deak, you know full well that there are those among us who would have demanded action countless times by now, even though there was nothing to act on until recently. Based on your own experience, tell me you wouldn't have come to the same conclusion."

"If you know I would have come to the same conclusion, then you had no reason to keep it from me," Deak shot back. "I could have been watching for the signs — preparing..."

"...which would have diverted you from other tasks that were important in the here and now. We had no way of knowing this would occur in our lifetime. Show a little faith in your leaders!"

Kayla knew the conversation between Deak and her mother wasn't over, but this wasn't the time or place. "Enough. We have to deal with what is before us."

"What does it matter?" Beniti insisted. "We're past the point of no return. The waters are coming and no one will survive. Any effort on our part will be an empty gesture."

"I disagree," Akhen responded. "The kin world in question only made that connection immediately prior to the onset of the flood. We've known about the facial recognition technology for many years in advance of a possible flood and those years have not been wasted. In our search for answers, we've opened more rifts than any kin world we know of. We've already lasted longer than all but a few high-tech worlds who've helped us along the way. As long as some Servators remain, we have hope. We also have one other advantage. The Levigator."

Beniti waved away Akhen's opinion. "The Levigator's role is to ease a burden — something he has already accomplished many times over. None of us would be sitting at this table without his efforts. As a result, those of us who remain now have time to say our goodbyes and prepare our hearts to meet the Maker. I've lost the opportunity to say my farewells, but the rest of you?" Beniti looked at each of them in turn, letting them see his pain. "Don't waste what little time we have left on a fool's errand."

Kayla raised a palm to silence the conversation. "It may be true that we can't prevent what's been set in motion. Does that mean we should ignore what is happening to our brothers and sisters who don't know the full extent of their peril?" Kayla looked directly at Beniti. "If, as you say, we should be spending time with friends and family, then we need to gather them and bring them to a safe place where they can do just that. I can't pretend to understand the depth of your pain, Beniti. I haven't lived long enough to appreciate the many connections you've made over the course of your lifetime. Even so, I can't imagine it's your wish for others to suffer that same loss or deny them the opportunity to have a little more time together."

Beniti lowered his head and said no more.

"As far as I'm concerned, the only plans we're currently considering involve the safety of those Servators who remain. Can we have a show of hands from those who agree?" Kayla waited as each raised their hand in turn, Beniti last of all.

"I'm sorry, my friends," Beniti spoke into the lull. "My haste to enter the comforting embrace of the Maker comes from my grief. It's not fair of me to project the weariness of my soul upon the rest of you. Please, forgive me."

"There's nothing to forgive," Jokan assured him. "You shouldn't be alone at a time like this, my friend. Come and stay with Esta and me. The quarters Kayla provided has a spare room. You know Esta sees you as a big brother. I insist."

Beniti nodded his head.

Kayla continued. "Then I recommend we evacuate Arapanus base and bring everyone here to Caralithica. With the recently completed Ports Vantos and Callan, we have two secure locations that are well removed from local populations and the prying eyes of the Breacher viewcorder network."

"You won't get any argument from me," The Chief Sentry of Arapanus answered. As one of the older bases, our security measures are woefully inadequate. We've been looking over the schematics you've provided for the security upgrades used in Port Callan. Unfortunately, we're limited by topography and by the city that has sprung up around us. It has hindered our progress in finding suitable solutions. With the current pace of Breacher attacks, I'm not confident we can prepare in time."

Kayla nodded. "After the second base fell, we began tunnelling to prepare more space at Port Callan should it become necessary. Things might be a little cramped at first, but we're expanding rapidly."

Deak seemed to have forgotten his anger at Cello now that his mind was engaged with a problem to solve. "The bigger question is how to get them here. There's no sure way to move that many people without drawing attention. The masks Leviticus created are no longer effective now that the Breachers have figured out what we've been doing. Leviticus has created a few new masks with identities that we've held in reserve, but they'll only be good for a few uses — certainly not a solution for a large number of people."

"How many are we talking about?" Cello asked.

Jokan thought about it for a moment. "As you know, Arapanus base maintains a smaller Servator Host. We took heavy losses after the plague, but I'd estimate there are approximately seven hundred remaining."

Deak shook his head. "Lighter Than Air transport, and sea transport are the only viable options if we want to move that many people overseas in a hurry. Water and air travel both offer a level of security once underway and beyond mainland communication networks. Unfortunately, both involve gathering in a public place before boarding."

Cello picked up where Deak left off. "We won't get away with that kind of gathering more than a few times before the Breachers notice. Air transports have a much smaller capacity and would need more time to load passengers. Even if we were able to land enough transports all at once, it would raise red flags."

Kayla lifted her hand to interject. "I have concerns about using air transport to Port Vantos. The mountains do a good job of hiding the passage of an LTA transport once they've entered the ranges, but there has always been exposure when transitioning from travel over sea to travel through the mountain valleys. It hasn't been a problem when no one was looking for us, but that's no longer the case. I've grounded flights for that reason. It's more important than ever to remain hidden, even from speculation. The last thing we need is for Breachers to start scouring the mountain ranges."

"Also, sea transports can load more quickly and carry more passengers," Deak mused. "We could dock transports at several ports along the coast. The berths are always filled with transports, so it won't draw attention in advance of boarding. It might be possible to coordinate boarding so all transports leave at approximately the same time. There will be a risk of Breacher stowaways if someone becomes suspicious."

"I have some thoughts about that as well," Kayla offered. "It will take several days to arrive by sea transport. That will provide time to search for infiltrators. We'll need some way to verify identities over the course of the journey. There is the mark of the Servators, of course, but Jokan, I assume you have records that can help with additional verification?"

"I do. In fact, I can arrange for groups who can vouch for each other to travel together — if that helps."

"Yes, that sounds good. Here's what I'm thinking. Port Callan is the logical choice because the undersea entry is nearly impossible to locate. The

difficulty arises when we transfer passengers from sea transport to sub-aqua transport. The subs are much smaller and will require many trips to offload passengers. Normally we would make that transition at the island transfer station in the shipping lanes. I don't think that's a safe option anymore. Instead, I'm imagining that we have the analysts create a template for a docking platform that can materialize on the side of the sea transports. We can arrange rotating coordinates as transfer points far from the shipping lanes - never the same place twice. Sea transports can offload their passengers at those locations using the mobile docking platforms.

Deak was warming to the idea. "That could work. We'd be able to see anyone coming from leagues away and disassemble the docking platform long before anyone got close enough to suspect what we've been up to. Additionally, once they submerge, no one will have any idea which direction the subs are heading. Two problems remain. First, we need to make sure the transfer point is far away from land so there is no way to guess the destination if someone were to discover what we're doing. We won't be able to unload all of the passengers at the same location, so that means the sea transports will need to be stocked for an extended voyage. The second is the risk of a stowaway onboard the sub. Most of that will be alleviated by whatever system we come up with for identification, but it only takes one stowaway to create a big problem."

Kayla took Deak's concerns in stride. "We won't be able to control all of the variables with an operation involving so many people. All we can do is minimize the risk as best we can. On the plus side, if a Breacher spy finds his way aboard one of our subs, he'll have no way to orient himself once submerged. He would arrive through an undersea tunnel, never having the opportunity to view a landmark that might give away our location.

"Once on base, options for a spy will be limited to the use of our communications network, or an attempt to escape to the surface. Assuming a Breacher were able to figure out how to use Q-tech to send a signal to a non Q-tech device, they still wouldn't be able to offer anything more specific than we're located in an undersea base. Good luck finding such a thing with the entire sea to search.

"As for escaping to the surface — I've already sealed all exits except one that is guarded by rangers. No one is allowed to surface under current conditions without authorization and the only destination available at the moment is Port Vantos in the mountains. As you know, there are no surface roads or passes to that facility and precious little way for someone to guess the location without having travelled there overland.

"I concede there is a small risk. If someone were able to make it that far, correctly guess the way out of the range, and survive the long journey without supplies — we'd have a problem. Even so, it would be difficult for a large Breacher force to find its way through the range without being spotted first. We would have time to retreat to Port Callan and collapse the tunnels."

Cello smiled. "I see you've given this a lot of thought. I knew you were the right person to replace me. Kayla's correct, nothing we come up with will be foolproof. Regardless, we have contingencies, and if we're thorough with our identification procedures, we may have nothing to worry about. We just need to be extra cautious about who is allowed to board the sub-aqua transports."

"If I may?" Jokan asked.

"Of course."

"There is a tradition among the Servators of Arapanus that is taught to our children so they always know who is friend or potential foe. We greet people with a common handshake, but if someone wants to confirm a fellow Servator, they will squeeze twice. The proper response is one long squeeze followed by two brief squeezes. It's very difficult for an outsider to notice what is taking place. All Servators from Arapanus will know the proper response if you initiate this handshake. It will give you a quick way to secretly add an extra check against the records I'll provide. I suggest you not try it until the point of transfer from sea transport to sub. That will limit the opportunity for the tactic to become known ahead of time."

"Thank you, Jokan. I think we have a framework we can build on. I'd like to get this underway immediately. I think we need to get everyone here as quickly as possible and worry about transporting personal belongings later. It will be safer to send small retrieval groups later for as long as it's feasible — until we discover that Arapanus base has been compromised. Deak, can you work out the details with Jokan?"

"We'll begin at once, Chief Sentry Vantos."

Kayla took in the haggard faces around the table. She knew she was pushing them hard. All of them were short on sleep. Without knowing what the Breachers were planning, they couldn't afford that luxury until everyone was safe at Port Callan. After that, they'd have a chance to catch their breath and develop a long-term strategy. Kayla glanced at the wall chrono. "I have to attend a report from the analysts, so I'm calling this meeting to a close. Thank you all — and please," Kayla motioned toward the uneaten food at the buffet table, "take some food with you. It would be a shame for it to go to waste and all of you need to keep your strength up." As an after-thought she added, "Let's not give in to despair. This plan will work. The Maker's not done with us yet."

Chapter 31

Hemish stared hungrily at the journals arrayed on the meeting room table. He was both upset and elated at the same time. When he'd learned that Leviticus had removed them from the archives in Kemetica, he'd travelled to Caralthica with Akhen in tow, to demand their return. Levigator or not, it was a grievous breach of both protocol and security. That was before Kemetica base had been attacked by the Breachers and the archives burned to ash. The thought of losing those irreplaceable documents, his life's study, was such a shock, it had bedridden him for several days. Seeing these precious saved remnants was both a reminder of what had been lost and a balm to his soul.

Lev was rifling through the parchments, searching for a particular text.

"Levigator, please," Hemish pleaded. "Be gentle, this is all that remains."

Lev made an effort to be more precise in his handling of the journals. Having found what he was looking for, he unfurled it and carefully placed weights to hold it open.

Hemish gasped, startling Lev who thought he'd been quite careful. Lev's face reddened as he followed Hemish's gaze to the underlined words and notes that were scrawled in the margins. Hemish said nothing, but indignation burned in his eyes at the desecration.

"I'm truly sorry, Hemish, but these journals were meant for me, and it's my right."

"How can you say such a thing? This is our shared history. It belongs to all of us!"

"Not these particular journals. They were meant to be read by another Levigator."

Hemish stilled. "What do you mean?"

"I mean, there are words embedded within the particles of the parchment."

Hemish, ignoring his insistence on careful handling, dragged the parchment closer and pulled out a magnifying lens. "Where? I don't see anything."

"It's only visible through pattern sight."

Hemish lifted a questioning brow to Akhen, who leaned over to look for himself. "I can't see with the same fidelity as Leviticus, but I can tell you that the parchment's structure has been modified in places that would seem consistent with lines of text."

"You've read these journals yourself, Akhen, why have you never noticed this before?"

"Probably for the same reason *I* missed it at first," Lev interrupted. "I only think to look for pattern changes in my surrounding environment. A journal is just an object *within* the environment. Reading words on a page is generally a cerebral exercise, not something you try to physically step into."

"It's really a very clever security measure," Akhen mused. "Very few would be able to read it in the first place, and as you say, one might not think to look at all for words behind words on a page."

"But why?" Hemish wondered. "What reason could a Levigator have for withholding information?"

Lev shrugged. "That's what I'm hoping you can help me understand."

"Maybe you should fill us in on what the hidden messages say," Akhen suggested.

"I've transcribed them on my Q-view." Lev tapped out some commands on his wrist.

"I've just forwarded the text — you can read through it later. For now, I'll give you a quick summary. There are two main themes. The first regards the current hostilities. According to Yuul Neem, Breachers aren't the real threat. We should have been worrying about the wastrels.

"The voices you heard behind the door in the Anarch's quarters," Hemish provided.

"Exactly. Do you remember how I mentioned that I felt an absence in the pattern beyond that door? Well, it's confirmed here in the writings of Bon Weiloos. Apparently, previous Levigators trapped wastrels by creating what they called void rifts — rifts leading to an abyss."

Akhen pinched the bridge of his nose as he tried to process what Lev was saying. "They created patterns of nothing? You must be reading that incorrectly."

Lev shook his head. "They use the words *void*, *abyss*, and *emptiness*. I don't see how it can have any other meaning. The wastrels, who Hemish tells me are insubstantial, are drawn into it — likely because the void has even less substance."

"Other ancient texts do make mention of wastrels being confined to the void," Hemish confirmed, "however, this is the first I'm hearing about Levigators creating a void and that there may be more than one."

Lev nodded, remembering their earlier conversation. "Bon Weiloos said that wastrels spread madness. Their influence is like a pinch of leavening — it multiplies and alters everything it touches. The steady whispers from an abyss are enough to corrupt any anarch in close proximity, creating the problems Servators have been fighting for generations. Bon Weiloos said if any were ever to escape, it would mean the end."

"I thought the facial recognition algorithm signalled the end."

"It's one of the sign-posts, but not the final indicator. In Yuul Neem's journal, he mentioned that they'd received a message just before the flooding of a particular kin world."

Hemish stared in rapt attention. "What was it?"

Lev reached for the journal in question and read it aloud. "Escape of a wastrel was the point of no return — the event that precipitated a world destroying flood."

Hemish slumped in his seat. "Maker, help us. We've been focused on the wrong thing all along. We've been fighting symptoms instead of the disease. If the Breachers had released a wastrel at any time over the past several hundred years, we would've been too late to stop it."

Lev hesitated. "Maybe not."

Akhen leaned forward, never a man content to do nothing. "Explain."

Lev sighed. "As I mentioned, Levigators created void rifts to capture the wastrels, which means they were loose at one time — we're still here. Bon Weiloos also mentioned that wastrels are drawn to power and nothing draws them more than the power of a Levigator."

"You think you could draw them in and recapture them before too much damage is done?"

"Yes — No — I don't know! I'm a Levigator — theoretically I should be able to." Lev turned pleading eyes on Akhen. "Please tell me you know how to create a void rift."

"I'm sorry, Leviticus. Even with this new context, I can't recall ever hearing of such a thing. Hemish? How about you?"

Hemish merely shook his head.

Lev threw his arms out in exasperation. "Well, so much for that idea."

"You said there were two themes," Hemish prodded.

"Right. That relates to another conversation we had previously. I'd mentioned that it seemed like the Levigators were more interested in flood worlds than technology worlds."

"I remember. You found something more specific?"

"Rushoen Nu Lon believed that if we could close the rift of a post-flood world and reopen it at a different location on the same world, we would discover survivors. All of the Levigators seemed to have the same notion. It leaves some hope that the flood is not the end."

Akhen gasped. "If that's true, it means the Levigators were never looking for technology. They were looking for flood survivors."

"Something none of them discovered," Hemish added. "Why would they go through the motions, pretending to look for one thing when they were seeking another?"

"As someone new to this whole Servator thing, I have a few thoughts," Lev replied. "Your traditions and expectations are pretty rigid. My guess is that they felt it would be easier to show you something irrefutable rather than to try and convince you."

Akhen snorted. "That cuts too close to the truth to be anything but."

"I've been told on a few occasions that there's a difference between those who follow the dictates and those who follow the Makers Way. If I understand correctly, one is a measuring stick and the other a choice. The common denominator seems to be a recognition of consequences for employing free will in a harmful way. Hemish, you told me that the dictates lead us towards order, but that a longing to change is also required."

Lev thought about his vision — how he felt pulled apart by the strands connecting him to the myriad kin worlds, but strengthened by a greater strand which he understood to be the Maker's Way. It didn't feel like the proper time to share that experience, but it helped him put things in perspective.

"Yes, Leviticus, that is what I told you. I can see you have something on your mind. What are you thinking?"

"The Servators have done a great deal of good. If the Breachers were left to do as they pleased, the world would be a much darker place. The Servators are driven by the dictates, so it follows that those have value. However, it seems to me that somewhere along the way, we became so comfortable with the task of measuring Breachers that we've failed to do much more than keep a balance. If this is all we've accomplished when wastrel influence is constrained, how will we fare when they're unbound?"

The room fell silent as the words settled. Akhen was the first to speak. "Considering the current Servator losses — if the wastrels are set free, the scales will tip so far in favour of the Breachers that they will flow over the face of the earth in a flood every bit as destructive as the waters that are sure to follow."

Hemmish shook his head sadly. "What could we have been doing to prevent this?"

"I believe that's what the previous Levigators were trying to learn. If we could speak to the flood survivors of a kin world, they may be able to tell us what we need to know. They might know a way to obtain a safeguard against the wastrels — something so powerful, it wouldn't matter if they escaped."

Akhen rubbed the back of his neck. "So, what are our options?"

"We could try to determine if there are other wastrel prisons and take possession of them," Hemish suggested. "We could post guards so the Breachers can't release any wastrels intentionally or otherwise."

Akhen waved that idea aside. "We no longer have the manpower to strike even a single Breacher stronghold and keep it."

"That won't work as a long-term solution anyway," Lev added. "When you have time to look at the notes I've sent, you'll learn that we already tried that once. The Servator guards were corrupted by their proximity to the wastrels and eventually formed the Breacher organization."

Hemish bolted to his feet. "The Breachers were once Servators?" Hemish was trembling as Akhen helped him return to his seat.

Hemish took a few calming breaths. "When I said I wanted answers before I died, Levigator, I didn't think those answers might be the death of me. However, this answers so many questions and I'm glad to learn the truth even though it pains me."

Lev placed a hand on the archivist's shoulder and gave it a gentle squeeze. "The only options I can see are to close and reopen a post-flood rift in the hope that we can talk to a survivor — pass through a post flood rift and go looking for survivors — or recapture the wastrels if they should escape."

Akhen slapped a palm on the table. "We've already talked about this, Lev. You can't risk passing through a rift. You could die, or go mad in the attempt. Supposing it even worked, with a whole world to explore, you might never find a survivor before it was too late for this world. That's assuming the theory holds true."

Lev shrugged. "That leaves closing and reopening a rift, or opening rift voids to capture wastrels. Currently, I can do neither of those things."

Akhen rubbed at the pain in his temples. "I'm sorry, Leviticus. I have nothing left to teach you."

"I don't blame you, Akhen. You've helped me more than you know. Both of you. I still have a little time to figure things out. With everyone safely here at Caralithica, I feel more comfortable leaving for a while. I think I'll revisit some of the post-flood rifts I've marked and see if I can figure out how to close them. If the wastrels should somehow escape before I find an answer, then I'll return and do my best to at least draw them away. Akhen, can you put together some kind of task force to monitor events that appear to be wastrel activity? We'll need some way to identify the threat as quickly as possible."

"Yes, I'll get started on that as soon as we adjourn."

Whatever happens now, I'm committed, Lev accepted. There were only a few possible paths remaining. It was a relief to finally have a direction, even if he had no idea what to do when he got there. Lev smiled fondly at the two men sitting across from him. He wasn't sure if he'd ever see them again. "Thank you, my friends."

It felt like he should say more, but he worried it would break his resolve. Instead, he rose and left before they could say anything that might change his mind.

Chapter 32

Kenric imagined a puddle of something slimy oozing from Tuk's feet onto the spotless floor of his chambers. He couldn't help it, the man looked greasy. He wished the meeting could be held anywhere else, but his chambers were the only place he felt confident that no one would overhear. Information was power and Kenric didn't get to where he was by being careless about who was privy to the information he gathered.

Tuk was his master of intelligence. For all of his hygiene issues, the man was a wizard at collecting valuable information from his informants.

"So, you're telling me that the hordes from Caralithica and Jaihuwan are also in Arapanus?"

"Yes, Anarch. Our own hordes are unable to move against Arapanus base. Tensions are high. Battle lines have been drawn with Arapanus as the prize."

"This is intolerable," Kenric fumed. "What have you learned about their leader?"

"My informants tell me that the Breachers of Caralithica and Jaihuwan fell in line with relatively little bloodshed. The new Second Anarch is clever and ruthless, knowing when and where to apply pressure. She actually reminds me of you, Anarch."

Kenric stopped pacing and spun to face his master of intelligence. "Did you say *she*?" He asked, a look of incredulity on his face. "Impossible! No woman could do this. Your informant must be confused."

"There's no mistake, Anarch. Many have witnessed her fight in the battles. She doesn't rule from behind. She joins the front lines."

A female? Leading in battle? This wasn't good. It reeked of the kind of narrative used to create heroes. Kenric had spent years seeding fear and doubt, but now someone was undermining his hard work by portraying an inspirational underdog. He'd be impressed if it wasn't at his own expense.

"Who is this nameless upstart?" Kenric demanded. "What do we know about her?"

"Her name is Tenika Sheridan."

"Sheridan, I know that name — wait — is she that woman Isau Jax was coddling?"

"Indeed. She served as Second Anarch Jax's right-hand man — I mean woman."

Kenric tugged at his beard in frustration. "Finding your way briefly into power is one thing. Claiming the title of Second Anarch and holding it is something altogether different. To maintain the position requires a true show of power. What possible proof of worthiness could she offer?"

Tuk squirmed in the presence of Trantor's growing ire. "She destroyed the Servator base in Jaihuwan as well as two Servator rehabilitation islands."

"Now I know your information is flawed. No one knows the location of those islands."

"The Sicari participated in those attacks and have confirmed the truth of the matter. The coordinates are known to them if you'd like to send a sea transport to confirm the rumours."

Kenric shot Tuk a warning look, and held up a finger for silence as he lifted a tote-comm to his ear. "Dagor, join me in my chambers."

Kenric tapped his foot impatiently as they waited for the Sicari to leave his post outside the door and enter.

"Tell me, Dagor, what do you know of recent rumours regarding the Servator rehabilitation islands?"

"The battle was glorious."

"You're saying it really happened? Was the attack led by a woman?"

"Tenika Sheridan discovered the island, but gave the Sicari free reign in its destruction."

"Aha! So she doesn't lead from the front after all." Kenric turned a smug grin in Tuk's direction.

Dagor shook his head. "You misunderstand. We did not contract to follow her battle orders. She rightly accepted that we would be most effective left to our own devices, but she fought alongside us."

"You speak as if you were there."

"I joined the first attack. That was before I contracted with you. A full complement of my brothers took part."

"A full complement! How could she afford to pay for your services?"

Dagor pulled an energy scythe from the sheath at his side and turned it on. "With these."

Kenric stepped back instinctively, eyes wide. Sicari were threatening enough without glowing blades. "May I take a closer look?"

Dagor turned away protectively. "I'll warn you once, Trantor. Never try to separate a Sicari from his weapon." He slapped the pommel to power it down, and slid it back into its sheath.

Kenric was flabbergasted. "The woman is dealing in technology as well?"

"As I mentioned, Anarch, she reminds me of you. I..."

"Shut up, Tuk!"

Kenric couldn't believe what he was hearing. How could someone have amassed so much power among the Breachers without his knowledge? "You're in charge of intelligence gathering, Tuk. How can someone take control of two hordes and I'm only hearing about it now?"

"Apologies, Anarch. Many usurpers have risen and fallen in the chaos. It's been challenging keeping up with events. Ms. Sheridan's ability to maintain control without challenge was unexpected. She's been moving swiftly ever since."

"You're to provide *me* with the information you gather. I'll decide what's important, not you!" *It's your own fault, you old fool. You became complacent when the other anarchs died.*

"Dagor, I want to contract you to assassinate Tenika Sheridan."

Dagor sneered. "You won't dirty your own hands? Unlike you, Tenika would face her victim."

"What?" Kenric scowled. "Do you admire this woman?"

"She's an impressive fighter and she doesn't ask others to do her dirty work."

Kenric let the insult slide. "Will you accept the contract or not? I'll pay double the standard rate."

Dagor shook his head. "No Sicari will accept this contract. Tenika Sheridan is currently under our protection."

Kenric scoffed. "I can afford twice what she's paying you."

"Tenika Sheridan has not contracted us for protection. However, many Sicari have a vested interest in her welfare and we do not interfere with the plans of our brothers."

Kenric stared at Dagor in disbelief. He'd formed countless contracts with Sicari throughout the years and he'd never heard of such a thing — it was unprecedented. What was so special about this woman that the Sicari would *volunteer* their protection? Did she discover a dangerous secret? Was there something only she could provide? It didn't make sense, unless... *the blades!* "She holds the technology for that weapon at your side." Kenric guessed.

Dagor didn't confirm or deny.

"Thank you, Dagor, you may leave."

"Is there anything else you need from me?" Tuk inquired.

"Are you still here? Leave! I need to think."

Tuk was almost to the door when Kenric stopped him. "Wait — I want you to contact Ms. Sheridan. There's no need for this aggressive stalemate in Arapanus. We should be killing Servators, not each other. Tell her I'd like to meet about a mutually beneficial arrangement."

"I'll see what I can do and report back, Anarch." Tuk closed the door and left Kenric to his thoughts.

Chapter 33

Tully had the map unfurled on the table. They were gathered in the makeshift headquarters he'd set up in the back room of a local tavern near the Breacher base in Arapanus. "The troops marked in red represent Kenric's hordes. Ours are displayed in green — here, here, and here."

"The troop tallies?" Tenika asked.

"About even. We actually have a small advantage."

Tenika moved her hair out of her eyes so she could see the map better. "So, unless Arapanus base picks a side, we're in a deadlock."

"It looks that way. This could have been worse. It appears Kenric didn't commit everything he had. Considering his recent invitation, I don't think he expected us to be here."

"I'm inclined to agree. What were his messenger's words, exactly?"

"He said that Breachers should be killing Servators, not fellow Breachers. He claimed that Kenric had a mutually beneficial proposition."

Tenika laughed. "I seriously doubt that a man like Kenric Trantor has ever made arrangements to benefit anyone other than himself. If he's serious, then he's desperate. If he's not desperate, then he's luring me into a trap. Where did he suggest we meet?"

"His private chambers, no less. I'm told it's a great honour," Tully grinned.

"He can't seriously believe that someone who gathered two hordes under her command would swoon in his presence and succumb to his charms."

Tully tried not to laugh. "For all of his cleverness, Kenric Trantor doesn't pretend to comprehend what he refers to as the fickle temperament of a female. He'd have no idea how to deal with you, but I would love to see him try."

Tenika knit her brows in thought. "Truly? He's naive enough to think that he might manipulate me because I'm of the *weaker sex*? If that's true, then there may be an opportunity here. If I can get him alone...."

Tully held up a hand. "I know that look in your eyes — I don't like it. You can't just walk alone into the lion's den."

"I could take a few Sicari with me, but I don't think it will be necessary. I'm only in danger if he thinks he has something to gain by killing me. I have to make him understand that removing me will only make things more difficult for him — that I'm more valuable alive than dead."

"How will you accomplish that?"

"Kenric will want to face me before deciding anything. When I'm in his presence, I'll contact you by tote-comm. He'll hear me instruct you to immediately attack his forces if you don't hear from me — with the proper password — on the hour, every hour."

"Do you really believe that will be enough?"

"Probably not, but it will throw him off balance. I want you to detain Kenric's messenger. Did you say his name was Tuk? Arrange for a Sicari to pose as one of Kenric's people, ostensibly to *free* Tuk. Meanwhile, we'll want that Sicari to feed information to Tuk. Shortly after I leave to meet with Trantor, I want you to arrange for the Sicari to free Tuk and deliver him directly to the Breacher base where I'm being *entertained*. I want Trantor to hear certain rumours while I'm still in Sumakad."

"I see," Tully nodded, "and what might these rumours be?"

"First, I want you to try and reach some of the Sicari who are known within the Arapanus compound. Offer an energy scythe to any Sicari willing to spread the rumour that the Sicari support me. Secondly, I want you and a few men to visit local taverns frequented by the Breachers from Arapanus base. Buy them drinks and tell them you heard that Kenric Trantor killed their Second Anarch so he could rule over Arapanus. Tell them Trantor is a coward who sends his people to die in battle while he profits from their deaths."

Tully grinned, picking up the narrative. "And Tenika Sheridan fights alongside her soldiers, letting them keep all of the spoils. Trantor is stuck in the past, while Sheridan represents a future where every Breacher has an equal opportunity to advance."

Tenika chuckled. "You've got the gist of it. Make it interesting enough that it will be repeated. If the people of Arapanus base hear it often enough, they'll begin to believe it, or at least repeat it.

"When Tuk is *rescued*, have our Sicari friend talk to as many Arapanus Breachers as he can while escaping. I want Tuk to hear the rumours being spread by Arapanus Breachers. It's important that Tuk doesn't have time to talk to any of his own contacts or conduct an investigation. When he returns to Trantor, all he'll be able to report is that the Breachers in Arapanus are leaning towards supporting me."

"That will put greater pressure on Trantor to make a deal with you, or risk losing Arapanus before he even gets started," Tully concluded.

"I only need him to hesitate — to be willing to get me alone where we can talk freely. If he's truly the misogynist you claim, he'll never deal with a woman where others can bear witness. I need to get him alone so I can learn the truth about his long-term plans and properly judge the threat he represents as my opponent."

Tully chuckled. "So, I need to convince some of the men to buy drinks with the boss's money and tell tall tales? I don't believe this will be too difficult to accomplish."

"Thank you, Tully. Now, if only we knew the location of the Servator Base here in Pekinau. That would be the filling in the pastry."

"On that note, we have a promising lead."

Tully unfurled a second map over the first. "We've been studying Servator bases that have been located by either our forces or those of Kenric Trantor. When we compare them to historic topographic maps, some interesting patterns emerge. The surface elevations have risen significantly over the centuries, suggesting that the bases weren't built below cities so much as cities grew over top of them. That's actually fairly common in ancient civilizations."

"If it's a common occurrence," Tenika commented dryly, "I don't see how that helps us narrow things down."

"Normally, it wouldn't."

Tenika rolled her eyes and let out an exasperated sigh. "Tully, what have I told you about dramatic pauses? Get to the point!"

"Where's the fun in that?"

Tenika stared him into compliance.

Tully raised his hands in surrender. "Okay, okay. It turns out that most of the Servator locations originated in natural depressions, so the gradual build up is difficult to discern. Arapanus, however, has always been overwhelmingly flat. The old district of Pekinau city stands out as an exception. Pekinau was originally known as the city on a hill. Yet, no hill should exist in that location.

"When you enter the old district from any direction, you ascend stone steps. The architectural records acknowledge that this was a constructed feature, but they claim it was created as a defensive measure, giving the citizens the advantage of higher ground in turbulent times."

Tenika's eyes brightened with interest. "You believe the Servator base is under that hill."

"I do. The impression given is that the steps were carved into the hill, but these steps interlock in a fashion that is consistent with a self-supporting structure. Builders don't use such a technique to support stone work that will be resting on compacted soil."

"How soon before you know for certain?"

Tully made some quick mental calculations. "We've found a section of stairs that were used for seating in an abandoned amphitheatre on the east side of the old district. It's become a gathering place for the homeless. The stonework there is badly deteriorated and hasn't received the same level of maintenance as the rest of the stairs in the district. I have some men drilling in an inconspicuous corner. If they find a hollow space beneath, I think we'll have our answer. They should be done in about three more hours."

Tenika narrowed her eyes. "You seem pretty confident that they'll find what you expect."

Tully smiled. "The homeless folk who live there say the place is haunted. They believe warriors are buried beneath the steps. When the amphitheatre's transient residents lay their heads on the stones to sleep at night, they hear the voices of the dead rising from the earth."

Tenika threw her head back and laughed. "Tully, I could kiss you! I want you to gather the Sicari we have on contract and fill them in on your suspicions. Work together to come up with a plan of attack based on a breach through the stairway in the amphitheatre. Prepare my horde for a quick deployment to that location. I want them ready to move when I leave for Arapanus. With any luck, the news that we've taken the Servator base at Arapanus will reach Trantor's ears shortly after Tuk gives his report.

"Tell my horde they're to kill any Servators they find, but then withdraw and leave the base intact. Once the Servator base is secured, I want you to tell the Breachers of Arapanus that the Second Anarch, Tenika Sheridan, has taken the Servator base and commands them to extract their revenge on their ancient enemy — tell them to plunder and destroy. They will greedily oblige. Their obedience to that first command will quickly lead to obeisance on the heels of my generosity. It will be all the proof they need that the rumours you spread about me are true."

Tully began rolling up the maps and clearing the table. "How much time do we have to prepare?"

"I'll be leaving in three days and travelling for two more. Do you think you can be ready in that time?"

"What if we don't find the base where I expect it to be?" Tully asked.

"It won't matter. It's just filling in the pastry, remember? If your suspicions fail to bear fruit, leave the horde where they stand and prepare to battle Kenric's army if he makes a move against us."

"I'll need to begin immediately." Tully gathered his maps and moved for the door."

"Tully?"

He paused in the doorway.

"You've been with me through thick and thin. If this works, I want you to be my voice in Arapanus, as Third Anarch."

Tully grinned and struck a rakish pose.

Tenika slowly shook her head. "Just go already."

Chapter 34

People were taking on busy work to occupy their minds. They'd recently been dealt another blow. Retrieval parties of fifty rangers had been making trips to Arapanus base to gather personal belongings left behind in the rushed flight to Caralithica. There had been three successful excursions, but the fourth ended in catastrophe. The retrieval team had noted an increased Breacher presence in Pekinau, but the activity seemed to be limited to the far side of the city, so they decided to risk one more trip to the base. It was a fatal mistake. The Breachers chose that moment to mount the attack everyone feared was coming.

This latest setback threatened to undo what little emotional healing the Servators had managed. There was a small consolation in that the lives lost accomplished an unexpected benefit — if it could be called that. The Breachers, not knowing how much resistance to expect, seemed to assume that the rangers they encountered represented the last of the Servators in Arapanus. The Breachers followed a pattern similar to their previous conquests. Once they destroyed a Servator base, they pulled out completely, their swath of destruction forgotten as blood lust drew them to new targets. It meant that the survivors from Arapanus were no longer being hunted. Unfortunately, that also meant that Caralithica was now the only remaining base — the combined focus of all Breacher searches. It was the reason for Kayla's recent consultation with Nico and Leviticus. They needed to be ready for anything.

The last few days had been busy as the three of them worked to further enhance security at Ports Callan and Vantos. It was critical, now that Caralithica was home to the remainder of earth's Servators. Altogether, their numbers made up little more than the equivalent of one Host.

In the few hours of each day that was free of meetings, Kayla and Nico spent time together. It was a precious gift for Kayla's troubled mind. When she was with Nico, there was no need to play the role of a strong and fearless leader. She could release the facade to share her fears and frustration. He was always ready with wise counsel and a comforting word. It was a quality of Nico's that made him a good leader and a better friend. People were drawn to his kindness and strength of character. Those who sought him out in difficult times usually left his presence feeling encouraged. She felt a little guilty hoarding him for herself, but she needed to draw on the strength of someone who didn't see her as a self-assured Chief Sentry. Sometimes she wondered who Nico turned to when he needed comfort of his own, but if he ever gave in to despair, it was something she hoped never to see.

Not for the first time, she thought he would've been a better choice for Chief Sentry. That role was changing as they wrestled with the complexities of creating a single body of Servators. The command structure was now under combined leadership. Jokan Pizzar, former Chief Sentry of Arapanus shared duties with Kayla as the joint Chief Sentries of Caralithica. They worked in shifts giving each other some much needed rest. Major decisions were made by consensus between Jokan, Kayla and her mother, who presided in an advisory capacity as a former Chief Sentry.

Caralithican Servators were asked to bring their concerns to Jokan, and likewise, the Arapanus Servators brought theirs to Kayla. It was important to quickly build a mutual trust in leadership. They needed to function as a united Servator Host. Much of what they might deal with in the days to come would require decisive action. They couldn't afford to have the Host second guessing orders from a particular leader. Things had gone well, so far. Jokan had a similar command philosophy to her own, which smoothed the transition immensely.

There was no point in having a structural separation between the Servators of Arapanus and Caralithica. Kayla wanted their guests from Arapanus to become family. They'd be together for the foreseeable future and they needed to feel that this was their home, too. She'd encouraged many of the Caralithicans to give up their quarters and move into some of the spaces they were excavating for the newcomers. She hoped it would foster new friendships to help with the integration process.

Not surprisingly, it was the young and adventurous who chose to take on new quarters while the more elderly opted for established quarters. The age division had worried Kayla at first, but it turned out to be exactly what they needed. The more senior of both groups had much in common, and bonds were quickly formed. That acceptance filtered down to the younger who followed the example of their mentors.

For their part, the younger Servators were excited to create something new after so much loss. That joint enthusiasm and creative energy forged new friendships with a common purpose. Kayla had decided to give them free reign to design new spaces for their quarters. Tunnelling crews were ordered to allow anything that didn't compromise structural safety. They had already come up with some interesting solutions and Kayla was curious to see what the final floor plan would be.

Things seemed to be progressing nicely, all things considered, but when Lev and Nico left early in the morning, she felt their absence like a deep regret. So much had changed — was still changing. *Will Nico and I ever have a chance to be together?* They both had responsibilities that kept them apart more often than she would've liked.

Kayla gripped the railing on the mezzanine level of the atrium as all of these thoughts played through her mind. She barely noticed the ebb and flow of activity taking place on the lower level as she gazed out over the space with glazed eyes. Deak interrupted her contemplation by leaning against the railing on her left.

"You look like you could use a break."

Kayla gave him a wry smile. "This *is* my break."

Deak grunted.

Kayla felt a lecture coming on. She loved Deak, but he worried too much. She wasn't working harder than anyone else. Experience told her the best way to avoid Deak's objections was to distract him with a problem. "How is Project Exodus coming along?" Kayla smiled as he took the bait.

"The analysts have already begun construction of a new memory stash for the Quantum Positioning Network and the high-power transmitter you requested."

That addressed one of the issues Nico had identified. The QPN employed a distributed network shared among the Servator bases. With the loss of those bases, they were experiencing serious lag time in the creation of tokens and the sharing of information. Some areas were experiencing a blackout and the loss of coverage was blinding them to Breacher movements. The Servators couldn't afford to lose their only remaining advantage. If Caralithica base fell, they'd lose the entire network.

"Any news on a site to safely house the archive?"

"Scouts have found a cave in a suitable location on a peak about five leagues from Port Vantos. It's oriented in the proper direction for transmitting to three of our largest repeater stations."

"What happens if we lose those repeater stations?"

"The Levigator had templates for a mini-repeater that Kade Brixton developed. It looks similar in appearance to a common component found on the public tote-comm network transmission towers. It actually works in that capacity while doubling as a QPN node. Surviving Servator supporters around the globe have begun to gather QPN coordinates for tote-comm towers world-wide. It will take some time, but once we've mapped the towers, our analysts will determine a pattern for best signal distribution and create the necessary repeater tokens for those coordinates. We'll have redundant coverage for as long as the public tote-comm network is functioning."

"That's good news."

Kayla breathed a sigh of relief. Project Exodus was a plan of last resort. If the Breachers ever discovered Ports Callan and Vantos, a few could escape by sea in the subs, but the majority would have no option but to flee into the mountains. At that point, they would be homeless and on their own. Their only hope of survival would be a functioning QPN network. The remnant would disperse in every direction, seeking some place where they could eventually settle anonymously for the remainder of their lives.

"And the beacons?"

"LTA transports have mapped five routes that can be safely traversed by foot through the ranges. Each beacon ultimately leads to civilization. Water sources have been identified along the route."

Deak continued before Kayla could ask her next question. "Survival kits are being prepared as we speak, with stun batons for protection or hunting. The kits include water bottles and emergency rations for a week. Analysts are generating templates for portable shelters and other emergency gear that can be materialized as needed. Once the new QPN transmitter is in place, everyone will be able to use their wrist Q-views anywhere in the mountain ranges. Those who decide to avoid civilization and remain hidden in the mountains will have all of the tools necessary to construct permanent shelter."

Kayla placed a hand on Deak's arm. "Thank you, Deak. I hope it never comes to that, but it comforts me to know there's an option for those who don't wish to risk their lives in a final confrontation. That's not a choice I want to make for these people. They've suffered enough."

Deak stared at her, trying to guess what she was thinking. "So you've decided."

"What I'll do if it comes to that, you mean? It's a Chief Sentry's job to protect her people. I can't do that if I'm running at the first sign of danger."

Deak turned Kayla to face him. "Cello and I have talked about this. We've both led full lives and are more than capable of holding the fort. There's no need for you to remain. You'll be more useful to the remnant if you're out there with them. If there's any hope of resurrecting the Servators, they'll need leadership."

Kayla's lower lip trembled at his words. The offer to sacrifice their lives to spare her own touched her deeply. This was real love, to freely give your life for another.

"That means a great deal to me, Deak, but if we're diminished to nothing more than a tiny remnant, there will be no rebuilding."

Deak started to protest, but Kayla cut him off. "You heard Akhen. When the Servators are no longer able to stop the Breachers, the prophecy will be fulfilled. The flood won't wait ten or twenty years for the Servators to rebuild. Have you ever viewed the rift of a flood world, Deak?"

"You know I haven't," Deak scowled. She'd touched on a sore spot between him and her mother.

"It's like looking through a window at the bottom of the sea. Even if you lay down on the floor in front of the rift and attempt to look up through the waters in search of the surface, you'll see nothing but more water. We're not talking about a seasonal flood that rises to the height of a man and then quickly recedes."

Deak had a dubious look on his face. "How can that possibly be?"

"I have no answers for you. All I know is what I saw, and that I don't want

208

to survive a Breacher attack just so I can drown. Perhaps that makes me a coward."

Deak considered her words. "No, you're right. If this will be our last stand, then the only hope for our world is to push the Breachers back. But know this — you won't be alone — your mother and I will be right by your side."

Chapter 35

"How long has she been down there?" Kayla asked.

"She's been in and out over the last three days, Chief Sentry. She doesn't seem aware of the hidden entrance to the base, so we've been trying to figure out what she's up to. It appears she's living in the basement storage area. She's slept there every night since we began monitoring." The analyst tapped on the bottom left hand corner of the screen. "You can see a pile of bedding here. We didn't want to bother you, imagining it was a homeless person, but then we cross-referenced her image with the archive and it brought up a red flag. We thought you'd want to know."

"Yes, thank you. We've been looking for her ever since her escape. I was convinced she fled the country. What could she possibly be thinking?"

Kayla watched as Tenika Sheridan, convicted felon, pulled what appeared to be a half-eaten apple out of a ratty looking bag and began to eat. She looked like she didn't have a worry in the world. *Could she be suffering some kind of mental collapse? What are you up to, Tenika?*

"What would you like to do about this, Ma'am?"

"Has she wandered near the hidden tunnel located in that room, or given any indication that she's searching for it?"

"No, Chief Sentry — nothing like that. She mostly sits on the bedding and reads from a tattered book — when she's there at all."

Something felt wrong. What were the odds that Tenika Sheridan would show up in the basement of the archive building — the same place where Kayla had once fled from Breachers who were chasing her and Leviticus Radix? Their mysterious disappearance through a hidden tunnel in a room with only one exit drew intense Breacher scrutiny. It forced her mother to abandon Caralithica base, deciding the risk of discovery made it nonviable as a headquarters for operations. It was a subject of great personal shame for Kayla. She'd redeemed herself over time and built-up Port Callan and Port Vantos as replacements, but she still hoped that one day the original base could be used again.

It had to be a coincidence. Tenika had never even heard of the Breachers before she was captured by the Servators and sentenced by Kayla's mother — Chief Sentry at the time. Tenika couldn't possibly know about Breacher suspicions, or Kayla's part in that fiasco. *It's a public building. This wouldn't be the first time a vagrant found their way into the basement. Still....*

"We need to bring her into custody, but let's do this right. No one is to use the hidden passage. We'll use the main entrance to the archive and take the stairs to the basement. I'll need four rangers to accompany me."

"Chief Sentry, do you think that's wise? The rangers are best equipped to deal with this. There's no reason to put yourself at risk."

"I hardly think I'll be at risk from one person while accompanied by four rangers. I have history with Tenika and I need to be present. It's possible she may say something in my presence that will provide valuable context."

"As you wish."

"Contact Deak Bosto and my mother as well, and fill them in. The former Chief Sentry can watch from this terminal, but by my order, she isn't allowed any closer until we have Ms. Sheridan in custody and properly restrained. There will be plenty of time for my mother to confront her then. Tell the rangers to bring some of the new masks provided by the Levigator. I'll meet them at the tunnel exit under the old rail transport station. We'll walk the quarter league to the Denmount archive building from there."

***

It had been quite some time since Kayla last walked the streets of Denmount, long enough that she felt it unlikely Breachers would be actively seeking her any longer. Of course, the Breacher viewcorder network was ever-present, but she had faith in Lev's masks. The trip to the archive building was uneventful. The group paused at the top of the basement stairs while one of the rangers conferred with the analysts on his wrist Q-view. They were recording everything and confirmed that Tenika was still there.

The rangers moved down the steps swiftly and quietly. Kayla followed at a casual pace. There was a startled screech followed by the voices of her rangers ordering Tenika to be still. When Kayla entered the dimly lit space, the rangers had Tenika surrounded. She stood timidly between the stun batons pointed at her.

The room looked much as Kayla remembered it. Pallets filled the confined space, stacked high with parchments. A few of the pallets held older documents written on animal hides. The unique smell of leather and ink permeated the air — a scent that would forever trigger a memory of this place.

Kayla stopped two steps from their captive and let her gaze travel from head to toe. "Tenika Sheridan — I never thought I'd see your face again. You look like you've seen better days."

"Well, if it isn't the spoiled little Servator Princess," Tenika spat.

One of the rangers prodded Tenika with the end of his baton in response to her insolence. Kayla held up a hand to prevent further action.

"The Servators don't have a monarch, but my Mother told you as much when you were last in Servator custody. What are you doing here, Tenika? When you escaped, you should have kept running. You had to know that if you remained in Denmount, you would be found sooner or later."

A feral smile split Tenika's face. "I was counting on it. I had really hoped it would be your mother who came to visit, but you'll do."

Kayla's body stiffened with alarm, but it was too late to shout a warning as six shadowy forms flowed from between the pallets.

"Sicari!" One of the rangers shouted. They quickly formed a protective perimeter around Kayla as two of the Sicari moved to block the stairwell.

The Sicara were carrying wicked looking blades that glowed with menace as the remaining four paired off with the rangers. The fighting was fierce, but brief. The ranger's stun batons weren't functioning and served as little more than useless sticks against the weapons wielded by the assassins. In less time than it took for Kayla to move to a corner of the room, it was over. The Sicari moved in her direction.

"No!" Tenika shouted as she reached down to pull a blade of her own from under the blankets that served as her bed. "She's mine."

Tenika slapped the pommel of her short-sword and it glowed like the others. She approached Kayla with a confident stride that showed none of the weakness of the previous moment. Kayla reached for her Q-view hoping to initiate one of the emergency shield tokens, but Tenika pointed her sword at Kayla's Q-view. It sparked and overheated, burning her arm.

"I'm sorry, my dear, but that device will be as useless as the batons your rangers were carrying."

Tenika held the tip of her weapon an inch from Kayla's nose. The skin blistered from the heat. She was about to jerk away, but Tenika deftly flicked her wrist and drew an angry red burn across Kayla's cheek. She gasped from the pain.

"Your family cost me everything," Tenika screamed.

"You have no one to blame for your circumstances but yourself," Kayla scoffed.

Tenika slapped Kayla hard across the face. "You're every bit as arrogant as your mother. How dare you presume to judge me based on your secret Servator laws. You have no officially recognized authority, yet you act as both judge and executioner."

"Servators don't sentence people to death. But you — you had Nico's parents murdered! Don't pretend you didn't deserve the sentence you were given. It would have been the same or worse under the Caralithican judicial system."

Tenika laughed. "I guess I should thank you. Your family took everything away from me, but you also gave me a gift. You showed me a world I never knew existed, a world where Sicari are my friends and Breachers are my servants."

Kayla grew faint as the words sank in.

"That's right," Tenika gloated. "I control the hordes that have destroyed several Servator facilities, but I won't be satisfied until Caralithica base is razed and your mother is begging at my feet. I might show some mercy if you give me its location."

"I think we both know that's never going to happen."

Tenika shrugged. "It hardly matters. We monitored your exit from the old rail transit station and the Breacher files contain a very interesting tale about your disappearance from this very room. Your reappearance confirms the base is nearby, most likely beneath the archive building. We've noticed that Servators like to locate their facilities under ancient buildings. Thanks to you, we now have two confirmed points of ingress, and while the entrances may be well hidden, sooner or later we'll discover the secret. If the search proves too tedious, we'll just start excavating from the surface in a line between the

two points. I have plenty of men who can wield a shovel as well as a sword. We'll find a way in. It is inevitable."

I can't believe this is happening again. How could I make the same mistake twice in a row? Kayla screamed in frustration as she batted Tenika's weapon from her hand and launched into her. Kayla landed two blows before Tenika rolled away and sprang to her feet.

"You want a piece of me, do you?" One of the Sicari handed Tenika her energy scythe. "Impressive, isn't it? I'm quite proud of the finished product. Provided enough power, it can cut through almost anything, but it's also capable of disrupting other technology from a distance. You've already witnessed that aspect in action. You might be interested to know that I took the technology from one of Nes Callan's research facilities. He was planning on using it for agricultural purposes. The man had no imagination."

Tenika gestured for a second energy scythe from one of the Sicari.

"I'd say the chances are very good that today you will die from wounds inflicted by a weapon birthed at your suitor's company. There's something poetic about that." Tenika tilted her head and laughed. "Don't look so glum — I'll give you a fighting chance." She tossed an energy scythe to Kayla.

"Hit the pommel to power it up. The Sicari won't interfere. You'll have your chance to take a pound of my flesh. You might even kill me. The Sicari won't let you leave here alive, but you might be able to take me with you."

Kayla energized the weapon without hesitation and threw herself into a flurry of forms. Tenika was caught off guard and backed away from the sudden onslaught, but soon she found her rhythm and was matching Kayla blow for blow.

Sparks flew as the scythes clashed. It was like fighting through a cloud of miniature suns, burning as they touched exposed flesh.

Kayla began to panic as Tenika took the offensive. Kayla was an expert in warkata swordplay, but Tenika wasn't using any of the familiar techniques. She was more like a street fighter, learning and improving moment by moment. Kayla had never fought someone with such raw intuitive skill. Tenika moved to sweep

Kayla's feet. Kayla jumped into the air to evade but it was a ploy. While Kayla was helplessly aloft, Tenika swung upward slicing deep into her forearm. Kayla screamed as her weapon flew from her hand. Grabbing her wounded arm, she backpedalled from the point of Tenika's energy scythe until she was stopped by one of the pallets of parchment.

Kayla moaned as Tenika placed the tip of the energy scythe over Kayla's heart, cauterizing the skin as she held it there.

"I gave you a chance — something your mother never offered me. You fought well. I could use someone with your skill. It's almost a shame to waste such talent..."

Tenika plunged the scythe through Kayla's heart.

"...almost."

***

Cello clutched the edges of the viewscreen and cried out as she watched the body of her daughter slide off the blade and drop to the floor. "Noooooooo! No — No — No. Deak, do something! Send a contingent of rangers, send the medics, we have to save her."

Deak held her tight, a tear rolling down his cheek. "You know we can't do that, Cello. That's what they want. They're watching for entry points to the base. You heard Tenika, she has control of the horde. There are probably hundreds of Breachers waiting outside."

Cello pounded her fists against his chest. "We can't just leave her there. She's dying!"

Deak lifted her eyes to meet his own. "She was pierced through the heart, Cello. She's already gone — I'm so sorry."

Cello collapsed to her knees, whimpering. "The Breachers keep taking from me. First my husband, then my friends, and now my daughter."

Deak lowered himself to the floor and rocked her gently as she wept, his own tears flowing freely. The analysts cleared the room and left them alone to mourn.

Chapter 36

"Are you sure you'll be okay?" Tark asked for the seventh time.

"I'll be fine," Lev assured him. "There's a town ten miles from here — an easy day's walk. I can find transportation there."

Tark looked torn.

"I'm serious, Tark. There's nothing more you can do here," Lev insisted.

"None of us are comfortable leaving you here alone."

"You know I can take care of myself."

Tark, Yori and Nico were more like travelling companions than a security detail by this point. Lev had capabilities that far surpassed any protection they could offer.

Tark shrugged. "I feel like we're abandoning you."

"I'll miss you too, my friend." Lev pulled him into a firm embrace.

It was the right thing to do. Tark and Yori were some of the best fighters Caralithica had to offer and Denmount needed their help far more than Lev did. He'd known for some time that the two rangers were anxious about friends and family back home. They wanted to be there, protecting the ones they loved, not wandering around in the wilderness watching the Levigator stare at things they themselves couldn't see.

The last few weeks had been a litany of bad news. A remnant of the Servators had gathered at Ports Callan and Vantos — the last refuge of a dying order. *If they can't hold against the Breachers...* Lev tried not to dwell on it. The

216

thoughts brought out feelings of helplessness. His actions as the Levigator seemed to result in one failure after another.

Lev thought he knew what he needed to do now. He had to figure out how to close a rift, but that was something only he could do. If he was honest with himself, he wanted his friends to leave, if only so he wouldn't keep failing in front of an audience.

Yori finished loading his gear into the ground transport and nodded for Tark to do the same. As Tark headed off to comply, Yori took his place. "It's been my life's greatest honour to know you, Leviticus."

"Come on, Yori — I'll be back in Denmount before you know it."

"You can't promise that, Lev. Things are moving quickly now and we don't know what may be required of us. We'll walk where the Maker leads, even if it's to the grave. You may arrive home only to find that the rest of us are gone."

Lev swallowed hard and struggled to hold back tears. These three men were his closest friends. The thought that he might never see them again — that he might not be able to save them — it threatened his resolve.

Yori held him by the shoulders at arms-length, looking more serious than Lev had ever seen him. "I know you think you're failing the Servators. You're always so hard on yourself. I need you to listen to me and believe what I say.

"You entered into a mess that was not of your making, one created by millions of people over hundreds of years. You were asked to take up a burden that no one should have to bear, and to perform an impossible task. I've watched you rise to the challenge. A young man who in a very short time became a seasoned leader bringing hope to many people.

"Some lives have been lost during your time as Levigator, it's true, but so many more lives have been saved because of your actions. No matter what happens, you've accomplished more than most people would ever have attempted and you've done it well. Not one person I've met among the Servators has a bad thing to say about you. I'm not sure you realize what glowing praise that is."

Lev wilted at the words. To have affirmation that he'd done at least *some* things right was a balm to his soul, bittersweet though it was. Yori gave his shoulders a firm squeeze, and left to take his place in the ground transport.

There was one goodbye remaining. Nico stood ten paces away looking off into the distance. Lev's heart went out to him. The news of Kayla's murder at the hands of Tenika Sheridan had left Nico broken. Lev and Nico had wept together until their eyes were dry. They sat in silence until Nico's grief turned to rage at the one who had robbed him of both love and a future. Not long after, he'd fallen into despair and guilt for not having been at her side to protect her. Through it all, Lev sat quietly, offering what support he could with his presence. He'd have given up all of his power if it would bring Kayla back to his friend.

Nico hadn't spoken since, and Lev wasn't sure what to expect from what might possibly be their last conversation. *Tell me, Maker, why must this be so difficult?*

Lev choked as he began to speak. "Nico... there isn't enough time to tell you everything I need to say to you... you've always been there for me. My sounding board, my stabilizing influence. You're my best friend and the brother I never had. I couldn't have made it this far without you. My heart aches with your loss, but I can't take this grief from you. I'm sorry. I'm so very sorry...."

"I know," Nico whispered, a tear rolling down his cheek. "Your family took me in after my parents died and you were by my side from that day forward. Don't think you haven't been there for me as well, when I needed you. I owe you, not the other way around, yet I'm the one who's leaving."

Lev shook his head. "You don't need to feel guilt for anything. I need you to be there for the funeral and for Cello. Give her my condolences."

Nico nodded as he wiped at the moisture on his face. It turned out that quite a lot could be said in a very short time, with very few words.

Lev clung to Nico ferociously for a minute and then, giving him a little shove, sent him towards the ground transport where Yori and Tark were politely looking in the other direction. A moment later, they were roaring down the road leaving a cloud of dust in their wake.

When Lev could no longer see them on the horizon, he sat on the ground, unsure what he should do next. He'd always known it would come to this — silence competing with solitude.

He switched his perception, letting noise from the pattern invade the quiet. The sound of a rushing wind emanated from the arch behind him as particles flowed from the kin world into their own. He glanced over his shoulder, then turned away again, piqued at the rift's refusal to release its secrets. Lev sighed at his petulance and stood to approach his objective once more.

Why can't I close this rift? Observing it from both sides opens it. So how do I accomplish the opposite? He'd tried many things without success and kept coming back to an idea he hadn't yet attempted. He'd discovered a way to open a rift by pushing a sight token through the thin space so he could view both sides at the same time. It made him wonder what would happen if he were to do the opposite — if he were to pass through the rift and attempt the same thing from the other side. It was a completely unscientific assumption with no positive potential outcomes. If he successfully closed the rift from the other side, he might be trapped there with no way to guarantee his return. The entire exercise would be pointless if he couldn't use what knowledge he gained to save his friends.

Even so, he couldn't let go of the notion. Analysts had tried sending small creatures through a rift, but every one of them perished. Akhen had warned him about the foolishness of attempting such a thing, but he'd had to acknowledge that Lev was somehow different. On a previous occasion, before he knew anything about the danger, he had passed his arm through a rift to grasp a token of a flower from the kin world on the other side. No one understood how that was possible. At the time, he was so mesmerized by the rift itself that he wasn't paying attention to what was occurring within his body. Without further hesitation, Lev decided to repeat the experience. Nothing had happened the first time — he risked little by trying.

Lev slowly passed his fingers through the rift — then his hand, and finally his arm up to his elbow. He wiggled his fingers. *Everything seems to be working. I can feel the warmth of the sun on my palm.* He pushed his second arm through and felt for a pulse on the first arm. He could feel a strong beat. *Synapses and blood flow are functioning across the frequency transition plane. The conversion must be instantaneous. How is that possible?*

Lev felt a cool numbness on his arm at the point where his flesh intersected the plane of the rift. He pulled his arms back out and decided to risk further experimentation.

He knew he was alone, but felt silly for what he was about to attempt and couldn't keep himself from looking around to make sure no one was watching.

Laying on his stomach, feet toward the arch, he began to push his way along the ground, through the rift. His thinking was that he'd proceed from the least to the most vital organs.

Everything was fine halfway through, but he paused just before he reached his chest. The thought of not being able to breathe was terrifying. Slowly, a little bit at a time, he proceeded — testing a breath every handspan of the way. He could feel his pulse pounding with fear, so he knew that his heart was still functioning as well.

Lev stopped at his neck. Akhen's warning screamed in his head. There was no way to know how his mind would be affected, even if the tissue itself survived. *What are you doing, Lev? You can't take risks like this. People are counting on you.*

Lev shook his head, got onto his hands and knees, and crawled back into his own world. A careful review of his body revealed no negative side effects.

Lev thought back to what he'd read about the previous Levigator's disappearance. No one knew what had happened to him. Lev grew more certain that Rushoen Nu Lon had intentionally passed through a rift. The question was, had it served any good purpose, or had he died?

Akhen was convinced that anyone who tried to pass through a rift would die or go insane. Something about that premise niggled at Lev. His body seemed to function fine in that other world. Why should his mind be any different? Akhen's whole premise was based on an assumption that the mind was somehow bound to the tissue that made up one's brain. That was the issue that troubled him.

It seemed strange to Lev that Akhen would hold such views as a believer in the afterlife. If the essence of who we are exists without the body, then it shouldn't be irrevocably tied to the flesh. More to the point, Lev had previously experienced a vision when he went through the process of mapping every particle in his body — at least he assumed it was a vision. He'd heard tales of people having out-of-body experiences when they were on death's doorstep. Perhaps it hadn't been a vision at all. Regardless, he had existed for a short period of time outside of his body as he mapped the particles of his brain. When he had completed the process, he drew back into his body. At the time, he hadn't expended much thought on how he had accomplished it. Reflecting on it now, he thought he remembered.

Lev entered pattern sight to test his theory. He called to memory a simple token and materialized it atop a nearby rock. He gasped. *I see it now!* The differences were subtle, but now that he knew what to look for, it was unmistakable. The space around him sang in a chorus of frequency shifts, each a pinpoint in space, having its own unique notation. Life on the other side of the rift resonated at a different frequency than in his own world, but that didn't mean that each world had only one frequency.

When Akhen declared that Lev was his own QPN, they had both assumed he was recording coordinates in the same way that the quantum network did. That wasn't it at all. He wasn't marking coordinates based on distance from the QPN network, or himself for that matter. He was memorizing frequency notations for every particle in the world around him. All of that time he'd spent practising, he thought he was mapping coordinates. In reality, he was subconsciously memorizing frequencies that remained the same, no matter where he was in relation to any given particle.

The conclusions were shocking and obvious at the same time. The reason he could surpass the efficiency of the QPN network was because he wasn't actually bound by coordinates. Looking closely, he could see that a particle's frequency remained the same even as it moved through the pattern. The only thing that changed was its relation to other particles. That was why he needed to watch a token materializing in order to commit it to memory, he was using an entirely different process than the QPN network.

This discovery of unique frequencies also explained how he had been able to move his consciousness outside of his body, and back again. He knew the frequency of the particles that were attuned to his ... his what? Essence? Soul? That was a whole other level of strangeness he wasn't ready to think about. There appeared to be yet another force at work. It had something to do with the tendrils he'd seen in his vision. They were *connected* to other versions of himself on parallel worlds. Perhaps they were more real than he'd assumed. If so, that would suggest that the whole of his being was definitely more than the grey matter in his skull.

Lev paced, trying to work through all of the ramifications. If what he suspected was true, then it was indeed possible for him to pass through a rift without going insane.

There were several arguments to support the idea. First, he knew that he could adapt the frequencies within his body instantly, without really thinking about it. Lev now understood that he wasn't changing the unique quantum level frequency of the particles that made up his form, he was just changing the modulation so each particle could find its place in the kin world.

Second, he knew that his greater self didn't exist only in his flesh. Therefore, he couldn't go mad based on some physical scrambling of brain matter. Besides, there was no reason to believe the matter in his skull would be damaged any more than the rest of his body was when he'd passed partway through the rift.

Finally, he felt certain that even if he was somehow separated from his body, he would recognize the unique frequencies necessary to find his way back, especially since he now understood the modulation differences between two worlds.

The sun was setting and Lev felt a headache forming. He decided to call it a night. *Tomorrow will be a day of experimentation. Finally, some answers.*

Chapter 37

"Welcome, Ms. Sheridan. Come in, come in. No need for your security detail. As you can see, it will be just the two of us this evening."

Tenika paused before crossing the threshold into Trantor's chambers. She pulled out her tote-comm as planned and spoke with Tully. "If I don't contact you with the password on the hour, you're to attack Trantor's horde."

"I assure you, Ms. Sheridan, that's completely unnecessary. You're in no danger here."

She nodded to her two Sicari escorts, indicating that they should wait in the antechamber. She couldn't believe that Trantor would allow her to be alone with him in his chambers. Perhaps he actually thought her defenceless. "I prefer that you address me as Second Anarch."

Kenric looked affronted. "As a rule, Second Anarchs are less formal when they're among peers. You may call me Kenric."

"And you may call me Second Anarch," Tenika repeated.

Kenric put on an ingratiating smile. "Very well, my dear. Have you had a chance to eat? I've had the kitchens prepare an evening snack."

"I'm not hungry."

Kenric sneezed. "My apologies, I seem to be coming down with something. I have a very fine wine that settles my stomach. Won't you join me?"

Tenika attempted to decline, but Kenric would have none of it.

"I insist. You'll not find this vintage anywhere else and it demands to be shared. Besides, I feel we have much to celebrate with this auspicious meeting. Why don't we retire to the sitting area? We have a great deal to discuss." Kenric walked towards some plush chairs carrying two mugs and a flagon, not waiting to see if Tenika accepted his invitation. She shrugged and followed.

Kenric motioned for her to take a seat. Tenika chose the chair beside a potted plant.

"What do you think of the place?" Kenric asked as he poured the wine. He handed her one of the mugs and coughed in her face.

Tenika turned her head in disgust. "Why have you invited me here, Kenric?"

"Must we turn to business so quickly? We're just getting to know one another. It's so seldom I can visit with — another Second Anarch."

That's right, Kenric, a woman is your equal. "That's just it, Kenric - I don't know you and I don't trust strangers."

Kenric turned to place the flagon of wine on a nearby pedestal. While his back was turned, Tenika poured half of her wine into the plant pot beside her.

As was customary for the host, Kenric took a sip of the wine to verify that it was safe to drink. His eyes widened in surprise when he noticed her mug was already half empty. A smug smile tugged at his lips.

Go ahead, Trantor, you keep believing I'm just a naive woman. "You said you had a mutually beneficial proposition. I've come a long way to hear it and I don't have time for games."

Kenric sighed. "Business first, it seems — as you wish. You've made quite a name for yourself in a very short time. You have done an admiral job of providing leadership to the Breachers in Caralithica and Jaihuwan during a difficult time. I've been doing the same here in Sumakad and Kemetica.

"It seems we both had the good intention of helping out in Arapanus. Someone needs to maintain order in the ranks. I wanted to discuss this current impasse before unnecessary blood was spilled. We are on the same team, after all."

"Are we?" Tenika asked.

"Of course, my dear. But as you must know by now, leading a single horde is a demanding job. You've taken on two hordes, with no previous experience. I worry that you'll overextend yourself if you take on a third. It's a dangerous thing for an anarch to lose track of all the pieces in play. Many schemers will be waiting in the wings to topple you. I've been leading Breachers for many years and can carry the burden of Sumakad while you strengthen your own position."

Kenric was interrupted by a knock at the door. It opened a crack and Tuk stuck his head through to peer into the chambers. His eyebrows rose in surprise when he spotted Tenika.

"What's the meaning of this interruption?" Kenric demanded.

"Apologies, Anarch," Tuk's eyes shifted between Kenric and Tenika, "I must speak with you immediately!"

Kenric rolled his eyes and rose from his seat. "Excuse me for a moment."

Tenika nodded and watched with interest as the animated Tuk shared his information. She couldn't hear, but she already knew what they were discussing. She poured the rest of her wine into the potted plant.

When Kenric returned to sit across from her once more, his pallor was decidedly worse.

You heard correctly Trantor, I have the hearts of the Breachers in Arapanus, and as a result, I now also hold favour with the Sicari. You should be very afraid.

"Are you feeling ill, Kenric?" Tenika asked sweetly.

Kenric waved away her concern with a shaky hand. "It's just this plague, it's a mild case — don't mind me. It seems congratulations are in order. I've just heard that your men captured the Servator base in Arapanus."

"Did they? That's very good news." Tenika was learning of the victory at the same time as Kenric, but she had no doubt the Arapanus horde now belonged to her as well. She couldn't keep the smile from her face.

Kenric responded with a scowl that was quickly replaced with his own smug grin when he noticed her empty wine mug. "You've done well ridding the world of Servators, though I understand you still haven't located the Servator Host of Caralithica. I'm happy to offer my services in locating that elusive remnant."

Tenika lifted her eyes skyward and pretended to consider his offer. "No, I don't think so. I have three hosts now — that should be more than enough to get the job done."

A vein in Kenric's neck stood out as his face purpled. "You insufferable shrew! You need me. I fostered the development of the facial recognition algorithm. I implemented the Breacher viewcorder network. It was *my* plan to destroy the Servators! You've nearly ruined everything with your meddling."

"Does this mean you no longer see a mutually beneficial partnership in our future?"

"Ms. Sheridan, I don't think you fully understand how precarious your position is."

Tenika pursed her lips. "I believe I only gave you permission to refer to me as Second Anarch. Not *Ms. Sheridan* or *my dear*."

Kenric bit off a retort and regained his composure. "I'm afraid I won't be referring to you with a title you've stolen and won't be holding onto for long."

"Is that a threat? If my people don't hear from me within the next fifteen minutes, my *three* hordes will attack your pitiful forces in Arapanus."

Kenric chuckled. "Now who's making threats? Empty ones at that. I had Tuk order my horde to withdraw. There will be no one there for you to attack. As for my comment about your title, I was only stating a fact."

"You seem quite confident for a man who no longer has Sicari support. They won't agree to an assassination contract."

Kenric shook his head with a pitying look in his eyes. "Do you actually believe the Sicari are my only resource? I've spent decades building up my network of agencies, corrupt authorities, and mercenaries. The Sicari are merely a tool I use for special circumstances that require their unique skill set. Believe me when I tell you that I have much more at my disposal than the Sicari or the hordes under my command.

"I will repair the damage done to my plans," Kenric sneered. "Those bumbling anarchs who preceded you couldn't stop me and there's not a chance someone like you could do any better."

"What do you mean, someone like me?"

Kenric snorted, "Someone born with the limitations of the weaker sex."

Tenika felt her blood begin to boil, but held her temper in check. She had to draw him out to get the answers she needed. "So it wasn't a lucky coincidence that you were the only Second Anarch to survive?"

Kenric gave her that pitying look again. "Poor thing — you really are in over your head. No, my dear, it wasn't a coincidence."

Tenika rolled her eyes. "Perhaps you could enlighten poor little me."

"I suppose it can't hurt at this point. You're as good as dead anyway."

Tenika stiffened. What had she missed?

Kenric ignored her reaction. "I'm sure you recall the plague that swept the world not that long ago. It's curious how selective it was. Some had minor sniffles while others dropped dead. If anyone had thought to investigate, they would've realized that those who perished were Servators or their supporters. Well, I guess it's no surprise the public failed to make that connection, the Servators being as secretive as they are."

"It's not possible to selectively target people with a plague, and the other anarchs weren't Servators."

"Very good, my dear. You're correct, but the plague isn't what killed the victims, it was only a trigger. The targets were infected with a toxin beforehand. The toxin only becomes dangerous when triggered by the plague which by itself was relatively benign."

Tenika's eyes widened. "The facial recognition algorithm ... you weren't using it so you could send kill squads, you wanted to infect Servators with the toxin and let it lay dormant until the right moment."

"You're smarter than I originally gave you credit."

Tenika had to admit it was an elegant scheme. All of the Servators would die and no Breacher lives would be lost in endless skirmishes. The logistics alone were unbelievable. At another time, she might have openly admired the plan, but at this moment, all she could think was, *Kenric killed Isau Jax*. Vengeful fantasies filled her mind and she struggled to remain seated. Her finger played with the ring that held another kind of toxin. "That doesn't explain why you killed your peers or how you administered the toxin to men who are suspicious by nature."

Kenric growled. "The fools were supposed to wait until all Servators were identified so I could finish administering the toxin to all of the targets. They became impatient and started attacking groups of Servators on their own. The Servators were becoming circumspect. I had to stop the other anarchs before the whole plan unravelled.

"As to how — it wasn't difficult. Such a large undertaking requires regular meetings. I was hosting one such gathering and my fellow anarchs were more than happy to consume my tainted wine after I drank from the same flagon. I of course had taken an antidote in advance — just as I did before your arrival."

Kenric stared at her in triumph, watching closely for her reaction. Tenika made a show of slumping in her chair with a frightened expression on her face.

"By the look on your face, I imagine you're finally putting two and two together. I also infected myself with the trigger plague. I can see you're already feeling weaker."

Kenric drew close to Tenika and forcibly exhaled in her face. "It won't be long now...."

Tenika didn't hesitate. She flipped the cap off her ring and embedded the poisoned tip into Kenric's neck. He jerked upright, startled. Tenika surged to her feet, shoving him backwards. She followed up with a thrust kick to his chest that sent him to the floor on his back. He lay there motionless, the fast-acting toxin already seizing his muscles.

"Your breath stinks, you pig!" Tenika kicked him several times in the ribs. "You killed Isau," she raged, "I loved him!"

The admission brought her up short. Is that what she felt? She'd never said so to Isau or allowed herself to consider the possibility. Now he was gone. The sudden realization that she was both capable of love and unable to experience a future with Isau consumed her as she sat on Kenric's chest and rained blows on the man responsible for her pain.

A groan escaped Kenric's lips. It was the only sound he could manage through his paralysis.

Tenika sneered. "In answer to your unspoken question, there are three things you should know. First, in case you forgot, I already recovered from your trigger plague after the first time you used it. I have immunity. I suppose it could still have triggered the toxin, somehow, except — and here comes the second thing — I didn't drink your wine. How stupid do you think I am? I poured it out in that sad excuse for a potted plant over there."

Kenric couldn't move, but the fear in his eyes was clear enough.

"As for the third thing," Tenika continued, her nose inches from Kenric's, "I'll finish killing off the Servators without you. It will be *my* name that goes down in history, but don't worry, you won't be forgotten. I'll make certain the history books include you in a footnote as the arrogant fool who was bested by a woman."

Tenika stood and looked around the room for a weapon. Pummelling a defenceless man had lost its allure now that her rage had diminished. She needed to finish him off before the effects of the toxin began to wane. There were plenty of ornamental swords hanging from the walls, but this called for something poetic. Her eyes rested on the half-finished flagon of wine that Kenric tried to use on her. *Perfect.*

Tenika grabbed the flagon and knelt beside Kenric's head. "You say it's a fine vintage? I'd hate to see it wasted and I know you wanted to celebrate our auspicious meeting." She poured the wine down his throat. It overflowed onto the floor, staining an expensive throw rug along its path.

Unable to swallow, Kenric began breathing rapidly through his nose.

Tenika patted him gently on the cheek. "Goodbye, Trantor." She pinched his nostrils shut and waited until the light faded from his eyes.

Chapter 38

Intelligence gathering had become all but impossible for the Servators. Forced to remain in hiding, they were unwilling to take the risk of making contact with informants or allies. Sadly, most supporters were dead because of their association with the Servators — any who remained were also in hiding. With so many bases compromised, the analysts were effectively cut off from anything other than local Servator reports and publicly broadcast news media. Unfortunately, the public sources knew nothing of the Breacher influences driving the increase in criminal activity.

Bits and pieces of information still filtered through from old spy token placements, but so much had changed in the Breacher structure that much of what they gleaned was no longer relevant. The analysts did the best they could at piecing the fragments together. Much of the bigger picture was missing, but some gossip was too persistent and relevant to ignore. The rumour of greatest concern was that Breachers world-wide were now united under a single leader. That development was disturbing enough, but the new leader's identity was what had prompted this emergency meeting.

Chief Sentry Jokan Pizzar was sharing the analyst report. "The evidence is compelling. Tenika Sheridan is now the sole leader in charge of all Breacher hordes."

Cello's face oscillated between fury and sadness, contemplating all she'd lost to Tenika's ambition. "I should have made an exception in her case and opted for execution. The woman is ruthless and hopelessly unrepentant."

Nico had asked Beniti Abrax to join them. Beniti wasn't there in any official capacity, but Nico hoped for his blessing for what he was going to propose.

Beniti placed an empathetic hand on Cello's shoulder. "You don't mean that Cello. It's not our way."

Cello continued, "Don't I? Look at the destruction wrought by this one woman because of her irrational hatred for the Servators. She blames us simply because she's unwilling to take responsibility for her criminal behaviour. Her mind is twisted and I seriously doubt there would've been any hope of rehabilitating her. Not that the option is open to us any longer. I think it's fair to assume that she was behind the destruction of the rehabilitation islands. This is all my fault."

"We don't know for certain that Tenika was involved in the attacks on the islands." Deak offered.

Cello choked up. "You witnessed Kayla's murder, Deak. You heard what Tenika said. She already controlled at least two hordes by that point and admitted responsibility for destroying several Servator facilities. She was furious that I tried to have her sent to the islands — it was her."

The impromptu meeting was taking place in the mountains. With so much depressing news of late, it felt good to be away from the undersea facility at Port Callan and spend a little time above ground. It was one of the few places left where they could freely walk outdoors. The trails were deep within the mountain range, hidden below the tree canopy. Nico had arranged for portable chairs in a clearing a short distance from Port Vantos. He looked out over the valley below and took in a deep breath of the fresh air. It helped to clear his mind and he needed that clarity now.

After Kayla's death, Nico had almost given up. Jokan and Cello had convinced him that they needed his strategic skills to deal with the Breacher threat. He'd been angry at first — how could they so easily set aside their loss and move on? How could they ask him to pretend nothing had happened and carry on with business as usual? Eventually, he realized that the tasks they had given him didn't make him forget, it just gave him something to live for. They were all grieving, but life continued whether they liked it or not. Kayla wouldn't have wanted him to turn his back on all she had worked for.

"I agree with Cello." Nico caught her eye. "Not that it's Cello's fault, but that Tenika is responsible. She was always driven and spiteful when she worked at Callan International. She had my parents murdered to advance her ambitions. You all know how she framed me for murder as well, to get me out of the way.

"Her behaviour is pathological. She won't stop coming for us now that she has the means. She intends to destroy all Servators and is well on the way to achieving that goal. The Servator remnant is not insignificant, but it pales in comparison to the strength of five hordes. If Tenika brings all of her forces to Denmount...."

"There's already an increased Breacher presence in Denmount," Jokan confirmed.

"It was no coincidence that Tenika chose to draw us out by appearing in the basement of the archive building," Cello added. "Tenika correctly deduced that the Servator base for Caralithica is somewhere below the Court of Learning campus. She's like a dog with a bone. She won't let go."

Nico shook his head in frustration. "If we'd had time to deploy the labyrinth strategy, we could have opened the false tunnels to the public as a tourist attraction and diffused Breacher suspicion."

"It was a good plan, Nico, but that transport has sailed." Deak pinched the bridge of his nose. "It's not a total loss. The Breachers may find the base, but the labyrinth will still keep them from discovering the tunnels to Ports Vantos and Callan."

"Maybe for a short time," Nico acknowledged, "but if they find the base empty when they attack, they'll know we're hiding somewhere else and the hunt will continue. At best, it will serve as a delaying tactic."

"So what do we do?" Jokan asked. "We can't sacrifice some of our people to feed Breacher bloodlust in the hopes that they'll move on like they did in Arapanus."

Arapanus had been evacuated just in time, but when some of Jokan's men returned to gather items left behind, they had been attacked and the base destroyed. The loss continued to haunt Jokan. He wouldn't allow that scenario to be repeated as a tactic even if they had willing volunteers.

"Agreed," Nico nodded, "we can't condone any unnecessary loss of lives."

"Who determines what's necessary?" Cello circled back to her original comment. "If we'd sentenced Tenika to death, only one life would've been lost and we wouldn't be having this conversation right now."

Jokan rounded on Cello. "You can't seriously be suggesting that we ask our own people to give their lives for the *greater good*. There is no *good* in that line of reasoning. It means giving in to evil because of fear."

"Don't twist my words, Jokan, I just meant...."

Nico loudly cleared his throat to forestall a pointless argument. "We're not sacrificing any lives, but there may be a way —"

"I knew you called us here for more than a walk in the woods," Deak sighed, "about time you got to the point."

Nico lifted an incredulous eyebrow.

"Sorry," Deak sighed, "we've all been under a lot of stress lately."

Nico nodded in understanding. "What I'm about to suggest will be difficult to hear, but I've considered all of the alternatives. It's our best chance if we hope to avoid loss of life."

Jokan sat straighter at the warning. "It seems like all news is difficult to hear lately. It's not like we have many options — go ahead, we're listening."

"We all know this only ends with the Breachers getting what they want — destruction of the base and the death of Servators. The base is already effectively abandoned and isolated, so that's not an issue, but we need to convince the Breachers that we're there and putting up a fight. To do that, we need to control the scene as if we were putting on a theatre production.

"We know the Breacher network continues to monitor Denmount campus. When we're ready, we'll have a few rangers go topside — maybe visit the market. They'll allow the network to track them to two of the base entrances where we'll disengage the false walls and basically leave the front door open. We want to control their points of ingress and there needs to be more than one."

"All of the attacks we've seen so far have brought overwhelming numbers," Deak observed. "Our point defences were never designed to take on a force that large."

"The Breachers won't know what to expect, but I don't plan for us to deploy *any* Servator defences. I want to play up their own expectations of a battle."

"You've lost me," Deak said.

"We'll direct them along predefined paths that are filled with monitoring tokens. Everything will be orchestrated remotely and will rely on careful timing. Breachers are more familiar with projectile weapons and explosives, so we'll create the appearance of that threat. It will be their first time encountering resistance from Servators who are using ballistic weapons. They'll see it as an act of desperation, but it will also disorient them and create the impression of a hard-fought battle."

"You want us to use lethal weapons?" Jokan wondered aloud.

"Why not?" Cello muttered, "They use them on us."

Nico was concerned about Cello's increasingly dark perspective. "No. As I've said, I want to put on a show. I want lights and sounds and smoke. I want the Breachers to recognize a familiar danger that will pump them full of adrenaline so they make mistakes — so they won't notice small details. They'll respond to the chaos with their own show of lethal force, creating real collateral damage, but we won't be there."

"Won't they wonder why they haven't seen anyone?" Deak asked.

"That's where the timing comes in. Once a sufficient number of Breachers have entered, we'll shut off power and kill the lights. In the following moments we'll make it appear that backup power has come online, but the lighting will be minimized. Hopefully each breaching group will assume other Breachers are responsible for the power failure, heightening the impression that the battle has already begun. At this point, it's critical that the tunnels are poorly lit and filled with smoke.

"As Breachers advance under reduced visibility, we'll begin to project viewcordings of Servators fleeing, always just beyond reach. The screen tokens we use for the projections will need to be disassembled immediately after use so the Breachers never come across evidence of the deception. We'll plan circuitous routes so we can keep the drama going for a while."

Deak had been listening intently, leaning forward with his elbows on his knees and his chin on his fists. He leaned back in his chair. "An interesting tactic, but it won't work. If there's a real battle, there will be death. Sooner or later, one of the Breachers is going to notice the absence of bodies. Even if Breachers accidentally kill each other in the chaos, there won't be enough dead to maintain the charade."

Beniti spoke up for the first time. "He already knows. That's where the uncomfortable part comes in. That's why you asked me here, isn't it?"

Nico grimaced and nodded.

Deak watched the silent exchange. "Does one of you care to fill the rest of us in?"

Beniti continued to hold Nico's eyes as he explained to the rest of the group. "We didn't have the time or manpower to bury the dead at Kemetica base. Instead, we sealed it and filled it with gas. The bodies are perfectly preserved until we have an opportunity to return."

Cello's eyes widened in shock. Jokan bolted upright, placing a hand on Beniti's shoulder. "You would dishonour the dead?"

Beniti patted Jokan's hand. "It's okay, my friend. You know the dead have gone to be with the Maker. The bodies are just empty shells. As for their memory, I think there is no greater honour than to allow them to save more of their brothers and sisters in this way. I approve."

"We'll want to gather them eventually," Nico added. "After this is done, we can give them a proper burial in the crypt above Port Callan."

"Assuming we bring the bodies here — how do we distribute them in a realistic manner?"

"It will be a grim task. Makeup will be applied so the deaths appear recent. We'll create false wounds. After that, the bodies will be positioned below the projector screens. As the Breachers advance, they will come across bodies that appear to have fallen to weapons fire. Some bodies will be held behind false walls and released as things progress. We'll begin to reduce the sounds of battle we've been piping in and allow the smoke to clear. It will give the impression that the battle is coming to a close. By then, there should be enough bodies to convince the Breachers that they've been successful."

Jokan looked like he'd swallowed something bitter. "When you said it would be an uncomfortable proposition, you were understating things."

"I don't like it either, but it's the only thing I could come up with that had a reasonable chance of success. I'm open to other ideas, believe me."

"Let's just put it to a vote," Beniti suggested. "All in favour of proceeding with the plan, raise your hands."

Beniti's hand was the first to rise, followed slowly by the others and last of all Jokan, who looked like he would rather be someplace else.

"It's unanimous," Nico whispered with a resigned slump of his shoulders. How had they come to this?

Deak rose and folded his chair. "I'll begin preparations to transport the bodies from Kemetica Base."

No more was spoken as they made their way back to Port Vantos, individually reflecting on their losses and all that might yet be required of them.

Chapter 39

Tuk sat across from Tenika in Kenric's chambers — well, her chambers now. Getting things under control in Sumakad and Kemetica was taking longer than she'd anticipated, so she needed to stay put for the time being. The Second Anarch's chambers were the seat of power in Sumakad. She needed to be seen as the sole occupant.

Tenika wasn't really needed anywhere else at the moment. Nash Koth, Isau's former assistant, was keeping an eye on things in Caralithica. Jaihuwan was well in hand under Quento Shung's guidance, and Tully was running things in Arapanus. Kemetica had been more or less under Kenric's thumb and it was close enough for Tenika to step in if necessary.

Sumakad was where she needed to be. It was necessary that she cement her power here — that was becoming abundantly clear the more time she spent talking with Tuk. The greasy little man was a wealth of information. He'd tried to hide from her at first, but the Sicari tracked him down. Once Tuk realized she wanted to retain him in his former capacity, with an increase in pay, the man seemed eager to answer her questions. He'd told her everything she might want to know and other secrets she wished he had kept to himself.

Trantor had his fingers in so many pies, it was proving difficult to root all of them out. His network was vast and his people were well embedded in each of the hordes except for the one in Caralithica. Tuk's first task was to locate those in Trantor's network who would willingly transfer their loyalty to Tenika. It was why he was before her now. "Stop your fidgeting Tuk!"

"Sorry, Anarch!"

"Don't apologize. Just sit still! You're putting me on edge."

Tuk made an exaggerated show of stilling himself which involved a great deal of fidgeting. He handed her a sheet of parchment. "This is a list of people who immediately agreed to submit to your authority. Most had no love for Trantor to begin with, so it wasn't a difficult decision. The monetary incentive you offered definitely helped. A lot of people are feeling uncertain about their future with the recent upheaval and are just hoping things will get back to some semblance of normal. As you can see, the list of names represents about eighty three percent of Trantor's total network. That's more than enough to keep you apprised of everything going on. I've operated the network with less than that on occasion and managed to maintain a high degree of reliable intelligence."

Tenika scanned the document. "Will the holdouts be a problem for us?"

"I don't think so. I've worked with most of them before — they're more cautious, is all. They'll come back into the fold when they're convinced there will be no reprisals."

Tuk handed her a second sheet. "This is a list of the business holdings I've uncovered so far. It's quite extensive. Most are legitimate enterprises that are completely unaware of their benefactor's true nature. Trantor's treasury is astonishing. You'll have no shortage of resources. Of course, I may never uncover all of it."

Tenika gave Tuk a hard stare that increased his fidgeting.

"I'm not stealing from you, Anarch! I swear! I've been completely forthcoming with everything I've discovered."

Tenika knew that wasn't true. It was to be expected in any criminal organization. The important part was making sure her people knew she didn't trust them. "What about those not directly under our employ?"

Tuk shuffled through his documents, happy for a change of topic. "This is a record of the civil authorities who Trantor has either bribed or blackmailed. He had magistrates at his beck and call in every corner of the world. I helped to secure a good number of them."

"Excellent!" Tenika grinned. "Now that we're all under the same banner, I want you to connect with Quento, Tully, and Nash to consolidate the intelligence networks of the other hordes. I want everyone to know that there's no place to hide from the eyes and ears of their Anarch."

"It will be done, Anarch."

"Good. Now tell me the outcome of the attack on the final Servator base in Caralithica."

"The hordes were surprised by the ferocity of the Servator defence. They were using Breacher style weapons and tactics. It was completely out of character, but I suppose that's to be expected from a last stand."

"Losses?" Tenika asked.

"We lost about twenty-five men, but the Servators didn't stand a chance. The final tally counted over four hundred dead Servators. No one escaped."

"So many in one base?"

"We believe Servators who escaped from other bases found their way to Caralithica."

Tenika took a deep breath and slowly exhaled. "So it's done then. Thank you for the report, Tuk. You're dismissed. Tell the guards that I am not to be disturbed until tomorrow morning. I have a lot to consider."

Tenika made a slow circuit of her new chambers. The vaulted room was ridiculously opulent. *Why does anyone need so much space?* It had bathing, dining and sleeping areas in a mostly open arrangement. Pacing wasn't limited to walking back and forth. She could march around the perimeter without ever needing to dodge furniture. *I could jog in here.* She noticed the lack of an exercise area. *I'll have to remedy that.*

My initial plans are almost complete. What remains unfinished? Tenika considered her revenge list. Kayla Vantos was dead and supposedly her mother as well. Tenika made a mental note to have her people search the Caralithican base for the body of Cello Vantos. She wanted viewcorder proof of the woman's demise. Trantor was also dead, having paid the price for killing Isau. *Who am I forgetting? Oh, yes! Halen Tu — that ungrateful little worm.* In what seemed like another life, her former lawvocate had been compiling evidence against her as an insurance policy. He handed it over to the Servators who used it to convict her. Ironically, she might not be in her current position if not for Halen's duplicity, but she wasn't about to thank the man for being a traitor. First thing in the morning she would invoke a Sicari contract to have Halen hunted down.

Tenika tried to think of any others who had wronged her in the past, but no one else stood out as worth the time or effort. She was above all of that now. No one would ever control her again. Tenika's laughter echoed in the open space, her mind moving on to future considerations. What should she do now that she'd met her immediate objectives? *Anything I want — what do I want?* Tenika thought about the kinds of things that she found interesting and challenging. It wasn't difficult to identify what drove her. She liked to make plans and succeed at them. It didn't matter what the goal was, but she wasn't content to function in a supporting role when she had a better solution. *And my way is always the better way.* Tenika chuckled at her arrogance, but it was true. She was able to see things better than most and devise an optimal strategy. It was what carried her to this point.

Now that she had a global criminal empire at her disposal, she found that she didn't actually want to run it. The ambitions were too small. What was the point of vice and violence just for the sake of money? With the combined war chests of five Breacher anarchs, she already had more than she'd ever need. She had power, but the uninspired criminal pursuits were — boring. Kenric, for all of his failings, understood that. He had invested in many legitimate business enterprises and research efforts. Much as she hated to admit it, they had much in common. She wanted to conquer more than the criminal world.

Trantor focused his efforts on eliminating the Servators. He wanted Breacher adoration. Tenika didn't enjoy the spotlight. Her affirmation came from getting away with something unthinkable, something behind the scenes. Trantor was a criminal with legitimate business holdings. Something about that was alluring to her — the idea of the so-called morally righteous owing their success to the very thing they hated. She would enjoy a goal like that — secretly subjugating a whole world.

It occurred to her that she had never enjoyed her life so much as when she was running Callan International. There was always a challenge to overcome, and while brute force worked on occasion, a clever manipulation was far more satisfying.

Tenika stopped her pacing as a revelation hit her. *I was trying to do exactly that — take over the world through a globe-spanning company — Callan International.* It was the ultimate challenge. No wonder she had been so angry when Nico Callan put all of that at risk.

This pondering brought up one more person who she wanted revenge on — Nico Callan. She wanted Callan International back. She wanted to take it right out from under Nico and then rub his nose in her final victory.

Tenika began to grin as she plotted. This time she had the backing of the largest criminal organization in the world, all eager to please her. Whether through bribery or blackmail, she owned lawvocates and magistrates. She had immense wealth and an enviable intelligence network. She could buy, crush, or manipulate her way into ownership of everything Nico possessed and she could do it all in ways that seemed legitimate and nonthreatening. He wouldn't know what hit him until it was too late. It was a worthy challenge.

Everything was coming together. It had been a long time since Tenika felt so energized. *No, that's not an adequate description, it's more like a burning lust for something.* The thought brought her up short and she stopped pacing. The sensation increased. Now that she thought about it, she'd felt the sensation every time she neared this part of the room. *In fact, it's strongest right here in front of this peculiar door.*

Tenika was aware of the ancient looking door, but hadn't had time to consider what lay beyond it. Some part of her imagined it was a place where Trantor carried out some twisted fetish and she was in no hurry to discover what that might be. Now that she looked at it closer, it seemed too heavy a door for something so trivial as intimate privacy. It looked far more suited to security. Tenika tried the handle. The door was locked. An old-fashioned keyhole was the only visible barrier. *What were you hiding here, Trantor?* Tenika laid her ear against the door and felt a thrill of desire. *It's mine now!* A sudden possessiveness had her frantically searching for the key.

"Where would you hide a key?" Tenika whispered. She stood in the centre of the room and slowly turned, taking in her surroundings. Kenric was meticulous in his professional planning, but everything about his personal space suggested reckless abandon. It was as if this was a sanctuary where he could let himself go. Instead of secrets, everything was on display. Maybe he wasn't hiding the key at all.

Tenika gazed at the door from where she was standing. Light fixtures bracketed the door on either side, attached to the wall. They were ornate, but out of place as if they were installed at the same time as the door which was in stark contrast to the rest of the decor. Each fixture was formed of intricately cast gold filigree that framed panes of glass. The filigree flowed beneath the light source to end in a dangling pendant. "It can't be that simple."

Striding to the massive door, Tenika took a closer look at the fixture closest to the door handle. The dangling portion looked like it could be a key, but there was no obvious way to remove it so she moved to the second fixture. The dangling portion looked similar, however the eyelet of the *key* was slightly flattened on one side. The ring that the key hung from had a thin

slot near the base. The ring appeared more like a hook on closer inspection. By matching the flattened eyelet to the slot, Tenika was able to remove it. It didn't look like any key she was familiar with, more of a rod with a series of grooves encircling it. Regardless, it was the correct diameter for the keyhole and she inserted it. Turning the rod didn't seem to do anything, so she left it in place and tried the handle. This time the door moved. She swung it open.

Tenika didn't understand what she was looking at, but waves of desire filled her. The space beyond was dark, but she was certain she could make out something just a few steps beyond the threshold. It seemed to flicker in and out of existence. It was beautiful. She wanted it — she needed it. Tenika glanced over her shoulder, suddenly afraid that someone would enter the room and take it from her. She rushed forward to claim it for herself.

Her scream was cut short, followed by a whimper and then silence.

The two Sicari guarding Tenika's chambers were tossing dice to pass the time. "What was that sound?" one asked. The other shrugged. "A drunk anarch celebrating her victory?"

"Should we check it out?"

"She said she didn't want to be disturbed until morning. Do you want to stick your head in there and get it chewed off?"

"Not particularly, no."

"Then stop stalling and roll. You're not getting out of paying my winnings so easily."

The Sicari returned to their game. No one was there to witness the disappearance of Tenika Sheridan and there was no one there to close the ancient looking door.

Chapter 40

"Block!" Akhen yelled. A transparent barrier materialized in three places just in time to obstruct the Breachers coming at him from behind and from either side. The barrier disassembled immediately after it served its purpose, creating confusion among those who had collided with it. It gave Akhen a few seconds to deal with two more Breachers in front of him. He laid one out with a swivel kick to the head and dispatched the other with a knife-hand strike to the throat. The first of those who had rushed him from behind was already on his feet. Akhen spun to face his attacker and winded him with a thrust-kick to the solar plexus followed by a vicious upper-cut that left his opponent unconscious on the ground. Yori and Tark slipped in behind the remaining two Breachers, employing choke holds that put the last of them to sleep. Treasury staff rushed in to tie up the would-be thieves and dragged them away.

Akhen nodded his thanks to the analysts of his team who stood apart from the combatants. Their timely intervention with token shields was a proven battle tactic by now. This particular group of Breachers had been attempting to gain access to a money lender's treasury when Akhen's team came upon the scene. It wasn't the first altercation of the day and it wouldn't be the last.

Akhen was exhausted, both physically and emotionally. For the past two weeks they'd been trying to mitigate unprecedented atrocities in the city. The suffering of so many people drove him to push on, but he needed to take a break soon or he would collapse and be of no use to anyone.

Criminal activity was surging across the city. There was a great deal of confusion among the analysts as to the reason. If the Breachers thought they had destroyed all Servators, what possible reason would they have to start attacking the general populace? Some speculated that the Servators were removed specifically for this purpose — so the Breachers would be free of Servator interference, to do as they pleased. That line of thinking saw the current trend as an inevitable outcome from the lack of balance provided by a Servator presence.

It wasn't the only theory. There were rumours that Tenika Sheridan had been assassinated and no one had stepped in to take her place. It would explain much, if the Breachers were rudderless and the current atrocities were the result of an *every man for himself* looting spree.

Regardless of the reason, Breachers were no longer working in the shadows. The entire horde was openly ravaging and pillaging — violently. To make matters worse, the City Sentinels seemed to be turning a blind eye to the destruction. Akhen had witnessed a victim approach a Sentinel for help, only to be killed by the one whom she assumed would protect her. The Sentinel had let out a roar and proceeded to murder two others who happened to be within reach.

If Akhen had reacted a minute sooner, he might have intervened. His hesitation had been a reaction to the wraith-like entity that circled the man's head, whispering in his ear. Whatever it was saying appeared to be driving the Sentinel's murderous rampage. The ghostly thing faded in and out of sight as if it didn't really belong to this universe.

A name popped unbidden into Akhen's mind. *Wastrel*. He'd never seen one before — they were thought by many to be nothing more than myth. Akhen knew better, he'd studied the journals of the Levigators. The thing he saw fit descriptions of past encounters. A chill crept up Akhen's spine every time he thought about it. Reading about wastrels was very different than seeing one in person.

Akhen had no idea how to fight such a thing, but he vowed never to hesitate again. He knew that Leviticus was off trying to learn how to form a void rift — the only known way to imprison a wastrel. It was an ability his predecessors possessed and he planned to rediscover the technique in a prescriptive attempt to prepare for this very eventuality. Unfortunately, no one had heard from the Levigator in some time. Was Leviticus even aware the wastrels were free?

Akhen recalled the written words of a former Levigator named Yuul Neem who warned that if the wastrels escaped, then all would be lost. Akhen pushed the thought to a corner of his mind. *It's not too late, we just need to slow things down until Leviticus returns.* Akhen didn't know if that was true, but the alternative wasn't something he wanted to consider.

Akhen was a little old to be roaming the streets looking for trouble, but as a former World Warkata Champion, his skills more than compensated for any age-related disadvantages. He looked around at the team he had assembled and his heart swelled with pride. Together they were making a difference, even if it was only a small one.

Among the Servators who were trained fighters of the Host, there had been a great deal of frustration at being forced to passively remain in hiding. When the Breachers began attacking innocent citizens, they wanted to help. It was in their nature to defend the underdog. Akhen found himself sharing their frustration.

The Chief Sentries had reluctantly agreed to let Akhen form teams of their best warriors to do what they could on the condition that they found a way to mask their Servator identities. The analysts needed information about what was happening beyond their self-imposed prison and that meant someone needed to venture out. Akhen's teams could serve both purposes, but it was imperative that Breachers continued to believe the Servators were eliminated.

Akhen had already given the problem some thought. They would wear City Sentinel uniforms and masquerade as a police squad. Hiding from the Breacher's facial recognition network was a more complicated proposition. The Levigator had come up with a masking technology that could convince the algorithm that the wearer represented one of several identities planted in the Breacher network. Unfortunately, the technology had been overused and when duplicate identities began appearing in different places at the same time, the Breachers caught on to the deception. The masks became useless at that point.

This time around, the analysts decided to distort the facial images created by the masks so the algorithm couldn't make a match at all. There would be no duplicate entries, just a number of incomplete match attempts. Sooner or later, it would arouse suspicion, but if the Breachers investigated, witnesses would say that City Sentinels were involved in an altercation. It would look like legitimate Sentinel action or possibly like another rogue Breacher element trying to gain authority. Regardless, Akhen's teams wouldn't be staying in any one place or following a routine, so they'd be difficult to track.

They encountered another problem when they realized they couldn't be seen using Servator weapons. The Breachers would definitely recognize the Servator stun batons. Options were limited for a team with an aversion to the lethal weapons used by Breachers and Sentinels. They decided to rely on hand-to-hand combat and the strategic use of their shield technology. The shields were nearly invisible when judiciously applied during the confusion of a battle. At least those would give them an edge.

Here, again, the analysts had come up with a clever solution. They developed a type of mini-repeater for the Quantum Positioning Network. A user could request a token at the repeater's coordinates which would be placed in a buffer within the device. As long as the user remained at those coordinates, the repeater could provide new coordinates anywhere within a five-cubit range of the repeater. A stored token could be dispensed instantly and repeatedly to the immediate surroundings without the typical QPN delay.

The drawbacks were the time required to fill the buffer during the initial request and the need to remain stationary in the middle of a battle. To overcome those limitations, Akhen had the teams train in sub-groups of three. One analyst for every two warriors. One warrior would fight on the fringes, taking on targets of opportunity while protecting the analyst. Meanwhile, the analyst would provide strategic shielding for the remaining fighter who operated as the point of the spear — striking aggressively and drawing attention to himself. It didn't take long to develop a cohesive fighting style that proved very effective.

Ten teams of elite fighters were deployed among the various city districts. They were constantly on the move as they patrolled the streets during the day. During the night, they slept in Servator safe houses — never staying at the same one twice in a row. The strategy appeared to be working, but the impact they were having seemed woefully inadequate.

Initially, the Breachers were responsible for most of the turmoil, but the world was becoming a much darker place as average people began to add to the chaos. Wastrel influence seemed to be reducing inhibition and encouraging base desires.

On one occasion, Akhen witnessed a man being robbed at knife point while his friend stood helplessly by his side. Akhen had stopped the thief who dropped the money bag to flee. When Akhen gave up the chase, he turned to see the victim's friend grab the bag for himself and run off. Trust was eroding, alliances were failing — mother turning against daughter, sister against brother, husband against wife. It was getting harder to tell who the innocent were. Akhen couldn't imagine what a world completely under wastrel influence would look like.

The teams began to avoid the streets at night when the public revelled in drunken orgies. The festivities often left behind the gruesome remains of murders that appeared to be part of a ritual. One of Akhen's men had quit the team after witnessing a mother sacrificing her infant child on a crude altar constructed of human skulls. There were so many demoralizing stories, that Akhen sometimes wondered if their small thankless victories were worth the permanent scars forming in their hearts and minds.

It felt hopeless, but they had to hang on. They needed to do what they could to push against the coming storm. *There's no one else who understands the threat.* The thought pierced Akhen like a blade. *Why have the Servators operated in secret all of this time? Why didn't we warn the world? We thought we were protecting people when we should have been preparing them.* The truth of it drove him to his knees.

Later that night, Akhen longed for sleep, but was kept awake by his revelation. He prayed for the Levigator's return and added a plea for the Maker's forgiveness for the foolish hubris of the Servators. He finally fell asleep with a small hope — *maybe it's not too late.*

Chapter 41

Useless... poser... weakling....
Lev lay, curled into a fetal position, weeping.
You've killed everyone you love... they died cursing your name....
"No!" Lev bolted upright, sleep fleeing from his mind. He rose to his feet, shaking his head to clear the dark thoughts that clung like cobwebs. Opening his eyes, he saw the shifting entities swirling nearby — too close.

He shifted into pattern sight so he could clearly see his accusers. They immediately backed away, but the whispers never stopped. Lev had learned that the ghostly beings didn't like it when he remained in pattern sight. The wastrels preferred to approach stealthily. They preyed on people who were unaware of the threat - taking advantage of their victims in moments of weakness. That didn't mean their efforts weren't having an effect on Lev, aware as he was. He already harboured insecurities about his decisions as a Levigator. He was filled with regret about lives lost as a result of his choices. The wastrels amplified his despair, making it difficult to focus on anything else.

That was the problem. He didn't have time to be distracted and he couldn't afford the brain fog that accumulated from the relentless, restless, nights.

Lev had wandered from rift to rift, without any real plan. He was hoping for inspiration — a clue that would show him how to close a rift. Unfortunately, staring at a rift for too long tended to stifle creative thought.

Travelling helped to shake things up. He let his mind wander, along with his feet, reflecting on what went right or wrong in his various attempts to teach himself the lost techniques of former Levigators.

Three weeks earlier, he had neared a small city on the way to his next destination. That was when the first wastrels noticed him. He'd entered the city to resupply and was shocked by what he witnessed. The place looked like a war zone without a military presence. There were no sounds of battle, yet bodies lay on the streets and screams echoed in the distance. The people he encountered avoided his gaze and quickly moved away, or stared at him with a predatory gleam in their eyes. It was profoundly disturbing and he felt a constant fight or flight response wearing at his nerves as he wandered the mostly empty market square.

The vendors were armed and wary as he purchased supplies. Only a few were selling consumables. Most were selling charms and potions to ward off evil — sorcery supplies that were usually found in the fringe districts of a city, not the main market. It was deeply disturbing.

Lev made to ask about it, but the vendor suddenly made a warding sign with his hands and shut the booth in Lev's face. Alarms rang in Lev's mind and the hair rose on his arms as he felt someone approaching. When he spun around, there was no one there, but he heard a voice that felt like a shout.

Levigator — power — influence.

Lev was caught off guard when something materialized before him and just as quickly faded. He entered pattern sight reflexively and the form retreated, but a dozen others soon joined the first. There was no mistaking what he was seeing — these were the wastrels he had read about in the Levigator journals. He recognized the voices as similar to those he had once heard behind a door in Kenric Trantor's chambers.

Lev was filled with dismay at the discovery. He'd thought he would have more time. It meant he would have to shift his energies from closing a portal to learning how to open a void rift. If he failed at that, nothing else would matter. The relentless whispering began shortly after, whittling away at his mental defences.

When Lev left that city, the wastrels followed him. He felt some small consolation knowing that the city would have a reprieve from their suffering as he drew the tormentors away. At the same time, he worried about how his friends may be suffering as a result of this new threat.

Failure — useless — incompetent.

Since then, more wastrels had joined his unwelcome entourage. Every time he neared a settlement, the numbers increased and he still hadn't learned how to form a void rift. Worse, the creatures seemed to realize what he was attempting and increased their clamour to distract him. They promised him power, they promised him pleasure, they promised him relief, if only he would follow their lead. He knew better than to give into temptation, but it was far more difficult to ignore the despair growing within him.

It was only a matter of time before the wastrels did so much damage that it would be too late to stop the flood.

Your friends are suffering — you've abandoned them in their time of need — it's all your fault.

Lev longed to return to his friends. The Breachers had decimated the Servators and now the wastrels were free. How would Caralithica fare? He needed to get back to Denmount. He should be there to defend the remnant. He was the Levigator. It was *his* hometown. Protecting family and friends was his responsibility. The twisted horrors he'd seen in various cities filled him with urgency.

Join us — we can help you save them.

Lev placed his hands over his ears. "Shut up — shut up — shut up!" He knew he couldn't go back. A swarm of wastrels would accompany him. He was a carrier of the worst kind of plague.

Who do you think you are? You were a fool to think you could help anyone.

Lev ground his teeth at the latest attack on his conscience. He knew what the wastrels were doing, but it still hurt because he believed it was true. Ironically, it also gave him the strength to go on. Even if he failed at everything else, he could still ease the burdens of many people if he drew the wastrels away from populated areas. He retained that power over them. It proved that the wastrels were liars and limited in their tactics.

It became his habit to travel to as many settled areas as he could and then retreat again into the wilderness. Each step meant a new voice and a heavier burden. Lev worried he might cross the threshold from sanity to madness and end up giving the wastrels what they wanted. Who knew what damage would happen as a result? Lev couldn't allow that to happen. He had to learn how to form a void rift before he lost his mind.

Lev forced himself to eat some dry bread for his breakfast and swallowed some water before settling himself in front of the rift he'd arrived at the night before. He stared at the rift using pattern sight, willing it to reveal its secrets.

There was something there, something he was missing.

If only he could focus. The wastrels increased their caterwauling in an attempt to distract him. Lev looked up. There were probably a thousand of them by now. The wailing and imprecations rained down on him as they circled in a threatening manner.

Selfish — coward — hiding in the wilderness.

Lev tried to ignore them.

Why do you live while those you swore to protect die?

"Shut up!"

Unworthy — you deserve to die.

"I didn't ask for this!"

End it — their souls cry out for justice.

"I'm sorry... " Lev whimpered. "I tried my best."

Not good enough — you failed the world — it's all your fault.

Lev wrapped his arms around his legs and placed his head between his knees, trying to block the voices. It was true. He'd failed everyone. The world was going to end in a flood because he pretended to be the Levigator. He was just a peculiar man with an abnormal mind. Maybe he'd been insane this whole time.

The wastrels drew close enough that he could feel their presence as a palpable entity. Lev drew his knife instinctively and slashed at the air, accomplishing nothing. He sobbed and dropped the knife on the ground where he sat. His eyes were riveted on the blade. He could end the voices and prevent the wastrels from using him against his friends.

You deserve to pay for what you've done — pick up the knife — end it.

Lev squeezed his eyes shut. His fingers touched the cold steel. He couldn't take it anymore. He'd never asked for any of this and now he was carrying the burdens of the world. It was all too much. Lev whispered a prayer. "Maker, help me."

A voice rang clear in his mind. It wasn't audible, but it cut through the clamour of the wastrels — encouraging rather than accusing. It comforted his troubled soul. "Enter the silence between the songs."

Lev's eyes flew open. The rift stared back at him. "The songs?" Lev closed his eyes and listened. The familiar frequencies of the particles around him sang out in harmony. "The songs..." he whispered, "...but what is the silence *between* the songs?" The wastrels became agitated at his words. Lev opened his eyes to pattern sight and looked with a fresh perspective. Particles filled his view, making up the very fabric of the world around him — like the tiny motes seen floating in the air when a sunbeam shines through a window. "Like motes floating in the air." Lev repeated aloud. He'd spent all of his time fixated on particles and frequencies, but never noticed the space around the particles — and why would he? There was nothing there.

Lev shifted his focus to the space between the particles and the songs began to fade until he heard nothing at all. The silence was a blessed relief from the wastrels and he stayed there for a time thinking of nothing at all — drinking in the solitude. Eventually, his mind returned to the problem at hand. The quiet allowed him to think clearly for the first time in weeks. He'd found the silence and entered it, but that did little more than offer a respite from his tormentors. There must be more to it than that.

Lev pulled out of the silence. *Actually, it felt more like a void.* Lev froze. The incessant babbling of the wastrels returned, but Lev was like a bloodhound with a scent and had a mind for nothing else at the moment. His eyes darted to the intersecting plane of the rift at this location. It was free of particles except at the edges. He'd seen this before — an emptiness behind the door in Kenric Trantor's chambers. The difference was that he could look through most rifts to see a kin world, so he never noticed the lack of matter in the intermediate space. What he saw with pattern sight, on the other side of Kenric's door, was nothing at all, a void.

He should have made the connection earlier. He already knew that wastrels were trapped in a type of rift, he'd just never considered what a rift actually was.

Lev's mind raced. Rifts were created at thin *spaces*. Those were locations between parallel worlds where there was a thinning of particles. Rifts were created when those fewer particles were pushed aside by quantum forces, enlarging the space between particles. If it was possible to create a rift between two worlds by simultaneously observing particles from each, then it should also be possible to open a void rift by simultaneously observing the spaces between the particles from two different perspectives.

Lev's mind struggled to grasp the concept. How was that even supposed to work? Lev had been opening rifts by passing a sight token through a thin space so he could view one side with his own eyes and the other via transmitted image. Those thin spaces already provided an opening about the diameter of his little finger. This was a different situation altogether. He couldn't very well pass a sight token through the microscopic space between particles.

A wave of encouragement flowed through him, along with an idea. *Could it really be that simple?*

Lev had once separated his mind from his body and he repeated the process now. He could feel the fury of the wastrels as they increased their attempts to distract him. Their protestations faded as he pulled away from his body and pushed his mind into the silence between the songs. He looked back at himself from across the void and in that instant, when the eyes of his essence locked onto the eyes of his flesh, the particles of his world fled apart from the unmistakable intersection plane of a rift. In that same moment, he reunited with his flesh.

Lev felt a moment of disorientation as his mind re-established its place within his body. He heard screeches of outrage as his body was buffeted by a stream of wastrels inexorably drawn into the newly created void rift open before him.

"Yes!" Lev shouted above the wailing of the panicked wastrels. He stepped to the side and watched until the last of his tormentors disappeared into the void. He was alone again.

Relief washed over Lev. He'd done it. He wasn't a total failure — now he finally had something to offer. Still, he felt like he was forgetting something. He remembered Hemish explaining how a void rift would lose its pull over time, and that previous Levigators had sealed the openings to prevent the wastrels from escaping.

A door in the middle of the wilderness would beg to be opened, so the idea wasn't practical or permanent enough for Lev. He scrolled through token options on his Q-view for ideas and settled on something simple. He began forming layers of rock over and around the rift. It took the remainder of the afternoon, but when it was done, a new rock formation graced the landscape. It extended out from the rift for eighteen cubits in every direction.

Lev stood back and took in his handiwork. He added a few modifications to make things look more natural. It would take a lot of work to dig through the dense rock to the core, reducing the temptation for anyone to make such an effort. Lev nodded, satisfied. "It will do."

Nico had given Lev some names to contact if he ever needed to use Callan International's resources for transportation. Lev wasn't sure how many wastrels had been freed around the world, but he was going to be doing a lot of travelling if he wanted to imprison them all.

Lev threw his pack over his shoulder and started back to the last city he'd visited. For the first time in a very long time, he had a hopeful spring in his step.

Chapter 42

Nico was on his third lap of the mezzanine overlooking the concourse. They'd had a little good news recently. Kade Brixton managed to make contact. He had survived the brutal attack on Chellea along with Selica and the island's children. Kade had been eager to share what he'd learned during their failed attempt to defend the island. He'd transmitted some novel uses of the QPN network that Nico thought they could modify for use at Port Callan. It was one of the reasons for his pacing. He was considering ways to improve on Kade's strategies.

Nico glanced down as he neared the railing. People moved back and forth on one errand or another. The main cavern of Port Callan was busy day and night. Nico found he didn't like to be alone with his thoughts these days, so he sought out crowds whenever possible. Ironically, he could concentrate better in the noisy environment. The sound of machinery and voices echoing off the cavern walls distracted him from the ghosts in his mind.

Nico had joined the many others struggling with the heavy losses of the last few months. He'd received a report from the medics that a number of people were complaining of having hallucinations or seeing ghostly apparitions in recent days. He imagined it was stress related — tensions were running high with the recent news. Sicari were arriving in Denmount by the hundreds and slaughtering everyone in sight. Akhen's teams had been forced to remain in hiding. It was like the assassins were playing some twisted game to see who could take the most lives.

He knew they were a bloodthirsty order, but there had to be a specific reason why they were here in Denmount.

One of Akhen's teams had gone silent two days ago. There had been no word from another team yesterday. He'd ordered the remainder to rendezvous at one of the old entrances to Denmount base. They hoped that no one would be monitoring it, since it had already been destroyed by the Breachers. If Akhen's people could make it there, they could escape using the sub rail transports. The labyrinth would help if they needed to lose any pursuers. Getting there would be dangerous, but it was the closest option for the scattered teams. They risked exposing the tunnels leading to Ports Vantos and Callan, but no one wanted to say what they were all thinking. Two teams were missing and the Sicari were master interrogators. There was a high probability that the port locations were no longer a secret. All they could do was hope that Akhen's teams escaped unseen. They'd deal with the consequences later.

A young analyst named Dosan ran across the mezzanine toward Nico. Everyone knew that Nico preferred to do his thinking on the move, but the senior staff grew weary of constantly searching for him. As a compromise, Dosan was tasked with fetching Nico when needed. Dosan waved to get his attention, then suddenly stopped in his tracks and began pointing at something beyond Nico's shoulder. Turning to see what Dosan was so excited about, Nico found himself face-to-face with a wastrel. He'd heard the descriptions from Akhen. This was the first one he'd seen for himself. Nico cautiously backed away. *This is why the Sicari are in Denmount. They're driven by the wastrels — wastrels who clearly know where Port Callan is.*

The wastrel faded and Nico spun to face a slack-jawed Dosan. "Report!"

Dosan blinked twice before coming to his senses. "We just received word that LTA transports are circling above Port Vantos. You're needed in operations, sir."

"Listen to me, Dosan, I need you to run to the harbour master with the message that we need to evacuate. Have him prep all of the sub-aqua transports for immediate departure and arrange for a sea transport to take on passengers at the muster coordinates."

Dosan headed to the lower level and Nico ran to the operations centre. He took a moment to catch his breath as he gauged the tension in the room. "What's our status?"

"Nico!" Deak waved him over to his terminal and pointed to the viewscreen. "About thirty minutes ago, some proximity alarms were triggered at the sea cliffs. I sent a sub out to get a visual. These images are live."

Nico shook his head. "What am I looking at?"

Deak enlarged the image, pointing to several spots on the viewscreen. "These are ropes. Several men rappelled down the face of the cliff. From their garb, I'd say they're Sicari. They all stopped at the same height and have been there for the last ten minutes. No, wait — there's movement. They're climbing back up. What on earth are they up to?"

Nico squinted. "What are those dark patches?"

"I'm not sure. Shadows maybe?"

"Can you enlarge the image some more?" Nico asked.

"It'll be fuzzy, but I can try." Deak stiffened. "Those aren't shadows..."

"...those are explosive charges!" Nico shouted seconds before a massive explosion shook dust from the ceiling.

Warning Lights were flashing and the room erupted in chaos. "Send out evacuation orders!" Nico commanded. "I want as many people on the subs as possible — immediately! Deak, is that sub still transmitting images?"

Deak pulled the image back up for a better view. There was a huge crater in the face of the cliff. Sicari were already swarming into the hole and placing more charges. Nico shook his head in dismay. "They're still a good 25 cubits above us, but once they've cleared enough space for an attack force, it won't take them long to start drilling down. I'd say we have about an hour before they infiltrate. Can you pull up a sight token from my estate above the cliffs?"

Deak tapped in a few commands and the image on the viewscreen changed to a view of the yard from Nico's house. He gasped at what he saw. Hundreds of Sicari were moving toward the sea cliffs.

"We never planned for something like this," Deak whispered.

"Gather as many fighting men as you can on the mezzanine level to cover the evacuation. I don't know where the Sicari will breach, but we'll want to lure as many of them into the main atrium as possible. Make sure everyone who stays behind has breathers and tethers."

Deak drew his mouth into a hard line and nodded. The main atrium wall could be triggered to dissolve, instantly flooding the chamber with seawater. It was a defence of last resort and there was no doubt the time had come. They had practised plenty of drills to prepare, but no one knew for sure if it was possible to survive the rush of water, regardless of the breathers or how well people were tethered to the walls. Still, they had a better chance than their attackers.

Nico pounded the table in frustration. It was too soon. They'd barely had time to start experimenting with Kade's modifications, let alone install any new defences. Now it was too late.

Nico looked around the operations centre. "What are you all waiting for? Go!"

"What about you, sir?"

"I have to take care of a few things before I can leave. Don't worry about me, I'll take the mini-sub from the estate emergency tunnel. I'll be right behind you."

Once the room was cleared, Nico tried contacting Akhen. He didn't pick up, but Yori answered.

"Yori! What's your status?"

"We made it to the tunnels, but not unseen. The Sicari will be tied up for a while in the labyrinth, but they know where to look. I'm sorry, Nico."

"They already knew where we were. Wastrels have been sighted in Port Callan."

Yori groaned. "We suspected as much."

"Did everyone make it? I couldn't reach Akhen."

"Akhen is busy sending the extra rail transports away by remote command. Once we make it to midway station, we'll collapse the tunnel behind us. We don't want to make it any easier for the Sicari than we have to. If they find their way into the tunnel system, they'll have a long hike before they reach the collapsed section. It will force them to backtrack and it might gain us some time. As for everyone else — only two teams made it to the rendezvous point."

Nico fell silent.

"That's not all, Nico ... Tark sacrificed himself so we could escape. He held them off at the entrance to the labyrinth."

Nico let out a shaky breath. "Of course, he did." Tark had been a Breacher once. When he decided to become a Servator and follow the Maker's Way, he was all in. Nico had never met anyone more loyal. From the moment the Servators had given him a second chance at life, Tark had been ready to lay that life down in return. Nico felt the moisture brimming in his eyes. Tark was a dear friend, but now wasn't the time to mourn. Many more lives would be lost before the day was through.

Yori broke the doleful silence. "We'll be back at Port Callan within the next twenty minutes."

"No, it's too late. There are hundreds of Sicari lowering themselves to a hole they blasted into the face of the sea cliffs. They'll be breaching soon. We're evacuating as we speak."

Yori's voice was filled with concern. "Where do you need us, Nico?"

"Make for Port Vantos and help with the evacuation. I'll be calling there next to initiate Project Exodus. Sicari are circling in air transports. No word if any have landed yet. This is very distressing, Yori. From your reports of what's been happening in Denmount, I don't think the Sicari will be satisfied with the destruction of Port Vantos. They'll hunt those who flee into the forests."

"Then we need a good head start. We're leaving now."

"Be careful, Yori. I've lost too many friends."

"And you, my friend," Yori replied. "It begins."

"It begi..." Nico was cut off by another explosion. This one shook the room. He looked up at the bank of viewscreens showing sight token feeds from public spaces around the base. Sicari were running through the tunnels.

Nico felt for the reassuring lump on his belt. He was wearing a QPN mini-repeater like those worn by Akhen's teams. He loaded a shield token into the buffer. It allowed him to erect a shield within five cubits of the unit for as long as he remained in one spot. They hadn't had much time to experiment with Kade's suggestions, but Nico had taken the time to make two specific modifications to his personal repeater. He had set the shield to collapse and regenerate in a rapidly repeating cycle — and he'd turned off the safety protocol that prevented a token from forming in the same space as pre-existing matter.

"Time to go."

"I don't think you'll be going anywhere."

Nico spun and was confronted by a large Sicari blocking the doorway. The man's eyes widened in recognition when he saw Nico's face.

"Well, well, well. If it isn't Nico Callan. I can hardly believe my good fortune."

Nico recognized the Sicari from still-views Kayla had shown him. "Qas."

"You've heard of me. I'm flattered. I've been looking for you for a very long time."

"Sorry to have been such an inconvenience," Nico dead-panned.

"I've never failed to fulfill a contract — until you. Your lack of consideration has tarnished my perfect record —" A grin slowly spread across Qas's face as he drew out a wicked looking blade. "- until now." Qas struck the pommel of his blade against his chest in a mock salute. The scent of ozone filled the air as the weapon began to glow. Nico pulled his own blade and pointed it at Qas.

"Very good!" Qas laughed. He looked at Nico's blade and then his own. "It hardly seems fair, though." Qas tilted his head in consideration. "Tell you what. I'll give you a fighting chance." Qas struck the pommel a second time and powered down the weapon so it was just a regular blade. "Let's hope you give me more of a challenge than your parents did."

Nico clenched his jaw at the assassin's taunt. He screamed and threw himself at Qas with a flurry of strikes. Qas deftly parried them all and began advancing. Nico held his ground — barely, but he'd already taken several small cuts to his forearms and ribs. He could feel himself tiring. The assassin was clearly a better fighter. Nico needed to change tactics. He had to enable the shield before Qas grew tired of toying with him. Qas continued to press toward him as he tried to figure out how to get five cubits away before engaging it.

Nico glanced around the room, considering options. *There!* He ducked just as Qas's blade whistled over his head. He dropped to the floor and rolled under the map table.

"You're only delaying the inevitable, "Qas taunted. "If you're not going to stand up and fight, then I'm not going to play anymore." Nico sprang from under the table and ran for the far corner of the room. He turned to face his pursuer and energized the shield. Qas took two running steps before he collided with the pulsing token. The result was explosive as particles of matter tried to share the same space at the same time. With each regeneration of the shield, more of Qas's body disintegrated as his momentum carried him forward.

Nico stared in shock at the gruesome display, slumping to the floor in exhaustion. The cuts on his body began to ache as the adrenaline left his system. His leg was bleeding badly. *Qas must have nicked an artery.*

He was too weak to stand and Nico realized he'd already lost too much blood. It looked like he wouldn't be going anywhere, but he hoped everyone else had gotten away.

Nico lifted his wrist Q-view and brought up a still-view of Kayla. He kissed his fingertips and touched her image. A tear slid down his cheek. "I'll be right there."

His eyes fluttered closed and Nico breathed his last.

Chapter 43

It had taken Lev several tries to enter Port Callan. He was eventually able to make his way via the tunnel from the office in Nico's house. It was surprising that the hidden panel hadn't been found, considering the excessive vandalism of the Callan estate property.

The damage to Nico's house was nothing compared to the destruction of Port Callan. The elevator refused to descend below the upper levels and he was forced to take the stairs for the final leg of his descent. He hadn't gotten far before water blocked his path. A short dive revealed that the entire face of the sea cliff was gone. Someone must have triggered the last-resort defence measure. Sea creatures were feasting on human remains. Mostly Sicari, from the look of things. Lev hoped that some of the Servators had managed to escape.

He'd left immediately after for Port Vantos, praying that he wouldn't find more of the same. The mountain port defences weren't as good, but the location was remote, so perhaps it remained untouched.

The false tunnel entrances used to leave Port Callan were still in place, so it was unlikely that those who attacked the base had found the sub-rail transport tunnels to Port Vantos. Lev had been both relieved and disappointed to note that the transports were waiting at the platform. It meant the Sicari hadn't found the tunnel, but it also meant that the Servators hadn't escaped this way.

Riding the transport alone had been unsettling. No one responded to his Q-view calls. The soft rhythmic clicking of wheels rolling along the tracks seemed too loud in the empty rail car. The quiet ride increased his anxiety minute-by-minute. Lev's anticipation of hearing a voice — any voice — had him so keyed up by the time he exited the transport, that he was left numb and shaking at the utter silence he found in the stillness of Port Vantos.

The place was like a ghost town. Anything of value was either gone or demolished, but there were no signs of struggle and not a single body in sight, living or otherwise. "They must have initiated Project Exodus." Lev voiced his thought to push back the silence, but the echo only emphasized the emptiness.

Making his way to the landing bays, he found the LTA transports all sitting in their docking clamps with their gas bladders slashed. His heart sank a little more. Everyone had left on foot. He tried his Q-view again. Nothing. The repeaters in the mountain range were showing as active. Perhaps the danger was still present and people were maintaining radio silence. Lev chastised himself for putting people at risk by broadcasting. The thought put him on alert. He'd allowed himself to get lulled by the finality of Port Callan's destruction and the silence found here in Port Vantos, but Sicari could still be roaming the woods. He was confident he could deal with any threat, but first he'd have to recognize it. Yori would be shaking his head at Lev's carelessness. Lev felt a lump form in his throat as he remembered Yori's goodbye. It had seemed so final. He forced the thought away.

I need to check the forest. Lev hesitated, not sure he wanted an answer to the nagging question. He left the base with a lot more caution than when he had entered. There were several hiking trails around Port Vantos with varying degrees of difficulty. *Which one would I take if I was fleeing?* Lev wondered. He supposed it would depend on how close the pursuers were. It was obviously easier to move quickly downhill. Also, paths leading uphill would soon end with no options for further escape. *I'm overthinking this — a portion of the population would have children or elderly with them. They'd start on the easiest path.*

The most travelled route, by far, was a wide meandering path that led to some popular outdoor meeting areas. Lev made a decision and headed in that direction. He discovered the first victim at the second clearing. Lev continued walking for an hour before he became too disheartened to continue, and decided to turn back. He didn't have the fortitude to try to determine the number of losses. What he'd seen was bad enough. *Better to carry on with the hope that some escaped.*

The slow walk back to Port Vantos was filled with self-recrimination. Dark clouds rolled in, matching his mood. If he didn't know better, he'd wonder if a wastrel was following him again — whispering accusations. *I should have been here. I could have saved so many people.*

Lev thought he'd been making progress when he discovered how to form a void rift. He'd created several on his way here, imprisoning hundreds of wastrels. Even so, it would take months to travel the world, searching for them all. He didn't have that kind of time. Meanwhile, the Servators seemed to be dying out anyway. Could the few ragged survivors hope to make a difference anymore? The Breachers and Sicari were roaming the land unchecked. Lev shuddered to think what was coming. "Why, Maker? Why appoint me to this role only so I could fail? I don't understand. You helped me with the wastrels — help me now."

It started to rain. Lev ran the last stretch to the base. He hung his wet clothes up to dry and took a hot bath. His tears joined the bathwater until he had nothing left to offer. Deciding he'd spent enough time in self-pity, Lev headed for the kitchens and found a few scraps of food that had been left behind.

At some point over the course of his meal, he began to realize that his task wasn't yet complete. His failures were overwhelming, but hadn't the previous Levigators been fixated on something else entirely? They weren't focused on overcoming the Breachers or defeating the Sicari. No — they were seeking survivors of the floods, survivors located on post-flood kin worlds.

Lev left the kitchens and locked himself in one of the guest suites for the night. He formed a steel barricade across the entrance to make sure he wouldn't be attacked in his sleep. Lev sat on the bed with his back against the wall, considering his options. If he could find a way to close a flood world rift, then he could try to open a new one to a different part of the same world. At least in testing Rushoen Nu Lon's hypothesis, Lev could say he'd tried everything.

Lev had already come to the conclusion that the Servators had been operating under a misguided premise. If previous Levigators were right, flood survivors could potentially provide the answers that would set them on the proper path. He needed to at least try to find those answers in the little time he had left. The closest rift that would serve his purpose was located in the Servator base below the Denmount Centre for Learning. He'd leave first thing in the morning. That decided, Lev lay down and fought his way into a fitful sleep.

Chapter 44

Lev arrived in Denmount later in the day than he'd anticipated. The quick trip from Port Vantos by sub-rail transport had turned into an hours long waste of time. The Denmount tunnel was blocked at the mid-way station and he'd had to return to Port Callan. He should have guessed that might be the case, since he had helped to plan the defensive contingencies.

From Port Callan, he made his way back to Nico's estate. Having originally come from that direction, he knew it was passable. He lost more time finding and repairing a ground transport among the vandalized collection in Nico's garage. The remainder of the slow and miserable journey was above ground.

The sky was black and the lights on his transport weren't working. Lev had been forced to navigate by the glow of intermittent lightning strikes and a hand held lantern he'd brought along from Port Vantos. The torrential rain made the roads slippery, with several washed out sections leaving the trail almost impassable. Lev's growls of frustration were answered with peals of thunder. The one silver lining of being accompanied by these angry clouds was that no one else would be stupid enough to venture out into the rain. If the Sicari were still in Denmount, it would be easier to avoid them.

Lev tried to access the Servator base from several entrances, but most of them were flooded, He was forced to look for options that were protected from the weather. That led him to the basement of the archive building, the place where his adventure with the Servators began.

Lev was dripping from head to toe by the time he made it into the building. Leaving a trail of puddles, he descended the stairs and was met by the familiar scent of ink and parchment. He looked around for something he could use to dry himself. All he saw were pallets of scrolls and other stored texts. With a shrug, he pulled some from a pile and began patting down his clothing. *It's not like anyone will ever be reading these again.* Lev reprimanded himself for the defeatist attitude. It wasn't over yet.

Lev recalled the last time he was here. Kayla had saved his life. It was a terrifying experience, but the impression she'd made forged a stronger memory than the fear. Lev smiled, remembering her cocky attitude. Such a poor representation of who she really was. His smile dropped as he suddenly remembered that this was also the place where she had died. Scanning the room, he spotted a blood stain on the floor. He knew the details of her death, but refused to watch the recording. *Another person I failed to protect.* She'd saved his life, but he wasn't around to return the favour. Lev closed his eyes and spent a silent moment honouring her memory. *I'm so sorry, Kayla. Please, forgive me.*

Opening his eyes, Lev turned from the pain and wove his way behind the pallets to the hidden entrance. This time, he'd be crossing the threshold alone. He found the familiar symbol of the Servators, and cleared the tunnel barrier. A moment later he was through, with the false wall reforming behind him.

Lev's footsteps echoed as he made his solitary way to the rift chamber. Water had found its way into the base and was pooling in low spots. He needed to descend to the lowest levels, so hopefully the water hadn't found its way there. The rift room, being the most secure place on site, gave Lev high hopes that it remained well sealed. It occurred to him then that the most secure place on the base might also house survivors. Lev quickened his pace and arrived at the heavy steel doors a minute later. There were signs that someone had tried unsuccessfully to breach with explosives, but the door remained as immovable as ever. He tried to temper his expectations as he entered his security codes and waited for the massive door to open. "Hello? Is anyone in here?" There was no response. Lev sighed as he strode into the chamber. Everything was intact. The slightly musty smell of a long unused room hung in the air.

Approaching a rift was always mesmerizing. So familiar, yet alien. Someone had replaced the red flower token he'd plucked by passing his arm through the rift into the kin world. That act had identified him as a Levigator, and now he was back where he started. His whole journey seemed to be about new beginnings. He prayed for one more.

Over the next several hours, Lev tried one thing after another, attempting to close the rift. He endeavoured to proceed systematically. If a rift opened by being observed from both sides, maybe it could be closed by repeating the process. Lev sent a sight token through the rift so he could view from the kin world side on his Q-view while observing from his side at the same time. It was a procedure he had developed and used successfully to open numerous rifts. Duplicating those efforts accomplished nothing.

What if I try changing the frequency of particles just this side of the intersecting plane to match the frequency of the kin world? That endeavour elicited an excitement of particles within its thin veneer, ending in their destruction. The sudden absence of particles left only the spaces from between them. The rift appeared to grow marginally as a result, definitely not a result he was looking for. Repeating the process on the kin world side brought things back into balance, but no combination of the technique caused the rift to shrink.

Lev's frustration grew with each failed attempt. In a fit of aggravation, he grabbed particles from his surroundings and flung them at the rift like a child throwing a stone at the town bully. To Lev's astonishment, the rift wavered. *What just happened?*

He tried it again, with the same result. When he increased the volume of particles, the rift seemed to vibrate. Lev thought it through. A thin space was just an absence of particles. In the centre of every thin space was a pinhole that broke through between worlds. Lev had watched rifts form while in pattern sight and knew that it pushed the thin space aside, allowing particles to bleed through. Rifts tended to stabilize at a diameter established by the volume of slow flowing particles from one universe into the other. If he could stop the flow — maybe the rift would revert to its former state as a thin space. Lev theorized that by throwing particles at the rift, he had filled the void enough to disrupt the flow. "It can't just be about a mass of particles though," Lev thought aloud. People had tried plugging a rift with formed tokens before. At most, they were able to place tokens in close proximity, like when he formed stones around the void rifts to prevent wastrel escape. Particles didn't seem capable of existing in that plane between the competing frequencies of parallel worlds. Either they flowed through or were repelled. *So what was the difference here?* Lev analyzed the action he'd taken. He hadn't tried to fill the rift with stationary particles. He'd set a volume of moving particles that were largely reflected. It must have impeded flow. What if he were to prevent the particles from being repelled by converting their frequencies at the threshold as he did when passing his arm through? By forcing a large volume of particles through the rift to match and counter the rate of flow from the other side, perhaps he could eliminate the particle bleed altogether. It was worth a shot.

Lev entered pattern sight and expanded his senses, identifying billions of frequencies from the world around him. He chose heavier particles, hoping that the additional mass would help. Lev had never filled his mind with so much information at once. At first, he felt limitations as frequencies began to elude him, but then he realized it was a matter of progression. When he allowed his mind to finish mapping a consumable number of frequencies, he found he was able to add more frequencies without issue. He just needed to control his consumption. When he felt he had enough volume, he began moving them toward the rift horizon. He had to split his focus to continue adding to his store of particles while at the same time converting their frequencies at the moment of transition. It was taxing and his head began to throb with the effort, but it was working.

The edges of the rift began to vibrate as if uncertain which side of the intersection plane was stable. It began to shrink as the flow of particles thinned. When the rift was at half its original size, it suddenly snapped shut, cutting off the flow. Lev stopped directing particles as they began to bounce back at him. Relief washed through him at the cessation of effort. He had a pounding headache, but that was a small price to pay for what he had just accomplished.

Lev had changed a rift back into a thin space, but it wasn't enough. He needed to close it entirely or it would just open to the same place. He began to gather the particles again, pressing them against the thin space, thickening it — squeezing it — forcing the void between the particles to disperse into the surrounding spaces until the thin space was no longer thin and vanished altogether. Lev's shoulders drooped in exhaustion. "I can't believe that worked."

Now came the moment of truth. If Rushoen's theory was correct, sealing the thin space would have forced it to relocate somewhere nearby. Lev closed his eyes and opened his senses to feel for a thin space. His eyes flew open a moment later. "No." It was gone. There wasn't a thin-space anywhere in the vicinity.

Chapter 45

"No, Maker — please." Lev dropped to his knees. "What do I do now?"

His mind was blank and into that absence of ideas a calm voice spoke clearly once more. "Move beyond the silence."

The words broke through a growing fog of despair. It was concise and he knew exactly what it meant. Without hesitation, he pulled his mind from his body and entered the void between particles. He pushed himself deeper into the void and emerged into that place he'd once thought of as a vision. He knew better now. This was as real as anything he'd experienced so far. Everything appeared the same as the first time he'd visited this place. He could see tendrils extending from his essence. One was thicker than the others and he knew it led to the Maker. The others led to versions of himself on parallel worlds where the consequences of his choices had splintered off new timelines, continuing to their logical conclusions.

So many fractured paths. Lev was dismayed by his poor choices, but he also recognized an important truth. Some part of him existed on many worlds and he realized he had a connection to those other paths. Lev could clearly identify the different frequencies associated with each tether. He recognized one in particular. It was the kin world whose thin space he had just closed. Surprise bloomed in his mind. A part of him existed on a post-flood world. He had survived the flood in that place. That meant a version of himself had answers.

Lev instinctively began to pull on that tendril, drawing it towards him. At the same time, he backed out into the void and then back into his body. After a moment of disorientation, he opened his eyes. His senses flared at the proximity of a new thin space directly in front of him.

Lev shook with excitement. He didn't bother with his normal procedure for breaching a thin space. Instead, he employed the method used when he created a void rift. He sent his mind through the small hole at the centre of the thin space and looked back at himself. The familiar sensation of a rift forming filled the chamber with the gentle breeze of particle flow.

Lev peered through the newly created rift. The flower token was missing and the scene was entirely different, but the frequency was unmistakable. This was the same kin world. Unfortunately, no people were visible at this location either.

It was the flaw in Rushoen's theory. With an entire world to search, the odds that a rift would open right where people were living was infinitesimal. It didn't matter though, because Lev knew a version of himself was alive on this kin world. Rushoen and the other Levigators had been right about finding post-flood survivors. More importantly, the tendril that connected him to his other self was still visible. He could track his alter ego anywhere on the planet and that meant he'd find other survivors as well. He could learn the truth.

Lev felt a wave of relief. He hadn't failed — not completely. He might not save this world, but his friends still existed in parallel worlds. They weren't completely gone. He realized they might not be present in the kin world that lay open before him, but Lev was no longer constrained by that single option. He could open a rift to any world he had a connection to, both pre and post flood. Certainly on some of those worlds he would have crossed paths with the same people in one way or another. It eased the burden of loss just knowing a part of them remained. He could see them again if he took the time to find them. It comforted him and cleared his mind to consider the broader implications.

Two things became clear to him. Life didn't end with the flood and the flood wasn't inevitable. He hadn't been able to prevent it on this world, yet here he stood with the opportunity to do better on countless other worlds. More importantly, he'd no longer be ignorant about what needed to be done.

The Servators were never meant to be protectors. The goal wasn't to stop the flood. The goal was to prepare hearts and minds for a better way. The Servators were meant to be examples and guides. They needed to break away from the dictates and prepare people to receive the promise of a future filled with hope.

Life wasn't about material possessions, power or accumulating pleasure. It wasn't about living a perceived role as if our mortal flesh could define the essence of who we were any more than it could contain us forever. Life was about the consequences of our choices when imposing our will — about recognizing our shortcomings and choosing better in the future. People were meant to be something greater, something unbroken, something less fractured.

With that epiphany, Lev understood his purpose. He would learn what saved the remnant from the flood and he would take what he learned to pre-flood worlds to help them prepare. He'd seek out Levigators and enable them to carry that message to the worlds he had no connection to. Maybe, just maybe, they could slow the endless splintering of kin worlds and ease suffering in the process. It was a worthy goal — perhaps beyond the ability of mortals. Yet somehow, Lev knew there was much more going on and he didn't need to have all of the answers. He just needed to move forward.

Fine words, but they mean little unless you take that first step. He still needed to pass through the rift and the fear of death or madness lingered.

There's no rush, you have time, he told himself, but he knew that wasn't true. He looked at his feet. Water had risen to his ankles.

Lev shook his head. He only had two choices at this point. Sooner or later the water would become an insurmountable obstacle. He had no place to go. The waters were rising too quickly. This base would become his tomb. Or, he could take a chance and step through the rift. If he died in the process, it would only hasten his demise by a few hours.

Wouldn't you rather take the chance and make a difference? It was a stupid question. As soon as he asked it of himself, he knew staying was never an option. If there was any chance to redeem his failings on this world, he would take it, no matter the cost.

Lev took a deep breath, placed his life into the hands of his Maker, and stepped through the rift.

Epilogue

Lev sat in the mouth of the tunnel overlooking the sea. It was a beautiful day. The sun was shining, the sea birds were riding thermal updrafts and the scent of saltwater filled the air — memories of home.

It had been a year since the Maker helped him to understand his purpose and encouraged him to step through the rift. Lev embraced his new role, but his doppelganger was less enthusiastic. When Lev first introduced himself, his counterpart had spent considerable time in denial. The other Leviticus had never even heard of Servators. Things changed when his eyes were opened to his innate abilities. Since then, he'd become almost as adept as his teacher. They'd spent a great deal of time formulating plans — those efforts were paying off.

Of the worlds Lev visited that had a Servator presence, few had Levigators and fewer still were as powerful as he was. It made things much easier when he approached them. They were universally eager to bring him into the fold and learn from him. It took time to change generations of tradition, but he'd made progress encouraging them down a new path. It was inevitable that sooner or later he would come across another Tark and Yori at a Servator base, and indeed, on one world, the two were companions much like they'd been on his own world. They were happy to study warkata under his tutelage and it didn't take long to build a friendship. Their histories were different, but their characters remained much the same and soon they had many new memories in common to draw from. It was the same with Akhen, Hemish, Kayla and Cello. In fact, he'd made new connections with all of his closest friends on kin worlds.

This world, however, was his favourite. Lev looked at his wrist-chrono. The two would arrive shortly if they stuck to their regular routine. He used his wrist Q-view to call up the spy token he'd placed when he first visited this world. He was currently sitting in the sea caverns where Nico's family maintained a crypt.

Right on time, Lev grinned.

"Nico, toss me an apple, I'm starving."

"You're such a mooch. You might as well move in, with the way you make yourself at home."

"Can I?" Leviticus asked.

Nico pitched the apple at Leviticus's chest.

"Ow! Hey!"

Lev sat in the tunnel and vicariously soaked up their antics. He had chosen not to make himself known here. The Breacher presence was limited and neither Nico nor Leviticus had any contact with the Servators on this world. They were just students with their whole lives ahead of them. It brought back memories of simpler times and showed him how things could be — should be. It reminded him what he was fighting for.

Lev watched for another hour and then reluctantly disconnected the feed. He rose and stretched before exposing the rift he'd hidden behind the tunnel wall. It was always difficult to leave, but he could visit at any time. Perhaps one day, when he was no longer needed, he would retire here, but for now, he still had a great deal of work to do. As he disappeared through the rift, a sea bird stood in the mouth of the sea wall, watching. It cocked its head in curiosity and then flew away.

I hope you enjoyed reading Leavening. Visit my website https://www.kallensamuels.com and subscribe to the mailing list for information about new releases and exclusive content.

www.ingramcontent.com/pod-product-compliance
Lightning Source LLC
Chambersburg PA
CBHW030809210726
48290CB00002B/505